ATHE

A Famine Tale of Love and Survival

CATHAL DUNNE

MERCIER PRESS
Cork
www.mercierpress.ie

© Cathal Dunne 2025

ISBN: 978-1-917453-94-3
eBook: 978-1-917453-95-0

All characters and events in this book, except for those who are identifiably real and recognisable in the public domain, are entirely fictional. Any resemblance to any person living or dead which may occur inadvertently is completely unintentional.

This book is sold subject to the condition that it shall not, by way of trade or otherwise, be lent, resold, hired out or otherwise circulated without the publisher's prior consent in any form of binding or cover other than that in which it is published and without a similar condition including this condition being imposed on the subsequent purchaser.

No part of this publication may be reproduced or transmitted in any form or by any means, electronic or mechanical, including photocopying, recording or any information or retrieval system, without the prior permission of the publisher in writing.

Printed and bound in the EU.

Dedication

In memory of my brother. Des, we miss you. This novel is also dedicated to all first responders globally, including my son Ryan, who put their lives at risk daily.

Contents

Acknowledgments   7

About the author   9

Author's note   11

A Quick Guide to Pronunciations *(in italics)* & Meanings   13

PART ONE: They Called Him Horse   15

PART TWO: Resistance   81

PART THREE: Rotten Lumpers   109

PART FOUR: Consequences and Piano   127

PART FIVE: Toy Soldiers and Assault   163

PART SIX: Concerts and Murder   173

PART SEVEN: Dingoes, Whales, Potato Orphans, and a Letter   209

PART EIGHT: Cradles and Snakes   305

PART NINE: The Air That Binds   347

Sources for Further Reading   381

Acknowledgments

Behind every author is a supportive network of family members, friends and colleagues. I am deeply grateful to you all who have supported and encouraged me throughout this journey. My heartfelt thanks go to my family, whose unwavering belief in me has been a constant source of strength; to my friends, who offered inspiration and comfort at every stage; to my publisher, whose expertise and guidance were invaluable. I also wish to acknowledge the countless individuals—named and unnamed—whose contributions, insights, and kindness have shaped this work in meaningful ways. Without your support, this endeavour would not have been possible.

First and foremost, to my wife, Kathleen for all the first readings and all the great suggestions. You are my rock and a huge part of this book. To Judy Savela, my friend and sounding board, who worked tirelessly with me throughout the writing process and whose intellect and literary talents have guided my work. Your patience, help with editing and generosity of your time has been incalculable. I am humbled and eternally grateful for your input into this book. A special note of thanks to Michelle Moe, another literary friend who brought her keen eye and attention to detail to the advancement of the chronology, plot and character development. I would like to thank my publisher Mercier Press, Cork and a note of thanks to Michelle O'Mahony, famine author and historical consultant who advised on the historical context and ensured historical authenticity throughout the characters' many escapades. Much thanks to my son, Ryan for your support and contribution. To my stepson Shaun I appreciate your insights and input for the cover imagery of *Athenry*.

I would like to remember with fondness, Malachy McCourt and his initial insights and thoughts on my early manuscript of Athenry. To my friend, Phil Coulter, thank you for taking the time to read my work. I wish to express my gratitude to the staff at the State Library of Western Australia, to Trove- the National Library of Australia, the staff at the Australian National Maritime Museum, to Pat Lengauer for your many proofreadings and to Cecilia Fabos-Becker for your assistance.

Finally, to you the reader, I hope you enjoy the book, and to my followers and supporters, thank you one and all.

About the author

Cathal Dunne is a professional singer, songwriter, pianist, author and storyteller. He holds a degree in Music from University College Cork. In 1979 he represented Ireland at the Eurovision Song Contest with his own song, *Happy Man*. Originally from Cork City, he now resides in Pittsburgh with his wife and family and continues to perform across America. This is his second book.

Author's note

With a background in music and entertainment, telling a story is part of my identity. Drawing on my passion for music, Irish history and culture, it was only a matter of time before I put pen to paper and let my imagination take flight. Initial inspiration came from Pete St. John's iconic song; *The Fields of Athenry*. A song widely beloved by the Irish at home and abroad, a song that has resonated around the world, and is synonymous with the Irish Diaspora. In three short verses, it captures a watershed moment in the lives of so many Irish families. After the Famine, nothing was quite the same, and those who survived, survived against all odds. The song tells a story of a pauper who stole food from his landlord to feed his starving family during the Great Irish Famine of the mid-1840s. Found guilty, he was transported to the Penal Colony of Botany Bay, Australia. Like others of his kind, he did not return. It is estimated that over one hundred and sixty-four thousand convicts, both Irish and English, men and women, were transported to the penal colonies in Australia between the years 1788 and 1886. Today, Athenry is a medieval town sixteen miles east of Galway City, attractive to visitors for its castle, stone walls, fortifications, and an Anglo-Norman street plan.

During my research for *Athenry – A Famine Tale of Love and Survival,* I came to realise that, because of the huge collective and intergenerational trauma in Ireland at the time of the Famine and the immediate aftermath, perhaps even to present day, that the plight of the victims, their experience of hardship and despair - to a certain extent - has lain unexplored. Daily life and love stories were forgotten in the search for food, and in later years, politicians and historians tended to focus less on individual victims of the Famine and more on the political debates of recounting history. The daily life of the Famine victims was beset by hunger - yet they watched the majority of the foodstuffs, which could have halted the rising mortality rates - leave the country as cargo in ships bound for Imperial Britain.

This novel is a tribute to the strength, resilience, love of family and forbearance of the Irish in the face of overwhelming adversity, given the uniqueness of their situation in the mid-1840s. It is reflected in the lives of two families, equally, terribly affected by the twists and turns of history and historical moments: the penal laws, land crises, land subdivision, and of course the Great Irish Famine, or its more historically accurate term - An Gorta Mór - The Great Hunger.

My fervent hope is that each reader especially those of Irish heritage will see elements of their ancestors in *Athenry's* characters, as I strive to bring the emigration and experience of so many together in one story. For others it is simply an epic love story that defies the odds. This year, 2025 marks the 180th anniversary of the arrival of the cataclysmic blight to Ireland in the Autumn of 1845. *Athenry- A Famine Tale of Love and Survival* is a testament to the memory of all of those who endured so much.

A Quick Guide to Pronunciations *(in italics)* & Meanings

Amadán – *OMadawn* – Idiot
Aoife – *EEfah* – from the Irish word 'aoibh' meaning radiance
Banjaxed – Broken
Bothán —*Buh-Hawn* – a lower class of dwelling, comprising one room, symbolic of misery
Bríd – *Breed* – from Brigid
Cathal – *KA-hal* —meaning brave warrior
Capall – *COPull* – Horse
C(h)ara – *KARrah* – Friend
Céilí – *KAYlee* – Irish dancing and singing
Colm – *KULL-m*
Connacht – *CON-uct* – One of the four provinces of Ireland
Craic – *Crack* – Fun
Craythur/ Créatúr – *CRAYthur* – Poitín
Currach – *KURuck* – traditional Irish fishing boat
Diarmuid – *DEAR-mudj* – Dermot or Jeremiah in Irish
Duine le Dia – *Din-eh leh DEEah* – translates from Irish as a person with God, often referring to a child with a disability
Dunguaire – *DunGOORah*
Hooley – *WHO-lee* – Party
Jumper – Irish sweater
Kumba – meaning black fruit tree in Aboriginal languages
Liam – *Le-um* – Irish for William
Máire – *Maw-ruh* – Mary
Meitheal – *MEHhull* – communal work in an agricultural setting, farmers helping one another gather crops
Órla – *OAR-lah* – meaning golden princess
Poitín – *puh-tcheen* – Irish moonshine

Porter – Irish stout
Róisín – *RowSHEEN* – Irish for little Rose
Saoirse – *SEARshah* – Irish word for freedom
Seán – *Shaun* – John
Siobhán – *ShoveAWN* – Joan
Sláinte – *Slawn-tcheh* – Cheers
Sláinte is saol – *Slawn-tcheh is see-uhl* – Cheers and life
Sláinte mhaith – *Slawn-tcheh woh* – Good cheer
Súgans/ Súgáin – *SUE-gawns* – Braided straw ropes
Tomás – *Tum ahss* – Thomas
Tomásheen – *Tum Ahss-heen* – Little Tomás
Turf – Irish peat
Yagan – Aboriginal word for brother
Yidaki – Aboriginal musical instrument – Didgeridoo
Úna – *oo-nah*

PART ONE

They Called Him Horse

Ireland 1843

'Horse' is what everyone called him, except his mother of course. Learning to ride Connemara ponies almost before he could walk, together with his seemingly natural-born skill with horses, earned Liam this nickname. Galloping astride Bridgey, his beloved Connemara pony, Liam scanned the craggy rocks at the edge of the beach. He knew he'd see his brother rowing on the choppy waters, fishing for their landlord's daily meals. Today the surf seemed unusually wild and rough, with the winds picking up by the minute. His family, once proud landowners, but now dispossessed of everything they'd owned, lived at their landlord's whim in a small bothán-like thatched cottage, on a tiny piece of land allotted to them by their landlord. They survived on their annual crop of potatoes, buttermilk, a few roaming chickens, and a sow.

From atop the cliff, Liam spotted Colm in his black currach. No more than a hundred yards offshore, his boat rolled over the rising swell as he hit for shore with his catch. Colm must have sensed his brother's eyes on him, for he paused mid-stroke and waved. As Liam raised his own hand to return the greeting, his gaze drifted beyond Colm to a wall of dark water, a huge rogue wave barrelled towards Colm. Frantic, he waved in warning. Not understanding the danger Liam was trying to convey, Colm waved again. The distance that had seemed so small moments before now felt like an impossible chasm. Liam shouted, 'Get up girl,' urging Bridgey forward. She took off in a massive burst of speed, furiously jumping stone walls and ditches as they neared the beach.

The menacing mountain of water continued to roll in. Almost as if in slow motion, the currach was lifted to the peak of the wave and then flung, toy-like, into a monstrous churn of white foam. Helpless within the overpowering swirl, Colm was swallowed by the sea. Resurfacing, his arms flailing above his head, and gasping what could be his last breath, Colm was pulled under again. Pulse quickening and heart pounding in fear, Liam rode Bridgey to the water's edge. Leaping off the still-moving horse, he ran the length of the rocky beach, tripping over rocks. Then, trying to keep his balance in the loose sand, Liam stumbled as he shed his heavy boots and tattered woollen waistcoat. His strong legs carried him to the water's edge where he came to a halt to watch for Colm to resurface, if at all. 'Colm! Colm!' he screamed, his voice lost in the roar of crashing waves. Scanning the waterfront to his right, Liam caught sight of the overturned currach as it smashed against the rocks. The shoreline's sharp rocks bit into the soft flesh of his feet as he continued to search. 'Coluuuuum!' *Oh God, Colm!* he thought. *No, God no!* Was he hallucinating, or did he see a spot of white? Or was it sea foam? He stared at the spot about fifty feet out, and again it bobbed into view. Colm's thick woollen jumper. Liam dove in, his system so brutally shocked by the freezing seawater that it took his breath away.

Liam loved looking at the sea with all its different moods but hated being in it. The coastal waters never got warm and were always a numbing ten degrees Celsius or colder. It was only at the insistence of their father that the O'Donaghue brothers had learned to swim. Too many of Tomás' good friends were lost at sea because they had never bothered to learn. 'What's the point in delaying the agony when there's no hope of being rescued? Just get it over with,' was their attitude. So Tomás was adamant that his sons learn at least the basics, just in case.

Fighting the strong current, Liam was glad he could swim,

but a champion swimmer he certainly was not. Angry now that he hadn't spent more time practicing, Liam feared whether he could even reach Colm, let alone save him. Stroking furiously, and not making any great progress, he swam and kicked harder. Exhausted, waves pounding him from every direction, he stopped to regroup and floated momentarily to look for his brother's jumper. Floundering and virtually paralysed by the cold, Liam was lifted up by an enormous wave and was demoralised to see Colm far out and off to his left. Barely able to lift his arms and kick his legs, he knew he was in deep trouble himself and losing his battle against the frigid water. Frantic thoughts screamed in his head. *I need to save myself. But what'll I say to Mam and Da? 'Colm drowned, and I didn't save him.' Their lives would be over. I have to try to save him, no matter what.* Mustering what was left of his flagging strength, he stroked and kicked his way towards his brother and finally reached him floating face down. Grasping Colm's jumper, Liam turned his limp body over, looked up to see which direction he needed to head for, and pulling Colm with one hand, began what seemed impossible – getting them both back to shore.

Somehow, the thought of Colm having any hope of living, gave Liam the last bit of strength he needed to stroke the water with one hand and kick his feet as hard as he could. Taking advantage of the swell of two incoming waves, he slowly swam the last few yards, until finally, his feet touched ground. Liam crawled the last few feet, dragging his motionless brother to safety, and collapsed beside him. The cold wind pierced Liam's wet clothes, and he began to shudder violently, but the gut-wrenching fear of losing his brother jolted him back to the task at hand – reviving him. He fought the paralysing numbness of the cold and frantically pounded on Colm's chest as hard as he could. He had learned this technique from saving many a newly-born heifer as it emerged from its mother unconscious. 'Push all the liquids out of their lungs and allow them to breathe,' was what his father had taught him. 'Colm come on! Come on!' Liam rolled Colm onto his side to help clear his lungs, then continued pounding. After what seemed a lifetime, Colm, bleeding badly from a head wound, spewed a mouthful of saltwater and his eyes fluttered open. Then, grimacing in pain, he coughed violently, purging the last bit of water from his burning lungs, and regained consciousness. Relieved, Liam pulled his brother into his chest, 'That's it Colm, good man. Get it up, get it up, good man.' Then smiling through tears, he ripped a strip of cloth from the hem of his shirt and tied it around the gaping gash in his head to staunch the bleeding.

Liam whistled for Bridgey. 'Down girl,' he commanded, and obediently she folded her forelegs and eased onto her knees. Liam was never more thankful that he had taught Bridgey to do this, a movement that amazed his family. Carefully, he lifted Colm up to straddle Bridgey. 'Up girl,' he commanded and, walking beside Bridgey while steadying Colm in the saddle, headed home. The family cottage in sight at last, Liam saw his mother Josie hanging out the washing, her apron billowing in the breeze. Glancing up when she heard Bridgey's approach, she gasped when she saw Colm slumped over the horse. 'Oh, Mother of God,' she cried, blessing herself. She ran towards them screaming, 'What happened? What happened?' 'A huge wave hit the currach, and Colm was thrown over against the rocks.' Liam gently slid his groaning brother down onto his shoulder and carried him inside.

Josie, shocked at the sight of her two boys – Colm groaning in pain and Liam, wet, shivering and exhausted – calmed her nerves and took control. She shouted orders to her two young daughters as she helped carry Colm into the cottage and laid him on the bed. 'Bríd, get Mrs O'Flaherty. Go on now! Hurry up girl. Tell her to come as fast as she can. Aoife, get some blankets and wrap them around the both of 'em. Give Liam some hot tea and put some poitín into it to warm him up.' Skilfully, Bríd jumped up onto her brown Connemara pony, Saoirse, and, champion little jockey that she was, raced to midwife Mrs O'Flaherty's house.

Some years before, an entire family, lifetime friends of the O'Donaghues, immigrated to America, and left their beloved Connemara pony to the O'Donaghues. They knew she'd be well cared for, knowing their love of horses. And even though she ate them out of house and home, Bríd was obsessed with her, so that was it – Saoirse was adopted!

Liam had been giving riding lessons to his younger sisters since they were wee little girls and, like her brother, Bríd was a natural. She loved racing her own pony, sometimes beating Liam and Bridgey, taking dangerous chances as they'd jump the many stone walls in the hilly landscape. They all knew it was to the doctor's house Bríd should be going, but she would be turned away; the doctor was only for the English and Anglo-Irish classes.

Mrs O'Flaherty did her best to attend to Colm. Although her specialty was delivering babies, as the last resort for poor Irish farmers and their families, she had experienced all sorts of medical situations. The Irish took care of their own because they had to. With hard-earned skill, Mrs O'Flaherty tended to Colm's serious wounds and, in her usual droll way, finally gave the family the news they were praying for. 'He's got a grand ould bang on his head, but he just won't shut up. He's the same cheeky ol' divil he always was, so he'll be all right. His left leg is broken, so I put a strong splint on it. He'll have to take it real easy for a couple o' weeks.' 'Thanks be to God and his blessed Mother,' Josie cried. Liam, unable to imagine life without his younger brother, went in to see him. 'Irish twins' they were, as Colm was born less than a year after Liam. Inseparable from the start, learning the tough life of farming from their father, and always into every mischief imaginable, that was Colm and Liam. He approached the bed where Colm lay keeping warm under the woollen blankets. 'You're all right then?' 'Yea, all I remember is a huge wave lifting me up in the air. Where in God's name did that come from? Mrs O'Flaherty said you saved my life – you and Bridgey.' 'I suppose you won't be going to the wake on Thursday then, will ya?' 'I dunno'. I won't be doin' any dancin', that's for sure,' Colm answered with a bright smile. And for the first time that day they laughed.

The wake on Thursday night was a farewell party for Paudie and Úna Casey, who were immigrating to America the following Monday. Their parents had saved enough money for their passage from Galway. In the 1800s, Ireland was no country for young people. Anyone lucky enough to get out, got out, but they were the very fortunate few. As they would likely never return again, this party was known as a 'living wake' or an 'American wake'. So, their broken-hearted family would put on a brave face for this final night together before the emigrants set off on the long journey to the docks of Galway.

'Don't forget yer tin whistle,' said Tomás. Over the years he had taught his sons to play the tin whistle and the button accordion, so Liam and Colm were infused with traditional Irish music from all the parties and céilís everyone enjoyed. Nothing better relieved the monotony of back-breaking and repetitive farming, constant rain, the daily challenges of surviving the Ireland of the west, and of course, the ever-present brutal British oppression. 'This is our gold – our music and our dancing,' Tomás always said. 'Whatever else they take, they can't take this away from us.' 'All right so, you go on, I'll see ya there,' said Liam.

The Casey's thatched cottage was larger than the O'Donaghues'. It had a loft where three daughters and two sons slept. Like most such cottages, the outside was whitewashed. It had the classic half door, the bottom usually latched to prevent chickens and other small animals from entering. The upper half was open to allow in light and fresh air, and to let out turf fire smoke. The cottage windows were tiny – not because the Irish liked tiny windows, rather, because the British, in their greed for every penny possible, levied a tax on windows by size. As always, the Irish did what they had to do – often eliminating windows altogether to avoid yet another tax.

Paudie and Úna Casey shyly greeted neighbours and friends as they streamed into the Caseys' tiny dwelling. Comprised of one room and the loft, its steep loft ladder had been removed to make more room for the adults gathered there. The children took in the festivities from their perch above.

Paudie and Siobhán Casey warmly welcomed Liam into their home. Stepping inside, he heard the chatter of family and friends sharing thoughts of the young couple leaving. Truly a sad time for the Caseys and for Úna's parents, the Keanes, this was a stark reminder to everyone else attending that they, too, could experience the loss of one of their own. Paudie Casey senior offered the men a little poitín – the illegal brew he had bartered from a master brewer friend who distilled it in the hills of Connemara. The potent drink immediately hit the men who showed their appreciation of its quality with smiles all around.

Liam saw Colm sitting alone on a small bench on the far wall. Colm was the more outgoing of the two, and Liam felt sorry for him, having to sit out one of his favourite things to do – dance. When Liam joined him on the bench, their father pulled out his button accordion. After a couple of warm up notes, Tomás broke into a lively reel. It was time to let go of everyone's sadness for a while. Feet started to tap as an older man took out his spoons and added a terrific beat. Paudie Casey tuned up his fiddle and played along. Two couples joined hands and walked onto the dance floor. Others joined in, forming two lines of eight. That was all it took to get things started. Fun began! Colm tapped his good leg furiously and took out his spoons to add to the frantic dance beat. They watched as dancers twirled by, one by one, laughing and whooping. Soon everyone was on the dance floor doing a Galway set – an elaborate mini symphony of several three-minute dances called 'sets'. The tiny cottage overflowed with dancers. So much so that several couples danced right out the half door, not missing a beat. The familiar, heart-racing sets continued outside with a cacophony of feet dancing on a few rough timber planks some neighbours had provided.

Liam, shy as always, and realising that Colm couldn't enjoy one of his favourite things, held back. Although they were as different as any two brothers could be, Liam, the shy one and Colm, a fearless force to be reckoned with, they were best friends. Through a break in the crowd, Liam caught a glimpse of a beautiful young girl, thoroughly enjoying the festivities. Her auburn hair flew as she was whipped around the dance floor. As she came closer, her green eyes caught his. Her flawless skin was flushed and glowed from all the dancing. And her smile lit up the room. *What a beautiful girl!* Mesmerised by her delicate ankles peeking out from the hem of her soft burgundy dress, Liam saw the way her slender body moved to the music with confident grace. He couldn't tear his eyes away. 'Who in God's name is that?' he asked Colm. 'That's Máire Donnelly.' 'You're jokin' me.' 'Yea, I'm as shocked as you, boy. What a change huh? She's been workin' up in Dublin in some fancy house for a few years. I picked a great time to break me leg, didn't I?'

Liam looked again, as Máire swung with abandon to the music's frantic beat. He remembered her now: that tall, skinny, freckle-faced tomboy of a girl, with a wild mop of dark red hair. In those gloriously innocent days, she was always wrestling with the boys and getting into as much mischief as any of the lads. He smiled, remembering the black eye she'd given him when he'd teased her for falling off her pony when they'd raced. She'd dusted herself off, gotten back up on her pony, casually ridden up to him, and taking a swing, hit him in the eye. 'As if you've never fallen off yerself, Liam O'Donaghue!' And off she galloped.

Máire walked back to her parents when the dance ended. Marvelling, Liam couldn't believe how, in such a few short years, she had transformed from that playful little girl into the most beautiful woman he'd ever been lucky enough to encounter. He wanted nothing more than to sample those lovely lips of hers. In all his twenty-five years, he'd never entertained such thoughts as these about any other girl. Colm was the womaniser in the family, and Liam had walked out with a few girls himself, but none of them had had Máire Donnelly's immediate, warming effect.

When the dance ended, Father Murphy stepped forward to get everyone's attention. It took several moments for the group to take leave of their conversations and turn towards the priest. Father Murphy called the young couple to the front of the room to give the emigrating couple his blessing. 'Ah, 'tis grand to be with you all this evening as we bid farewell to Paudie and Úna before they begin their long journey to America on Monday. 'Tis a sad time to be sure, but we ask God's merciful blessings on them as they start a new life for themselves in the new world. Paudie Junior and Úna, may God keep you close in his heart, bless you with many children, and look out for you always.'

Father Murphy's blessing deeply touched these hardened men and women, strong and tough, because they had to be. Yet they couldn't help themselves now; they sniffed loudly, and their usually stoic faces jerked with anguished emotion. Tears began. Young Paudie and Úna, their shaking hands gripped tightly with feelings of loss, clung to each other for comfort. They looked at their broken-hearted parents, shoulders slumped and devastated, yet hopeful for their children's future in the new world.

Addressing the young couple again, Father Murphy continued, 'You come from strong Catholic families who will pray for you every day of their lives. May the Lord bless you, Paudie and Úna, in the name of the Father, and of the Son, and of the Holy Ghost.' 'Amen,' they all whispered, voices struggling, nearly silenced by lumps in their throats. In the awkward silence that followed, only Tomás had words. 'Horse, play somethin' for them.' Liam shyly took out his tin whistle and glanced around the room, taking in the young couple one last time. And then, reflecting the sadness of the occasion, he began to play a slow and haunting air he had recently composed.

On many of his rides atop Bridgey, he'd witnessed the most beautiful ocean sunsets with skies of orange, red, and all shades of purple, the sun brightening the closer it got to the horizon. As the sun kissed the water, he could almost hear it sizzle. All around him, wildflowers draping the hills of Galway bloomed gloriously. Watching wild hares and pheasants busily building homes for their young, Liam was enchanted by the emotion he felt for God's beautiful creations, a feeling which flowed from his lips to the tin whistle, and into his song, as it did now for this gathering. Tears flowed freely from everyone present, knowing that they would never see this couple again.

Liam played on, eyes closed, concentrating on the melody with all its subtle inflections and grace notes. He played as a master tin whistle player, steeped in the West Clare/Galway tradition. Had he opened his eyes, he would have seen Máire staring at him, weeping and remembering her long-ago crush on him, then a strapping, pimply teenager. Now, as she looked at him, she couldn't believe the man she saw: white shirt, sleeves rolled up revealing his strong arms, and tweed waistcoat – standing six feet two, skin glowing from his long days working in the fields, and playing the tin whistle with quick strong hands and agile fingers.

Liam was known as 'black Irish' – a person born with thick black hair, darker than normal skin, and piercing green eyes. During the eighteenth and nineteenth century, a thriving wine industry had grown up in the city of Galway. Spanish ships would dock in the city for weeks loading and unloading their goods. Since the sailors did what sailors often do, numerous Galway kids grew up looking a lot more Spanish than Irish. As this marvellous infusion of foreign blood coursed through the veins of many an Irish person living on the west coast, the name 'black Irish' came to be.

Liam finished his tune and everybody applauded. Then Tomás and the others started to play another lively set, and the dancers took to the floor once more. Watching Liam pocket his tin whistle, Máire remembered how shy he had been as a boy, so she knew that a first gesture at renewing their friendship would have to be hers. Having spent a few years in Dublin working as a housemaid for a wealthy English family, she had seen considerably more of the outside world than had the sheltered folks back home in West Galway. Now she wasn't as shy as she used to be. Wondering how Liam had come on over the years she'd been away, Máire worked her way towards him, wending her way through the clusters of people engaged in conversation. As she approached, Liam locked eyes with her and then shyly looked towards his brother. Assuming that she was coming to talk to Colm, who usually got the looks from the girls, he heard her speak above the din in the room, 'You're a fine tin whistle player, Liam O'Donaghue, and are ya as fine a dancer?' Startled and trying to find his tongue, he blurted, 'Well I dunno'.' Máire took a step closer and said, 'Well come on then.'

Having enjoyed big sips of their drinks, the musicians started playing again, and Máire, smiling her perfect smile, extended her hand to Liam. He grinned, slowly pulled himself to his feet, and took her hand. They reached the dance floor, joined hands formally, and faced the opposite couple. In and out they danced, three steps in, three steps out, repeat. Then they skilfully danced seven steps to the left, three steps standing, repeat, and seven steps back. Placing his left hand on her waist and holding her elbow with his right hand, they swung and twirled together in small circles in time with the music. They stopped, faced the next couple and repeated the same dance pattern, swinging wildly together.

Too soon, Máire and Liam were back to the sevens left and sevens right, when the dance ended. Still laughing and catching their breath, their eyes locked and held for a moment. Their hands slipped apart and Máire, breaking the spell, left him standing alone on the dance floor, calling over her shoulder as she walked away, 'So you can dance too, Liam O'Donaghue.' Smiling, she rejoined her parents and sat down.

The small cottage was filled with the mixed scents of burning turf, boiling food, drink, and hot dancing bodies. Mrs Casey reached for a huge steaming pot of crubeens, a traditional dish of boiled pigs' feet, simmering over the fireplace. Carefully, she carried the heavy pot to the table. The grateful guests went over, grabbed a plate, picked one out each, and started eating the heavily-salted dish, quenching their thirst with sips of poitín.

'Horse,' said Colm, wiping his mouth with the back of his hand, 'will ya go over there and talk to her? I saw the way she looked at ya.' 'What could I say to her, down from Dublin and everthin'?' 'Yerra, I dunno', but I saw the way you looked at her, too. You'd better ask her out before she goes back to Dublin. Take her horse riding or somethin'.' Nudging him with his elbow he said, 'Go on Horse, go on, before ya lose yer chance!'

Liam, feeling a bit more encouraged by Colm, mustered up all his courage and walked over to Máire; to Liam, the few steps felt like a mile. 'I remember you now from the hedge school long ago before we moved to Mrs O'Connor's shebeen,' he said shyly. He recalled that Catholics were not allowed an education back then. Nevertheless, dedicated teachers and priests moved about to teach religion, reading, and writing. But if they were caught by the redcoats they could be hanged, and many were. So they taught secretly up in the hills, usually hidden by thick hedges, thus their classrooms became known as 'hedge schools'.

'And I remember you. You were a great one for the ponies,' she said. Liam smiled, remembering those carefree days. 'I suppose you're going back to Dublin tomorrow.' 'No I'm not. The family I work for has gone to London for a wedding, so I have a few days off.' More confident, Liam knew this was his chance. 'Well then, would ya like to go for a horse ride tomorrow?' 'That would be nice, but I haven't been on a horse in years.' 'Ah don't worry about that. Sure I'll be there to help if need be.'

Awakened by the sound of chickens cackling and glimpsing a bit of light peeking through the tiny window brightening the cottage, Máire rolled over, put her arms above her head, and gave herself a long stretch. She woke with a dreamy smile. It seemed her thoughts all night long were of her old friend Liam. He certainly was no longer that young boy! She got out of bed and rinsed her face at the washbasin. Then she ran a brush through her long hair, pulling it back to tie it loosely with a ribbon at the base of her neck. Looking forward to spending time with Liam today, she dressed, ate a small bowl of porridge, sipped a quick steaming cup of tea, and then set out to Liam's cottage.

Liam had been watching for Máire to come over the little hill, eager to have time alone with her, but when she first came into view, he didn't recognise her. He saw a lovely figure with long hair tied back. She was dressed in elegant riding attire – a dark green jacket that accentuated her hair, tweed riding pants, and at her neck, a white scarf. It was as fine an outfit as was only seen on the backs of the well to do. And then, when she was closer still, and he realised who it was, she took his breath away. He was dumbstruck.

With a half-smile Máire said, 'Well are ya ready to go

ridin' Mr O'Donaghue?' 'My God, woman. I thought you were a landlord's daughter. Where did ya get those fine clothes?' 'Yerra. The lady in Dublin's gone off to buy the latest riding outfit in London, so she threw these out. I thought I'd sell 'em at the fair in Clifden this weekend to pay for my trip, but first I'll get a bit o' use out of 'em today.'

Liam had already prepared the horses for their ride. Bridgey and Capalleen were tied to a small tree by the cottage. Liam had named the pony Capalleen because she was smaller than most Connemara ponies. Though diminutive, she had a strength and proud air about her that Liam loved. Liam was wearing a pair of rough pants, a traditional blue grandfather cotton shirt, a tweed cap, and the same waistcoat he'd worn at the wake. A ray of sunshine peeked through the clouds as they came to the horses. 'Say hello to Capalleen,' he said, untying her rein from the tree.

Máire patted her gingerly, put her leg up into the stirrup, and pulled herself up, holding onto the ancient saddle. As Liam jumped up onto Bridgey, his mother came out of the cottage. 'Hello Máire, 'tis grand you're lookin'. Here Liam, I made some hot tea and bread for ye.' Josie handed him a small cloth bag containing buttered bread and an old whiskey bottle they normally used for the poitín. Today, the bottle full of milky, sugary tea, was tucked into a thick woollen sock to keep it warm. 'Go on, off with ye now.' She waved as they left the cottage and headed out onto the dirt road. It was a glorious spring morning with a light warm breeze blowing the green fields of barley all around them to swirl in a natural ballet. They headed towards the ocean. As they cantered slowly along sun-kissed fields, Liam looked at her admiringly – Máire all decked out in her lovely riding outfit, looking like a champion rider. 'You have it Máire.

You look like you've been doin' this all yer life.' 'Go 'way outta' that. Sure we're only walkin',' she laughed nervously.

Soon they arrived at Liam's favourite place, the spot he came to whenever he wanted to be alone. It's here he'd play his tin whistle amongst the gorse and heather and the green fields descending to the ocean. The sky looked bluer today than he had ever seen it before – not a single cloud. Waves lapped gently ashore, their calming sounds barely audible in the distance. Liam jumped off Bridgey and walked around to help Máire dismount. She felt his strong hands holding her gently as she eased down the side of the pony. For a moment, he was so close that she could feel his breath on her face. She felt her cheeks redden, and as she looked up into his eyes, he hesitated, then broke away shyly.

Hitching the horses to the only tree nearby, Liam untied a rolled-up blanket from Bridgey's saddle and grabbed the bag Josie had given them. At a soft grassy area, he opened the blanket, spread it on the ground, and invited Máire to sit next to him. Opening the bag, he pulled out the bottle and poured tea into two brown pottery cups, handing one to Máire. Besides the brown bread slathered generously with her rich homemade butter, Josie had packed a small jar of gooseberry jam and a knife. Liam opened the jar and offered it to Máire. She delicately scooped up some jam, spread it on her bread, and handed the jar back to Liam. Digging into the jam roughly, Liam smeared his slice generously. Food never tasted so good to the young couple, thoroughly enjoying the scenery before them. After a while, their bread devoured, they drank more tea. Without thinking, Liam reached over and gently wiped a trace of jam from the corner of Máire's mouth. She smiled. "Tis nice here.' "Tis,' he replied. And then there was an awkward silence, for Liam was once again at a loss for words. When he leaned forward for another slice of bread, Máire noticed his tin whistle in the inside pocket of his vest. 'Will ya play me somethin'?' 'What would ya like to hear?' 'I dunno', I liked the tune last night, but t'was very sad. Play me somethin' lively.' 'All right so.' He put the tin whistle to his lips, gave it a quick blow to clean it out, and then began playing a lively reel. Máire was mesmerised again by how quickly and gracefully his fingers flew over the holes, stretching the instrument to its limits as he moved up and down the octaves with a master's ease. She looked out towards the ocean and closed her eyes to take in the tin whistle notes and the gentle waves coming ashore – a pleasing duet. When she opened her eyes again, she saw two dolphins rollicking in the waves, submerging and reappearing, leaping out of the water, then crashing down loudly as though applauding Liam's brilliant playing. Smiling, she looked back to Liam, this strong, silent man, eyes closed and transported to another world for a few brief moments.

Máire felt a strange stirring in her core that she didn't quite understand. She only knew that she loved being there with Liam today, and as she watched him play, she found herself leaning closer to him. He was startled when he opened his eyes to find her so near. Without thinking, he leaned in and kissed her softly. When he pulled away to continue the melody, Máire rested her head on his shoulder. Delighting in the feel of her tender kiss, Liam tucked the whistle back into his pocket and smiled. He reached up and removed her riding hat, loosening her auburn hair to fall around her face. He kissed her gently again, and they fell softly to the grass, lips still touching. Liam was in heaven, but considering what he'd love to do next, he was already dreading Saturday night's confession with Father Murphy. They lay there silently looking up at the blue sky. Máire slipped her hand into his. 'Can we do this again tomorrow, Liam?' 'That sounds good, but I have to plant the ould potatoes tomorra', and with Colm banjaxed, it'll take me all day.' 'Sure I can help ya. I did it all the time before I went to Dublin.' Gazing at this vision in her smart riding outfit, Liam was taken aback by Máire's offer. He couldn't imagine her slaving in the fields to plant potato seeds – dirty, back-breaking work. Yet, the thought of being with her again tomorrow was enough for him. He was overjoyed. 'Well that'd be great then, if ya don't mind.' Sitting there close together, they watched the clouds dance across the sky for a while, and knowing they must eventually head back, they eagerly looked forward to tomorrow.

Liam breakfasted on boiled potatoes, eggs, and buttermilk and then went out to the mud-thatched shed to collect the sack of potato seeds. Potatoes were all that allowed the Irish to survive from one year to the next. One acre of 'spuds', the easiest crop to grow, planted twice a year, would keep a family of five alive for almost a year, together with buttermilk, cabbage, a few chickens, and, if a family was lucky enough to own a pig, some bacon.

The O'Donaghue family farm had been ruthlessly taken from Tomás' father by the British when, one day, a British captain and ten regular redcoat soldiers rode up to his cottage and announced: 'As of tomorrow, by order of His Majesty King George IV of England, your lands are now granted to Colonel Fairchild who shall henceforth take ownership of all your crops, livestock, and farming equipment. Should you resist, your cottage shall be burned, and you will be evicted from this land forthwith. Long live the king!'

Some years later, Colonel Fairchild died without a son, and the land was re-granted to Lord William Kitchener, an arrogant, retired English colonel, who, having fought for Queen Victoria in Afghanistan, was thus rewarded with the O'Donaghues' land in Ireland, and many other local farms as well. Aging and lazy, Kitchener quickly recognised the farming abilities of Tomás, healthy and in his early fifties, and his two strapping sons; Liam twenty-five and Colm twenty-four, the O'Donaghues could serve his purpose. So, rather than evicting them from their farm altogether, he rented Tomás' own tiny cottage back to him, along with a small bit of land, in return for growing crops and raising sheep and cattle for export to Britain. Life for Tomás' family was to become subsistence at its lowest level, but they knew that they were among the lucky few to still have a roof over their heads.

Early next morning, Máire knocked on the O'Donaghues' half door, entered, and with her hands on her hips, asked, 'Well are ya goin' to sit there all day, and watch me do all the work, Liam O'Donaghue?'

Turning to the door, Liam caught Máire's comely smile, and his mood immediately brightened. When he saw that Máire, tall and lovely, was wearing a simple, long, dark blue dress of cotton and work boots, he knew that she was serious about helping him with the planting. Her grin and sense of devilment warmed his heart. 'Well now, aren't you a grand sight indeed on this fine day Máire Donnelly?' Liam threw the heavy sack of potato seeds over his shoulder, and they walked to the small potato patch facing the thatched cottage.

The most popular, easy, and reliable potato seeds were called lumpers, which, when planted, produced a bountiful crop of large knobby, brown-skinned, but not-so-tasty, yellow potatoes. They were nourishing enough, however, to keep a family alive, and the moist Irish climate was perfect for this crop. As they began sticking each seed into the ground, Liam appreciated all the more Máire's volunteering to take Colm's place. This gesture cut the monotonous job in half, and she easily kept up with him. Kneeling, they paralleled each other, inching down the potato patch, elbows touching occasionally.

It was another warm spring morning, and thankfully, other than covering them with soil, the seeds didn't need any fancy planting care. Patience, waiting for the rich autumn harvest, was all that was needed now. Máire's face was beaded with sweat, and her hair fell loosely from its ribbon as they finished the first run. Liam's heart burst with admiration as he watched her work just as hard as he did. Reaching into the rough bag to grab more seeds, Máire's hand brushed against his, and they both paused, surprised. She straightened up and looked at him. Across the bag of seeds, they both leaned forward and Liam cupped her face. He kissed her softly, gently pulling her close, the monotony of his dreary existence forgotten. Slowly and shyly they pulled away, and dug back into the bag. Máire broke the silence. 'Come on now Liam O'Donaghue; we gotta lot o' seeds to plant still.' Then turning towards him she smiled, 'I like planting seeds with ya.' They began another run of planting, both sensing that their lives had changed. The last thing she wanted now was to go back to Dublin. Liam was certain that all he wanted was to be with her every second for the rest of his life.

After a long day of back-breaking planting, they were finally done, and Josie had dinner ready for them. The fare was boiled potatoes as usual, but this time prepared with the luxury of butter, along with bread and blackberry jam preserved from last year's summer hedge picking. Buttermilk was their beverage. 'So Máire, when are ya goin' back to Dublin?' asked Josie. Máire and Liam looked sadly at each other, lowering their heads. 'So it's like that then, is it?' Josie recognised that look of longing, desperate love. Pleased, but at the same time alarmed, she knew what they were thinking; they want to marry, but they'll have no place to live.

Tomás was born to farm, possessed of the skills needed to reap bountiful yearly harvests despite anything Mother Nature threw at him. An expert fisherman, Colm kept her Ladyship's kitchen well stocked with fresh fish and lobsters for her lavish dinners. Liam's horse training skills were invaluable to the landlord. Lately he'd been teaching Kitchener's daughter the fancy sport of show jumping and, under his guidance, she was becoming a promising rider. But if Liam left, the O'Donaghues might be thrown off the estate to make way for another family having the same farming and fishing abilities as Tomás and Colm. Would her family's skills hold enough sway with Lord Kitchener that he would allow Liam to build a cottage here?

Lord Kitchener's son, Edward, in striking contrast to his diligent sister Emma, showed the classic traits of a spoiled brat born into privilege – laziness, drinking, and gambling – and he was still only in his mid-teens. Lord Kitchener was content to allow the O'Donaghues to stay on his land, working for virtually nothing, to keep him and his family living the good life he had become accustomed to here.

'I'll ask your Da to have a word with Kitchener about what we can do about ye.' Máire and Liam's spirits rose at Josie's amazingly insightful instincts. He reached out and held Máire's hands. 'Thanks Mam. I'd have never thought of that.' 'Well he'd never listen to a woman, but maybe Tomás can get him on his good side – if he has one.' They smiled hopefully. 'Go on now Máire. Go back to Dublin. The more ya learn there, the better chance you have of gettin' work in the big house.' Realising that Josie was right, they slowly walked to Máire's home, but knowing she'd be leaving for Dublin tomorrow, Liam couldn't bear the thought of being apart from her for even a second. He stopped, drew her close, held her fast in his strong arms, and kissed her passionately. 'Marry me, Máire. Stay with me. Don't go back to Dublin, Máire. Stay here, please. These last few days have been the happiest of my life. Don't go.' He kissed her again. Máire taken aback by Liam's passion, felt likewise. She'd heard exactly what she'd hoped he'd say. Although thrilled that he'd asked her to marry him, like Josie, she was more pragmatic. 'Liam O'Donaghue, yes, I will marry you, but your mother's right. We've nowhere to live. Let Tomás talk to the master and see what happens. I'm sure he wouldn't want to lose ye all, and I could work in the big house with all I've learned in Dublin.' When they reached her cottage, Liam kissed her one last time, and with a loving smile she ran inside, then turned and waved from the half door. 'Come back soon, Máire.'

''Tis a very good season sir,' said Tomás, giving his annual spring report to John Bishop, Kitchener's bailiff, and hated rent collector. 'Sixty-five lambs, and forty-three fine, healthy calves, seven of 'em bullocks,' he recited. 'Good.' 'I think the master will be pleased.' 'He wants more barley and oats planted this spring, at least ten acres.' Hearing this demand, Tomás assumed that his Lordship's son Edward must have lost more of his family's money gambling, and he was still only in boarding school. 'Is the master here?' asked Tomás, not knowing if he was away in London or Dublin, as he often was. 'Why do you want to know?' inquired Bishop, suspicious because it was he who handled all affairs of the estate. 'I need to talk to him about Liam.' 'What about him? If he has a problem, tell him to come to me and not waste his Lordship's time.' 'Yes sir.' And heeding Josie's wise advice, Tomás decided to go with Liam the next time he went up to the big house to give Lady Emma her riding lesson. Kitchener might be there and would probably be in a good mood watching his pride and joy jumping low fences in her perfect little riding suit, all the while displaying the courage he wished her older brother had.

'Hurry up and clean out the chickens; we haven't got all day,' barked the head kitchen maid to Máire. Still half asleep after the exhausting trip back to Dublin, Máire picked up the pace and gutted two plump chickens for evening dinner for the master's family. Like the Kitcheners, the Prescott family were English and were preparing for Dublin's spring society party season. In addition to a country estate given to them by the queen for services to Her Majesty, they also owned a fancy townhouse in Dublin, Britain's second jewel in Her Majesty's empire.

Dublin was built in a splendour comparable to that of London. The landlords and their wives, the aristocrats of their day, enjoyed a luxurious standard of living, partying, gambling, and socialising amongst their own, creating their own little London of the day. Cork, being the second city, also had some fine architectural homes and buildings. Their staff, all Irish, were worked hard for paltry wages, but they knew that they were the lucky ones. They could be let go at any time for the flimsiest of reasons, and there were plenty of others waiting in the wings for a 'good job' in one of the fancy houses.

Máire, the happiest she'd ever been, was giddy and in great form despite her tiredness from her journey. However, she couldn't confide in anyone. If one word got back to the mistress about the possibility of her leaving, she would be sent packing. No, she'd wait until she heard how Tomás fared with Kitchener. Carrying heavy china dinner plates up one floor, Máire looked about the splendid dining room with its massive hand-carved table and chairs overhung by a glittering crystal chandelier. The scene was set with brightly flowered wallpaper and silver cutlery perfectly arranged. For a few magical moments, she imagined herself in her ideal setting, in her ideal wedding gown with Liam at the head of the table, her parents and siblings to the right, and Tomás, Josie, Colm and his two younger sisters to the left, about to enjoy the wedding feast. Her heart teemed with love and happiness, as she revelled in the fantasy – Liam, so handsome in a fine suit, beaming with pride as he raised his goblet to toast his beautiful bride. And then she heard the other maids placing heavy pewter candleholders onto the perfectly laid out table. Her wedding feast was over, but she could dream.

How can life be so cruel? she thought. *These are the most selfish, spoiled, lazy people I've ever met. They have everything that life can offer them, and yet they look down on everyone. How can God allow this?*

Máire knew that, while his wife was back in their country estate running the house, the master was in Dublin conducting 'business', – cheating on her with his mistress. And Máire had seen most of her master's men friends doing likewise. One of them had grabbed her breast one evening after dinner as she was serving brandy and cigars. When he drunkenly groped her, she 'accidentally' dropped the snifter of brandy on his lap. 'Sorry sir,' she said, feigning regret. He cursed her as she pulled away. Thankfully her master hadn't seen this exchange, and the man didn't complain, so there were no reprisals. But she observed the shallowness and hypocrisy of their privileged lives daily. *By God, I would rather sleep next to Liam on a bed of straw, have his children, and live in a tiny cottage for the rest of my life, than live like these people.*

Josie already had potatoes and cabbage boiling, as her family dug into breakfast. She was a gifted cook, proven by the way she prepared the flavourful cabbage and onions which her sons had bartered or stolen from the bountiful yearly harvests. Mercifully, Bishop, the bailiff, turned a blind eye to the smattering of vegetables Josie grew on their little patch of land. 'I'm giving Lady Emma her jumping lesson tomorrow Da, and the master is home.' 'Fair enough, Horse, I'll be there. Bishop will be away selling a few heifers, so it's as good a time as any to speak to him.' Josie had given her husband the news about Máire and Liam, and had coached him in what to say. 'Praise the little girl like she's the only girl that ever rode a horse, Tomás. Tell him she'll be a champion fox hunter soon. Then tell him the good news about the lady of the house getting a housemaid trained in Dublin, if Máire and Liam marry. When he realises how pleased his wife will be, just let him know that they need to add a bit more to the cottage, which will take no time at all.' Grateful for her backing him in his dream of marrying Máire, Liam smiled at his mother's crafty logic and dearly hoped that Tomás could pull it off tomorrow.

On another grey and dreary day, clouds blanketed the lush green hills and valleys. Emma, in her trim riding suit and hat, easily prompted her horse Lilly to soar over the four jumps Liam had erected in the field behind the big house. Liam was teaching her to ride cross saddle as against side-saddle, the gentrified style of the time. Kitchener, an ex-cavalry man, was all about control of the horse. 'Twisted and packed onto a side-saddle no more,' were his instructions to Liam. 'Fashion be damned,' he said, 'I want Emma to gallop and jump in complete control of her horse.' He told Liam that he got Elizabeth away from side-saddle riding as soon as they came to Ireland. Liam was encouraging her, down by the first fence. 'Don't look down, Lady Emma. Look straight ahead, head up.' She cleared a fence. 'Good, good, good… now turn as quickly as you can, that's it, good girl.' Emma smiled proudly at her beaming father, as she cleared the last fence. 'Good girl, Emma,' he shouted as she turned and jumped the fences again. 'She'll make a fine fox hunter soon sir,' said Tomás as he walked up to Kitchener, watching her turn and jump again. 'By God, Tomás, I think you're correct,' he beamed. 'I was in the cavalry myself, and she's already as good a rider as many a man I had in the regiment. And she's still only eleven. Liam has the knack doesn't he?' 'Yes sir, ever since he was as young as Lady Emma, he was riding the ponies. We call him Horse, you know.' Kitchener smiled and seemed more relaxed than Tomás had ever seen him. Making his play, Tomás said, 'Congratulations on the Lady about to give birth, sir.' 'Thank you, Tomás, but I'm getting too old for this I'm afraid.' 'Not at all, sir. Sure look at Lady Emma. She must be thrilled she'll have another brother or sister.' 'Yes, she'll boss him or her around just like she does the rest of us.' 'Well, maybe I might be able to help her Ladyship, sir.' 'What do you mean?' 'You know one of your tenants, the Donnellys?' 'Yes, of course. What about them?' 'Well they have a daughter, Máire, working for the Prescotts in Dublin.' 'Oh yes, I know the Prescotts. Good family.' 'Yes, sir. She's been a housemaid with them for the last four years, trained to do everything in the kitchen, cook, clean, and organise big parties. Lady Prescott is very pleased with her.' Kitchener shook his head, half listening. 'Well, she and Liam are getting married, and she's looking to come home, or maybe both of them going to America,' said Tomás, adding his own little white lie for Kitchener to worry about. 'Maybe her Ladyship, in her condition, could use more help now. With everything Máire has learned up in Dublin, she could be of great assistance. She's a very hard and honest worker, sir.' Kitchener looked at Emma as Liam helped her dismount, and she ran to him. 'Lovely jumping, Emma, you're getting better every time I see you. Mama will be very pleased.' She smiled. Turning to Tomás as he walked away, he said, 'I'll ask her Ladyship if she thinks she needs some further help.' 'Thank you, sir.'

Later, Liam anxiously awaited Tomás' return from his afternoon chores, and the moment he entered the cottage, Liam asked, 'Well, how did it go?' 'He said he'd tell his wife about Máire, and he'd let me know.' 'Did you ask him if we could build somethin'?' 'No, he walked away and said he'd let his wife know about Máire.' Sensing his son's impatient annoyance at wanting everything to happen yesterday, Tomás advised, 'Patience, Horse. If the lady says yes, then I'll ask him about your building somethin'. If he says no, he'll have to make sense of his decision to his wife.' Liam walked away, bitter as always at the stranglehold the landlord had over him and his future happiness.

Dinner was served in the Kitcheners' dining room by two kitchen maids, each worn out from running from the kitchen to the lavish dining room. Each carried a tray heavily laden with two plates topped with silver lids to keep the food warm. In the old English family mansions, the kitchen was never located below or near the dining and family rooms, as the landlord and his family should never be bothered by cooking odours. Tonight the maids walked briskly from the kitchen, through the wine cellar, across the entire basement area of the house, and finally up the stairs to the dining room. Placing a plate before each family member, they lifted the silver covers with a fancy flourish to reveal the main course of roast pheasant, mashed potatoes, carrots, and turnips. Then the maids stepped back, to await further instructions or complaints.

'I hate turnips. How many times do I have to tell you?' shouted Edward, glaring at the head maid. With a flick of his wrist, the pieces of turnips flew off his plate and fell to the floor. 'Edward,' said his mother sternly, 'that sort of behaviour is not allowed at the table.' One of the maids crouched down, picked up the discarded turnip slices, and put them in her apron. 'But Mother, I don't want to eat it. I hate it.' The maids eyed each other in unspoken disgust, but they were pleased to know that, once out of sight of the family, they would eat the discarded vegetables. The head housekeeper watched the servants like a hawk, keeping on Lady Kitchener's good side by reporting any stealing or slouching exhibited by anyone on staff. A bitter old woman, Peig Shea was from another parish and had never married. The mistress trusted her, and over the years, Peig had worked her way up to her position of authority. Nobody was ever going to take her place as long as she was alive.

'William.' Lady Kitchener addressed her husband and looked to him to do something. 'Edward, apologise to your mother for your terrible table manners.' The maids were invisible in this drama, and none of the family even considered offering an apology to them. They were nothing, merely help. Head down – fist clenched, Edward sulked. 'Edward!' said his father sternly. 'I'm sorry, Mother,' he said unconvincingly, and they began eating. 'Mama,' chirped Emma, 'I didn't knock any fences down today, and Liam said they were three feet high.' Elizabeth's face softened, beaming at her beloved daughter's innocent passion. 'That's absolutely smashing Emma. You're getting so good.'

'Liam says I'm going to be a champion hunter when I grow up. 'You're our little champion already, my dear.' 'I heard some news today,' said William. 'Liam is getting married.' Emma looked up at once, surprised and worried. 'Is he going to go away? Who will teach me?' 'No, no, no, dear. He's staying right here,' said her father. 'Who is he marrying?' asked Elizabeth. 'One of the Donnelly girls.' 'Aren't they very young?' 'The eldest girl apparently has been working in Dublin for the Prescotts for the past four years.' 'And she's going to give up a fine job like that?' 'Well, perhaps you might consider taking her on here, given all her experience, especially now when you're about to have a baby. I'm sure another pair of hands would be helpful for you.' 'Yes, we could do with an experienced housekeeper. The maids are virtually useless. I can never get them to do exactly what I want, no matter how many times I show them. Perhaps you could interview her when you're in Dublin next month. If the Prescotts will vouch for her and her housekeeping experience, tell her to come down. I'm sure they can easily find a good replacement for her in Dublin.'

Elizabeth rang a bell summoning the maids to remove the dinner plates. Hurrying down to the kitchen, they placed the plates by the big water tub. Peig had desserts ready on another tray – warm apple pie topped with a generous dollop of fresh whipped cream. The exhausted maids hurried back to the dining room to serve them. Leaving, they heard their mistress quarrelling with young Edward about school. 'Edward, your spring report is vastly disappointing.' 'I don't like school,' he complained. 'It's so boring, the food is horrendous, and nobody likes me.' 'You have three years left before you go off to college. You won't get into Trinity unless you pull up your socks and study. What do you do at boarding school? Obviously not homework.' 'I study, Mother.' 'Well obviously not hard enough,' said his father sternly. 'You can join the Army like I did and do it the hard way. Is that what you want?' 'No, Father.' 'Well then, you'd better get down to it for the rest of this year, or it's the Army for you, my boy.' Edward angrily attacked his dessert.

Colm hobbled around on the crude crutches Tomás had made for him from two sturdy hawthorn branches, bent at the top by strong, constant western sea breezes. Restless and bored from being confined to the relatively flat area around the cottage, he was sitting just outside the half door, mending his fishing nets. ''Tis gonna' be a cold one out there today, Horse.' 'Yea,' said Liam, gathering up the nets. 'Don't drown yerself now boy,' he teased. Laughing, Liam walked down to the shoreline, the heavy nets on his back. He pulled their new currach into the water, jumped in, and rowed away from the rocky beach. Kitchener expected a constant supply of fresh fish as part of the O'Donaghues' rent. Never mind that Colm was grounded; a supply of fresh fish was expected three days a week. No excuses.

When the herring or mackerel shoals ran in the summer, it was easy to throw the wide nets out and land a decent catch. In the springtime, though, casting the nets was far more difficult and physically demanding. Heavy stones were attached to the base of the nets, so that they would sink and be dragged along the seabed. Fighting against the current pulling him back to shore, Liam needed all his strength to row against the tide, the wet nets getting heavier as he snared a few herring. He dragged the nets towards the currach, and with a strong pull, tried to heave the sodden nets into the boat, almost tipping it over. Liam dropped the nets, and to his relief, the boat righted itself. He wished he had his brother's natural fishing skills. Colm could pull the nets into the boat, timing the motion perfectly to keep the currach in balance, and make it all look easy. Liam tried again and got half the netting into the boat. Looking down at the remaining nets in the water, he saw that he had caught a few nice fish frantically trying to escape. With a few more pulls, the nets were back in the boat. He emptied the fish into a big bucket of seawater to keep them fresh and then rowed out to cast the nets again. Exhausted after repeating these motions several more times, he rowed ashore. Jumping out, he pulled the currach up the beach and spread the nets out to dry. Grabbing the half-full bucket, he thought *I'm no fisherman*. Colm nearly always had a bucket full of fish, some of which his family would enjoy. Not today.

Liam walked over to the rocky shoreline and scanned the tide pool for Lady Kitchener's most favoured catch of all – lobster. It was almost impossible to see them as they slowly slid along, well camouflaged by the rocks. Sometimes Colm would get lucky and grab one, knowing exactly where to latch onto them safely. Liam half-heartedly looked about, knowing that he didn't have Colm's timing, and dreading the moment when he would have to commit his hand to nabbing one. One mistake and he could lose a finger from a lobster's razor-sharp claws. Presenting a lobster to Lady Kitchener kept Liam's family in her good graces; no luck today, though, so he picked up the bucket and headed to the big house.

Shouting orders to the kitchen girls as they washed the breakfast dishes, Peig Shea was there when Liam delivered his catch. 'Well, O'Donaghue, what have ya got for us today?' she asked in her heavy-handed tone. He entered the basement door, the staff entrance at the back of the house. Peering into the bucket, Peig groused, 'The mistress was hoping for a lobster. When will yer brother be able to go out again? You're useless, so you are!' Liam wished he did have a lobster – to throw at her. He imagined the lobster's claw grabbing onto her nose and her screaming and roaring trying to shake it off. She'd soon lose that high and mighty attitude of hers. 'It'll be a while,' he said. 'The mistress wants to see you.' Thinking the mistress would hire Máire immediately, he was delighted to follow Peig down the long dark corridor, up a staircase to the first floor, and then into a little side room. This was where the maids waited between courses to be summoned by the bell to remove dirty dishes. 'Wait here,' Peig snarled, wondering to herself what in God's name her mistress had to say to him. *I'm the one who dishes out the mistress' demands to staff and tenants.* Peig entered the elegant drawing room where Lady Kitchener was reading by the fire. 'Beggin' yer pardon ma'am,' she said, curtseying. Lady Kitchener looked up. 'Yes, Peig, what is it?' 'You asked me to bring Liam O'Donaghue to you, and I have him here.' 'Good, bring him in.' Peig was shocked that a tenant was being allowed into the big house's drawing room. *Lord Kitchener would never countenance such a thing.* She walked back to the little side room and barked, 'Follow me.'

Liam followed her into the immense drawing room and couldn't believe the luxury there – two imposing gothic windows, lavish draperies, large sofas, an overpowering fireplace, multicoloured rugs, magnificent oil paintings, and impressive hunting murals. 'Hello Liam,' she said warmly. Having never seen this side of her before, Liam was taken aback. Usually, when he was teaching Lady Emma, this woman, like her husband, was aloof. Peig remained, waiting to escort Liam out after Lady Kitchener finished her business with him. She had no intention of missing what her mistress had to say, and she thought she had every right as the head housekeeper to be present. 'That will be all Peig, thank you.' Stunned and utterly speechless for once, Peig looked at her mistress, who gave her a curt smile and dismissive nod. Turning, she saw Liam, eyebrows raised, wearing a smirk. She walked out of the room gritting her teeth. 'Please close the door, Peig.' Furious, Peig thought, *How could my mistress embarrass me like this? And what is so important that she hasn't confided in me whatever matter this is? And after all I've done for her!* She closed the door slowly.

'Congratulations Liam. I hear you're getting married.' 'Yes ma'am, to Máire Donnelly.' 'Yes, my husband told me all about it, but I don't remember her. What does she do for the Prescotts?' 'She's a housekeeper, ma'am, making sure everything's clean, and she's a nanny to their young child.' 'Really?' she said. 'I told my husband to inquire if she's suitable. If so, and if the Prescotts will let her go, we would hire her.' 'That would be great ma'am.' 'Will she be moving in with your family once you're married?' Liam couldn't believe this was happening – exactly the way Josie predicted. Realising she actually seemed to have a softer side than her husband, Liam decided that, rather than ask her husband, he'd ask her about adding a room onto the house. He was also fully aware that she would be getting a great deal, since Máire would be working for slave wages if she did get the job. He decided to look her in the eye, face to face. Tenants were never allowed to do this, as they were always expected to remain meek and humble. 'Don't you ever dare to forget your place,' was constantly drilled into the Irish. It was difficult for Liam to be meek and humble though. Quiet as he was, his pride was never too far below his skin. Heart thumping, he said, 'We were hoping to add a little room to the cottage, ma'am, if the master will allow us.' 'I see,' she said. 'I'll have a word with my husband, if he thinks Máire will work out.' 'Thank you, ma'am.' Then, forgetting his station briefly, he added, 'I'm sorry I wasn't able to catch a lobster for ya today.' She gave him a slight smile, something she'd never done before. 'When will your brother be able to go out again?' 'Soon, ma'am. He's the fisherman in the family.' Smiling, he nodded his head, careful not to bow, his own little hint of rebellion, and left the room. Waiting in the anteroom, Peig reasserted her authority and quickly escorted him out the back door. Walking away with a happy gait, Liam took out his tin whistle and played a cheerful reel. *Next month, Máire will be in my arms forever.*

Lord and Lady Prescott's Dublin home was a Georgian townhouse on Leeson Street, not as formidable as those on St. Stephen's Green; nevertheless, it had a grandiose Georgian door and elegant steps. Landlords and their wives used these city houses for the annual social seasons, debutantes' balls, gambling, business, and for sexual pleasuring with their mistresses.

The butler took Lord Kitchener's hat and showed him into the drawing room. 'William, good to see you. How is Elizabeth?' 'Hello, George, very well thank you, and with child again, I'm afraid.' George walked over to the drinks cabinet and poured two glasses of port, handing one to Edward. 'Congratulations, my dear fellow. When is she due?' 'Sometime in October.' 'Cheers,' he said as they clinked glasses, 'but aren't you getting a trifle old for that sort of thing?' he teased. William smiled. 'I think it actually happened the night of your daughter's ball.' 'Sorry about that old boy, but Elizabeth is a beautiful lady, and of course, much younger than you,' he joked. 'So, to what do I owe this visit?'

'Well, you have a maid called Donnelly working for you.' 'Oh yes, a housekeeper and nanny. Margaret is pleased with her. Why do you ask?' 'She's the daughter of one of my tenants.' 'Oh yes, I remember.' 'Well, she's marrying another tenant of mine, and I would like to kill two birds with one stone, as it were.' 'How so?' asked George. 'Well, the fellow she's marrying is my daughter's horse trainer. Along with possessing many other skills, he's a very good worker. With Elizabeth expecting a child, she could use an experienced domestic, so if you could do me a favour and let the Donnelly girl go, it would be very much appreciated.' 'I'm sure that would be okay, William. I shall ask Margaret tonight and send word to you. Beats them both leaving entirely of course.' 'Yes,' said William, 'I was thinking about that. I wouldn't like to lose him, you know. Best tenant I have. So, how was your calving season? Profitable I hope.' They talked about each other's business, and after a while, William left.

Later that evening, while William was reading in the drawing room, the butler delivered an envelope just arrived from George Prescott.

Dear William,

Margaret is happy to hear the good news about Elizabeth and sends her best wishes. She is willing to let the servant go, albeit reluctantly, as the girl is a good worker. No doubt, she'll find a replacement quickly.

Enjoyed your visit,
Yours,
George

Two weeks later, Elizabeth, an excellent rider herself in every local fox hunt, came to watch Liam and Emma train.

Resplendent in a new riding outfit for this week's horse jumping lesson, Emma had mentioned that her father was back from Dublin at last. Expecting Kitchener to come to observe Emma's progress, Liam hoped for good news. Elizabeth, now visibly with child, encouraged her daughter as she jumped, landing perfectly. 'Lovely, Emma darling, watch your timing now.'

The fields were rampant with spring's wildflowers. Lambs and calves ran and played in the field nearby, revelling in how far and fast their legs could carry them. Liam remembered the time long ago when this was O'Donaghue livestock, running on O'Donaghue land. Now all his family did was work for nothing while watching Kitchener sell the animals and get richer every year. Liam was jolted from his bitter memories, when Emma yelped. Lilly had buckled coming down from a jump and thrown Emma headfirst, landing with a sickening thud. The horse collapsed and turned over, its legs flailing dangerously close to Emma who lay motionless. They ran to her. 'Emma!' screamed Elizabeth. Stunned, Emma raised her head, looked at her mother, and screamed with fright. Elizabeth pulled her close, 'It's all right child. Thank God you were wearing your hat.' The horse moaned, tried to get up, but fell again. Clearly her leg was broken, and she would have to be put down.

Dressing himself, Kitchener watched the scene in horror from his bedroom window. He raced down, reaching them as Liam helped Emma to her feet. She was shaken but otherwise fine. 'Emma,' he said, 'are you okay, dear?' Full of love and pride he watched her pull herself together, brush herself off, and give him a brave smile. With a tear of relief in his eye, he thought, *By God, she's a Kitchener all right*, and he drew her close for a hug.

Liam cried as he gently talked to Lilly, rubbing her head, calming her, as the others walked to the house. 'I'll be back shortly,' said Kitchener. Liam knew he'd gone for his gun and soon would be back to end her suffering. Liam was there when Lilly was born and had trained her from the start. She'd become an excellent jumper and a gentle rider. Kitchener had larger champion horses, also trained by Liam, but Lilly, as Emma had named her, was a fine small grey Connemara pony. She was perfect for Emma's age, always gentle, and willing to ride for as long as anyone wanted.

Kitchener returned with his pistol. 'Okay, let's get it over with then,' he said coldly. Liam bent in front of Lilly, looked into her eyes, gave her a gentle kiss, and moved aside. Kitchener stood in front of her, aimed and shot a bullet between her temples. The pony's head jolted back violently. She gave out a huge sigh and then leaned over dead. 'Jolly bad luck,' said Kitchener. 'She was a good pony. Get this mess cleaned up and get the brown pony ready for her next lesson. She has to get back up on a horse immediately.' *The brown pony!!! Bríd's pride and joy? Oh, Mother of God, what am I going to say to her? That ugly bastard is going to break her heart.* Kitchener knew Saoirse was Bríd's pony. It was the only thing she had. He had seen her riding it several times, but that was no matter for him. *How will I tell my sister she'll have to share her beloved pony with our landlord's daughter? Or that she might never ride Saoirse again?* Kitchener walked away, then stopped and half turned. 'Oh by the way, the Donnelly girl is going to work for us shortly. When the Prescotts find a suitable replacement, she'll start here straight away.' Despite Kitchener's condescending tone, Liam couldn't believe what he'd heard. *Máire is coming home, and we're going to marry.* Thank you, sir, and that little room I'd like to add onto our cottage, sir. Did the Mistress tell you about it?' Kitchener waved his hand dismissively, 'Yes, yes, go ahead,' and without any good wishes for Máire and Liam, he turned and walked back to the house. Liam's wildest dreams were coming true. Máire Donnelly would soon be Máire O'Donaghue. He could already see the little thatched room added on to his family's cottage. Maybe it would even have a small window. Perhaps a loft. He began to fantasise about their first night together, making love for the first time. His dreams interrupted by the buzz of flies flittering around the dead pony, Liam returned to the immediate reality – disposing of Lilly's carcass. He walked to the stables at the rear of the house, purposely not visible from any of the mansion's windows. He gathered up a few stable boys, heavy ropes, and shovels. Together they hitched two large workhorses to a flat-bedded cart, loading it with twigs and heavy branches. Then tying the pony's hind legs to the cart, dragged her a half mile or so down the lane. They entered a small stony field, looked for the least rocky area, and started to dig. Digging a pit seven by seven and three feet deep, in rocky ground, took a huge amount of time, sweat, and strain. That done, they threw the twigs and branches into the hole, setting them afire, and then stoked the pyre with branches one by one until it burned strongly. Finally, they dragged Lilly over and pushed her into the fire to cremate her. Though the smell of the burning flesh was disgusting, they had to remain until the carcass was consumed, so that the fire wouldn't spread. They stood upwind, turned their backs to the fire, and put their hands to their faces to lessen the smell. At last, cremation was complete, they extinguished the flames and then made their way back to the stables exhausted. Kitchener, watching from his library, saw the smoke in the distance and was happy he'd designated that field half a mile away; he wouldn't want his family to be nauseated by the smell.

Despite Bríd's heartbreak, it was a great night in the O'Donaghues' little cottage. Liam pulled Josie to the middle of the floor and swung her around happily as Tomás played a lively Irish reel on his button accordion. 'Will ya stop Liam, you're goin' too fast for me. You're gonna' make me fall,' she screamed, a big smile on her face. With the fire blazing and the poitín flowing, and some whiskey from local distilleries, Liam and his family celebrated the great news. Colm played the spoons furiously, just two large spoons in the hands of a master, adding great excitement to Tomás' fast reel. Aoife joined hands with Josie and Liam and they swung happily around in circles. 'Liam's getting married, and we love Máire, too!'

Lasting friends, the O'Donaghue and Donnelly families had been through hell and back over the last twenty years. They'd survived by sticking together, sharing whatever they had when the other family was short, and helping around the little bit of land each had whenever anyone needed an extra hand or two.

Tomás and Josie had watched Máire grow up, blossoming from a lovely innocent little girl into the beautiful woman she'd become. They too, were delighted when she'd gotten the job in a fine house in Dublin, knowing she would never go hungry. That was every Irish family's worst nightmare; would the stored potatoes be enough to last the year? Though there were two harvests each year, springtime and autumn, frequently the crop didn't last through the season, so they would have to scavenge for berries, rabbits, and, as a last resort, steal some of the landlord's grain and vegetables. They did this on a tiny scale, knowing how savagely they would be treated if they were caught. Somehow, they managed to survive until the next season's potato harvest.

As he saddled up Bríd's pony for Emma's lesson the next morning, Liam's head pounded. As much as he'd been on top of the world last night, it was hard, then, to remember that he was due for an early start today. Now he regretted the overindulgence of that damned poitín, *but it tasted so good.* As he drank it, he could feel the heat of it going straight to his toes and then exploding right back up to the top of his head. He also knew from bitter experience that, if he drank a drop of water this morning, he'd be flying again. So, as he headed out to give Lady Emma her riding lesson, no breakfast for him.

Elizabeth and Emma were waiting when he brought Saoirse out. 'Good mornin', ma'am. Mornin' Lady Emma.' They smiled silently. Liam mounted the pony and began a gentle trot. Saoirse was a little taller than poor old Lilly, but Emma would have been ready to go to a bigger horse soon anyway. Liam had broken her in, and she respected his expert touch. They trotted to the end of the field and approached the first fence. It was a thing of rare beauty, doing together what they were born to do, the two as if one. They rose and landed and then sailed over the next four fences effortlessly. Liam turned her around and they jumped the fences again. He trotted over to Emma and dismounted. 'Well, what do you think of her, Lady Emma?' 'I miss Lilly,' she said sadly. 'I know you do, Emma dear,' said Elizabeth, 'but Daddy is giving you this lovely pony for your very own. Why don't you ride her and see if you like her?'

At these words Liam nearly vomited. He wanted to scream. *This is our pony. Bríd's pony! How can you stand there with no shame at all about what you and your husband have taken from us? How can you say you believe in God, yet have no conscience when you see the awful things happening all around you?*

Emma gingerly put her left leg in the stirrup and pulled herself up into the saddle. Putting her right leg into the other stirrup, she dug her heels gently into the pony's sides, and they walked out into the field. 'Okay, Lady Emma,' said Liam, 'now speed up a little.' He saw her confidence growing, as she became comfortable on her new pony. Liam lowered the fences to just one foot high to get her used to jumping again. 'Very good, Lady Emma. You're doing fine. Now try jumping one fence.' She saw how low they were and easily jumped all five. Emma smiled proudly at her mother, and Elizabeth clapped in response. She would be delighted to tell William that his darling little daughter got up on her new pony, conquered her fears from her fall, and was great. Emma dismounted, handed the reins to Liam dismissively, and, engrossed in conversation with her mother, walked away with her, hand in hand. There wasn't a word of thanks to Liam from either of them. Liam walked the pony back to the stable and handed her off to the stable boy.

Walking home full of excitement, Liam began planning to build a little house. Even though it would only be a small extension to his parents' house, it would be Máire's and his home. *I'll build Máire a fine strong house*, he thought happily. Living on the west coast of Ireland, where brick-like rocks were abundant, he would select the most suitable ones for the job. Although it was difficult to grow most vegetables in that region other than potatoes, at least he was in luck when it would come to building a sturdy house. He had rocks. If he were farther inland, he'd have to build using mud bricks. That work was pure drudgery: digging out suitable mud, mixing it with reeds for strength, moulding it into thick bricks, stacking it like turf to dry, and finally, building the hut with a thatched overhang reaching almost to the ground to keep the mud from collapsing from the relentless Atlantic rains.

He'll have to have a meitheal – in happier times, on dry summer days, men gathered in each other's fields to cut and then store hay to feed their cattle over the winter. He knew exactly who he'd have to get to help him build his little thatched addition. As the men toiled in the rocky fields, their wives would serve them sandwiches and hot milky tea from bottles kept warm in thick woollen socks. Then, when everyones' hay was in, there would be a big feast with drinking and dancing all night in someone's thatched cottage. But those were the old days. Now they worked solely for the master, and they were forced to live in tiny, thatched sheds.

After Sunday mass, everybody gathered at the O'Donaghues' little cottage. Apart from the staff in the master's house, who were obliged to work almost twenty-four hours a day, seven days a week, they were all there, willing to give up their only day off to help Liam and Máire build their little dream house. The farmers spread out and began the drudgery of digging and prying out rocks, which, comfortably embedded into the earth and weeds, didn't give themselves up easily. Extracting the bricks and stones took up most of the day. Over and over, Bridgey faithfully pulled the heavy cart full of stones from nearby fields back to the cottage. After selecting the most suitable rocks for the foundation, the men dug a trench, beginning against the end of the O'Donaghues' cottage and started mounting the rocks onto each other. As they built higher, they tapered the rocks inward to lessen the impact of gale-force winds blowing in from the ocean. After several hours of hard labour, the stonework was complete. The technique for this build was the same one used when building dry stone walls. The men were experts at this. Since they didn't have gates to access the various fields, every time they needed to move cows from one field to another, they quickly opened a gap in the stone wall, put the cows into the new grass-rich field, and then re-stacked the stones to fill in the gap.

The next step was sealing the walls. The wives had been baking medium-sized limestone rocks in a kiln. When the stones broke down from the kiln's intense heat, the women ground them into a powder. Then they mixed the stone powder with water and clay to create a paste. The men plugged all the gaps in the wall with this mixture, which would take several days to dry and harden. 'With a bit 'o luck, this good weather will hold, and we'll be back next Sunday to finish the walls and the roof,' said Máire's father.

That night there was a hooley in the O'Donaghues' cottage to show their gratitude to everyone for their hard day's work. Josie offered up the little they had for dinner, then Tomás played his button accordion, and of course, the poitín and whiskey flowed. 'When will Máire be back?' asked an old neighbour and great family friend. 'I don't know, Seán,' said Liam pensively. 'Every day I walk out over the bridge, hoping to see her. That's all I can think about, seeing her comin' down that road.' 'Ah, she'll be here soon, Horse, and she'll get some surprise when she sees what we all did today.' 'Thank you Seán, you didn't take it easy out there.' 'Ah sure, t'was nothin',' he said modestly. 'Wouldn't it be great now, if she didn't come back 'til it was all finished, roof and all?' 'I don't think I can wait that long.' 'Ah yes Horse. Sure isn't love a wonder when first it's new, as the song goes? I remember those days meself.' 'What was it like?' asked Liam, sensing that Seán wanted to ramble on a bit. Sure enough, a big smile lit up Seán's craggy, weather-beaten face. 'Ah Horse, sure t'was grand altogether. We couldn't keep our hands off each other. She was mad and cracked and shameless, but t'was only when we were alone. Sure you'd think butter wouldn't melt in her mouth, but when we were alone, and the humour was on her, sure she was a divil, and there was nothin' like it. Even after the kids arrived, we were still mad after each other, though t'was hard to get away from the kids. I miss her every day. And the nights.' He looked off into the distance, shaking his head, 'Those long-damned nights are a killer.' He caught himself and gave Liam a smile. 'I hope you'll be as happy as we were. Sure, we had it better than me father's time. He survived the famine back then. They were rough times. We had our little cottage, the kids, the music, and the porter, and enough to feed ourselves'.

He took a swig of whiskey and continued. 'Did ya ever notice Kitchener? He never seems happy. I know he's poison, but he's not the worst of 'em. He goes around worried and fretting like he might lose everything all the time. I hope he does someday, the ould bastard.

Liam spent the next week scouring the beaches for driftwood, the odd thick log or plank, and riggings from shipwrecks. This would be his only source for timber for the roof. He gathered up as much suitable driftwood as he could find, hardly enough, and hauled it home in the cart pulled by his faithful Bridgey. This rough assortment of timber would be used as framework for the thatch roof. The following Sunday everyone returned to finish Liam and Máire's modest dwelling. Since the week had been dry, they found no draughts in the stone walls. Some of the men began building the stone fireplace, while others cut Liam's salvaged timber into equal lengths and began building the roof frame. Lacking sufficient timber, there was a wide space between each of the joists, so to strengthen the roof, the men lashed thick branches of hazel rods horizontally to the frame using súgans – braided straw ropes.

During the week, at the end of their landlords' daily farming obligations, the farmers had been cutting scraw, thin layers of top sod in twenty-foot lengths for Liam's thatch roof. They delivered their rolls of scraw in their donkey carts. Perfect as an under-thatch layer for insulation, scraw provided a firm grip for the dozens of scallops the thatcher would need. Scallops were long, twisted hairpin-shaped rods of thin, bendable hazel or willow branches. The thatcher would push them through the bundles of straw, and then into the scraw, tying them down from the inside with súgan ropes.

Séamus the thatcher had been coming and going in his donkey cart since dawn, hauling five to six-foot bundles of last year's wheat reed straw, lashed together, and carefully thrashed by hand to ensure that the stems remained unbroken. The hollow, dried-out straw stems had a natural coat of wax which would give the roof total protection from rain. Liam was amazed at Séamus' skill. Not having had any interest until today in how a roof is thatched, he received an up-close lesson on how a master thatcher, using all locally-sourced material, created his masterpiece. Séamus instructed Liam and the men on how to lay the scraw over the roof, grassy side up. They pierced the outsides of the scraw and lashed the súgan ropes to the branches and timber joists below. Once they had the underneath layer secured, Séamus started laying the bundles of straw on the roof, securing them with the scallops. Carrying bundle after bundle of straw up the ladder, Liam watched Séamus with admiration.

After a short break for tea, thatching resumed. Séamus

worked until he had about a twelve-inch thickness of straw laid down securely, covering the entire roof. Using a sheep shearer, Tomás trimmed uneven bunches of straw hanging from the roof, creating a smooth-looking finish to the eaves. Meanwhile, Séamus instructed the men to tie heavy rocks to each end of twenty-foot-long súgan ropes. They strung the ropes over the roof about three feet apart, with the stones hanging about two feet lower than the thatch, further protecting the roof from the Atlantic coast's gale-force winds. Finally, the workers started applying the same paste mix they had used last week to seal the gaps, sloshing it on roughly all over the outside stone walls. Once dry, this application would give Máire and Liam's new little dwelling the typical whitewashed look of an old Irish cottage, one with simple yet effective rainproof walls. 'That's a fine strong house you've got there, Horse,' said one of his neighbours. 'So where're ya gonna' find a soft feather bed for the fine lady from Dublin ha?' teased another. Liam, the shy strong lad in the O'Donaghue family, was like a little boy with a new toy. Casting aside his self-conscious loner ways, he walked about the yard eagerly hugging his neighbours and friends, thanking them for this generous gift – a home for his bride. Tears of joy? Exhilaration? Gratitude? Liam could contain none of these. His delight was all the workers needed as thanks for their toil, for it was little victories like these which held them together; the best of humanity flying in the face of their demeaning daily existence. The thatch job needed one last touch, and Liam could do this one alone. To keep dirt and bits and pieces of sod from falling from the scraw, he used rough sackcloth bags to cover the ceiling. The job complete, Liam thought, *It's finished now, Máire. All done. Hurry home! Come see!*

Máire was summoned to Lady Prescott's lavish drawing room in Dublin. Her heart beat rapidly with nervous excitement. After six long weeks that felt like six long years, she hoped for word that she could finally go home to Liam. Lady Prescott, sitting stiffly on the sofa, sipped her tea. Máire gave her a small, respectful curtsy, face bowed – the gesture which all housemaids were instructed to do when in her presence. 'So Máire, you want to leave and go back home?' 'Yes ma'am, I'm getting married.' 'So I hear,' she said, no emotion in her voice. 'This came as a complete surprise to me. Very bad timing really, now that we're in full social season.' 'I'm sorry ma'am,' Máire replied, her heart dropping. *Dear God. She won't let me go!* 'However, Lord and Lady Kitchener are good friends of ours, so in this case I'll agree to their wishes and make an exception, especially as Lady Kitchener is with child.' Máire wanted to explode with joy, but with great difficulty, she controlled her emotions and listened as Lady Prescott gave final instructions. 'The head housekeeper will give you your final wages on Sunday. The new help will need your bed, so I expect you to be gone Monday morning. Am I clear?' 'Yes, ma'am. Thank you, ma'am.' She curtsied and almost floated out of the room, thrilled that soon she'd be returning to Liam to spend the rest of their lives together. The fact that she didn't receive a word of thanks for her four years of hard, low-paid work bit into her, but thoughts of a happy future, back with her own people, carried the day. In two days, she'd no longer have to put up with the haughty, overbearing Lady Prescott and her equally obnoxious family and friends. She went to bed that night exhausted but happy, wishing tomorrow could be Monday. The next day, Máire finished her work and rushed across town to book her ticket home. Finally, the big day came and, tearfully, Máire bid sad farewell to the other maids who had become good friends over the years. They'd consoled each other through times of profound loneliness, shared hopes and dreams, and, out of earshot of course, the odd laugh at the Prescotts' expense. Genuinely excited for Máire's future, they offered her their prayers and best wishes.

Máire had booked passage to Galway on a Bianconi horse-drawn coach, the only regular mode of mass transport available. It was relatively cheap and certainly faster than the alternative – walking. Thankfully, she had saved enough to cover her trip, including the nights she would have to stay in inns situated along the staging points where the coachmen changed horses. She had heard all about Carlo Bianconi starting the first mass transport in Ireland. Kitchener boasted endlessly at dinner about the Duke of Wellington defeating Napoleon at the battle of Waterloo, leaving thousands of quality cheap horses and horsemen out of a job. He told everyone admiringly how this colourful Italian saw his opportunity and took it.

The horseman, a German fellow, would be Máire's coach driver today. The passengers lined up at the staging area which reeked of horse manure. When the coachman took Máire's ticket, she handed him her heavy bag; it held all her clothing and the fabric for making her wedding dress. He stuffed it into the middle of the coach, which was already packed with several mailbags and the other passengers' furniture and suitcases. Placing Máire and several other travellers on the left side of the light-wheeled carriage, he then directed the remaining passengers to the right, doing his best to balance the weight. Once seated in two back-to-back rows, the travellers braced for the journey, their legs resting on a footboard which projected over the wheels. In his clipped German accent, the coachman shouted, 'Hold on,' snapped the reins, and the horses pulled away slowly. Máire teared up with excited anticipation. *I'm going home for good!* roads were bad, the coach was open to the elements, and frequent showers drenched them mercilessly. They shivered, poorly clad for the weather, some in black shawls or warm woollen blankets, others wearing long black overcoats and top hats. The lucky few opened umbrellas.

Bianconi coach transport provided no luxuries, but at least they weren't walking. At every steep hill they reached, and there were many, the men, the younger women, and the children had to exit the carriage to make it lighter. Dozing, Máire was startled when the coachman blew his horn, signalling to a family walking up ahead to move to the side of the narrow road. The sound was so pathetic, a wheezing rather than a solid attention-getting honk, that everybody aboard burst out laughing. The family moved over, and as the coach passed, the mother of the family roared cheekily at the German coachman. 'Hey you, yer old horn sounds like death warmed up – 'tis as hoarse as me old grandma. Give it a drop of the ould craythur or it'll die of consumption before ya reach Galway.' Everybody laughed at her engaging sense of humour. Despite being destitute, she walked spiritedly with her family to God knows where. The German coachman wasn't amused! Finally, after several long days, they reached Galway. Máire stepped down, retrieved her bag, and began the rest of her journey home, a long walk west.

It was nearing sunset when Liam put the final touches to their bed. Scouring the beaches once again, he had found a hefty, long log that had probably been a ship's mast. It was thick, and long enough to make side rails. With plenty left over, he used the narrower pieces to complete the bed's foot and headboards. He'd search again tomorrow for a suitable base for, as his friend teased, their fine feather bed. When the neighbours heard that Máire and Liam were going to be married, they started collecting chicken feathers which Josie happily accepted. Using a base of soft hay, she added the feathers, ultimately making a grand soft mattress for the soon-to-be-wedded couple.

Liam walked down the sea road and rested against a stone wall, deciding to catch one of his favourite miracles of nature – sunset. He watched in awe as silver rays of light pierced the grey clouds, their heavenly beams creating a multicoloured, majestically visual symphony between earth and sky. The powerful opening prelude played out beautifully before him, the ever-changing and building crescendo of nature's panoramic glory, and soon, its inevitable coda – the sun's elegant finale. Moved by what he'd just witnessed, and in homage to God's glorious creation, Liam took out his tin whistle and put forth the soulful melody he'd played at Paudie and Úna's farewell party. The distinctive high tones of his tin whistle carried through the still night air.

Absolutely exhausted from her day-long walk home, Máire finally crossed the tiny bridge and, softly in the distance, heard that familiar and haunting air calling her back into Liam's arms. The man who was her only reason for living, the man who would hold her in his arms for evermore was just steps away. Her whole being responded with the most overwhelming emotions she had ever felt. Liam heard soft footsteps, opened his eyes, and there, standing before him, was his lovely Máire, his beautiful miracle. Tears flowing, she laboured to speak. 'Hello, Liam,' she whispered. Liam stepped forward, pulled her to his chest, and tucked her into his sheltering embrace. 'Am I dreaming?' 'I'm here, Liam. I'm here.'

Weeping, caressing, and softly kissing, they clung to each other, cherished. Liam had been waiting for this moment for what seemed like forever, and now he had another special treat to share. He picked up her heavy bag, smiled, and said, 'Come on, I've somethin' to show ya.' As daylight ebbed, they walked hand in hand, and when they came to the corner of the little dirt road, Liam paused. With a mysterious grin, he said, 'Close yer eyes Máire.' 'What?' 'Go on. Close yer eyes.' 'What are ya up to, Liam O'Donaghue?' she asked, shaking her head. 'Close yer eyes. Don't look 'til I tell ya.'

Liam took her hand, lead her around the corner, and stopped before their new home. 'Okay, open yer eyes.' With the moon's glow softly shimmering down in all its most romantic glory, Máire opened her eyes to behold a brand new little thatched cottage with its own half door and tiny window, situated right up against the O'Donaghue cottage. ''Tisn't as grand as where ya just came from, Máire, but 'tis ours,' Liam said humbly. Máire looked at Liam, still in shock and full of love and admiration at what he'd done in such a short time. Weeping, she whispered, 'Liam O'Donaghue, 'tis the finest house I've ever seen.' Nodding, relieved that Máire liked it, and overwhelmed with emotion, Liam took her hand and lead her inside. She stared in disbelief at the imposing brick fireplace stacked with turf, a fine big pot hanging over it ready for cooking. She saw the tiny, perfectly neat little window, and then she saw the timber bed in the corner. 'And this is ours? Really ours?' 'Yes, Máire, it's ours,' said Liam, holding her close and savouring the moment. 'We've all been workin' on it hard for the past few weeks. Mam told Da what to say to Kitchener, and when he said, 'yes' there was no stoppin' us.' Máire looked at the huge bed with no base or mattress on it yet. 'My God,

Liam O'Donaghue, you could chase me round and round that bed and you'd never catch me,' she teased. 'Oh, I'd catch you all right, Máire O'Donaghue.' He said it slowly and lovingly, letting her take in what would become her new name. Hearing him say 'Máire O'Donaghue' for the first time, she looked tenderly into his eyes, smiled, and said, 'I like that Liam. Thank you. Thank you for everything.' And then she kissed him gratefully.

Róisín Brosnan, the local seamstress, was busy putting the finishing touches to Máire's wedding outfit, as she measured the length from Máire's waist to the floor. "Tis fine long legs you have Máire, God bless ya.' 'D'ya think you'll have enough material, Mrs Brosnan?' 'Just enough, ya measured it well. So what d'ya think?' Máire was relieved, for she had no way to obtain more fabric without making another trip to Dublin. For her wedding Máire would have loved to wear any of the dresses she had seen adorning entitled landlords' daughters at Dublin social gatherings. Hers would be French silk, in blush pink, with long puffy sleeves, a jewel neckline, and at least twenty buttons from the nape of her neck to her waist. But she settled for fabric a step above the usual domestic material, heavy, plain fabric made from unbleached cotton normally used for bags, but versatile and serviceable enough to make a wedding garment for her station in life. The blouse and skirt would be powder blue. Mrs Brosnan had said she could easily hide the buttons on the blouse with a fabric panel, and she would embellish the panel using the nicest parts of a few scraps of lace a friend had given Máire as a parting wedding gift. The lace would also grace the cuffs of the sleeves, and the skirt would be long and flared. Máire's younger sister Órla was thrilled that Máire included her in the wedding plans.

As she watched Máire delighting in all the excitement and fuss, she dreamed of the day when she, too, would be fitted for her wedding. The sisters, lanky, freckled-faced tomboys, with only sixteen months between them, were always up for a little innocent mischief. Róisín didn't have the luxury of a full-length mirror, so Máire stepped back a little to see her first full view of Róisín's creativity. ''Tis perfect,' said Órla, admiring Máire, looking every bit like the queen of Ireland. And after the wedding, this would be Máire's Sunday best.

Later when they were enjoying a cup of tea, they froze when a chicken jumped up onto the half door squawking. It looked around and jumped onto Máire's skirt and blouse lying on the table. 'Oh, Mother of God,' screamed Róisín, making a dash for her broom. 'Get away outa' that. Don't you shit on that skirt or you'll be Sunday's dinner!' Máire raced to the half door and opened it. She watched in dread as the chicken walked all over the blouse and then shook it violently as she pecked on a sleeve button, trying to eat it. Clobbered by a perfect hit to its behind from Róisín's broom, the chicken took an unplanned flight and landed dazed by the half door. It shuddered for a moment, stood up, and then, squawking angrily, was unceremoniously propelled into the yard with a swift kick from the bride to be. 'Oh thank you, God,' said Máire, as they laughed, relieved. Then, tragedy averted, they sat down again to finish their tea.

'So, Máire,' said Róisín, 'two weeks to go before the big day. Are ya all set?' 'I think so. Father Murphy said Saturday week was available, so if the dress is ready by then, we'll be fine.' 'Don't worry a bit. Sure, 'tis nearly done. They tell me your little cottage is looking great.' 'Yes, I still can't believe what everybody did for us, all that work and for no payment.' 'Sure, why wouldn't they? Everybody knows your parents have lost enough already. Your mother would be dead in a year if you two went to America. Ye girls are the apple of your mother's eye. And what would Josie and Tomás do if Liam left?' Máire and Órla thanked Róisín once again and headed for home with wedding plans swirling in their heads.

The ladies and children had done their best to make the old church look as bright and welcoming as it could for this happy occasion. Normally dark and dreary, today the damp little church looked unusually colourful, its altar teeming with brilliant wild-flowers. A bank of homemade candles added a soft, romantic glow. The excited villagers were dressed in their Sunday best clothes. The men, uncomfortably self-conscious in ancient shiny suits, crammed their battered old tweed flat caps into suit pockets, and revealed their equally-shiny, baldy white heads. Everyone was delighted to be witnessing such a big event as Liam and Máire's wedding. Lacking the luxury of a church organ, four local musicians played elegant old Irish tunes as wedding guests gathered. A chorus of twelve eager children sat beside the altar waiting to sing Máire in.

Handsome as ever in their first-ever suits, Liam and Colm stood at the foot of the altar watching for Máire's entrance. Liam was focused and fidgety. Not Colm, though. He was well again and up to his usual devilment. Trying to put Liam at ease, he pretended to conduct the musicians. Surprised and delighted, the children squealed in innocent laughter. Órla had had a secret crush on Colm for ages and fantasised that this was their wedding. Watching Colm being Colm, so handsome and full of fun, made her laugh and melted her heart. Sadly, he didn't know she existed.

At the appointed time, vested in a cassock, and a chasuble hand stitched by Mrs Brosnan, Father Murphy entered the church's front door accompanied by four boys wearing cassocks and surplices. As they walked briskly to the altar, everyone rose. 'Good morning, everybody, on this grand day. We are gathered here for the marriage of Máire Donnelly and Horse O'Donaghue.' Everyone giggled. Father Murphy caught himself and with an embarrassed smile said, 'Eh, Liam O'Donaghue. Please remain standing as we welcome Máire to the church.' Máire and her father Diarmuid had been waiting outside for Father Murphy's signal to enter. Smiling, she appeared at the entrance, arm in arm with her proud father. The children's choir began a sweetly-simple old Irish song. Their innocent voices touched everyone present, as father and daughter walked slowly towards the flower-filled altar. Beaming, Máire heard the women guests gasp in admiration as she made her way past them to her intended.

Liam beheld a vision that would remain with him forever: a strikingly-beautiful woman, radiant in blue, her face framed by silky auburn hair. Máire smiled. Liam remembered seeing her at the céilí, dancing gaily to the music and then holding her for the first time as they swung together. He remembered their first kiss in the field when he played his tin whistle for her, and then the awful separation that felt like an eternity. *At last, Máire, we're about to marry.*

When the children's choir finished the entrance song, Father Murphy began the mass in the ancient Latin service, adding to the mystique of the wedding. 'In nomine Patris et Filii et Spiritus Sancti. Amen.' Throughout the mass, everyone responded in Latin. Together with slow airs from the musicians and well-known Irish hymns sung by the children's choir, the wedding was as perfect as it could be. Father Murphy beckoned Liam and Máire forward and asked. 'Do you Liam O'Donaghue take Máire Donnelly to be your wife?' 'I do,' answered Liam, looking straight into Máire's eyes. 'To have and to hold, through sickness and in health, 'til death you do part?' 'I do.' The priest asked the same vows of Máire. 'I do,' she answered. 'Could we have the ring?' Colm, standing at Liam's left, gave the priest the ring.

Though fashionable for the wealthy to have wedding rings, no such tradition existed for the Irish. Josie had a tiny wooden box where she kept a few precious keepsakes handed down in her family for generations. Amongst them were two miniature pewter baby's spoons. Tomás had had a local blacksmith forge one of them down into a narrow wedding ring. Having seen several ornately-jewelled wedding rings on the fingers of wealthy Dublin girls, Máire knew she would always cherish this ring, no matter how humble.

'I bless this ring in the name of the Father, and of the Son, and of the Holy Ghost.' Everyone answered, 'Amen.' Father Murphy handed the ring to Liam. Trembling, he lifted Máire's left hand into his and placed the ring on her finger. Watching Liam, Máire blinked back tears of loving emotion. 'I now pronounce you man and wife.' The bride and groom turned to face the wedding guests, and everybody applauded as the choir and musicians began the recessional music. 'Hello Mrs O'Donaghue,' said Liam. 'Welcome to the family.' 'Hello Mr O'Donaghue.' Standing hand in hand, as they faced their applauding friends and family, Liam and Máire felt that they could face whatever would come their way. Together was all that mattered.

Father Murphy and the altar boys genuflected, turned around, and began the procession from the altar. They were followed by Máire and Liam and their parents, and finally the guests. From the church, the newlyweds and their guests walked to the cottage where Máire was born and raised. Everybody congratulated Liam and Máire together; according to tradition; to congratulate Máire separately would be rude; it would imply that she had been 'lucky' to have gotten someone to propose to her. Only Liam and Máire sat and ate at their wedding breakfast. It was tacitly understood that the guests didn't need it, it being an honour just to have been invited to share their day. And practically speaking, the cottage was simply too small to seat so many guests. The guests would, however, receive traditional wedding cake which Máire's mother had baked – a simple cake sweetened with treacle. Again, following tradition, the guests didn't eat their slice of cake at the reception. It was given to them as they departed.

Wedding festivities lasted well into the night, and after the usual long Irish goodbye, everybody finally left. Máire and Liam walked the short distance to their own little cottage. When they opened the door, the high summer moon gave the inside a soft, welcoming glow. Hands clasped with fingers entwined, they paused at the door to regard their tiny dwelling: the turf fire waiting to be lit, the small table and two chairs, and a little dresser with cups and plates. In the other corner, compliments of Galway's wild seashore and Liam's successful efforts, was their bed, with Josie's soft feather mattress tempting them to lie upon it together for the first time. 'It's beautiful, Liam.' He regarded his new bride, perfection in her wedding dress, bathed in moonlight, and radiant with happiness. 'You're beautiful Máire.' He kissed her softly. 'Well, will we go in then?' she said nervously.

Liam lit the peat fire, and soon the blazing turf warmed the chilly cottage. After the few drinks he'd had at the reception, he wasn't as shy as he usually was. Arms encircling Máire's shoulders, Liam looked into her eyes, 'Hello Mrs O'Donaghue,' and kissed her harder and more passionately than he'd ever done. She returned his kisses eagerly, and they embraced in the comfort of each other's arms. He kissed her lips, then her neck, then her lips again, savouring every moment. She pulled away, her eyes fixed on Liam's and released the top button of her blouse. 'I want you,' she whispered. Wordless, he slowly released the remaining buttons. He placed both hands gently on her shoulders and pushed the blouse down to fall loosely upon her open arms. Máire slipped her hands out of the sleeves, and the blouse fell to the floor, revealing her breasts. Liam gasped at the sight and froze. Sensing his shyness, she gently led his hands to her breasts, and he cupped them softly. Emboldened by Liam's nearness, one by one, Máire unfastened the buttons of his white flannel grandfather shirt. The last button undone, Liam pulled the shirt off and cast it aside. Passions flared as Máire removed her skirt and underclothing and stood before him naked. 'My God, Máire, you're the most beautiful sight I've ever seen in this world.'

Eyes fixed on his bride, Liam shyly unbuttoned his trousers, dropping them, and kicking them away. Then, clearly aroused, he quickly lifted her up and they fell together onto the bed. No longer able to contain his passion for Máire, Liam lay on top of her, nudged her legs apart, and strongly thrust. At that she gasped in pain. 'Easy, easy,' she whispered. Liam stopped. Nobody ever discussed the actual 'act'. Unschooled in the art of lovemaking, his only experience was watching bulls and ponies do it. Everything 'down there' was a sin. Concerned and embarrassed that he had hurt her, he quickly pulled out. 'No, no, Liam. Nice and slow,' she softly encouraged. 'They told me to expect a bit of pain at first. Just be gentle.' Soon they were making love passionately, all shyness and inhibitions abandoned. They lost their virginity that glorious night in their tiny cottage. And as they lay together later, with the turf fire giving off its warm assuring glow, everything in their little world was perfect.

Two days later, Máire was a bag of nerves walking up the long drive to the imposing Kitchener mansion, its outside walls covered in stunning scarlet ivy. Designed with massive pillars, heavy wooden doors, tall gothic windows, and stables, and surrounded by meticulously manicured lawns, it was the finest house within miles.

In Dublin, Máire had more or less been another invisible kitchen maid with occasional babysitting duties. Now she faced the daunting challenge of working for her own landlord. Lord Kitchener was likewise the landlord of everyone else for miles around. She knew she had the job, but she wondered how well she would get on with this family and their staff. She was heartened somewhat by Liam's opinion of Lady Kitchener. 'She's better than Himself, so you should be all right. Lady Emma is spoiled, but she's a nice little girl. Stay away from their son Edward, though, he's a right amadán.' She walked around to the back of the house and knocked on the staff entrance door. Peig Shea opened it. 'So, you're Máire Donnelly,' she barked. 'No, I'm Máire O'Donaghue,' said Máire, emphasising the O'Donaghue part of her name. Liam had told her that Peig was a bitter old maid, and she'd learned in Dublin that, if she didn't stand up to a bully from the start, her life would be miserable. 'Lady Kitchener will see you at noon,' Peig said in her bossy tone. 'Come on, I'll show ya the kitchen.' Máire followed her in and noticed that it wasn't as big nor as grand as the Prescotts' kitchen. She became more confident when she saw that the setup wouldn't be any bother to manage. 'You can start by washing the pots, pans, and dishes from dinner last night,' said Peig. 'I'll bring ya up to her Ladyship later.' 'All right then. So,' said Máire, 'what will I call ya?' 'Peig. What else do ya think you'd call me?' She looked at Máire and raised her eyebrows condescendingly, thinking, *Oh my God, why do ya keep sendin' me these amadáns?* 'Go on now. Get to work. I'll be back soon.' Handing Máire her servants' clothes, Peig turned and walked out briskly. Conservative and plain in style, so as not to be mistaken for the lady of the house, the uniform Máire put on was a long, almost floor-length black dress, completely covering her arms and shoulders. The dress was way too big for her, surely another intentional act by Peig, the jealous old maid, when she saw how beautiful Máire was. A white waist apron and a white head cap finished her outfit. Máire got down to work, and in no time the table and kitchenware were clean and shining. She quickly learned the kitchen's layout. As she put various items away, she saw several instances where, to save time and effort in preparing meals, she could reorganise the kitchen to operate more efficiently like the kitchen in Dublin. But she knew she would have to clear any such rearrangement with the bold Peig. Her confidence grew, and as she began to relax, thoughts of the last two glorious days with Liam flooded back. They'd made love again within minutes of waking up that first beautiful morning. And as their initial shyness faded, their passion for each other was insatiable. She smiled in reverie.

'Okay,' said Peig loudly, bustling businesslike into the kitchen and interrupting Máire's happy thoughts. 'Her Ladyship will see you now. You know the rules: curtsy when you first see her and don't look her straight in the eye when she's talking to you. Call her ma'am at all times. Understand?' 'Yes.' She followed Peig up the stairs to meet Lady Kitchener who was waiting in the drawing room. 'Here she is ma'am,' said Peig, not mentioning Máire's name out of spite. Her imperious countenance, perfected by years of entitled society affairs, Lady Kitchener looked Máire up and down and found it difficult not to reveal how surprised and impressed she was by Máire's beauty. Despite her lofty position, her natural human instincts kicked in. Facing Máire – perfect, younger than herself, someone who might have been the toast of Dublin had fate otherwise decreed – Lady Kitchener felt inexplicably insecure and vulnerable. Dismissing these thoughts, she resumed her official position as lady of the house. 'Good morning, Máire.' 'Mornin' ma'am.' Máire curtsied before her with practiced humility, restoring Lady Kitchener's sense of control. 'The Prescotts speak highly of you.' 'Thank you, ma'am.' 'You have experience in every area, including as a nanny, I hear.' 'Yes, ma'am, I worked in every part of the house, cleaning, cooking, and serving, and I've looked after her Ladyship's daughter since she was born. She's three years old now.' 'Very good, I'll be needing your help in a few months, as you can see.' 'Yes ma'am,' said Máire. She figured that Lady Kitchener was about six months along. Peig listened to every word, watched her mistress' body language, and worried that her position as head housekeeper could be diminished by the access that Máire would have to Lady Kitchener as her new baby's nanny. *I'll have to keep this one on a tight leash.* 'Well, Peig, I'm sure you have plenty of work for her to do then?' 'Yes, ma'am,' said Peig. She felt better hearing acknowledgement that she was still the boss. Dismissed, they curtsied and Peig led Máire back to the kitchen.

As the day went on, Máire met the butler and the other maids and was warmly welcomed by them. They all either knew her or her family, unlike the maids and butlers in Dublin who came from all over Ireland, and who oftentimes were cliquish and distant. Here, her family was nearby. She would go home to Liam every night. There would be no more of the overwhelming loneliness she'd endured in Dublin.

She walked home happily that first day, looking forward to cooking Liam his first meal using the two onions she'd secretly tucked into her skirt pocket. Máire and Liam's life together was blissful. Their lovemaking was passionate, constant, and intense. Máire had heard all the 'dirty' stories her fellow Dublin maids gossiped about during long, boring hours in the Prescotts' kitchen. Sharing the almost incredible stories they'd heard about what other people got up to sexually, they regaled each other with fantasies of what they would love to do with a man, and Máire and Liam delighted in fulfilling those fantasies. Liam was a willing and eager partner, loving every moment of their intimate times together, especially when they coupled on warm summer nights in his favourite cliffside field, with the crashing waves below, the perfect backdrop to their wild lovemaking.

Serving dinner one evening, Máire came face to face with young Edward Kitchener for the first time. He had just returned from boarding school in Dublin. Carrying a heavy platter across the room, she felt his stare. She sensed that he was mentally undressing her, as he lewdly took in her every move. He didn't care a whit about the discomfort he was imposing on her. She was, after all, just the hired help. Máire figured that he was about fourteen, and she couldn't stand him already. He was tall for his age, pimply, skinny as a rake, and unfortunately for him, as homely as his father. She had experienced many similarly obnoxious versions of Edward up in Dublin – spoiled, entitled young men – and she was disgusted to realise that she would have to deal with him until he went back to school at the end of summer.

Máire served everybody roast beef and potatoes and, when she came to Edward, as she leaned down to serve him, he turned his head in her direction, pursed his lips as if he would kiss her and watched her as she straightened up. She saw his randy eyes and sneaky smirk and was sorely tempted to dump the whole platter onto his crotch. Dinner served, Máire left to wait in the anteroom for the bell to signal that they were finished and that she should come in and clear the dinner plates. Edward swallowed his food as quickly as he could, then got up and rang the bell. When Máire opened the door, Edward shouted, 'More beef!'

Máire ran down the stairs, crossed the basement to the kitchen, placed a few slices of beef on a heated plate, covered it, and ran back upstairs. She knocked on the dining room door and then served Edward more beef. Again, he followed her down as she bent over to serve him, but this time, careful not to be seen by his parents, he stuck his tongue out in a slow, lewd, licking fashion as he faced her. 'I'm glad to see your appetite has picked up, Edward,' said his mother, unaware of her son's smirking at Máire. It took all of Máire's self-control not to smack him in the face. *It's going to be a long summer.*

As she relayed her infuriating Edward drama that night to Liam, he smiled to himself, *if only you could see yourself through my eyes.* Looking at his beautiful bride bursting with fury as she went on another long rant about one of the Kitcheners, Liam tried to listen. Instead, he was aroused by her passion, beauty, and honesty. And unless it was a serious issue, it nearly always led to Liam's kissing her softly, pulling her into his strong arms, slowly rocking her from side to side, making her feel safe again, and eventually, ending up in passionate lovemaking. Máire knew how lucky she was to have Liam. When she endured ignorance and lack of respect at work, her body language was immediate, no matter how hard she tried to control it. He was always able to calm her down and unruffle her feathers by reminding her that they had each other, their cottage, their cliffside walks, and their bracing horse rides. His reassurances, strength, and their passion, helped her cope with another day. He was her rock.

Waking up one crisp fall morning, Liam was surprised to see Máire smiling at him. 'Good morning, Da!' Sleepily, Liam tried to understand what she had just said. When the word 'Da' registered, he bolted upright, eyes wide open. 'Are you?' 'Yes, I haven't bled in two months.' Liam's eyes began to mist up. 'How did that happen?' he joked. 'Well, what d'ya expect when you won't leave me alone, Mr O'Donaghue?' 'Oh, Mother of God,' said Liam beginning to grasp what was happening. 'What're we gonna' do?' She pinched his cheek laughing, 'We're going to have a baby. What do ya think we're going to do?' Tearing up, he shook his head, 'Mother of God,' he said again, and, as he held her closely, he kissed her softly and they cried happy tears.

Part Two

Resistance

In the first few months of their life together, Liam's farming and horse training and Máire's duties in the big house consumed most of their days. Sunday was their only day off, and the first thing they did was fulfil their Sunday obligation to go to mass before breakfast. No food and not even a drop of water was allowed after midnight the night before, as that would have broken their fast, thus not allowing them to receive Holy Communion the next morning. Liam and Máire put on their Sunday best and walked to church for mass where their beloved priest, Father Murphy would preside. Everyone knew him and his family. They knew that he was fully on their side, administering the sacraments, guiding them on their path to Heaven, and in celebrating the Holy Eucharist with them. They all truly believed that they were receiving the body and blood of the Lord Jesus Christ, their main reason for going to mass. Their faith was total.

Father Murphy did all of this while also being in the nearly impossible situation of not inflaming the locals' hatred of the British establishment with his sermons. Sadly, he knew that there were a few parishioners who, if they heard any hint of sedition in his sermons, would report their suspicions to their landlords to curry favour with them. Like everyone else, Father Murphy managed to survive the unjust conditions of the day, while doing his best to serve his flock. From Sunday to Sunday, everyone looked forward to gathering outside the church after mass. It was where the locals talked and exchanged all the latest news – who was pregnant, who was sick, who died, the weather, the next dance, news of cousins in America. It kept them going.

Announcing that she was having a baby, Máire was the centre of attention today. Every woman offered unsolicited advice about pregnancy and delivery, and many teased her about her condition. 'Ah sure, isn't it always the quiet ones that get ya into trouble?' 'So Máire, ya liked his little whistle, ha?' 'It isn't that little,' she said, blushing mischievously. Then, pausing for effect, she burst out laughing, giving them some gossip. She was amongst her own, and every bit as capable to give as good as she got.

It was also the place where pockets of resistance met without arousing the suspicion of local soldiers. What looked more natural than people gathering after Sunday mass? Most of the younger men were living lives similar to those of Liam and Colm: bitter about losing their lands and cattle, they were slowly losing their identities, their language and their Gaelic sports. The daily grind of their labour and the low-to-nothing pay from their landlords was emasculating them little by little.

The British divide-and-conquer method, a technique brilliantly used throughout their colonial days, was always front and fore of the British occupation of Ireland. So, well aware of British 'pay for information' tactics, secrecy was vital. Colm and Liam were the local resistance leaders, the remnants of the Whiteboys of the early 1800s. Pockets of activists involved in agrarian agitation still existed, keeping a small, trusted body of young Irishmen privy to their plans. Neither Máire nor their parents were aware of any of this. The brothers felt that the less their families knew about it, the safer they were in the long term. The men were biding their time, waiting for little opportunities to inflict damage. When they heard about an especially cruel bailiff or rent collector acting outside even the landlord's harsh rules, they 'took care' of him. In blackened faces, and in total silence, they would ambush him and gave him the beating of his life. If he didn't get the message this time, the next time he would vanish in a bog, never to be found.

British soldiers rarely ventured out alone, for several of their comrades had mysteriously vanished when they'd done so. Worried about local resistance, the British military and aristocracy were eager to squelch it. Remnants of the Whiteboys still existed in sporadic places in Ireland involved in agrarian agitation. When a rebel was caught, the British military would interrogate the prisoner with hard hitting body punches to extract information about accomplices, and then, to deter future resistance, the prisoner would be sentenced to prison, publicly hanged, or deported.

Liam, Colm, and their fellow agitators were well aware of what would happen if they were caught but witnessing the daily injustices they and their countrymen were forced to endure, they determined that they couldn't just stand by and do nothing. They were in their prime and did their best to help the older and weaker amongst them when they could. Often when a family was on the cusp of starvation, food – often stolen – would miraculously turn up outside their door, keeping them alive.

Elizabeth Kitchener was having a difficult pregnancy, threatening miscarriage, so her doctor had confined her to bed for her third trimester. Most days William was away in Dublin for business. Due to her condition, as a precaution, Elizabeth was advised by her doctor to sleep in another room when William was home, in case he got 'any ideas.' Máire and Emma had the most daily contact with her, while Edward virtually ignored her. Though Peig was efficient, loyal, and dependable, Elizabeth couldn't ever imagine having any personal conversations with her, their having nothing in common. During those long and lonely three months, however, as she was served her daily meals, an unlikely friendship grew between Máire and Elizabeth. Vulnerable, alone, bedridden, and usually feeling awful, Elizabeth opened up to Máire – a relationship which, under normal circumstances, neither of them could have ever imagined.

Máire was a good listener, possessed of an elegance and grace that resonated with Elizabeth throughout the rest of her confinement. Both pregnant, with remarkable changes happening to their bodies, they shared conversations which, when they were alone at least, rendered them equals. Despite the loftiness of her entitled position, Elizabeth laid bare her insecurities and frustrations. She told Máire about her two earlier pregnancies, something which helped Máire understand her own sudden mood changes – Máire had thought she was going crazy. They laughed at the outrageous demands Elizabeth had made of her kitchen staff at all hours of the night during her pregnancy with Emma.

Elizabeth admitted that coming to Ireland was the last thing she wanted to do. 'William and I married after he finished military college, and within a few months, was sent to fight in Africa. He was stationed there for three of the longest years of my life. I had Edward six months after he left, and were it not for my parents, I would have gone insane. When he finally came home, I assumed that he would never go away again, but six months later he was sent to Egypt for another two years. I received one letter every two months. As captain of his troops, he described the awful things he was ordered to do, and he kept promising he would soon come home for good and retire. He was sick of it all. That promise kept me going. When he finally came home, he was offered land in Ireland as a reward for his service to the queen. He convinced me that we could live better here than we ever could in England, so I agreed. But I miss my parents, my brothers and sisters, and all my friends back home. It's just not the same, I'm afraid.'

Máire winced at Elizabeth's nonchalance about putting the Irish off their lands to achieve William's goal. Even though Elizabeth and Máire had shared more than a lady and a housemaid ever should, Máire couldn't understand the superiority and imperialism so ingrained in Elizabeth and so taken for granted. It seemed that, once she came to Ireland, she became the kind of entitled person who saw everyone as a servant. Máire knew that, once Elizabeth's baby was born, the relationship between them would revert to the way it had been before – Lady Elizabeth, the head of the house, and Máire, the Irish kitchen maid. Still, Máire warmed to Elizabeth more than she had to any other English man or woman she had ever met. She actually felt sorry for her; she had seen Elizabeth's human side, separated from her parents, and, given what she had revealed to Máire, seemingly stuck in a loveless marriage. Nearly every night, Máire came home with stolen vegetables or fruit hidden in her dress – her way of rebelling. This varied diet kept Liam and Máire and their unborn baby healthy. Liam enjoyed the stories Máire shared over dinner, especially learning about the lives of the Kitcheners before they came to Ireland.

Every British man was a legitimate target for the activists. Máire's warming up to Kitchener's wife wasn't exactly something Liam had anticipated when he and his men were plotting to destroy any and all landlords and if necessary, their families. How would he explain to Máire the actions they might take? Yet, she had seen all of the injustices forced upon her and her parents, had endured slave labour in Dublin for four years, and was living in a tiny, thatched room, while her landlord and his family were living in luxury, completely unimaginable to the ordinary Irish peasant. Liam felt confident that, despite her feelings for Elizabeth, Máire would understand if he were to rebel against the Crown.

Elizabeth was about to give birth and the Kitchener mansion teemed with anticipation. Nervous, William paced up and down the hall. Emma sat near the bedroom door listening and hoping for a baby sister. Edward had persuaded his father to have him excused from boarding school for a week so that he could be home for the baby's arrival. Máire brought hot water and towels from the kitchen as the family doctor attended to Elizabeth. For the actual birthing, only the doctor was allowed to be in the huge bedroom. Clammy with sweat, Elizabeth screamed in pain, unnerving everybody waiting in the hall. She pushed and pushed, until finally came the marvellous sound of a baby's first cry. And with that sound, everybody uttered a collective sigh of relief. Shortly, the doctor opened the door and announced: 'It's a boy.' Lord Kitchener went in to see his exhausted wife holding their newborn son.

While the doctor completed necessary post-birthing procedures, Máire quietly entered to remove bloodied linens. In the fourth month of her own pregnancy now, she certainly wasn't looking forward to childbirth, especially after everything she'd just heard. She decided that, unlike the circumstance of Elizabeth's cold and clinical delivery, when it was her time, in addition to the midwife, she would ask her mother to be present. It never occurred to her to ask Liam. This being women's business, men simply were not allowed, and they certainly didn't beg to be present.

Walking home that night, she could not help feeling sorry for Elizabeth, so alone in her fine mansion. The landlords and their families attended and held showy dinners and banquets to impress each other. The women had big, beautifully-decorated houses with all the domestic help they needed. The men had mistresses and gambling. And though their children attended the best schools and had nannies, horse riding, and every luxury showered on them, absent were strong family bonds and loyalties that really mattered. As she approached her humble cottage, she knew Liam was waiting for her, looking forward to seeing her, and she him. Her loving family was close by, and she knew that her mother and mother-in-law could not wait for her to have her baby, so that, when she was at work, they could take care of it and spoil it completely. She understood now why Elizabeth wished she were back in England with her family and friends. That night for dinner, on their tiny handmade table, was the added luxury of a few stolen carrots, making more palatable the usual boiled potatoes and buttermilk. Dessert was stolen too – a few huge strawberries.

After dinner, Liam lit a turf fire and the couple sank into the comfort of the rocking chairs Colm had made for them as a wedding gift. 'You can rock my nephews and nieces in these,' Colm had joked when he'd presented them. 'They should last for a good dozen or so.' As the turf glowed, Máire gave Liam a virtual blow-by-bloody-blow of the birthing of the new Kitchener boy – what she had heard of it, at least. When she described Elizabeth's screaming and roaring during the final few minutes of labour, Liam winced and lost his appetite, unable to touch a single bright red strawberry.

Máire wondered what new duties would be required of her with the Kitchener baby. 'If I have anything to do with bringing him up, I'll teach that boy manners. He's not going to be a shit like Edward. He didn't even go in to see his new baby brother when he came home from horse riding. And Kitchener did nothing about it – just let him go to his room. Can you imagine that?' Liam relished Máire's fiery passion and determination. He watched with loving pride as she expressed her disgust and outrage about the Kitcheners' abysmal child-rearing ways. Always 'a divil', he leaned back in his chair, and with a big open smile teased her. 'Well now, Máire O'Donaghue, if you have a girl, will ya allow her to be the mad tomboy that you were?' Caught off guard by his cheeky remark, she considered their own reality. They were soon to have a baby of their own, and the responsibility of bringing the child up right would be enormous. Yet, she smiled at the memories of her wild days as a carefree little girl who got into everything. She'd always climb the cliff that little bit higher than the boys, and she rarely allowed any boy to beat her when they raced their ponies. She smiled smugly remembering that she'd never lost a fight with any of the boys. 'Yea, I was a tomboy, wasn't I?' Liam smiled, paused for a few seconds, and said, 'If our baby's a girl, I hope she'll be just like you.' 'And if it's a boy?' asked Máire, giving it back to him, 'Sure 'tis a wonder you're still alive Liam O'Donaghue. Will you allow your little boy to get up on a pony before he can walk and let him race like mad all over the place like you did? Will you let him wander the countryside on his own, chasing badgers and foxes and God knows what else?'

Liam pondered Máire's questions for a minute, remembering those marvellously carefree days when he and Colm were growing up. Wild they were together, doing mad stuff all the time, getting away with all sorts of mischief. Then he had a wild thought, leaving him nearly dumbstruck,

'Mother of God, Máire, what if we have one of each?' They burst out laughing. 'It'd be interesting. That's for sure,' said Máire. 'That it would.' Then, lost in their own thoughts, they gazed into the comforting glow from the fireplace. Rocking back and forth, there was no need to keep the conversation going as they listened to the wind giving its own natural concert outside with its sweeping rise and fall and erratic but soothing tempo. Completing the mood, the gentle crackling from the turf fire soon had them both nodding off. Barely awake, Liam stood, and taking Máire's hand, gently helped her rise from her chair. They walked a few steps, fell together into their bed, and soon were sound asleep after another hard day's work.

The following morning, Liam and Colm began to dig up the summer potato crop from the lazy bed's bountiful harvest. Within a few hours they had picked and stored this priceless food source which would sustain their family until the end of the year. 'I swear, Horse, someday we'll plant whatever we want, whenever we want.' Bitter about this never-ending, dreary existence, Colm mopped sweat from his forehead with a dirty sleeve. While Liam shared his brother's pain, he was grateful for the solace of Máire in his life. Every night he and Máire talked about anything and everything, helping each other get through whatever challenges were thrown at them. And given the excitement of impending parenthood, they felt invincible, despite the Kitcheners' constant, selfish demands. Other than Liam, Colm really had no one in his life that he could talk to. Since the wedding, Liam wasn't as available as he used to be. 'Yea,' said Liam, aware of Colm's constant need for action. 'I think we'll have to sort Spencer out. He's given Mary Lowry one last warning to pay her rent or be evicted.

She's in a desperate state since poor old Jocko died, leaving her and the five kids penniless.' 'Spencer's one of the worst of 'em,' said Colm. 'I'll have no problem at all sorting him out. What's the plan?'

Edmund Spencer from Bath, England was a bailiff and rent collector for a landlord five miles north of where the O'Donaghues lived. The landlord Spencer worked for, like many landlords of the day, spent most of his time in Dublin or London. Landlords such as these were called Absentee Landlords and too often let their bailiffs and rent collectors run riot – no questions asked – as long as they pulled in monthly rents from all of their unfortunate tenants. 'Paddy McNamara has been watching him for a while,' said Liam. 'Every Saturday night he visits the landlord's sister up at the big house. She's been over from England a few months since her husband was killed in India.' 'Mother of God,' said Colm. 'Her husband isn't even cold in his grave, and she's sleeping around already, and with Spencer of all people. Shit, he has to be the ugliest man in Ireland! God was asleep when he came along.' 'Well,' said Liam, 'they say she's no beauty either.' Shaking his head, Colm quipped, 'Well, all I can say is that's why God invented whiskey. So ugly people can have sex too!' Liam laughed, then laid out the plan. 'We'll take care of him next Saturday night. It'll have to be quick so he can't shout out for help. Paddy says there's a turn on the road between the big house and his place, and that's the best place to grab him. I'll let Jackie Casey know; you tell Paudie O'Brien.'

On a lonely cow path of a lane, at around three a.m. on a damp moonless night, four men with blackened faces waited for Spencer to walk into their trap. At the ready, Liam, Colm, Jackie Casey, and Paudie O'Brien hid behind the wild and uneven low hedges. Hearing someone coming from the big house whistling, the men got ready, two on each side of the lane. They heard approaching footsteps and were relieved to discern that it was only one person. As Spencer turned the corner and walked the few steps approaching them, Liam recognised him, let him pass, and then jumped out from behind him. Clamping his hand over Spencer's mouth, he almost lifted him up. Then Colm, now fully recovered from his broken leg, faced him and dealt a crushing blow to his stomach. Spencer couldn't see Jackie Casey beside him, but when Casey swung a stick to his legs, Spencer's knees buckled and he came down heavily on them. Paudie O'Brien jumped in from the other side and pushed a black hood over his head. The ambush took mere seconds. 'Scream, and it'll be the last thing you ever do, you English bastard. Understand?' said Colm. 'What the fuck is this?' gasped Spencer, down but not out. 'If you evict Mary Lowry, THAT will be the last thing you do; we won't be as nice to you next time. This is your first and last warning,' said Liam. 'Fuck you,' said Spencer. Liam lashed out and landed a heavy blow to Spencer's face, breaking his nose. 'As I said, leave her alone, or you'll drown in the bog,' said Liam. Another blow to the face from Colm finished the encounter – no mercy – a tactic they learned from the British. Spencer collapsed to the ground, bloodied and unconscious. The lads vanished into the night.

The local constabulary ordered more night patrols and did what they had always done; they tried to divide and conquer by spreading money around to buy information from the locals, but they got nowhere. Mary Lowry and her family were not evicted.

Nearly five months pregnant and tired, Máire washed pots and pans from the Kitcheners' previous night's dinner. Once again, she felt the bubbles – the little flutters. Liam had chuckled when she'd first described these sensations. 'What are ya laughin' about? It's not funny.' 'It's fartin'. That's all it is,' said Liam. 'I hate to tell ya Máire, but the O'Donaghues are huge farters, all of us, so that's what it is, it's just fartin.' Máire burst out laughing, giving him a friendly dig. 'Go way outta' that, but that's exactly what it feels like, all right.'

The maids' bell rang loudly in the kitchen, jolting Máire from her daydream. Elizabeth had slept through the night and was awake and wanted breakfast. The doctor had been in to check on her and the baby, pronouncing them both fine. Luckily another housemaid had cared for the baby boy through the night, allowing Máire to go home. Máire knocked on Elizabeth's door, brought in the breakfast tray, and set it on the bedside table. 'Good morning, ma'am, a little breakfast for you,' she said softly. Elizabeth pulled herself up gingerly, as Máire placed a few pillows behind her head. 'Will I open the curtains, ma'am?' 'No, don't do that. I want to go back to sleep once I've eaten and nursed the baby.'

Máire looked around admiringly at the opulent bedroom: a four-poster bed, mahogany bedside tables, and on the opposite end of the room facing the bed, a huge mirror. The matching dresser was flanked by stately bay windows adorned with red velvet drapes and valances. 'Your son is a fine healthy boy,' said Máire smiling. Clearly in no mood for talking, Elizabeth stared straight ahead with a strained, defeated look. She lowered her head and then went through the motions of eating her breakfast: tea, a boiled egg, bread, and jam. 'Tell the maid to bring him to me after breakfast, so I can feed him.' 'Yes ma'am,' said Máire, and she left the room. As she walked back to the kitchen, disturbing thoughts flooded into her head. There seemed to be no joyfulness in Elizabeth about just having given birth to a healthy child. *Is this how I'm going to feel after I have my baby? Does it take everything out of you? Lady Kitchener doesn't seem to have any desire to be with her baby.* Máire felt comfort in knowing that her mother would be with her for her birthing, and surely Liam would be waiting right outside the cottage, thrilled about becoming a father. And he'd be home every night sharing their happiness with their first baby. She wondered how the Irish could be so different in showing affection towards each other. Sometimes it took a few drinks to loosen up for sure, but the bond was tight between families and neighbours. The cultural contrasts became more significant, the more she observed how the Irish and English interacted amongst their own. She was happy to be Irish.

Over the next two months, while everything at the mansion revolved around the Kitcheners' baby, given the name Harry, every-thing at Liam and Máire's cottage revolved around their unborn baby, and its now familiar kick. A frontal attack, it accompanied the indignity of Máire's belly button's having recently popped out. At seven months, the baby's kicks felt like jabs, waking Máire constantly during the last few weeks. Mrs O'Flaherty said it was a good sign – that the baby was fine and healthy. Yet Máire wondered, *Does this baby ever sleep?* Liam stroked her tummy every night, delighting in the feel of the baby's erratic movements. And while Máire loved this gentle side of Liam, obviously coming from his breeding, delivering, and nursing so many horses over the years, she was blissfully unaware of his violent resistance to the English reign of terror in Ireland.

Everyone was concerned about how withdrawn Elizabeth had become. She wasn't rebounding as quickly as she had with her first two children. Wandering listlessly around her country manor, she was fearful and anxious, cried for no reason, and showed little if any interest in bonding with her baby. She seemed incapable of thinking clearly and was unable to focus when having to make simple household decisions. Máire took on all the extra duties that Elizabeth should have done for baby Harry – bathing and changing him, burping him and rocking him to sleep – everything except nursing him.

'She's all mixed up right now; 'tis part of it sometimes, especially when she didn't want another baby,' said the wise old Mrs O'Flaherty. When Máire asked her if there was anything she could do to help Elizabeth, the midwife said, 'You've got to get her out of bed, and out of the house. Whatever you do, keep her busy. Make her walk her baby every day. Bring her down to the horses and make her watch her daughter riding. That'll get her well again. It'll take a bit o' time, but she'll be all right in a few weeks. Don't take "no" for an answer.' Bringing up Elizabeth's breakfast the next day, Máire acted the tough Reverend Mother. She opened the heavy drapes to let in some daylight, ignoring Elizabeth's protestations. She sternly ordered Elizabeth to get dressed; they were taking the baby for an outing in his baby carriage, and she would only take 'yes' for an answer. Though Máire had absolutely no authority to demand any of this, she was hugely relieved when Elizabeth got out of bed and started to get dressed. After a good refreshing walk, albeit taken in silence, they walked over to the stables where Liam was about to give Emma her riding lesson. As she jumped over the challenging fences, Emma was delighted to hear Elizabeth's, 'Well done!' and so, having been ignored for weeks, Emma smiled proudly. 'They're five-foot fences, Mama.' Elizabeth's countenance changed, transforming into a happy smile for the first time in weeks. 'Yes, Emma, I can see that, and you jumped over every one. You're really getting good. Isn't she Liam?' 'Yes, ma'am. Would you like to see how well she can gallop?' 'Oh yes! Emma, show me, but be careful now darling.' Emma trotted down to the tree line, and then galloped back up to the jumping area, coming to a sudden stop, in masterful control of her horse. Elizabeth's smile broadened and she clapped in delight at her beautiful daughter's riding skills.

Máire could see the burgeoning turnaround in Elizabeth's attitude. Returning to the house, the baby began to cry. Elizabeth stopped, lifted Harry up and held him close. As they walked, she rocked him gently in her arms, Máire pushing the baby carriage, made of wicker and wood, which had been shipped from London's finest nursery store. Máire got Elizabeth out of bed daily for the next week, until at last she started to come down to the dining room for breakfast on her own. They took walks with the baby carriage every day, and soon Elizabeth had Harry's crib brought into her bedroom. Although her post-delivery depression was all but gone, Máire never received a thank you.

The parish church was full for mass that spring Sunday morning. As Father Murphy distributed Holy Communion, Máire waddled unsteadily up the aisle, leaning heavily on Liam's arm. Expressing reverence for the sacrament, with Liam's help, Máire slowly knelt down at the altar railing, extended her tongue, and received the Eucharist. She blessed herself, and with equal difficulty, pushed herself up slowly, holding onto Liam's hand. Turning to enter their pew, Máire winced with an unexpected pain. A few minutes later as mass was coming to a close, she realised what was happening when another pain began. She turned around nervously, and with a frightened look, nodded to her mother seated behind her. 'It's coming Liam. I think I'm going to have the baby right here,' she whispered in terror. 'What?' he gasped, 'Right here in the church?' Panicking, Liam shifted around in his seat, not knowing what to do. The commotion caught the attention of Mrs O'Flaherty sitting nearby. Ever the midwife, she calmly told her husband to go home and fetch the donkey and cart. She rose and came over to Máire with a reassuring smile. 'Máire, you just sit there now 'til Dinny gets the ould ass and cart. We'll get ya home all right.' 'He'd better hurry up,' said Máire with a pained expression. Tears welled up, as she leaned back into the seat and took short, shallow breaths. 'You're doing fine girleen,' assured Mrs O'Flaherty. 'The baby isn't going to come 'til we get ya home, okay?'

The whole parish looked on as Father Murphy blessed Máire. This unexpected drama at mass gave them enough fodder for conversation for months. The congregation turned as one when Dinny rushed in. Quickly, Liam, Colm, and a few other strong young lads carried Máire out and placed her up onto the donkey cart. She groaned as they began the short journey home. Dinny, guiding the donkey, did his best to avoid the many bumps and potholes in the road. Máire's mother Nora had run on ahead and already had water heating in the pot hanging over the turf fire. She quickly stripped the bed and spread a few rough towels on it. Once Máire was carried into the cottage and laid on the bed, Mrs O'Flaherty ordered everybody out but Nora. 'Breathe nice 'n easy now, Máire girl, nice 'n slow, c'mon now,' instructed Mrs O'Flaherty. Máire was almost breathless from her quick, panicked, tiny breaths. 'Nice 'n slow now, Máire, relax, nice 'n slow.' With Nora holding her hand, encouraging her all the way, Máire tried taking a few slower breaths and relaxed a little, but the contractions became more intense and frequent. 'It's coming! I think it's coming!' she screamed in pain. 'Okay Máire, push as hard as you can,' instructed Mrs O'Flaherty. 'Push!' Máire tensed up, eyes closed in concentration for the task at hand, and screaming uncontrollably, bore down with all the strength she could muster.

Listening outside the cottage, Liam, Colm, Órla, Bríd, Aoife, Tomás, and Máire's father Diarmuid, shuddered at the clamour just inches away – desperate, disturbing – everything beyond their ability to help. Liam gripped Colm's arm harder than he had ever done. 'Jesus, Mary, and Joseph, help her,' he sobbed quietly. 'It'll be all right,' said Tomás, reassuring his son, having been through this ordeal many times. 'Just a little bit longer, and it'll be all right.' 'But it's taking forever,' said Liam. 'Hey,' said Colm, trying to relax him, 'remember all those times you stayed up all night delivering the ponies? It's probably the same thing, ya know. It takes time.' 'Hey, she's my wife, she's not a feckin' pony, all right?' 'Hey, I'm sorry,' said Colm, realising he'd just put his foot in it. 'No, no, no. I know she's not a pony, but ya know what I mean.'

Pushing one last time, Máire let out a shrill scream, delivered her baby, and fell back exhausted. Mrs O'Flaherty cleaned the baby's mouth and within seconds the baby gave out its first sound, announcing, 'I'm here!' with a strong belter of a cry. 'It's a fine baby boy, Máire,' smiled Mrs O'Flaherty. She tied off and cut the umbilical cord, wiped the baby clean, swaddled him, and then placed him in Máire's waiting arms. 'And he's perfect, Máire,' said Nora, as she cleaned her tired daughter, covering her so that Liam could come in and see his newborn son.

Liam entered enraptured. The sight of his smiling Máire holding their son in their tiny little cottage would be etched in Liam's memory forever. With his brother, sisters, and two proud grandfathers standing behind him, Liam knelt, kissed Máire, and wept. He looked at his wife and son with pride, speechless and awestruck by this miracle. As Tomás tapped Liam's back proudly and reassuringly, Liam hesitantly touched his son's little hand, and the baby grabbed his finger firmly. 'He's a strong little divil.' 'That's no wonder, Liam. He's your son,' said Máire. 'Okay then,' said Mrs O'Flaherty, ushering them all out of the cottage, 'It's time to let Máire rest now; she's done enough for today.' Liam kissed Máire again, tenderly, and they all left. Máire thanked Mrs O'Flaherty, and she left too, her work done kindly and well. Máire looked at her perfect, tiny baby sleeping away, blissfully unaware of all the drama that had just taken place. Nora stayed with her, the both of them entranced with their new little bundle of joy. Agitated, the baby let out a big cry. 'He's hungry,' said Nora. Máire knew what she had to do next but was suddenly terrified at the thought of breastfeeding. A mother of four, Nora took this in stride. 'Okay, little fella,' said Nora, 'your mother will feed you now.' Máire opened her nightdress, took the baby into her arms again, and led his mouth to her breast. She waited for him to latch onto her nipple, but nothing happened. 'He's not sucking,' said Máire nervously. 'Touch your nipple gently against his top lip, and get him to open his mouth,' said Nora. At this prompting, the baby started sucking. 'It's sore,' said Máire. 'I know, Máire, it feels a little uncomfortable right now, but it will get easier. And he'll be hungry every few hours from now 'til tomorra',' said Nora. The baby sucked strongly on Máire's tender nipple. After ten minutes, she switched sides, and continued to feed him, until he stopped sucking and fell asleep again. Exhausted, Máire lifted the baby up to her mother, and soon was sound asleep herself.

Liam felt that Tomás had to be a mind reader, for as soon as they were out the door, his father said, 'C'mon lads. Dinny O'Flaherty asked us over to celebrate. There's aytin' and drinkin' ahead of us boys. We have a new O'Donaghue in the family,' he said proudly. Liam couldn't wait for the taste of that first drink. Josie brought food over for Máire and Nora, knowing they'd be hungry after their day's labour. And she couldn't wait to see her first grandson. Enthralled, she watched mother and baby sleeping peacefully as Nora whispered quietly, telling Josie all about the drama that had just unfolded.

The arrival of the new baby lifted the spirits of everyone in the tight-knit little village. As her time approached, their daily prayers had included Máire, and when the happy news quickly spread that she and Liam had a perfectly healthy baby boy with no complications, they felt that, for once, their prayers had been answered. The joy of new life gave everybody a lift and a sense of hope, in the face of relentless oppression.

'Take it easy, there boy,' said Josie. 'You've gotta' wife and new son to go home to later.' She'd seen Liam knocking back shot after shot of whiskey. To let off some steam at the impromptu party, Liam had given his tin whistle quite the workout, and now he, too, was spent. Leaving her cottage, he thanked Mrs O'Flaherty for all she had done for his wife and baby on that long, exhausting day.

When Liam arrived home, he saw Nora seated by the turf fire rocking gently, her first grandchild sound asleep in her arms. His new life, his everything, was sleeping there before him. Rising, Nora held the baby out for him to hold. Terrified, he sat in his rocking chair but hesitated. So, Nora showed him how to hold his newborn son, supporting his wobbly head. Nervous and awkward at first, with Nora's assurances that the baby wouldn't break, Liam rocked his son and relaxed into fatherhood. Then, satisfied that Liam wouldn't drop the baby, Nora said, 'I'll leave ye alone now, and be back to check on ye tomorra'.' 'We'll be grand now. Thanks,' said Liam.

Cuddling his son and nuzzling his little neck, Liam stood, delighting in this new experience. He paced back and forth in their little cottage, stretching out his arms, just looking at him, this tiny sleeping bundle, his son, wondering what sort of life he would have. He watched Máire as she slept, and he knew that he would gladly lay down his life to protect his new family of three.

Waking with a start, the baby grew anxious and, his eyes still closed, began to cry, drawing Máire out of a sound sleep. She opened her eyes and saw Liam looking lost and terrified as the baby howled, not knowing how to calm him. She smiled weakly, and said, 'It's time to feed him again.' Liam handed him down to Máire. The baby knew exactly what to do, and clearly the most comfortable of the three of them, started sucking as if he'd being doing it all his little life. In awe, Liam watched his wife nurse the baby. 'I'm jealous,' said Liam, smiling as he pulled his rocking chair over to the bedside. 'Ah, go 'way outta' that. It's the drink that's talkin',' said Máire laughing. 'Maybe so, but ya missed a mighty bit o' craic at the O'Flaherty's tonight. Everybody's talkin' about Dinny bringin' ya home on the ould ass and cart, and you screamin' and roarin' like a madwoman all the way down the road. Mrs O'Flaherty said 'tis a miracle ya didn't have the baby in the church.' 'I thought I was going to,' said Máire. 'I'm glad I gave 'em somethin' to talk about, the nosy buggers.' 'Yerra relax girl, they're all happy for ya,' said Liam. 'It was mad tho' wasn't it?' 'Yea,' smiled Máire, 'I'm glad it's over.' She moved the baby to her other breast, and as she looked at Liam said, 'Well is it going to be Tomás then, like your father?'

Until now, they hadn't seriously talked about names for their baby, and Liam was delighted that Máire wanted to follow tradition and name their firstborn son after Liam's father. 'Thanks, Máire. Da will be thrilled.' 'Tomás,' said Máire, looking down at their baby's sweet face. 'It suits him. Tomás O'Donaghue. I like it.' The baby's hands opened and relaxed, and he drifted off. 'He'll be hungry again in two hours; he's worse than you,' teased Máire. 'He's gonna be somethin' Máire; I can feel it,' said Liam proudly. 'Teach him everything you know Liam, and he'll be fine.' 'I will,' said Liam, 'and Colm will make a fine fisherman outta' him. When he grows up, he'll be a fine catch for some lucky girl, I tell ya, the pride o' Galway.'

The love Liam already felt for his son touched Máire deeply. 'Will ya stop?' she smiled. 'Let me enjoy him for a few years. How can ya think of this little fella married already?' She held him protectively, rocking him gently. 'We've a long way to go before all that stuff happens.' She handed him over to Liam and soon was sound asleep again. The following morning, Colm, thrilled to be asked to be Tomás' godfather, brought him, as per tradition, to be baptised by Father Murphy. They were all well aware that babies in poor Irish families often didn't survive their infancy. And they believed that, if Tomás died before he was baptised, they couldn't bury him in the church graveyard.

Peig Shea wasn't so heartless as to demand that Máire turn up for work just a few days after giving birth. She had seen how Máire had helped Elizabeth during her recent pregnancy and delivery. Had Máire not been there, Peig would have been obliged to care for Elizabeth, something a bitter old maid like Peig wanted no part of. She begrudgingly gave Máire a break of two weeks, there being little pressing to do with the Kitcheners away in Dublin for that fortnight. Nora was a godsend, looking after her grandson until Máire came home each night. Josie was also delighted to help, so the little lad received unceasing grandmotherly love those first few months. Another woman in the village had also recently given birth, and she nursed Tomás while Máire worked.

The newest O'Donaghue family adjusted well to the unfamiliar rhythm of life with an infant. Máire nursed the baby several times a night with neither she nor Liam getting much sleep. Liam and Máire worked as hard as ever for the Kitcheners to provide for their son, taking joy in everything Tomás did: the grimacing, smiling, and frowning in his sleep; turning his head to a new sound, staring back at them and studying their faces; and cooing when they sang to him.

Elizabeth summoned Máire to the Kitcheners' sumptuous mahogany-walled library, its shelves replete with hundreds of leather-bound volumes. 'Máire, I'm promoting you now to the position of Harry's chief nanny. There will be a little pay increase with this added responsibility, but I want you to keep this arrangement between us.' Máire was thrilled.

Elizabeth didn't spend much time with Harry, apart from feeding him and putting him to bed each night, so she had Peig hire another kitchen maid to relieve Máire of some of her kitchen duties, allowing her to spend more time to look after Harry.

Máire delighted in taking Harry for walks in his baby carriage around the mansion's carefully tended gardens. They enjoyed bath time, Máire singing old Irish airs as he splashed in the tub. Smitten by the little fellow, Máire was intrigued by Harry's development: the first time he rolled over, when he began to crawl, how he'd hold a rattle in one hand and pass it to the other, how he'd imitate funny sounds Máire made for him. She delighted in knowing that soon her own wee Tomás would be doing all of these things, too.

When Harry was almost a year old, Máire began to notice changes in him. He wasn't as responsive as he used to be. He rarely made eye contact. Yet, Tomás would babble away happily, smiling and following her eyes like a hawk. Harry's reaction to Máire's frowns, smiles, scowls, or laughter, was one of complete indifference. And he had lost all interest in his toys. Comparing Harry's progress to Tomás', it was clear to Máire that there was something wrong. She worried about bringing this up to Elizabeth; Nora had told her that every child developed at its own pace, but she was still greatly concerned. This happy, normal baby was increasingly listless, lacking interest in anything. Máire was torn about approaching Elizabeth about this; she risked losing her job, and thus vital income for her family, but she loved Harry.

Somethin's wrong with this baby. There must be somethin' I can do to help him.

The usual routine at the end of the day was for Máire to bring Harry up to his bedroom so that Elizabeth could nurse him, put him down for the night, and then join her family for dinner. Normally, Máire would make small talk with Elizabeth about what she did with Harry that day and then head for home. She was relieved when Elizabeth gave her an opening to express her worries, 'Have you noticed that Harry doesn't smile anymore?' 'Yes ma'am, just in the last few weeks,' she said apprehensively. 'I'm worried about him,' said Elizabeth, 'I think the doctor needs to see him.' Máire was relieved that she could now confide openly to Elizabeth. 'Yes, ma'am, I think that would be a good idea. He's not himself lately. I've tried everything ma'am, playing with him, talking to him, but he doesn't have any interest.' 'Yes, I know. He never looks at me. And he doesn't smile like he used to. Oh, God!' Elizabeth began to cry, 'I couldn't live if there's anything wrong with him.' 'I'm sure the doctor can fix it, ma'am. He'll be all right,' said Máire, doing her best at mother-to-mother reassurance. Máire left, happy that, for the good of little Harry, she could now share her observations and concerns openly with Elizabeth.

'It's because of what they've done to us,' said Liam. 'Didn't yer mother ever tell ya about amadáns? It's God's revenge on people for the sins they've committed. He gives them children like Harry to punish them.' 'I never heard of that,' said Máire, 'but what about Harry? He doesn't deserve that.' Liam went over and lifted Tomás from his crib, hugging him tightly. 'How's my little Tomás? Are ya the best little boy?' Tomás smiled and babbled some baby talk. 'You're the smartest little lad in Galway, aren't ya boy?' prompted

Liam proudly. 'I don't know, Máire, I feel sorry for the little lad, but I don't feel sorry for Kitchener. He deserves it, the ould bastard.' 'Well, the doctor's comin' tomorrow, so we'll see,' said Máire, taking Tomás from Liam, and feeding him. She didn't sleep much that night, worrying about what the doctor might find. She prayed that the doctor would give Elizabeth good news, and that a bit of medicine would make little Harry better.

The doctor arrived at around noon. Walking Harry in the garden, Máire was summoned by one of the housemaids to bring the baby in right away. She came in, lifted Harry out of his baby carriage, and handed him to Elizabeth, nodding a little smile of encouragement. The doctor didn't acknowledge Máire as he and Elizabeth entered the lavish drawing room, closing the door, and leaving Máire to sit in the hallway on her own. She put the baby carriage away and then sat for what seemed like hours. Finally, the doctor emerged and quietly took his leave. Soon, Elizabeth came out. It was obvious that she had been crying, and Máire feared the worst. Holding little Harry, Elizabeth stood in the hallway looking stunned. Taking Harry into her arms, Máire asked quietly, 'Are ya okay, ma'am?' Elizabeth slumped into a chair as if her legs had lost all their strength and sobbed, heartbroken. Máire's natural instinct was to hug her, but household staff wouldn't dare overstep their rank like that. Yet, she felt her motherly pain. *Where in God's name is her husband?* thought Máire, as Elizabeth sat there devastated. *He should be right here supporting her.* 'The doctor thinks Harry is going to be slow in everything,' Elizabeth sobbed. 'He says he might never talk, and there's nothing we can do. He says it will just get worse and worse as he gets older.' 'Oh ma'am, I'm so very sorry,' said Máire, stunned. 'I'm going for a walk with Harry on my own now.' said Elizabeth, 'Please get his perambulator.' 'Yes ma'am,' said Máire, surprised that she didn't give her an order as she usually did but had used the word 'please'. *It's strange the things that bring people down to earth*, thought Máire.

She went to the kitchen, and thankful that Peig had no more work for her, left for home. Her heart, too, was broken after hearing the doctor's diagnosis. She remembered how vibrant and full of life Harry had been just a short while ago, and she thought that, if anyone might know how to help Harry, it would be Mrs O'Flaherty. *I'll stop at her cottage*, thought Máire. *Surely, she'll have some advice to give me. Sure, she must have delivered nearly half the children of Galway and has probably seen everything.* 'Hello, Máire,' greeted Mrs O'Flaherty warmly, ''Tis well yer lookin'. How's Tomásheen?' 'He's fine, growing like a weed, so he is.' 'He's a grand laddeen, just like all the O'Donaghues. Will ya come in and have a cup o' tea?' Over the comforting tea, Máire explained all she knew about Harry's condition. 'Well, I'm glad he's not a duine le Dia. That's the saddest of all isn't it? I've seen what's happenin' with baby Harry all right, and I'm afraid it's going to be hard, Máire. There's no easy way of puttin' it. Some o' them can do all right, and others are in a world all their own, and they don't want anyone in it.' 'Is there nothin' I can do to help him?' asked Máire. 'Well, if ya can find somethin' he likes, do it with him. Do it 'til the cows come home. He'll get mad at everybody and anythin' stopping him, but that's the poor lad's way of lettin' ya know he wants to do it again. Don't let him just do nothing Máire; that's the worst thing you can do. Keep him busy.' Always the champion of the underdog, Máire silently pledged to be Harry's earthly angel, believing that he could indeed learn, despite the doctor's dismal opinion.

PART THREE

Rotten Lumpers

Part Three

With the dawn of 1845, everyone had high hopes for good health to survive another year. They prayed for another good season of potatoes and vegetables, and for the ability to pay their rents to avoid eviction. As usual, the O'Donaghue men planted their stock of potato seeds in early spring on the almost acre or so of land around their parents' cottage and Liam and Máire's addition. June broke hot and dry, and the green potato leaves sprouted quickly, turning into their classic healthy colours of lilac and gold. Liam and Colm were constantly busy on their landlord's farm that summer looking after the livestock, fishing, breaking in and training new Connemara ponies, and tending to and gathering up bountiful harvests of corn, barley, and grain. Up in the nearby hills, they hunted foxes which were a constant threat to the newborn lambs.

July was unusually grey and foggy, and it never stopped raining in August. Mercifully, the lumper potato was impervious to all sorts of inclement weather, a reliable staple, vital to the peasant Irish classes. One late August morning, a foul and stomach-turning smell woke Liam abruptly. He was surrounded by the stench, but where was it coming from? He had never smelled anything like it before. Nauseous, he ran out the door to vomit, and to his horror, saw that their beautiful, living pantry of healthy potato leaves had turned overnight into foul-smelling, dark rotting leaves. Looking closer he saw that more than half of the potato leaves had turned black. He held his nose and ran over to what seemed like the worst of the discolouration by the hedge. He knelt down and dug frantically into the stinking soil, revealing the true horror of what was happening – the potatoes had turned into mouldy, inedible sponges of stinking lumps.

Colm and Tomás appeared at the cottage door, their dread obvious when they saw the tragedy that had befallen their land overnight. Stepping back into the cottage, they grabbed rags to cover their faces. 'What's happened?' asked Tomás, unable to process the impossible scene of destruction before him. Hopeful, Liam tried digging where the leaves still had their colour. 'There're some that are still all right. Come on, we'll dig 'em up before they go bad too.' By now everyone was up and horrified at what they saw and smelled. Máire handed Tomás to Josie and helped the men as they quickly unearthed the healthy potatoes, bagged, and stored them, all the while battling the oppressively putrid smell. Keenly aware that this was a do or die effort, in a few hours they had gathered and stored all the edible potatoes – only about half of what they needed to get through the year. 'Oh my God and His Blessed Mother,' cried Josie. 'What have we done to deserve this? Jesus have mercy on us. What are we going to do?'

Exhausted, they looked towards their neighbours' fields and saw similar scenes in their patches of land. Just the day before, their healthy potato crops had bloomed amidst the lush Irish pastures. Now all they saw was black, rotting foliage. Their life-sustaining potato patches had become grotesque, plague-infested cemeteries. 'Mother of God!' cried Liam, in helpless desperation. 'What's happening?' Máire hugged baby Tomás close and, putting her scarf over his mouth to prevent him from breathing in the foul smell, went back inside the cottage.

As Liam made his way to work that day, he noticed that the oats, wheat, barley, and corn crops were fine. And as he passed the acres and acres of golden wheat, performing their usual elegant dance in the wind, everything seemed normal – everything was normal except for the potatoes. He had heard of the potato crop failure in the last century, causing so much death and destruction, but that was long ago. *How can it be happening again now?* he wondered. Bishop gave his report at the end of the day. 'I think it's some blight that has spoiled two crops, sir, the potato and the tomato.' 'Thank God for that. Are you sure?' 'Yes sir, all the other crops are fine. I checked everywhere, no sign of any infection.' Kitchener was relieved. 'Thank you, Mr Bishop, we're looking at a bumper crop this year, so all's well then?' 'Yes, sir. Hopefully it's just a fluke.'

Máire brought Tomás to work that day, to get him away from the smell, her first ever time doing so. She hoped Peig would understand. Word about the destruction in everybody's potato patches had quickly spread, and fortunately, Peig didn't object this one time. Little Harry was now almost two years old and, despite everything Elizabeth and Máire did to motivate him, nothing had worked. Harry seemed to be withdrawing more and more into his own narrow little world. Máire started her usual routine, washing the pots and pans from last night's dinner. She sat Tomás on the floor and placed a few big, upside-down pots next to him. To keep him occupied, she showed him a large wooden spoon and banged one of the pots with it. When she handed the spoon to Tomás, he happily began to bang away, making quite a rumpus.

Walking with Harry in the hallway, Elizabeth heard the kitchen commotion and went down to investigate. She was surprised to see Tomás, almost eighteen months old now, having the time of his life banging away on the pots while his mother did the dishes. Máire turned around to pick up another pot and saw Elizabeth looking at them. Startled, she knew she'd been caught doing something never allowed – taking your child to work. 'I'm sorry ma'am, but I didn't want the baby getting sick. The smell was awful. I just couldn't leave him.'

At breakfast that morning, Elizabeth had heard about the potato scourge and, thankfully, understood. She smiled at Tomás banging away happily on the pots and pans and bent down to say hello. She looked at him for a long, bittersweet moment, a perfect little baby amusing himself. *If only,* she thought. Agitated, Harry screamed and writhed, nearly falling out of Elizabeth's arms. Then he pushed away from her, leaning towards Tomás. Elizabeth and Máire were shocked. They had never seen Harry so excited. 'Do you want me to let you down, Harry?' Elizabeth eased her squirming son down to sit next to Tomás. With that, Harry grabbed the wooden spoon out of Tomás' hand and started banging furiously on a pot. Losing his spoon, Tomás bawled, so Máire quickly handed him another.

Soon both babies were banging away with abandon. Elizabeth gave them each another spoon, set out a few more pots, and she and Máire looked in awe at the amazing transformation in Harry. He was more relaxed and active than either of them could remember in a long time. The little drummers were having fun, crawling over each other to different pots and banging them, sometimes even in unison. Máire remembered Mrs O'Flaherty's wise advice and let them bang away to their hearts' content as Elizabeth went to get her husband. Máire curtsied when Lord Kitchener came in to witness what seemed like a miracle. He stood there awed by the babies' babbling happily together, as if they never wanted to stop. Although he never uttered a word, Máire sensed that he'd left so she wouldn't see that he was crying.

By the time Máire got home that night, Liam and Colm had burned the rotting mess on their potato patch and the stench had almost dissipated. She told Liam about her day's excitement at work and, despite the huge worry they now had of running out of food that winter, she thanked God for answering her prayers for Harry.

The following day, Máire tended to her usual kitchen duties, and then headed upstairs to care for Harry for the afternoon. The minute Harry saw Máire, he began to scream wildly, his rage stunning Elizabeth and Máire. Taking Harry from his mother, Máire rocked him gently to calm him down, but Harry wouldn't stop. 'I don't know what's wrong with him ma'am.' 'He can't be hungry,' said Elizabeth. 'I just fed him.' 'Maybe he wants to play with the pots and pans again.' 'Yes, that's it,' said Elizabeth, recalling yesterday's kitchen mayhem. 'Let's bring him down and let him play.' As they made their way to the kitchen, Harry's screaming continued. Máire took a few pots and pans down from the rough timber shelf as Elizabeth let Harry down to sit. Máire reached forward to hand Harry two large spoons, and he angrily swatted them away in a furious tantrum. His screaming, increasingly loud and shrill, Harry just sat there, shaking his little head in defeat. Then it dawned on Elizabeth. 'He wants Tomás. He saw you with him yesterday, and he associates him with you.' Máire realised that she was probably right, and cringed at what she knew Elizabeth was going to say next. 'Bring Tomás to work with you tomorrow and let them play together.'

Remembering Mrs O'Flaherty's advice about finding

something Harry was interested in and letting him do it 'til the cows come home, never in a million years did Máire think Tomás would be that something. He was the joy of both his grandmothers' lives, and she knew it would break their hearts if they didn't get to look after him when Liam and Máire were at work. Tomás was happy and secure in the care of his grandmothers. How would he react if this new situation became permanent? 'Yes, ma'am.' Once again Máire felt helpless, employed at the whim of a mistress who, without a second thought, could selfishly demand any and everything from her servants. She lifted a still screaming Harry into his baby carriage and went for their daily walk in the garden. Eventually, cried out, he fell asleep exhausted.

Elizabeth had instructed Máire to bring some pots and pans up to the living room and, sure enough, as soon as Harry saw Tomás, he showed the same wonderful excitement as yesterday. There were no tantrums from Harry as they happily drummed together on the floor. Elizabeth was delighted by the dramatic change in Harry's demeanour when he was with Tomás. When the babies eventually tired themselves out playing and drifted off to sleep, Elizabeth delivered the news that Máire was dreading. 'Máire, I can't believe what I'm seeing,' she whispered excitedly. 'It's truly amazing. I would like it if you would bring Tomás with you every day from now on.' 'Beggin' yer pardon, ma'am, but it'll break his grandmothers' hearts if they don't have any time with him,' said Máire, bravely standing up for her family. 'I can appreciate that, Máire.'

Elizabeth never imagined herself being in this position, a mother, desperately in need of a miracle for her child, and knowing that only her maid had that cure in the form of her baby. Elizabeth was used to getting her way; the entitled and impersonal line drawn between her and her staff was a given. But now she found herself in this unfamiliar and vulnerable situation, lacking control. For once, one of her household staff had leverage over one of the most important concerns Elizabeth had, her child's wellbeing. She couldn't just take Tomás from his parents like a piece of property. This conflicted with her conscience; she wouldn't be able to live with herself if she did such an evil thing, even though she could have, such were the times.

'Máire, I'm dreadfully worried about Harry. I haven't slept in months. I didn't want another baby, and you know what happened when I had him. I was lost and just wanted to sleep all the time. But for you, I'd still be in bed feeling sorry for myself. You made me get up, and you helped me pull myself out of the way I was feeling.' Máire couldn't believe what she was hearing: Elizabeth not quite saying thank you but speaking from the heart, one woman to another, no class distinction evident in her tone. 'As far as I can see, the only hope for Harry to get better is to have Tomás around him every day, and I will be forever grateful to you if you will do this.' Máire felt helpless. She knew Elizabeth was right, but what about Josie and her mother? How could she tell them about this without breaking their hearts? If she said no, would Elizabeth revert to character and use her authority to just take Tomás from her and quite likely evict everybody? 'I heard about what happened to your potatoes yesterday, Máire, and that you probably won't have enough to last the year,' said Elizabeth. 'I promise you this, Máire. If you help Harry, none of you will go hungry.' Máire was stunned.

Elizabeth was offering them exactly what they were saying the rosary for in the O'Donaghue cottage last night:

food, hope, life itself. Before Máire could reply, Elizabeth told her how she would fulfil her promise to Máire. 'I will instruct Peig to give you food every night before you go home. This will just be between you, me, and her.' Clearly, Lord Kitchener was not to be privy to any of this. Máire couldn't say no. She wanted to help little Harry more than anything, and by doing so, they would have a secret stock of nourishing food to keep them all healthy and alive, despite the calamity of losing half their potato crop. 'Okay, ma'am. I'll bring Tomás to work with me from now on.' 'Thank you, Máire. From the bottom of my heart, I thank you. You're doing the right thing.' Máire brought Tomás to work with her from then on. Sure enough, Harry had fewer tantrums and was noticeably calmer. And Elizabeth kept her word to provide Máire with precious food to keep her family alive when, indeed, their stash of potatoes ran out that winter.

Lord Kitchener was keeping a close eye on developments throughout Galway; the general conclusion was that the 1845 potato crop failure was an aberration, a once-off, unexplainable event. Liam and Máire heard reports of people starving in certain areas of Ireland and were thankful to have a roof over their heads, and enough food to survive the winter.

With spring's arrival, hopeful farmers planted their potato seeds once again, but they were sourced from last year's infected potato crop. The seeds were of poor quality, so together with the unusually wet and damp weather that spring, conditions were ideal for the infected seeds to replicate, and once again destroy the crop from within.

Colm was out fishing again, catching a bountiful supply of herring, mackerel and lobster for his Lordship's table, along with a precious few extra fish which he gave his mother when he was sure Bishop, or any of his local spies, were well out of sight.

Harry was almost three years old now, and with Máire and Elizabeth's help, was making slow but positive progress. Comparing the toddlers, their differences were remarkable: Tomás would eat anything, while Harry only ate potatoes – ironically – and mashed carrots, and drank lots of milk. That was it. He refused to eat or drink anything else. Harry still made very little eye contact and seldom expressed affection, a heartbreak for his family. Surprisingly, the one thing Harry loved to do was feed Tomás his dinner and hug him when he cried. When Tomás began to speak his first few words, Harry, almost five months older, was still babbling incoherently, so Máire would choose a word her son had spoken and say it over and over to Harry. Occasionally he would repeat the word – a huge victory which didn't go unnoticed.

The doctor recommended showing Harry pictures of cats, dogs, horses, and farm animals to teach him new words, and Máire showed each picture to him, saying what it was repeatedly, month after month, until Harry learned each animal and could name them. Tomás, meanwhile, was becoming bilingual; his native tongue being Gaelic. Here he was, learning English at the Kitcheners' mansion, and speaking Gaelic at home. Very few Irish people knew much English at this time. Being employed by the Kitcheners, Liam had learned some basic English – enough to get by. Máire on the other hand, having spent four years in Dublin with the Prescotts, was fluent.

Around midsummer, Liam was awakened by that too familiar stench. 'No, no! This can't be happening again,' he screamed, running out to see his worst fears cruelly realised.

There again was that dreaded coating on withered, black stalks. As he had done the year before, Liam clawed wildly at the soil expecting to salvage something from the crop, but his hopes were dashed when the few healthy-looking potatoes he unearthed crumbled in his hands. The one crop they depended on was gone. All of it.

Facing certain death by starvation, the Irish peasantry watched as their only hope of existence, grain, corn, beef, and sheep, sailed away daily in ships bound for Britain. Crops and livestock which the tenant farmers had produced for just pennies for their ruthless landlords were gone. And had there existed a modicum of mercy, a small percentage of these crops could have saved so many. But the interruption of commerce was not allowed under the political policies of the time.

'THEY MAY STARVE,' was essentially the reply of Sir Charles Trevelyan, Assistant Secretary to the Treasury. Unfortunately for the Irish, the British government of the day believed in the laissez-faire approach. In essence, this meant letting things take their own course. The administration believed that famine relief would encourage laziness in the pauper class.

With limited supply, the price of any remaining un-blighted potatoes and grain shot up to the point of being completely out of reach for most Irish people. Soon diarrhoea and dysentery broke out, as starving people desperately ate diseased potatoes. People were reduced to foraging for wild berries and seaweed (in the coastal areas). Meanwhile, under the constant threat of eviction which would mean certain death, in order to pay their rents, many tenants sold or bartered what sparse valuables they had left.

Kitchener's bountiful grain harvest was stored in his

warehouse, waiting to be brought to Galway for shipment. He was aware of a general change in the status quo: robberies were on the rise; protests were breaking out all over the country; desperate people were demanding help; horses carrying corn to harbours were shot; people were breaking into bakeries for bread; and protesters pelted soldiers with stones. Even so, feeling no imminent threat of anything happening locally, Kitchener hadn't taken any extra precautions beyond ordering his warehouse doors padlocked. Aware that Kitchener hadn't posted guards, Liam, Colm, and their few resistance fighter allies prepared to rob the warehouse. Tomorrow its contents were to be brought to the Galway pier to be shipped to England. Faces blackened, they carefully pried loose a few boards from the back warehouse wall. The men grabbed a few bags and then set about distributing a few more days' worth of priceless grain to the grateful locals. Kitchener called in the local military the next day, but to their consternation, nobody had seen nor heard a thing. After this raid, Kitchener had Bishop and his lackeys doing nightly patrols.

Everyone began the winter of 1846 hungry. It was the worst winter in years, lasting well into 1847. Freezing winds, rain, snow, and hail were relentless, tolling the death knell for thousands upon thousands of Irish families, evicted when they couldn't pay their rents. Entire families, ravaged by dysentery, scurvy, and typhus roamed the dirt roads. Already weakened from unrelenting hunger, their immune systems were susceptible to the deadlier strain of measles, then rampant in the countryside. Children were even more vulnerable. With no help forthcoming, these desperate souls eventually died by the roadside, succumbing to the frigid weather. The unyielding frozen ground and their weakened condition prevented these wandering families from burying their fallen dead, so as the catastrophe worsened, peasants were paid pennies to dig shallow trenches for graves. Thousands of paupers were buried in mass graves, covered with quicklime to prevent further outbreaks of typhoid fever. Liam and Máire witnessed numerous instances of bodies being transported to the graves in reusable coffins, often with two or three bodies per coffin. The road systems in the poorer areas of Ireland's west were primitive at best, and food relief was often too far away for emaciated famine victims to make the harrowing journey in search of food or work.

In 1847, known as 'Black 47' (due to the rising levels of mortality), food prices increased daily. Relief shipments to Ireland were few and far between. The British government were undecided about the best course of action. Some more empathetic politicians advocated for additional workhouses to be built in an attempt to house the starving masses. Entering a workhouse meant almost certain death. Entry into the workhouse meant the pauper had to fulfil the destitute rule, and as a consequence, the starving masses went there as a last resort. The destitute rule ensured that only the lowest class of pauper would be granted admission to a workhouse. Once inside the workhouse walls, typhus, dysentery and workhouse ailments quickly took their toll. Meanwhile, inmates often slept four or five to a bed, in overcrowded conditions which frequently was double the capacity of the workhouse. The British administration pressured landlords to assist the peasants. Some landlords were philanthropic and distributed food and soup. Greedy absentee landlords, safely away from the sickness and strife, exacerbated the situation by installing bailiffs to undertake massive evictions.

This set the scene whereby some landlords, receiving less revenue, began to feel financial hardship.

Given their own experience with suppression, in a moving expression of empathy with the starving Irish peasantry, the Choctaw Nation of Oklahoma in America stepped up and donated $170 (equivalent to $5,000 in today's dollars) for hunger relief. Their generosity was spurred on by the fact that it had only been seventeen years since their own displacement. They felt tremendous compassion for the Irish, having themselves been dispossessed of their lands.

Liam and Máire heard rumours of a society of friends distributing soup to the starving on the other side of the county. The Quakers, mostly based on the east coast, distributed vegetables, clothing and small amounts of money. Alas, they had very little presence in the worst-hit areas.

Máire's daily allotment of food from her agreement with Elizabeth, together with the fish Colm caught and withheld from his daily catch, allowed the O'Donaghues to survive that dreadful winter of the failed potato crop. One beloved family hadn't been so fortunate. On a bitterly cold November morning, Máire baked a loaf of bread and brought it to the O'Flahertys. Approaching their home, she noticed that there was no smoke coming from the cottage chimney. She shouted, 'Mrs O'Flaherty, it isn't the soldiers. It's Máire O'Donaghue.' When there was no answer, she pushed in the door and was horrified to see what looked like the skeleton of a man slumped in a chair. Clinging to each other on their straw mattress were the emaciated bodies of their three youngest children. Máire assumed that, in a final desperate attempt to survive, Mrs O'Flaherty and her four teenage children had gone to the workhouse in Galway. Or perhaps she might have had some money saved from her midwifery, and she and her remaining children had been able to make it on a ship to America. Liam and Colm buried Mr O'Flaherty and his children in front of their cottage.

Emaciated, nearly skeletal people started coming to Kitchener's back door seeking help, and Peig would summarily dismiss them. But soon, waves of sickly people came, desperately begging for mercy. Grabbing onto her for support and wracked by fits of coughing, some of them sprayed her with their sputum. Peig turned hundreds of them away every day, until Kitchener ordered Bishop to close the front gates, and place armed guards there to prevent entry by any further trespassers. But the damage was done; Peig became violently ill. Called to examine her, the doctor diagnosed Peig as having typhus. He advised Elizabeth to dismiss her immediately to avoid contamination of other household members. Within days, Peig died, heartbroken and alone.

When Kitchener heard that typhus had invaded his home, he moved the family to their Dublin townhouse to keep them safe and healthy. Edward, as was customary for the nobility of the day, undertook a grand tour of Europe. As a graduation gift for finishing boarding school with honours, Elizabeth and William had given him a year off before he attend Trinity College. They hoped he would do a lot of soul searching while on his journey and, hopefully, realise that he would get nowhere without a good college education.

With Peig's recent passing, Tessie O'Brien was declared head housekeeper. She had been Peig's second in command for the last few years and had proven herself reliable. Knowing that she couldn't trust Tessie to keep to herself her secret arrangement with Máire, Elizabeth left for Dublin without telling her about it. Máire no longer had access to extra food to sustain her family while waiting for the potato crop to come back healthy again. Like everyone else, the O'Donaghues were now on their own in that awful winter of Black 47.

Bishop kept Liam and Colm busy during Kitchener's absence. There were new heifers and lambs to care for and crops to be planted. Everything their bellies needed was right there in front of them, but they couldn't touch it. And because the cost of everything had risen sharply, they were buying less and less food with the pennies Bishop paid them. Máire did her best to smuggle a few vegetables out in her apron every day, but Tessie O'Brien kept an eagle eye on all the staff as they left for home each evening. Peig had taught her well.

Now three years old, Tomás was no longer being breast-fed, and the biggest concern for Liam and Máire was to keep him fed and healthy. They couldn't forage for wild berries yet, as it was still springtime, but they were able to collect some carrageen moss which grew along the shore. Liam and Máire went down and gathered it during low tide. To rid it of its salty flavour, Máire rinsed it in fresh water and then spread it out to dry. Then she chopped it up, soaking it again before simmering it slowly. Sometimes she would add a precious potato, if they were lucky enough to buy one, and whatever vegetables, if any, she had managed to smuggle out that day. The seaweed provided them with nutrients, vitamins and minerals similar to those in land crops. Although they were able to subsist for a few weeks on the seaweed, hundreds of people had already been foraging at the seashore before Liam and Máire were forced to do so. Eventually, this nourishing food source was harvested so relentlessly that, no longer able to replenish itself, within a few weeks it was depleted entirely.

Colm came out one morning to find that all of his fishing nets were gone, most likely stolen by a starving peasant who would try to sell them for desperately-needed food for his family. Since the Kitcheners were in Dublin and didn't need his daily catch, Bishop wouldn't give Colm the money to replace them until the family returned, and he didn't know when that would be. Bishop didn't know about the fish Colm stole, so when it came to changing Bishop's mind, Colm had no recourse. Both O'Donaghue families were now in serious trouble. All of their extra sources of food were gone. The money they earned barely covered the rent, and there was nothing left to buy food.

Since fishing and hunting were by license only, and the Irish were not allowed to hunt or fish, Liam and Colm, often under the cover of darkness, tried to poach the odd trout from the local stream. People who were caught poaching would be arrested and dealt with severely. The combined fear of punishment for poaching – together with the massive exports of crops, livestock, and other foodstuffs – ensured Ireland's poor now faced a humanitarian disaster of deathly and incalculable proportions.

Part Four

Consequences and Piano

Word came that Liam, Colm, Jackie Casey, and Paudie O'Brien, the local resistance group, were required to raid a warehouse full of grain on the Galway pier on Saturday night. Every able-bodied man was going to be needed as it was heavily fortified. The men had no choice. Raid for food or painfully watch their families starve to death. Liam was torn about whether he should tell Máire about his involvement in the resistance movement and about the upcoming food raid in Galway. There was nothing he wanted more than to tell her everything; still, he felt that the less she knew, the safer she and Tomás would be. Paid spies were everywhere. One loose word could have them evicted. It was the only secret he'd ever kept from her.

Liam set off to work the next morning as usual, or so Máire thought. 'I'll be back soon.' He kissed her and Tomás, and with one long last look at the both of them, he left when Colm appeared at the door. They joined up with Jackie and Paudie and headed out on the road to Galway. As they passed villages, they saw several food riots breaking out. They also noticed there had been a huge increase in troops deployed to contain the rioting. Day turned into night, and as they walked the lonely roads in the darkness, they were frequently nauseated by the smell of rotting potatoes. They passed hundreds of emaciated men, women, and children – ghastly skeletons – crouched over in defeat, barely able to walk, their mouths green from eating grass and weeds, all begging for help.

The 'safe house' for everyone to meet Friday night was Seán McNamara's cottage, a few miles on the other side of Galway. The sixteen strong men, many of them meeting for the first time, focused on the following night's raid. Liam marvelled at the rake of priceless potatoes and buttermilk Mrs McNamara fed the ravenous men. It was as if there was no shortage whatsoever. They all stared at the feast, then at her – in complete disbelief. 'I have my ways just like yerselves,' she smiled mischievously. 'You're some woman, God bless you,' said one of the men gratefully. Her husband Seán, a fine cut of a Galway man and a born leader, outlined the plan. 'There are eight soldiers guarding the warehouse, day and night, two of them guard the entrance to the pier, and the other six guard the warehouse itself. Two of you are going to start a fight on the pier to distract the two guards, so that we can row two currachs up the side of the pier without being noticed.' So far, Liam was impressed with the plan. Seán continued, 'There's a back window facing the water about eight feet up. The back of the warehouse juts up to the edge of the pier, so there's no way to guard the back of the building. We're going to row up to the pier, climb up into the window, grab the bags of grain, and hand them down to you with ropes. It looks like rain tomorrow, so hopefully the guards will be inside their huts. Once we get the grain, we're going to stampede a load o' cattle down the front o' the pier, and head straight out for at least a mile, cut across, and then come back to the little beach.' Seán then told each man exactly where he wanted them to be and what he wanted them to do. 'Any questions?' 'How will we climb up to the window if there's no place to stand on the pier?' asked Liam. 'C'mon outside lads, I wanna show ye somethin'.' Seán brought them around the back of the cottage and proudly pulled an eighteenth-century Irish war pike resting on the side of the cottage. 'We'll pull ourselves up from the currachs with this little beauty.' He smiled confidently, as he banged the ground with a twenty-foot spear-like weapon, with an angry-looking hook protruding near the top. 'We'll use the hook to latch onto the window, and that's it,' said Seán. 'Mother of God,' said Liam, 'where did ya get that?' 'My grandfather had a pike leftover from the 1798 rebellion. He hid it in the landlord's field, right under his nose all this time hidden by the stones of the ditch.' The Irish didn't have guns to fight with, so these long pikes had been the preferred weapon for fighting the British in several prior uprisings. The spear kept the aggressors' swords at bay, while the hook, cleverly situated just below the spear, was used to pull soldiers off their horses. 'Sounds good,' said Colm later on, as they went for a walk together. 'So what'ya think?' Liam tried to picture it all in his mind. 'Yea, it's a good plan. 'Tis risky tho'.' So many soldiers. God, it better be rainin' tomorra' to give us any chance. Any moon an' we're dead.'

He thought of Máire, worried sick when he didn't come home last night. Ever since they were married, he had never not come home. It was becoming more and more dangerous to be out and about, especially at night, so he knew she had to be thinking the worst. If all went well, he hoped she'd forgive him for not telling her about his rebel activities. Surely, she'd condone his absence when he turned up with enough grain to last them the few more precious weeks until the potato crop would be ready for digging. *Just a few more weeks. It can't fail again*, he thought.

That night, Seán's wife Eileen led the rosary, as sixteen hardened men humbly bowed their heads, all praying that everything would go as planned tomorrow night. Liam answered the Hail Marys by rote, thinking of Máire back home, another night alone with the baby. What kept him going was knowing that she and Tomás were going to bed hungry and that he was going to fix that.

As they started to put their plan into action the next night, it was pouring rain as they'd expected, and the soldiers were all in their huts sheltering from the storm, just as the rebels had hoped. The two soldiers guarding the pier were making quick inspections, stepping out briefly, then darting back into their tiny guards' hut. On a sandy beach, just around the corner, and out of view from the pier, the men were waiting for the all-clear signal to launch the currachs. When their lookout man ran back and motioned for them to launch, they pushed out into the choppy surf and rowed towards the pier. As planned, two of the men approached the pier, singing and roaring drunkenly. They paused and began to quarrel, calling each other names. The two soldiers posted at the start of the pier came out and laughed condescendingly as two tipsy Irishmen, drunk out of their minds as usual, argued with each other. Had they looked out at the water, the guards would have seen the men in two currachs approaching the pier, turning, and then rowing up the side towards the warehouse. Then the lads started throwing punches at each other. With that, the soldiers ran towards them shouting, 'That's enough Paddy, cut it out!' The lads kept at it, brawling closer to the soldiers, until they crashed into them, the noise alerting the soldiers guarding the warehouse farther down the pier. Exiting their guard huts, they started walking towards the ruckus, amused by the scene – their colleagues thrashing about on the ground, trying to pull the drunken fighters off each other.

Seán and his band reached the warehouse and stopped. He carefully extended the pike and latched onto the windowsill with the pike's hook. He stood up carefully, holding onto the pike for balance, and with great strength, pulled himself up the wall slowly, finally reaching the window. To everyone's relief, the hook held his weight as Seán knew it would. The old wooden-framed window, eight feet from the ground, didn't need a lock, as it faced out to sea. Seán pushed it open with one hand, and climbed in. As he looked around for bagged grain, Liam, Colm, and another man hurriedly scaled the wall, and in a few minutes, they were all inside. They quickly wrapped súgan ropes around several bags of grain and began handing them down to the lads waiting in the currachs. Indeed, not only were these ropes, perfect for tying thatch to roof cottages, but necessity being the mother of invention, they were also perfect in this case. Seán had thought of everything. As quickly and as silently as they could, they handed down eight bags of grain. Unexpectedly, the rain stopped and the wind died down. The men had no choice at this stage but to keep going as quietly as they could. Seán scaled down the wall, followed by his mate and then Colm. Liam was climbing out the window when a soldier emerged from his hut to relieve himself now that it was finally dry. He walked over to the pier's edge and started peeing into the water. Just then a wave pushed the currach up against the pier wall. The pike jerked in Seán's hands, pushing the spear into the window, and broke the glass. Following the sound, the startled soldier looked up and saw Liam hanging out the window. 'Who goes there?' The soldier pointed his gun at Liam and shouted, 'Halt or I'll shoot.' Liam knew he couldn't get down to the currach without being shot. Hanging there, he was an easy target. The soldier looked down and saw the men in their currachs. He pointed his gun at the men below, then pointed it back at Liam. And then began the commotion: dozens of cattle charged down the pier, three lads running behind them, whipping them into a frenzy. The sound drew the other soldiers out of their huts, disbelieving what they saw. 'Get outta' here!' screamed Liam. 'It's either me or all of us.' He saw that, if he jumped, he'd land in the currach, and tip it over, and there wasn't time to row out and back in again if he jumped. Paralysed for the moment, nobody knew what to do. If they rowed away, they knew that Liam would be captured and probably hanged. Seán shouted, 'He's right, we've gotta' get outta' here.' 'No!' screamed Colm. 'We can't leave him.' 'If we don't go right now, we're all dead,' shouted Seán. 'Row!' As the men rowed furiously, the cattle drew closer. The soldier's sense of self-preservation kicked in, and he ran into the warehouse promptly followed by the other soldiers, all of them missing the cattle's charge by seconds. The soldier shouted to his colleagues, 'There's a rebel stuck up on the window ledge, and there're two currachs in the water!' The soldiers ran up the stairs, looked out the window, and saw Liam scaling down the wall. The currachs had vanished into the darkness. 'Hold it right there, or you're dead!' Liam looked up to see four rifles pointed at him. As the cattle had passed and were now almost stopped at the end of the pier, four more soldiers ran out to aim their rifles at Liam. If he jumped, he knew he'd be shot. 'Come back up, you Fenian bastard, or we'll shoot,' shouted one of the soldiers. Liam shook his head and climbed back up. They grabbed him and dragged him roughly through the window, furious that his fellow rebels had escaped.

When Seán and his men met on the sandy beach, they dragged the currachs up to an old shed and hid them under a heap of filthy-smelling straw. Wordless, they felt that they had abandoned one of their own, and they were trying to come to terms with what that would mean. 'If he talks, we're all dead,' said one of them. Colm charged at the man and punched him in the face. 'Fuck you,' he said. 'My brother's no snitch.' The others pulled them apart. 'Take it easy lads,' said Seán. 'Look! Shit! This wasn't part of the plan. If only that feckin' rain hadn't stopped. We've gotta' get outta' here. They'll be sending out patrols soon, so take the bags, and get going. Colm, we'll send word to ya as soon as we know anything. Fuck this,' said Seán. 'I'm sorry Colm, I'm sorry.' Colm could see how terrible Seán and the men felt about Liam, but his mind was already racing to the next time he'd see Máire. *Christ Almighty, what am I going to say to her? How can I tell her? Why didn't I get caught? Why did it have to be Liam?* As he and his two friends headed home, their immediate worry, now, was not to get caught with four bags of grain.

Liam was brought straightaway to the Galway gaol. The soldiers tied him to a chair, and the interrogation began. 'What's your name?' demanded the sergeant at arms. When Liam said nothing, he received an almighty blow to his face knocking him and the chair backwards. The soldiers yanked the chair upright, and the torture continued. 'I said, 'What's your name?' you Fenian bastard!' Liam remained silent and another vicious blow hit the other side of his face. 'Talk or you're a dead man,' and another blow followed, this one to the stomach. Liam knew he was already a dead man, so he wasn't going to give an inch. Another blow, and he was out cold. They dragged him to a cell and threw him in.

In and out of consciousness all night, Liam shivered in his cell. He was brutally awakened next morning, when a soldier threw a bucket of water on his bloodied face. 'Wake up, you bastard,' barked the soldier. 'The magistrate wants to see you.' Four soldiers shackled Liam and led him up to the courthouse, into an impressive mahogany-panelled courtroom with a balcony full of observers. There waited the white-wigged magistrate in his judicial robe. Wasting no time, he asked, 'You are charged with stealing Her Majesty's grain from the pier last night. How do you plead?' Liam said nothing; he just stared ahead. 'Have you anything to say before I hand down your sentence?' Liam knew this was a sham hearing. The sentence would be death, no matter how he pleaded. 'I'd do it again, yer honour, but next time, sure I wouldn't be stupid enough to get caught.' This smart remark put the courtroom into an uproar, and people started to applaud and cheer loudly. They were all there wanting to see who this brave Irish fellow was, as word had quickly spread about the last night's daring raid on the pier. The magistrate was infuriated by Liam's impertinent remark and didn't appreciate the support he was receiving from the balcony. Banging his gavel down loudly to restore order, he said, 'I sentence you to hang by the neck until you die. This sentence will be carried out next Saturday morning at dawn.' When he smashed his gavel again, the crowd booed in the balcony. 'Clear the building immediately,' he shouted to the constabulary. As he was led back down to his gaol cell, Liam heard the salmon weir raging on the Corrib river nearby. He never felt lonelier in his life. Waiting for the hangman, his only solace was knowing that at least Máire and Tomás would have some of the food taken in last night's raid.

Colm managed to get home safely, but now he faced an impossibly heartbreaking task; he had to tell Máire everything. He had to reveal his and Liam's double life fighting the British occupation when and wherever possible. He dreaded telling her that Liam had been captured trying to steal food for their survival. And worst of all, he'd have to tell her that Liam's penalty would be death by hanging. And finally, and most cruel of all, even when she understood all of this, she couldn't visit Liam in gaol. If she did, Liam's identity would be revealed, and the O'Donaghue family would be evicted in a shared punishment to face certain death on the road.

Máire was thrilled to see Colm at the cottage door. She expected Liam to walk in behind him. But he didn't. One look at Colm's face, and she knew something was terribly wrong. He burst out crying. 'I'm sorry Máire, Liam.' Máire's knees felt like jelly, and she slumped to the floor. 'What happened?' Grabbing hold of a chair, she began to pull herself up, grasping Colm's arm for support. 'What happened? Where's Liam?' She screamed, 'Where is he?' When Colm told her everything, the awful reality slowly sank in that her Liam was never coming back. 'I want to see him,' she cried. 'Máire you can't,' said Colm softly. 'I have to see him one last time. I have to Colm.' 'Máire, they don't know who he is, and if they find out, they'll evict us all or worse.' 'But I have to see him,' she sobbed. 'I have to, just one last time.' Colm blamed himself for Liam's capture, unavoidable when that damned rain and wind stopped so quickly, ruining Seán's perfect plan. He knew that, if Máire had to see her husband one last time, he had to make it happen somehow. 'Seán said he'd get word back to us,' said Colm. 'As soon as I hear anything, I'll let ya know.' 'I wanna' be there, Colm, no matter what they do to him,' said Máire bravely.

By now, news of the daring warehouse raid had spread throughout the countryside, and it gave the desperate people something to cheer about. They marvelled at the clever plan, so brilliantly conceived and carried out. That there were men willing to risk their lives and fight back against the Crown greatly lifted their morale. Knowing that one of the rebels, sentenced to death was inside the Galway gaol, people gathered outside and began shouting and throwing rocks. Liam's smart remark to the magistrate had electrified them. He was an instant hero. Each day the crowds grew larger and angrier, so additional constabulary officers were stationed in front of the courthouse to contain them. As the crowds pressed closer and closer to the great courthouse doors, they screamed obscenities. By Friday afternoon, as the scaffolding was being completed, the crowds numbered in the hundreds. The worried magistrate was holding an emergency meeting in the courtroom with the captain of the guards, several city leaders of commerce, and some of the more prominent landlords in the county. 'The natives are desperate, sir. God knows what might happen if you hang the prisoner tomorrow. There will almost certainly be a riot, and we haven't enough troops to contain them,' said the captain, sharing his assessment of the situation. 'And if we hang him, we'll be giving them another bloody martyr, won't we? That's the last thing we want right now,' said the magistrate, well aware that hanging the prisoner would surely create another dead Irish hero to inspire future rebellions. With a hungry, angry, desperate mob just outside his courtroom door, and with insufficient guards to quell the situation if it got out of control, he was also worried about his own skin. 'Dismantle the scaffolding immediately,' he ordered. 'This should calm things down. Captain, once the scaffolding is removed, announce the new sentence. I'll have the order ready for you in an hour. Prepare your men to escort him to Dublin tomorrow. The mob should be gone by then but be sure to let people see him leaving Galway.' A huge cheer rose up from the crowd when they saw the authorities beginning to dismantle the scaffold. Soon after, the captain came to the front door, stood on the courthouse steps, and read the sentence. 'By order of his honour, Lord Faulkner, magistrate for the county of Galway, the prisoner shall be spared his life.' With the pronouncement that Liam would be spared the gallows, a resounding cheer erupted from the crowd, but when the captain continued, they were utterly crushed. 'In his infinite mercy, the magistrate sentences the prisoner to be deported for life to the Penal Colony of Botany Bay for stealing Her Majesty's grain, this sentence to be carried out forthwith.' When the crowd reacted with angry howls and loud boos and began flinging more rocks, the captain ordered the soldiers to fire warning shots over their heads. 'I order you to disperse or we will shoot the next person who throws a rock.' Fearful, the crowd slowly began to drift away. Seán was amongst the huge crowd, and he dispatched one of his men to get word of Liam's sentence to Colm.

By the time she received the news that Liam's life was spared thanks to the support of the Galway protesters, Máire was utterly exhausted – drained of all emotions. And while she was grateful to know that he wasn't going to die, she couldn't accept that, deportation meant that she would never see her love again. *How will we survive without Liam?* She was angry with him because of his secret life and for what his participation in it was going to cost their family. *Liam's gone. Now I'm alone. Why did he do this? Why didn't he tell me? Everyone but Liam got away. Why did he have to get caught? And why am I now the only one suffering?* Hungry, Tomás started crying. His needs brought Máire back to the immediate reality. Thanks to the raid, she had enough food to keep them going for a while, and they at least had a roof over their heads, unlike so many other poor souls. Until

Elizabeth Kitchener and her children returned, Máire was only required to work two days a week, but this wouldn't be enough money to pay the rent and buy food when the grain from the raid was gone.

To deflect suspicion about Liam's involvement in the raid, Máire, Colm, and the entire O'Donaghue family contrived a credible story: in desperation for food, Liam went out fishing and didn't return. This cover story would allow them to remain in their cottages and not be evicted. They told this trivial lie to Father Murphy and, at mass that Sunday, he had all the surviving parishioners include prayers for the soul of Liam O'Donaghue, who was tragically lost at sea. The condolences Máire received after mass were comforting to her, as this was exactly how she felt – widowed. Liam was cruelly lost and taken away forever from her and her family.

At dawn the following morning, with just a few stragglers on the street, Liam was moved to Dublin. Seán and a few of his men watched the prison gates discreetly as a flatbed prison cage, drawn by four horses, emerged from the prison gates. Four mounted soldiers were at the front, and four took up the rear. The four-wheeled, flatbed cart swayed heavily from side to side and frequently sank with heavy thuds, as it dug into the uneven road. To allay suspicion, Seán had his wife and children with him. They casually walked closer and were shocked when they saw Liam holding onto the prison bars to keep his balance. He was barely recognisable. His eyes were almost completely swollen shut, and his face was a mess of black and blue welts from beatings. As instructed, the soldiers made no effort to stop Seán and his family; they wanted the Irish to see the prisoner officially leaving Galway. 'How are ya doin' Horse?' asked Seán. Liam could barely see him out of one eye. 'I gave the bastards nothin',' said Liam. 'I know Horse. I know. Where are they takin' ya?' 'To Dublin, then they're putting me on a ship to England, then to Australia.' 'I'm sorry, Horse,' said Seán, weeping. 'Tell Máire I'm sorry, will ya? Tell her I'll think of her forever.' 'All right then, move away,' ordered one of the soldiers, as they began to pick up speed. 'Tell her I'll come back to her; tell her I'll find a way. Tell her how much I love her and Tomás.' 'I will. We'll make sure she's all right. I promise ya that,' Seán shouted. 'We'll never forget ya, Horse.' As Seán and Liam were speaking in Gaelic, the soldiers were none the wiser. Soon, they turned a corner and were gone.

1847 was the worst year of all; the potato crop failed again. People were dying in the thousands from hunger, dysentery, and fever. The entire west coast of Ireland, from west Kerry to Cork, right up through Clare, west Mayo, and Donegal, was especially hard hit. Evictions were the order of the day; tenants had no money to pay their rents. Heartbroken families would watch as their cottages were demolished with huge battering rams and set on fire, preventing their return. Entry into the workhouses was seen as a last resort; if the homeless and hungry couldn't reach the workhouse in time, they would eventually have died by the roadside.

Torn farther away from everything and everyone he had ever known, day after day, as he was transported to Dublin, Liam saw numerous bodies along the roadside. Provided with little food in the horse-drawn prison cage, Liam arrived at Kilmainham gaol in Dublin, dirty and hungry. As he was dragged out of the cage shackled, he saw before him an intimidatingly austere limestone building. Five grotesque shapes stood sentry above its doors, representing the five worst crimes: murder, treason, theft, rape and piracy. Shoved into a cell with two other prisoners, he was at last able to lie down. It was the first time in days. Exhausted, he fell into a deep sleep. He awoke the next morning to a breakfast of bread and milk, the only food to sustain him until he left that prison. Put to work sewing uniforms for soldiers, he was allowed an hour's exercise daily in the limestone-floored prison 'garden'. His thoughts were always about home. *How is Máire doing? Tomás? Will Seán keep his word and look after them?* He kept his sanity by imagining his smiling Máire, the angelic, innocent face of Tomás, Galway's blue skies, and riding his beloved Bridgey. He had no idea when he'd be transported to Australia.

After nearly two weeks in Kilmainham gaol, Liam was awakened one morning by two burly prison guards who ordered him to get up. Within minutes, he and several other prisoners were shackled together by the ankles and marched to the prison gates in a pouring rain. 'We're going to the ship,' said one, though none of them really knew their immediate future. Would they go directly to Australia or go to England to await a prison ship there? They had heard that most of the convicts left from England. They began their long, wet, walk to Dublin's quays, guarded by a dozen well-armed soldiers. Adding to their humiliation, curious onlookers stopped and gawked at their sorry state as they passed by. Liam felt like he was part of a cattle herd walking to slaughter. When, finally, they reached Dublin's port, they saw the ship that would transport them to God only knows where. Liam had never seen such a massive vessel. It had two huge masts and looked sturdy enough to carry a man anywhere he wanted to go. In a hive of activity, noisy cattle and sheep balked as they were loaded onto the main deck aft, while at the other end, provisions were being brought aboard and lowered to the deck below. Tough-looking sailors, hardened by years at sea, shouted orders in rough English accents which Liam had never heard before. Drenched by the rain, they were finally ordered aboard and led to a metal-grated hatch on the main deck. Two sailors heaved back the hatch, and two armed soldiers stepped down the ladder first. The prisoners were ordered to follow and descended the ladder one by one. When they were all below deck, the soldiers unshackled them from each other. 'Any trouble,' said one of the soldiers, 'and ye'll be shackled again 'til ye reach yer destination.' 'Which is?' asked one of the prisoners bravely. 'London!' The soldier clambered up the ladder, and the hatch slammed shut with a clanging thud, sealing the prisoners' only way out. If it was possible to deflate that sorry bunch of men any further, hearing London and not Australia, did exactly that. They all knew that this meant more gaol time in one of Her Majesty's fine prison cells to await a convict ship, which could take forever. To a man, they slumped to the wet floor, broken. As the ship left the dock to make its way slowly out of Dublin harbour, the prisoners were awakened by the cacophony of orders being shouted from the main deck. Housed in the midlevel deck, and lacking portholes, all they could do was listen. They could hear the main sails dropping and were jostled about when the wind caught them. As the ship settled into its journey to England, the prisoners began talking. 'How long did they give you?' asked a man of a young boy, barely twenty. 'Seven years.' 'For what?' asked another convict. 'I stole a bag of corn. How long did you get?' he asked. 'I got fourteen years, for stealing two silver spoons.' 'They were going to hang me, but they gave me life,' said Liam. 'For what?' asked another. 'Yerra.' said Liam lackadaisically. 'The judge didn't like me.' They all laughed.

The ship docked at London two days later. When the hatch opened, soldiers climbed down and chained them together again. Climbing up the ladder, the prisoners got their first glimpse of the river Thames. They saw a gritty navy yard with industrial-looking buildings of all sizes at quayside. Huge, menacing warships were docked everywhere, and sailors milled about on ship and on shore. As Liam took in these surroundings, he felt like he was already a million miles from Ireland. The reality of his separation and sense of isolation began to hit him; there was no green open land anywhere. 'Okay, you lot,' shouted a soldier, 'follow me.' Shackled closely together, they inched their way off the ship only to be marched about a mile downriver where, docked at quayside, a massive old warship came into view. This 'hulk,' no longer seaworthy, its rigging long removed, was to be their prison until they sailed to Australia. Nearing the timber vessel, the prisoners saw how massive it was. It had six decks of various sizes and, on three of its decks, menacing-looking portholes which had been used for cannon warfare during its heyday. Liam shuddered at the thought of spending a single night, or worse a week or a month, on this forbidding, rotting old warship, to await his transportation ship. The prisoners were led aboard, and once again led down a hatch where hundreds of other prisoners, all shackled to the floor, looked up at them. The new arrivals shuffled to an unoccupied area, were unshackled from each other, and then were chained to the floor. 'Welcome to the Warrior in beautiful Woolich, mate,' said one of the British convicts. Liam sank to the floor. He shook his head, put his hands on his forehead, and closed his eyes. 'It's all right mate. You'll get used to it. We'll get a bit o' fresh air again tomorrow, when we see Her Majesty's wonderful naval docklands,' said the convict reeking sweat and sarcasm. Liam looked to see who this unusually cheerful Englishman was. 'Billy Vickers. How do you do?' 'Liam,' he answered, not giving his last name for safety's sake. 'An Irishman?' He reached out to shake Liam's hand. 'Yes,' said Liam, taken aback by this friendly gesture from an Englishman. Recovering from his surprise, he extended his hand. Oddly, there was no sense of superiority in Billy's body language, no looking down at an Irishman. It was just one prisoner acknowledging another. *Well, this is a first,* thought Liam. He found an empty spot on the floor, lay down, and slept soundly.

At dawn, the prisoners were marched to community washrooms and toilets. Then they were led up to the mess area for awful-tasting gruel. Liam got his first taste of things to come when, next, they were marched down to the filthy naval dockyards. He couldn't believe how expansive the area was with several ships docked there. The men passed three gigantic shipbuilding slips and two dry docks, each housing ships under construction or under repair. They entered a gate and were marched into the biggest building Liam had ever seen. There, in what appeared to be a huge pond, he saw a half-built warship, propped up by a lacework of timber beams. Steam rose from an aft chimney. Near to where Liam stood at the front of the ship, another enormous chimney belched clouds of dirty smoke. 'Welcome to HMS Trident, gentlemen,' said the sergeant. 'The captain will give each of you your assignments for the day.' 'Follow me, gentlemen,' said the captain, dismissing the sergeant. The captain picked out the strongest-looking men for furnace duty and delegated his other officer to escort them aboard.

Liam and four other prisoners were brought down to the sweltering furnace and taught how to shovel coal. As he marched back to the hulk each night, Liam hardly had the energy to think. His back ached and his arms felt like jelly. Once fed, he'd fall asleep exhausted. For two weeks, he and his furnace-from-hell companions shovelled coal in daily ten-hour shifts. His next work assignment was much easier, and more satisfying – repairing ships' damaged engines. The job demonstrated by the foreman, Liam showed an extraordinary knack for remembering exactly where to put engine parts, rarely making a mistake.

Back in Dublin, Lord Kitchener, like other landlords, had a major problem. Over the last two years, his annual income had declined steeply. The deaths of so many of his tenant farm workers had resulted in the harvesting of a fraction of his crops; desperately hungry people had poached many of his cattle and sheep, and income from the few remaining tenants able to pay their rents was hardly enough to sustain his accustomed lifestyle. His bills were mounting at an alarming rate, and he was several months behind on his Dublin townhouse mortgage. Because property prices were declining rapidly, he knew he would have to act quickly to avoid bankruptcy. He reluctantly decided to sell his townhouse, and, once it was sold, Elizabeth had just a week to oversee the packing up of the household and prepare for the bittersweet journey back to their country estate. Having been away for a year, Elizabeth realised now that she was eager to return to Galway, for she felt more at home there than in their elegant Dublin townhouse. Even so, she knew that, for her family's sake, she would have to be careful to avoid close contact with any of the thousands of disease-ridden, starving people wandering the roads. So, her husband hired four heavily armed men as protection. The guards rode alongside the Kitcheners' comfortable horse-drawn carriage to keep the peasants from touching it, and to order them to clear the road as they passed by. The endless stream of paupers, gaunt and hollow-eyed, begging for help, was simply too much to behold; Elizabeth kept the curtains closed for the entire journey.

Bishop had kept the Kitcheners apprised of all that had happened in Galway during their absence. Still, it was a shock for Elizabeth when she arrived home to a very different situation from what she had left. Several stable boys and maids were dead from the fever. The fires hadn't been lit consistently throughout the house, so it was damp and cold. The pantry was almost empty, and Colm hadn't delivered any fresh fish. Máire was summoned to Elizabeth's elegant study. 'Máire, I'm so sorry. I heard what happened to Liam.' 'Thank you, ma'am. It's been very hard.' 'Yes, I'm sure it has been. I liked him. He was a fine man.' 'Yes, he was ma'am. I miss him every day.' And that was it. No caring chat about Máire's awful loss, how it happened, nor how she and little Tomás had survived since Liam's death. It was back to business as usual. 'Máire, I would like you to be my head housekeeper. I trust you, and you do a good job.' Knowing that Tessie O'Brien was still employed as head housekeeper, Máire was truly surprised by this promotion. 'Thank you, ma'am.' 'I've discussed this change with Tessie, and she understands.' Máire nearly burst out laughing, thinking of how 'understanding' Tessie was likely to be. Tessie O'Brien was a belittling old busybody, and now she would have to take orders from Máire, and not the other way around. *Well, this is going to be interesting,* thought Máire. 'Please stock the kitchen immediately, and please instruct Colm to slaughter a cow and a sheep. I will ask William to buy new nets, so that he can get back to fishing.' 'Yes ma'am. Thank you, ma'am,' replied Máire noticing a different tone altogether, *and she even said 'please' twice!* Then Elizabeth stunned Máire when she said, 'I want you and Tomás to move into Peig Shea's quarters. With all the sickness going around, I can't risk your contracting anything and infecting any of us. Remember what happened to poor Peig?' Even though it was a request motivated by pure self-interest, it made every bit of sense to Máire. Until the nightmare of pestilence finally ended, Tomás would be safer living with her here.

'This is from Liam,' was all that Seán ever said, followed by, 'I'm sorry Máire.' For, despite the near impossibility of fighting a rebellion on empty bellies, Seán, the leader of the agrarian rebels and his men kept their word to Liam. Máire and Tomás received a weekly supply of fresh vegetables and milk which she shared with the O'Donaghues and her family. This precious bounty kept them alive, albeit barely. Máire never questioned how they obtained the food. If she moved into the big house, Máire reasoned, Tomás' and her share of food from Seán could be shared by both families, and there were fruits and vegetables in the Kitcheners' larder which she could hand to Colm when he delivered his daily catch. *God have mercy on Peig*, she thought. *But never again will I have to worry about her watching my every move.* The potato crop had failed for three years, and there was no indication that this year's crop would be healthy either. Virtually no one had seeds to plant, for the farmers had either eaten or bartered them to survive, so Máire was torn about the prospect of moving into the big house. While she knew that it was the right thing to do to survive, she also knew that it was the Kitcheners and his kind who had sent her Liam away.

'How is Harry, ma'am? I think about him every day.' It had been a year since she had seen him, and she was hoping to hear good news. But the look on Elizabeth's face revealed otherwise. She sighed, gave a sad half smile, and looked off into the distance. 'He seems to be gone from us. Gone from everything. He doesn't talk at all. He's angry all the time. We took him to the best doctors in Dublin, but they said there was nothing they could do. We're all exhausted dealing with Harry. There's no break; it's constant.' Remembering Mrs O'Flaherty's wise words about finding something that interested him and running with it, Máire tried to offer Elizabeth some hope. 'Well ma'am, maybe Harry can play with Tomásheen again. Remember that time in the kitchen when they both banged on the pots and pans?' Elizabeth smiled, 'Yes, I do. That was the last time I remember him being happy.' Then, crestfallen, she said, 'I don't think he knows what happiness is.' Máire felt her pain, mother to mother, and so was looking forward to bringing Tomás tomorrow and seeing Harry's reaction when he saw her son again. Rather than continuing to talk about Harry, Máire felt it best to distract Elizabeth, so she discussed the steps needed to get the house up and running smoothly again. Who would light the fires? Who would look after bedrooms? What menus would Elizabeth want? She thought of the pain that moving out of her cottage and bringing Tomás with her would cause to both families, but she felt that they would understand, given the dangerous conditions all around them. Walking home that night she decided. *This is what Liam would want me to do.*

Máire spent a tearful evening explaining her decision to her family and Liam's. Mercifully, they had all survived the past few years thanks to having roofs over their heads, and their instincts to survive. The regular supply of vegetables Máire sneaked out of the big house, the fulfilment of Seán's promise to Liam to look after Máire and Tomás, and everyone's constant foraging for mussels and edible berries, had kept them healthy enough. 'I'll be able to get more food to ye now, when Colm brings his fish every few days. I'll hide it in his bucket.' 'Oh, that'll stink to high heaven Máire. There's nothing worse than fishy-smelling onions, yach,' teased Colm. 'Well, you try to find some lovely fat onions next time yer out and about,' quipped Josie. 'Máire girl, I know Liam would want you and Tomásheen to be okay. You're doing the right thing going to the big house.' 'Josie's right,' said Tomás. 'Bring yer little boy up fine and healthy. That's what Liam would want ya to do.' Máire cried, 'I miss him so much.' 'We all do Máire,' said Tomás, 'but wherever he is, I'd bet my life that he's thinking about gettin' back to us all someday, somehow. So never give up Máire. God is good.' 'I hope so,' said Máire, encouraged by their fortitude and thankful for their understanding.

Lying in bed that evening, Máire had an inspiration. *I'm moving into the big house. What a nice wedding present it would be for Colm and Órla if I gave them the little cottage to start off their lives together, just like Liam and I did. I'm sure Liam would agree.* She decided to wait a while, until just before the wedding, to surprise them. She slept well that night for the first time in weeks and dreamed that Liam was giving Tomás his first riding lesson. The dream was beautiful, just the three of them, but it was far too brief.

Liam excelled with maritime engines and was now an invaluable member of the repair team, a development which, ironically, would delay his transportation to Australia. He learned everything he could about the new state-of-the-art steamship engines. The foreman noticed Liam's engineering talents, and, wanting him to perform to the best of his abilities, promoted him after a long, nine months on board the Warrior, where he'd barely survived on the repetitive daily rations of oxtail cheek soup and mouldy biscuits. With the promotion, came better living quarters and better food. He was no longer marched nightly in chains back to the Warrior hulk, but was housed with several English, Welsh and Scottish boilermakers and repairmen in a nearby shack. The dock was heavily guarded, with no chance of escape, but his circumstances were much improved. Liam's colleagues soon got to know the new Irishman amongst them, a man so favoured by their foreman that he was now to be housed with them, rather than in the convict ship. They all respected his abilities and liked his honest ways, but he was still Irish with little English and, of course, he was still a convict. As the months went by, Liam's English became fluent. His mechanical suggestions were respected by the foreman, and many were implemented. By then, his English colleagues had become friends, and they no longer heard his accent. He was one of them.

In Connemara, there was great excitement in the O'Donaghue and Donnelly cottages as they prepared for another wedding. Over the last few years Colm had courted and fallen in love with Máire's younger sister, Órla. She had blossomed into a beautiful young woman with a gutsy attitude and a sharp sense of humour. Throughout the worst years of the famine, the sisters had become inseparable. Órla was a willing shoulder to cry on during Máire's darkest moments of loneliness and despair. But today it was all about the joy of both families coming together once again. Josie was up to the nines getting everybody ready for her son's wedding. She gathered and tucked in all her men's clothes, tightening waistbands due to their lack of nourishment. At his mother's feet, young Tomás played with their new kitten. Máire was making last-minute alterations to the wedding attire that she graciously offered to Órla for her big day. Bittersweet emotions stirred in Máire as she beheld Órla looking lovely and innocent in the clothes that she herself had been so happy wearing just a few years before. 'It's perfect Órla. You look stunning.' 'I remember when you wore it, Máire. I never saw such a beautiful outfit. Are ya sure you can watch me getting married in it?' Máire was trembling and tearing up. 'I'm sure,' said Máire, pragmatic and kind as ever. 'You'll turn everyone's hearts when they see you. You'll look beautiful for your big day, and that's the way it should be.' 'I only wish Liam was here. It's not fair,' said Órla. At this, Máire let out a deep, guttural cry, straight from her heart, and the tears she'd been holding back let go. She turned away and picked up young Tomás. Smiling at her son, she whispered softly, 'He's here, Órla. He's here in our son.' Touched, Órla embraced them both warmly and then brightened. 'If ya change yer mind and want to move back into your place, just let me know. It'll feel funny being in your bed tonight.' Máire wiped her tears and let Tomás down again. 'It's yours, Órla. Liam would want it this way. I'm sure of that. I hope you enjoy it as much as we did.' Órla let out a naughty little giggle. 'Yea, I know. Colm can hardly wait.' Máire laughed, 'Just like his brother!'

Wedding guests in the little church looked around and saw the many empty pews where their friends had sat just a few short years before, so Órla's wedding mass was a bittersweet occasion. Unspoken grief came to the fore, as they thought of those friends, now either dead or living in another country altogether. These were the folks they had sung and danced with at joyful parties not so long ago. Máire smiled remembering the fuss and craic at Mrs Brosnan's, during her final bridal outfit fitting. *If Mrs Brosnan hadn't given that damned chicken a good swift kick up the arse, it might've laid an egg on my skirt or pecked the buttons off my blouse.* Her smile changed to sadness as she remembered that the poor woman was also gone. *God bless her sweet soul.* Máire looked over to the second row where Mrs O'Flaherty and her family always sat, but their pew was empty. She remembered her friend's enduring wisdom and kindness. She hoped and prayed that Mrs O'Flaherty and her three remaining children had made it to America. *And poor old Mr O'Flaherty. I'll never be able to erase the awful memory of him, the poor soul, and the sight of his three emaciated children clinging to each other, all dead. God bless that family.* Today, however, everybody put on a brave face as they eagerly awaited Órla's walking up the aisle. And beautiful she was, a sight lifting everyone's spirits as Father Murphy and three altar boys stepped onto the altar to await her approach. Father Murphy seemed to have aged thirty years in the past five. He'd never had it so busy between mass burials, baptisms and deaths. It would be no surprise at all if, at some point in the future, not all baptisms and records during the famine years would be entered correctly; poor Father Murphy had little time to keep up with such administrative duties. Several little children stood at one side of the altar and sang an elegant, traditional song in Gaelic, and everyone stood up. To create a tiny ring for Orla's wedding, Tomás had had the local blacksmith melt down the remaining little pewter spoon luckily still left in the old wooden box. Tomás, his grandfather's proud namesake, captured everybody's hearts; he preceded Órla and her father Diarmuid up the aisle carrying Orla's wedding ring in a tiny scrap of emerald green linen sewn into a small tweed cushion. *He looks so sweet in his Sunday best,* thought Máire. *Thank God he made it all the way up to the altar without dropping it!* Truth be told, she'd stolen a scrap of linen from Elizabeth's sewing basket for the occasion. At Father Murphy's signal, the musicians sitting at the other side of the altar played Órla in. Colm, waiting nervously at the altar, looked to the church entrance. There, in her stunning wedding outfit, he saw his bride begin to walk up the aisle, on the arm of her father. Colm was still taking in how beautiful Órla looked, when Father Murphy welcomed everybody and the wedding mass began. 'In nomine Patris, et Filii, et Spiritus Sancti. Amen.' Thus began another Donnelly and O'Donaghue love story. Máire sat there with little Tomás at her side, smiling as the happy couple exchanged vows. Two of her most beloved people in the world were getting married, and she had no doubt that they would be happy together. But slowly, except for anger, her strength and any other emotions she had, abandoned her, as she watched the ceremonial drama playing out. Feeling more alone than ever before and knowing that in a few hours Órla and Colm would be clinging to each other in their marriage bed, it took everything for her not to scream her thoughts: *IT'S NOT FAIR!!! WHERE ARE YOU, LIAM? WHY AREN'T YOU HERE WITH ME TODAY?* Everyone clapped when Father Murphy announced, 'And now, under God, I pronounce you man and wife.' The applause jolted Máire back to the present. She pulled herself together. *Today is Órla's day.* Within a few months, everybody was delighted when Órla announced that she was going to have a baby.

Tessie. 'Let's go up together and talk about it with Lady Elizabeth when we bring her her afternoon tea,' said Máire. Tessie said nothing, but the nod of her head, albeit ever so reluctant, signalled to Máire that she had given Tessie the respect she felt she deserved, thus defusing the situation. They worked together as usual in the kitchen, cleaning pots and pans, peeling onions, and preparing lunch and dinner. It was an uneasy silent truce for a few hours, neither of them giving orders to each other. Máire noticed that Tessie still had all of her belongings in the bigger bedroom. Together, they brought Elizabeth her afternoon tea. Today, Emma was resuming her piano lessons in the music room with Elizabeth and Harry watching from the sofa by the bayside window. It was Máire's first time seeing Harry, after such a long time, and she was shocked at what she saw. He seemed to be in a trance, rocking back and forth on the sofa, his eyes closed. Emma earnestly struggled through her simple classical piece, on the brown mahogany grand piano. Her piano teacher Mrs Best, the Church of Ireland minister's wife, sat next to her, encouraging her softly, and patiently placing her hands over the correct keys.

When Elizabeth pointed to the parlour, Máire and Tessie brought the tea trays to a table there. Elizabeth and Harry followed them in. Máire went over to hug Harry. 'Hello Harry, how are you? It's so good to see you again.' Harry didn't respond. She could see that he didn't remember her at all, or so she thought. He just stared down at his feet, still rocking back and forth. Crushed, she looked tearfully at Elizabeth. Meanwhile, Tessie poured Elizabeth a cup of tea. Surprised that they were both serving her her afternoon tea, Elizabeth asked, 'Is everything okay?' 'Begging yer pardon, ma'am, but Tessie is upset, and we were wondering if

Máire wondered how things would be, now that she was going to live full time in the big house. Would Harry and Tomás get along? It had been well over a year since they had seen each other. As they walked along, she looked at little Tomás' fine mop of thick black hair. He was four years old now, a smaller version of Liam, the image of his father, quiet and strong, fearless but cautious. Every time he smiled, she saw Liam reflected in him, breaking her heart a little bit more. That smile reminded her of how real their love was, and how much she missed her husband. But that smile also gave her strength, bringing Liam closer to her through their son. She held his hand tighter as they walked along. Walking up the impressive driveway, she considered how Tessie O'Brien was likely to react to being demoted and having to move out of Peig Shea's room into a much smaller, closet-like room. She soon found out. When she opened the basement door and entered the kitchen, Tessie gave her the silent treatment. 'Good morning, Tessie.' Tessie ignored her. Máire decided to nip it in the bud there and then. 'Tessie, please turn around.' Tessie turned around reluctantly, but she didn't look at Máire. 'I didn't make this decision Tessie, Lady Elizabeth did. I was happy enough doing what I have been doing all along.' 'Well why don't ya tell her that then?' replied Tessie angrily. 'I kept the house going for the last year, and this is what I get the second she comes home. It's not right. It's just not fair.' Máire felt that Tessie had made a good point. Indeed, the house was in sad condition under her hands. She also knew from Tessie's constant complaints, that Kitchener wasn't sending her near enough money to pay for everything needed for the upkeep of such a huge house. But from her Dublin experience, she also knew how to balance budgets better than you would reconsider your decision about making me head housekeeper.' Incensed, Elizabeth loudly replaced her cup and saucer on the silver tray, sat up straight, and said, 'This is my house. I say who I want as head housekeeper, and I say who does what and when.' Scowling at Tessie, she said, 'Tessie, I told you yesterday that I was appointing Máire as head housekeeper, did I not?' 'Yes, ma'am,' answered Tessie timidly. 'I told you that she was moving in full time here today. Now, if you have a problem with that Tessie, let me know here and now, and I will find someone to replace you. Am I quite clear?' With this rebuke, Tessie lost all her fight and attitude. 'Yes ma'am,' she said meekly. 'Now, please go back to work.' They curtsied, quickly left the room, and headed to the kitchen. Máire knew that Tessie was crushed. She decided that now was as good a time as any to make their time together as comfortable as possible. Graciously, she poured them each a cup of tea, and with a friendly smile, faced her. 'Look Tessie, we'll be all right. We can work together here without killin' each other. Can't we?' At these words, Tessie's lips quivered and she began to sob. 'If I leave here, I'll die. I've nowhere to go. All my family are dead, I'm the only one still livin'. I can't leave here.' 'You don't have to leave Tessie. We can do this together. Sure, we can share everythin'.' Máire put her arm around her and held her as she sobbed quietly. 'I'll move my stuff out of the room. Sure, you and Tomás will need the space more than me.' 'Thank you, Tessie. That'll be fine. We'll be all right.' Thus started another unlikely friendship between two strong Irish women, forced to work together to survive the worst time in Irish history.

 Later that day, Máire was cleaning the Kitcheners' bedroom. The worst part of that chore was cleaning out the massive fireplace and replenishing the heavy logs needed to keep it blazing throughout the day. This kept the large room from becoming damp. As Máire toiled away, little Tomás amused himself making all sorts of sounds with Liam's tin whistle. Although the noise was irritating, it brought her back to all the beautiful tunes Liam had played for her. She softly hummed that first haunting air she'd heard him play. Though so very sad, it had become her favourite of all his compositions. Elizabeth happened to be passing the bedroom with Harry. They stopped and looked in. Agitated, Harry let go of his mother's hand, ran to Tomás, grabbed the tin whistle from his hands, and tried to play it. Tomás began to cry, angrily grabbing it back, and started playing it again, dodging Harry's attempts to get it back. Harry went wild with frustration. 'I'll ask Colm to bring another one tomorrow, ma'am.' She bent down, looked straight into Tomás' eyes, and said, 'Okay Tomás, now share with Harry. Come on, take turns.' Tomás was none too pleased. 'Come on, Tomás, share with Harry.' Tomás reluctantly handed the whistle to Máire. She walked behind Harry, bent down, took his hands gently, and showed him how to place his fingers over the holes. Harry blew hard and the tin whistle screamed. 'Softly, Harry, blow gently.' Harry did, and he blew his first real note. 'Well done, Harry,' encouraged Máire. 'Now, lift one of your fingers off the hole. He did, and another note came out. 'Now, put your finger back on the hole and blow again.' He did, and another sweet note came out of the whistle. 'That's how you play it, Harry, by lifting your fingers off the holes on the whistle and putting them back on again.' Harry was in a world of his own discovering different notes, calm for the first time in months. Elizabeth was amazed. 'He loves music, ma'am. Maybe he should have piano lessons too.' 'No, I don't think he could do that. It's far too difficult for him,' said Elizabeth, 'but please get that other whistle. I haven't seen him so amused in ages.' 'Yes, ma'am,' said Máire, wondering how Liam's father would feel about parting with his priceless tin whistle for the amusement of his landlord's son.

As Órla's time grew near, Colm became increasingly excited about teaching his son everything he knew about fishing and farming. He listened to all the 'experts' with their old wives' tales predicting that it would be a girl, but he was positive they were going to have a son. ''Tis said,' stated Nora, blunt as ever, 'that little girls steal their mothers' good looks.' Her daughter's skin had broken out almost from the day she got pregnant, and Nora took that as a definite sign that Órla's baby was a girl. Josie had done the 'ring test' a few weeks earlier and was of the same opinion. She tied Órla's wedding ring to a string and hung it over her pregnant belly. 'If it goes round and round, 'tis a girl. If it goes side to side, 'tis a boy.' Órla and Josie, and even sceptical Colm, were fascinated as it went around and around in a circular motion. Colm shook his head at their silly superstitions. 'Ye're all mad, so ye are. 'Tis a boy she's havin' I tell ye.' 'You're going to love her,' teased Máire.

Adhering to Wednesday's housekeeping schedule, Máire was cleaning the dining room. Dusting furniture and removing crumbs from under the table, she heard piano music coming from the drawing room next door. Hearing the music gave her great pleasure, and she fantasised about learning to play piano herself someday. As Elizabeth asked her to bring little Tomás to Emma's piano lessons, she was now familiar with the music. *Ah, Emma is practising her classical piece*, she thought. Harry threw terrible tantrums during Emma's lesson, until finally Elizabeth and Máire figured out that he wanted Tomás there with him. Once together, he sat and listened quietly, giving everybody some welcome peace and quiet. Máire realised that Emma had perfected the piece; she'd played it as flawlessly as her piano teacher. Knocking on the door quietly, she went in to congratulate Emma on her huge improvement and was stunned to see that it was Harry who was playing. Without looking up, he played the piece again, and again, and again. In complete shock, Máire searched the house for Elizabeth to no avail. Running down to the kitchen, she asked Tessie 'Where's Lady Kitchener?' 'She's over in the stables with Lady Emma, what d'ya need her for?' Máire didn't answer. She turned and raced to the stables, where she found Lord and Lady Kitchener watching Emma getting a riding lesson from a stable boy. The stable boy was on the opposite side of the horse as Máire entered, so she could only see his legs, and for a few beautiful seconds, she was back in happier times expecting to see Liam's smiling face when the horse turned around. When she saw that it was just the stable boy, her heart sank. *Oh Liam, I miss you so much,* she sobbed. She was overwhelmed by her sense of loss at the strangest times. She would get by for weeks looking after Tomás, doing her daily duties as head housekeeper, and babysitting Harry for a few of the longest hours of her day, to give Elizabeth a break. But every now and then, something would set her off, bringing her back to that awful emptiness deep in her broken heart. She knew they were lucky, compared to so many of her friends now nearly all gone, but she couldn't help longing for what should have been. 'What is it Máire?' asked Elizabeth. Jolted back to the present, she brushed a tear from her eye, and with a huge smile said, 'Come quickly, all of you.' 'Is everything all right, Máire?' asked Elizabeth. 'Yes, yes,' she said excitedly. 'It's Harry. He's playing the piano!' 'What?' asked Lord Kitchener, puzzled. They ran to the house, and hearing the music as they neared the drawing room, they began to believe the impossible. Emotions rose as they entered and saw the inexplicably lovely sight of their troubled six-year-old son playing the piano masterfully. Their faces glistening with tears, they stood there and took it all in as Harry played the same piece over and over. Kitchener's personal shame about having a son who wasn't 'right' was never too far from his thoughts. 'Why me? Why us?' He felt ashamed every time he looked at him. The child was a disappointment, a major letdown to his family name. 'Play something else, Harry,' asked his father proudly, but he just kept repeating the same piece. 'Send for Mrs Best immediately,' ordered Kitchener. 'Yes sir,' answered Máire. She went down to the kitchen and instructed Tessie to fetch Emma's piano teacher.

Mrs Best was shocked to realise that Harry was playing little Emma's piano piece better than she could play it herself, exactly the way she had tried to teach it to Emma. She asked Harry to stop and let her play another piece for him. She opened the piano bench and selected the piano arrangement of Franz Schubert's *Ave Maria*. She played the perfect four-bar introduction, with its majestic rising and falling six-note chords, paused, glanced at Harry, and then played the magnificent first page. She got up, placed the music in front of Harry, and asked, 'Now Harry, can you try to play it?' Harry, completely silent sat down again, placed his little hands on the keys, and without looking at the music, played it perfectly, exactly as Mrs Best had played it. He stopped at the end of the first page. They were all absolutely amazed. 'Carry on Harry. That was beautiful. Now play the second page,' said Mrs Best, and she pointed to the place where Harry should play next. Harry played the first page over and over again and again. Mrs Best was the first to notice the obvious. 'He's playing from memory,' she said, absolutely stunned. 'Watch.' She asked Harry to let her play again. He stopped, and Mrs Best finished the Schubert piece. She got up, and once again Harry repeated exactly what she had played. 'I've never heard nor seen such a thing,' said Mrs Best. 'It's a miracle. I think the Lord has sent you a strange genius,' and she started to cry, grateful for what she had just witnessed.

Colm, Josie, Thomás, and Órla's father paced up and down outside the cottage. Órla had asked her mother and Máire to be present for her birthing. Luckily Máire had come home from work just a few hours before her sister delivered a perfect baby girl. When Colm came in, Órla nervously pulled back the coverlet to show him their baby daughter, watching his face for disappointment. Stepping closer, Colm looked down, and all he saw was his very own family. He lifted the swaddled infant, surprised by how weightless she seemed. He studied his daughter's delicate features for several moments, wordless, and then nuzzled her little neck, just under her chin. Clearly smitten and looking at Máire, he said, 'Liam was right. This is the sweetest part of a new baby.' Watching Colm's tender reaction, Órla was relieved. And she was enchanted by how tiny their baby looked, cradled protectively in her father's embrace. 'She'll be a fine fisherwoman someday Colm,' said Máire reassuringly. Tears flowing, he gently nestled his daughter back into Órla's arms, and then, determined never to fail her, caressed Órla's hand softly and said, 'She'll be whatever she wants to be.'

Part Five
Toy Soldiers and Assault

Edward Kitchener had just finished his second year at Trinity College, Dublin studying engineering. Since 1793 Catholics had been allowed to enrol there – the university having been founded in 1592 by Queen Elizabeth I. Luckily for Edward, he had a talent for mathematics. Ironically, as lazy as he was, he passed his tests, which of course contributed to his cockiness and sense of superiority. With his family no longer owning a house in Dublin, Edward had to return to the family estate in Galway for the summer, forcing him to miss out on all of his usual Dublin action. It was the last place he wanted to be, but his tuition and lodging were stretching Kitchener's budget to the limit.

Máire was preparing his clothes and cleaning his room when Edward appeared at the bedroom door unannounced. Her back to him filling his dresser with clean socks and underwear, he had forgotten how beautiful she was. He stared at her slender figure and silky auburn hair and decided then and there to have her as his mistress. She's not that much older than I am, and her husband's been dead for years. She must be dying for it, he thought smugly. At least it will while away the tiresome three months I'm stuck here. Máire turned around and saw his eyes all over her. She had almost forgotten how much she despised him, standing there with that condescending look of his. 'Sir,' she said as she curtsied, 'you surprised me.' 'Hello, Máire, I didn't mean to startle you. I'm just back and wanted to drop my stuff off before dinner.' 'Yes sir. Welcome home. Your room is ready.' 'It looks fine. Thank you.' Máire sidestepped a little to avoid touching him as she walked out of the room. As she was making her way to the kitchen, she realised that his attitude was better than she remembered. *And he even said, 'thank you'. But I still hate that look,* she thought.

As Máire served desert that evening, she was surprised when Edward, who never showed any interest or generosity towards his younger brother, said, 'Harry, I've a present for you.' Harry kept his head down as always, ignoring Edward as he retrieved from his pocket twelve, two-inch-tall lead soldiers in colourful uniforms. The family had never seen the likes of them before, and this gift caused great excitement. 'I won them in a card game. The chap I won them from said that they're German and are quite rare,' he said proudly.

Edward placed the soldiers on the table in battle formation, each in unique battle positions, some with guns and some with swords. He took one of the soldiers and pointed it at Harry. 'Would you like it, Harry?' he asked. Without lifting his head, Harry moved to take it from Edward's hand, but Edward quickly pulled his hand away. Harry screamed angrily. 'Look at me,' said Edward, 'and I'll give it to you.' Harry just screamed and roared. 'Look at me,' Edward replied loudly. Harry flew into a tantrum. 'For God's sake Edward, just give it to him,' said William angrily. Harry had been quiet throughout dinner, and now he was shrieking, bellowing, and banging his hands on the table with rage. 'No,' said Edward, 'I'll teach him manners. If he wants it, he must look at me.' Elizabeth rose, and, as she had done so many times before, pulled Harry out of the room, to give William some peace. Angrily, William grabbed his newspaper, shook it loudly, and started reading. Later, Máire tucked Tomás into his cot and got into bed. Still annoyed by the chaos Edward had started at dinner, she closed her eyes and thought, *It's going to be a long three months.*

The next morning, Máire had Tomás and Harry painting quietly in a corner, while she and Tessie washed pots and pans. Edward knocked softly on the kitchen door, and, with a little smile and bow of his head, acknowledged the two women. He came in, walked straight over to the two little boys, knelt down to face Harry, and took out one of the lead soldiers. 'Would you like this, Harry?' he asked. Without lifting his head, Harry went to grab it, but once again, Edward held onto it and pulled it away. 'Look at me Harry. If you want it, look at me. Where are your manners?' he asked angrily. Once again, Harry flew into a tantrum. 'Would you like one, Tomás?' he asked. Tomás looked at Edward and reached his hand out. 'No, Tomás, you can't have it. It's not yours,' Máire said strongly. Then, Tomás, too, flew into a furious rage. 'What are you trying to do here? You know he won't look at you,' said Máire angrily, forgetting her station in a moment of frustration. She knew how long it would take her to settle the boys down again. 'I know he wants it, and I'll give it to him when he looks at me. Harry,' he shouted, 'look at me and you can have it.' With his little head down as always, Harry kept on screaming. Edward stood up and looked at Máire. 'He'll look at me if it's the last thing I ever get him to do,' he said. And then he stormed out. Tessie had never witnessed Edward's charm before. 'He hasn't changed a bit,' said Máire.

After dinner that night, Edward produced the twelve soldiers again, setting them out in battle formation as he had done the previous night. With his father away on business, Edward knew he wouldn't have to suffer his reprimand again. 'Would you like one of these, Harry?' he asked. Without looking up, Harry went to grab it out of Edward's hand, but Edward held onto it firmly. Harry started to scream once more. 'Edward!' said Elizabeth angrily. Edward ignored her and kept at it. 'Look at me Harry and I'll give it to you.' Harry kept on screaming. 'Look at me, Harry, look at me,' Edward screamed right back. 'Edward, stop shouting at him!' said Elizabeth angrily. And then the strangest thing happened: Harry lifted his head up and looked straight at Edward. Delighted with his victory, Edward put his hand out with the soldier and Harry took it, then lowered his head once again. Elizabeth put her hands up to her mouth, absolutely shocked. 'Would you like another one, Harry?' and he extended his hand with another soldier. Once again, Harry lifted his head, accepted the toy soldier, and lowered his head. 'Would you like another one, Harry?' asked Edward. Harry lifted his head and reached to take it, but Edward grabbed his brother's hand. 'I'll give it to you if you look at me, okay Harry? Keep your head up and I'll give two of them to you.' Amazingly, Harry kept his head up, and Edward handed him two more soldiers, letting go of his hand. Elizabeth was in tears, watching this little miracle playing out before her, Harry looking straight at his brother for the first time ever. Edward handed a soldier to her and nodded at her to give it a try. 'Harry, would you like another soldier?' she asked. Harry looked directly at his mother for the first time since he was an infant. Elizabeth wept as she handed her son the toy soldier. 'Can I give him one?' asked Emma, and the same joyful little drama played out. Soon Harry had all twelve soldiers and began positioning them on the table. 'Edward,' cried Elizabeth, 'I'm absolutely amazed. Thank you, thank you, Edward. I'm stunned. Look at Harry. His head is still up. Wait until his father sees this. Thank you, Edward, you don't know how much this means,' she said gratefully. 'I just wanted him to look at me. I knew he could do it if he wanted to.'

Elizabeth knew that Edward couldn't possibly be aware of the enormity of the victory he had just achieved. Edward was away at school most of the time and had absolutely no concept of all the heart-wrenching struggles his parents had experienced with his brother. Sharing what had just happened, her instruction to everyone who would deal with Harry was: 'If he wants something, demand that he look at you first.' Within a few weeks, Harry was looking at people, even when he wasn't asking them for anything. Elizabeth and Máire shared in the delight of this wonderful change in Harry, and they rose each morning thinking of other ways to help Harry become as normal a young boy as he could be.

Tomás and Harry were playing toy soldiers one morning, while Máire scraped carrots. Tomás was making all sorts of noises as he earnestly tried to rout the enemy, but Harry was silent as usual. When Harry noticed the carrots, he became agitated. Máire knew that he loved them and had an idea. 'What do you want Harry?' Harry howled and pulled Máire to the kitchen sink where the carrots were. This is what he always did when he wanted something. She pointed to the potatoes on the shelf. 'Do you want a potato?' she asked. Harry kept on howling. She pointed to a vase of fresh flowers. 'Would you like a flower?' she asked. Harry became even more agitated. She took his hand, held it out straight, and started pointing at everything in the kitchen. 'Tell me what you want, Harry. Point to it for me.' She kept leading his hand around until she came to the carrots in the kitchen sink. There, he stopped her from moving his hand. Pointing straight at the carrots, he shook his hand. 'You want a carrot?' she asked, taking her hand away. Harry just kept pointing at the carrot, and Máire, delighted with another victory, gave him a carrot. 'Harry,' she asked, knowing that it was in the top kitchen cupboard for safekeeping, 'where's your tin whistle? Where is it, Harry? Point to it.' When Harry pointed to the cupboard, Máire reached up and opened the cupboard door. 'Do you want to play it with Tomás?' Harry kept pointing obsessively, but without throwing his usual tantrum. She reached up, took out the two tin whistles, and gave one to each of them. Harry calmed down, and soon the boys started playing a tune they had practiced together.

'He can understand everything we say, ma'am, I'm sure of it,' Máire said excitedly, as she told Elizabeth about that morning's miracle. 'Thank you, Máire. I think he can; I really do. Edward said he got him to say his name after weeks of trying. He's coming back to us Máire, and it all started with Edward giving him the toy soldiers.' 'Yes, ma'am, Edward is very good for him,' said Máire, giving Edward some praise, despite her opinion of him. Was he changing for the better, she wondered? She would soon find out. She had been avoiding Edward as much as possible. She cleaned his room when she knew he was out. She hated serving him dinner, as she felt he was undressing her from the second she entered the dining room.

Tessie was in bed sick one morning, so, doing double duty, Máire was milking the cows in the barn. Seated on a low wooden milking stool, she expertly squirted the milk into her bucket. 'I like the way you do that,' said Edward, who had sneaked up behind her. 'Mother of God!' said Máire as she turned around terrified, 'You scared the livin' daylights outta' me.' Edward smirked, knelt down, and grabbed one of the cow's udders. He started to fondle the udder, up and down, as though masturbating. Then he smiled at her with a leer and raised his eyebrows suggestively. Máire pretended to ignore him and kept on milking. Edward pointed the udder towards Máire, aimed, and squirted milk on her dress. 'Oh, so sorry,' he giggled, and he moved to wipe the milk from her clothing, stroking her breast up and down. 'Stop it, sir,' Máire said angrily, as she pushed his hand away. With her back against the stable wall, Edward had her trapped. 'You like it, don't you, Máire?' he said, putting his hand on her dress again. Slowly he moved his hand down to grope between her legs. 'I said, 'stop it!'' she said loudly. Edward leaned over and tried to kiss her, but she jerked away, giving the stool a strong kick as she stood up. Grabbing the bucket of milk firmly with both hands, she aimed, and with a strong heave, the milk went flying, drenching him.

Shocked, he wiped his eyes with his shirtsleeve and shouted, 'You little bitch! How dare you? Who do you think you are?' Furious with rage, he grabbed her by the throat and forced her down onto the straw. He landed on top of her and began kissing her roughly. Máire tried to free herself, but he was far too strong. A boast she'd overheard as she'd served dinner one night flashed into her head. 'I'm the champion wrestler in Trinity; nobody has ever beaten me.' True. She couldn't move as Edward pulled her dress up, his hands all over her.

And then a familiar grunting sound came from near the barn door. Edward looked over and saw Harry's little silhouette just inside the barn. Clearly angry, Harry ran towards them grunting loudly and tried to pull his brother off Máire. Edward stood up, brushed himself off, and stormed out, ignoring his brother. Grateful to him for saving her from being raped, Máire, near tears, asked, 'What are you doing out here on your own, Harry?' But Harry just kept making angry noises. 'It's all right Harry; I'm fine now. Thank you.' She tidied herself up. *I'll finish the milking later.* As they walked back to the kitchen, Harry calmed down and then reached out his little hand and held Máire's. It was only for a few seconds, and then he let go, but it meant everything to Máire. It helped her cope with what had just happened.

Given the trauma of Edward's attack, Máire decided that, henceforth, she would go home every night after serving the Kitcheners their dinner. There was no point in complaining to Elizabeth, as she wouldn't believe a word she said about her sainted son, especially now, with all the breakthroughs Harry had made since Edward came home.

Part Six

Concerts and Murder

Tomás looked increasingly like Liam. He was now bilingual and becoming an excellent tin whistle player, thanks to his grand father Tomás who adored him. He was also learning to play the piano for, whatever Harry learned, he insisted Tomás learn too, although he lacked the genius of young Harry. It gave Máire the greatest satisfaction to see little Tomás seated at the grand piano, in the opulent drawing room of the big house, being taught by the local Church of Ireland rector's wife. He had not a clue about the absolute irony of the situation; he just took it all in stride, becoming a confident, inquiring little boy.

As Harry made steady progress, he was now able to speak almost complete sentences. He had been receiving intensive home schooling from a private English tutor who visited the Kitcheners and other nearby landlords, to teach their children English, mathematics, history, and geography. Harry, however, flew into a rage if Tomás was not in the room with him during his lessons, simply becoming unteachable. This unusual situation was untenable in light of Lord Kitchener's colonial thinking. He was being forced to educate one of his tenant's children, but he had no choice. Harry was making good progress, but without Tomás, he would not. Little Tomás O'Donaghue received the same priceless education as Harry and was likely the only local Catholic child of his day to have found himself in this situation.

Washing pots and pans in the Kitchener scullery, Máire happily hummed the haunting air Liam had composed so many years ago. She had lulled Tomás to sleep to the melody every night since he was born, so it came as no surprise to her when Tomás began humming along as he chased Harry's new puppy around the kitchen. 'You know, your father made that tune up,' Máire said, smiling at Tomás. Tomás looked surprised. 'Yes, he liked music too, he used to play it on his tin whistle. He was very good. Is Harry nervous about tonight?' 'I don't think so. He doesn't ever get nervous playing the piano.'

Besides the arrival of Órla's baby, the big excitement for Máire was Harry's piano concert to be held at the mansion that evening. Harry's piano teacher had suggested that it would be good for Harry if he were to give a piano concert, now that he had mastered several pieces. When Mrs Best discovered Harry's amazing capacity to remember exactly what she had just played, she had begun to teach him, slowly but surely, to read music. To the relief of everybody, with intensive tutoring he had become accomplished at this.

Elizabeth had instructed Máire earlier: 'Pick out some of Harry's clothes for Tomás to wear; I don't want Harry getting anxious if he isn't there.' Knowing how well dressed their guests would be, for the Kitcheners it was important to have them assume that Tomás was Harry's friend and not a tenant's son. Perception was all important to the Kitcheners.

At around five that afternoon, the guests began to arrive in ornate brougham and clarence carriages and coaches. Máire had Tomás looking splendid in a crisp white shirt, short grey pants, black socks, and well-polished black leather shoes. The ladies were offered sherry, and the men, generous portions of whiskey. The beverages were served in Waterford crystal glasses and decanters from one of the first crystal collections that Waterford had produced in the 1790s, adding beauty, class, and distinction to the occasion.

After their initial conflict, Tessie O'Brien had settled into her new role as second in command to Máire in the kitchen. Although over the years they had become closer, Máire didn't share any personal information with Tessie, purposely keeping the conversation light. Reluctantly, Tessie had come to appreciate Máire's no-nonsense talent at kitchen organisation, as well as her skill at estimating the family's weekly food requirements, sparing them both Elizabeth's frugal ire. Thanks to her experience working in Dublin, Máire was also able to prepare delicate-looking appetisers of smoked salmon, cold meat slices, and assorted cheeses. She and Tessie served hors d'oeuvres to the appreciative guests in the drawing room, sustaining them until the post-concert dinner.

As Máire was serving a nearby landlord, she overheard him making small talk with Harry. She'd often heard the Kitcheners refer to the man as a total idiot, which was exactly what she thought of him as well. 'And what are you going to play for us Harry my boy?' 'Bach. I like Bach.' 'Oh yes, very good, good choice,' said the landlord, nodding agreeably, 'I like Bach too.' Máire rolled her eyes and wanted to scream. *You wouldn't know Bach from brussels sprouts, you pompous little ass!*

Presently, William and Elizabeth graciously greeted their guests; after all the difficult early years, they were eager to show off Harry's amazing abilities. Emma, now a beautiful young lady, stood out amongst all the other women there, her arms and neck bare in a red, simple, slim-fitting silk and velvet gown which flattered her tiny waist. She looked relaxed and comfortable, compared to the other ladies who looked stiff and constricted in suffocating corsets and heavy bustles. 'Ladies and gentlemen, if you would kindly be seated, the concert will begin,' said William.

The twenty guests began to take seats facing the grand piano, purposely placed before two tall bay windows overlooking the front gardens. Along with the concert, the guests could admire vivid prized roses in the prettiest pink, interspersed with regal rhododendrons. They also saw Italian concrete statues of cherubs holding circular birdbaths aloft, and small, precisely-manicured squares of low-cut hedges dotting the estate's acres of freshly-cut grass.

When everyone was seated, Harry approached the piano and the guests applauded politely. He didn't bow or acknowledge them; he simply sat and placed his hands on the piano keys. Anxious, he scanned the room looking for Tomás and saw him standing in a corner at the back. Relieved, he turned and began playing the haunting opening bars of a Bach Adagio. Within moments, even the most hardened, vile landlords present were visibly moved, as Harry played the most beautiful music they had ever experienced. Máire watched proudly as Harry, alone at the piano, without Thomas or his piano teacher for support, confidently gave his first solo concert before an audience in this formal setting. When he finished his first piece, the audience broke into sustained applause. Harry looked down; then he slowly turned to look at the audience and briefly smiled.

He literally attacked the piano with his next piece, a frenetic prelude and fugue, stunning the audience as his hands raced up and down the keyboard at truly virtuoso speeds, and with perfect technique. With a dramatic flourish, he finished to rapturous applause and shouts of 'Bravo!' When the group rose as one for a standing ovation, Harry stood and looked around, bemused by their reaction.

Overcome with emotion, William worked his way to his son's side, relieved by the tremendous response of his peers. His personal shame, about having a son who wasn't 'right' and a major letdown to his family name, dissolved as he put his hand on his son's shoulder and beamed with fatherly pride. He remembered the piano teacher's words when they had heard Harry playing the piano that first time: 'I think the Lord has sent you a strange genius.' William finally began to accept his son as he was.

Máire watched as Tomás applauded his friend and, although proud of Harry's achievement, she was once again sadly reminded that her son had never known the love of his father nor his embrace. She went to Tomás and put her arm around his shoulders. *I wish your father could hold you like this, my Tomásheen.*

While Máire worked every day at the Kitchener mansion, Tomás and Harry continued lessons with various tutors. Harry was as nearly as 'normal' a boy as Tomás, having made tremendous strides, but he still wouldn't study for his tutors unless Tomás was sitting next to him. Harry's piano teacher had suggested that, for Harry to continue to improve, he needed a more advanced tutor. Considering the success of their son's memorable concert, the Kitcheners agreed, so they hired a traveling concert pianist to give Harry a monthly lesson. Under this tutelage, Harry showed such remarkable improvement, that there was talk of him possibly having a career as a concert pianist.

With Máire's workday at the mansion finished, she and Tomás discussed Harry's prospects in music on their way home. Tomás complained that he didn't want to take piano lessons anymore. 'I hate it. I just hate it. Harry is so good, I feel stupid.' Although Máire understood how he felt, she wanted her son to take full advantage of the unique opportunity before him: private lessons from a concert pianist! Employing a little bit of the Irish guilt to get him to continue with the lessons, she said, 'Your Uncle Colm would love to learn the piano, but he can't. He would never be allowed into their house, never mind getting piano lessons. And you know how much he loves music.' 'But it's so boring, and I'll never be any good.' 'I think you're very good. Is Harry as good as you on the tin whistle?' 'No, but that's easy.' 'You think it's easy because you're good at it. Harry will never be as good as you on the tin whistle. How do ya think Harry feels about that?' 'I dunno;' he doesn't play it anymore.' Her encouragement continued, 'Well if you don't practice, you won't get better.'

Liam had spent more than three long years in Woolich, watching thousands of others imprisoned on the hulk being allocated to various convict ships. But his natural talents with machinery were invaluable to the foreman – they made him look good to his superiors. Finally, with no work expected to be lined up at the factory for months, the foreman put in a good word for him, and the hulk's captain ordered that Liam be moved to the next departing convict ship. The timing was fortunate for Liam, as a ship was taking on convicts farther down the Thames.

The annual Galway Hunt was one of the highlights of the local landlords' social calendar. Originating in England in the sixteenth century, hunting clubs dated as far back as 1743 in Ireland. It was definitely a rich man's sport, as it required the keeping of horses and foxhounds, dog kennels and food, the storage of hay and oats to feed the horses, and straw for bedding, as well as the employment of saddlers, and frequent veterinarian visits.

With plenty of cheap tenant labour at hand, landlords were able to enjoy a marvellous day out riding throughout the stone-walled fields of County Galway to hunt foxes in their wild and natural state. William Kitchener was master of the Galway Hunt Club and eagerly anticipated tomorrow's hunt. He possessed the finest dog pack in Ireland and owned excellent Irish sporting horses which he had spent many years breeding.

Mating Irish draught horses with some of his thoroughbreds, he had produced several excellent horses perfect for the sport – sure-footed animals for the soft bog lands, deep ditches, narrow slippery streams, and gorse thickets. These horses were also brave, smart, and athletic enough to jump whatever was in front of them. Kitchener selected the horse he would ride for the next day's hunt and ordered the stable hand to ready it for the morning. Then he checked on one of his most cherished possessions – his pedigreed pack of Irish foxhounds. Weighing sixty to seventy pounds, and about two feet high, these beagle-looking foxhounds were bred exclusively for the sport. Kitchener looked at the splendid job his huntsman and his assistant had done getting his pack of ten ready for tomorrow's hunt. Like Liam, these men were his tenants, so he would never consider complimenting them on their expertise to their faces; it was simply expected that they would have the pack ready to go.

Later, when Kitchener was enjoying a brandy in his study, the butler knocked on the door. Upon hearing Kitchener's 'you may enter,' the butler handed him two letters on a silver tray. One was from Trinity College and the other was from the Prescotts. Reaching for his enamelled letter opener, he carefully opened the Trinity College letter first. Sent from the college provost, much to Kitchener's horror the missive was delivering shocking news:

Dear Lord Kitchener,

I am sorry to relate to you that your son, Edward, has not been attending his college lectures for the past month and is in serious danger of failing his third year of engineering.

I am writing to you as a courtesy, trusting that you might hopefully investigate and rectify this serious situation.

Yours respectfully,
Charles Woodbridge,
Provost, Trinity College, Dublin.

Fearing more unwelcome news, he dreaded opening the Prescotts' letter. He took a sip of brandy, and once again reached for the letter opener, and sure enough, it was shockingly worse than he thought:

Dear William and Elizabeth,

Although I hesitate to do so, I must share with you that a rather intimidating brute of a fellow appeared at our door today demanding to see Edward. I informed him that he was not here. I didn't tell him that he was with you for Christmas, of course.

He threatened that unless I or Edward repaid a gambling debt of one hundred pounds to his boss in a fortnight, there would be serious retribution.

This is an enormous amount of money for Edward to lose. I will of course pay the blaggard when he returns, and you can repay me when I see you next, but I must confess it shook me up rather badly. Luckily, Margaret didn't witness this extremely unpleasant exchange.

Edward comes and goes as he pleases at all times of the day and night and completely ignores both of us when we try to offer our advice. He cares not a whit about our feelings or routines. I dare say that, unless you nip this in the bud immediately, his future will be in serious jeopardy.

As this situation has become too stressful for us, especially for Margaret, I am sorry to let you know that we no longer wish for Edward to stay with us during his final year.

Yours regretfully,
George

Kitchener was furious. Grabbing both letters, he stomped up to Edward's bedroom and burst in startling his son where, as usual, he was sitting at his table dealing cards to imaginary friends. 'You ungrateful little bastard,' he shouted, wielding the letters. Seeing the letters, Edward realised that he was in for a serious confrontation. Still, as he rose from his chair, he stared defiantly at his father regarding him with utter contempt. 'After all we've done for you. This is how you repay us?' demanded Kitchener, shaking the letters in his fist angrily. 'Well, I've got news for you, sonny boy. You're on your own from now on. You're just a worthless gambler who'll probably end up dead on some Dublin street for all I care. You're a major disappointment to me and your mother. You always have been and always will be. This is the last straw.' Then William paused, took a deep breath, and said: 'As of now, you are disinherited.' He turned to walk to the door, then turned back and spoke. 'I want you out of here before Christmas.' With that, he slammed the letters angrily on the table and stormed out, his actions scattering Edward's carefully laid out cards, some of them falling to the floor.

Stunned, Edward sat again and began flicking cards angrily around the room, stewing on what his father had just said. Outraged by the insults, he thought, *How dare you talk to me like that? I've always despised you. Emma was always your favourite, and even stupid Harry is now better than me in your opinion.* Fuming and bitter, he sat there, fully the victim, taking no responsibility for his actions whatsoever. *I'm your elder son; this is MY inheritance. I'm the rightful heir to this property and land. How DARE you threaten to disinherit me?* He picked up the letters, crumpled them, and threw them disgustedly into the fire, convinced that he had no choice in what he'd decided in those moments to do.

Edward spent the night sleepless, playing out in his mind several ways to be rid of his father. Whatever it was, he had to do it before William could take any legal action, and before his mother became privy to her husband's intentions. He knew that this evening, his parents were hosting some of his fellow landlords and their wives for dinner, so personal family affairs wouldn't be discussed. Luckily for Edward, William and Elizabeth now slept in separate bedrooms and, as always, his father would stagger up to his own bedroom late into the night after too many brandies. *It's got to be tomorrow,* he decided. A truly diabolical scenario played out in his head, a brilliant but twisted scheme where he would never be suspected of killing his father. If everything went according to plan, it would all look like a tragic accident.

The following morning, Kitchener and a coterie of fellow hunt club members, dressed in battle-red riding jackets, formal white shirts, tan jodhpurs, black riding hats and leather boots, cut an impressive sight on their prized, spirited horses. The ladies wore similar outfits, but their formal jackets were black or green. The riders gathered on the gravelled forecourt of the Kitcheners' granite-stone mansion, which was covered in scarlet-red ivy. Enjoying the traditional pre-hunt glass of champagne, the hunters made small talk while, barking and restless, the thirty or so foxhounds made known their eagerness for the hunt to begin. 'I hope we won't have a blank day, William,' said his neighbouring landlord, hoping that they would at least give chase to a fox, and not come up empty. They knew full well how cunning and crafty a fox was, and how it used many tricks to lose the hounds. A fox would often run through a small stream or run the length of a high wall to throw the hounds off its scent. 'Well, it's a splendid day for a hunt, whatever,' answered Kitchener enthusiastically. A host of elements heightened the thrill of fox hunts: watching the hounds' scenting powers and then the dogs' following the line of the fox; seeing fellow hunters and their hounds at work, galloping through the fields, jumping low stone walls and hedges, and crossing over shallow rivers and streams; and enjoying spectacular fall colours. This, not necessarily the killing of a fox, is what they all lived for as the hunt date approached.

Earlier that morning, Edward had carried out the first part of his foul plan. He'd watched and waited until the stable hand had saddled his father's horse. When the stable boy left the barn, Edward slipped in the back door. Selecting one of the cinched saddle straps underneath the horse, he carefully cut it without going all the way through, just enough that a sudden jolt from the horse would snap it apart. Luckily for Edward, Irish sporting horses are the most placid of animals, so it neither flinched nor made a sound. The stable hand didn't notice anything amiss, when later, he brought Kitchener's horse to him to begin the hunt.

The champagne ceremony finished, Kitchener blew his hunting horn, and everybody headed out, anticipating an enjoyable day. Elizabeth and Emma joined in behind Kitchener, while Edward took to the rear. Watching from a distance, the 'gate shutters and openers,' witnessed an impressive sight as the hunters trotted along the riverfront: thirty riders in blazing red, green, and black jackets, beautiful horses of all colours, and barking hounds, with the russet tones of autumn leaves above them. It was a remarkable sight.

Soon, the dogs caught scent of a fox. Converging on thick gorse bushes, they flushed the fox out from its hiding place. Kitchener blew his horn and the chase was on. The fox ran across an open field with the dogs giving chase. It ran through a shallow ditch which separated two fields. Filled with water, the ditch wasn't the best place to cross, and soon it was a muddy mess from the pounding of heavy horses' hooves. Some of the horses jerked, losing their footing for a second in the deeper-than-expected ditch, and several riders fell off ending up wet and filthy, head to toe. Everybody laughed and teased them as they gallantly mounted their horses, signalled that they were okay, and continued on – good fodder for the banter sure to be exchanged later on at the inn. Elizabeth patted her horse on the neck, grateful for its having gotten her safely across the ditch, clean and dry.

During the ditch interlude, the fox made tracks to get ahead of the pack, and for a while the hounds lost its scent. Over the years, to heighten their enjoyment of pheasant and fox hunting, landlords had their workers carefully maintain hedges for the horses to jump, and thickets in which foxes and other small animals could breed and hide. On hunt days, the gate shutters and openers skilfully and quickly dismantled stone walls for younger riders as they galloped towards them, then quickly sealed the opening after they had gone through. The adult riders jumped them effortlessly.

Soon the riders were passing Dunguaire Castle, a sixteenth century tower house situated on a rocky, elevated outcrop looking out on Galway Bay. The views were astonishingly beautiful, as they rode along the rocky shore and nearby quaint harbour. The fox made a mistake and headed back towards the hounds. Alerted by the dogs' barking, Kitchener blew his horn, pointed to the fox, and everybody began to gallop after the pursuing hounds. The fox changed course and ran through a hole in a hedge into an adjacent field. Soon, the foxhounds followed it, causing a bottleneck at the hedge, since the hounds could only get through the hole one at a time. The excited hounds barked loudly; some of them climbed up the hedge and continued the chase by sight, not by scent. Soon the riders approached and jumped over the hedge. Their adrenaline pumping, they saw the hounds closing in on the tiring fox.

Kitchener galloped towards the hedge, but without warning, his horse balked and stopped suddenly. Though Kitchener held on for dear life, the cinch strap snapped. He jerked forward violently, propelled headfirst over the ditch, and landed in a heap, face down in the muddy water. Watching in horror, Elizabeth dismounted, climbed the ditch, and ran to her husband lying motionless in the filthy water. Several others quickly joined her to help pull William out of the water and onto level ground. 'Wake up, William,' she screamed, but he didn't move. The local doctor, himself an avid fox hunter, attended to William. Seeing Kitchener's head pitched to an awkward angle, he knew that he was seeing a broken neck. With his hand in the crook of Kitchener's neck, he felt his weak pulse slip away to nothing. There was nothing he could do. 'I'm sorry, Elizabeth,' he said sadly. 'He's gone.' Elizabeth screamed in pain at these words. Emma moaned, collapsing into Edward's arms, as everyone stood around Kitchener's body, stunned into silence at such an unexpected tragedy. Edward put his arm around his shocked mother, acting every bit the dutiful son. Several fellow landlords lifted Kitchener's body onto his horse for the long, sad journey home. Nobody saw the fox being torn apart by the foxhounds, killing it instantly.

When the stable hand put Kitchener's saddle away later that day, it was clear to him that somebody had cut the failed saddle strap. He wasn't about to bring it to anyone's attention though. Like everybody else in Kitchener's service, he despised the man and was glad to see the last of him.

'There's no good in him,' was Tomás' opinion of Edward, when the news quickly spread about the awful accident. There was a heaviness in the air amongst the Kitchener tenants. They all shared Tomás' opinion of the man who was to be their new landlord. Nobody had a good word for him.

The following Saturday, the Kitcheners, their friends from near and far, fellow landlords, bailiffs, and various business associates, filled the local Church of Ireland for the solemn funeral service. Lord Kitchener's coffin was draped in the British flag, the Union Jack. His sword, favourite riding boots, and several war medals were placed atop the coffin amidst a sprawling spray of white lilies. Mrs Best played a repertoire of well-known hymns from the Church of England hymnal. The church organ heaved while the entire congregation dutifully sang along. No tenants were allowed attend.

Kitchener's fellow landlords and Edward shouldered William's coffin and walked the short distance from the church to the small Protestant graveyard. As the minister recited the committal prayers, they slowly lowered the coffin into the grave. Finally, as the gravediggers started to throw earth onto the coffin, Edward began to relax. *I've done it, I've pulled it off without any suspicion. What happened was just a very tragic and unfortunate accident.*

The reception at the Kitchener mansion after the funeral was a busy affair for the kitchen staff, strained to the limit catering to so many guests. As Máire served drinks, she saw Edward's sly smirk, the expression she so hated. He didn't seem to be too upset by his father's death, and she wondered, *Was it really an accident like everybody said?*

It wasn't long before Edward put his personal stamp on 'his' estate. He ordered Bishop to impose a stiff increase in rent for every tenant, which put them all to the pin of their collar to pay every month. After all, he would need new lodgings for his final year in Dublin, and now, finally able to control the estate's purse strings, he could purchase a fine townhouse such that he deserved, one that would reflect the successful young gentleman he considered himself to be.

In the last days of 1850, Liam got his first look at the ship that would transport him to the other side of the world. This ship was much smaller than the Warrior. It had two tall masts and looked like most of the other modern ships docked nearby. The dock was awash with activity. Wagonloads of supplies were pushed up the gangplank. And as Liam had seen once before, terrified cattle and sheep reluctantly boarded. As their superiors shouted orders, sailors busily checked sails and other riggings. The ship would soon put out to sea.

Liam counted twenty-seven fellow convicts and himself. They were marched aboard and formally handed over to the ship's master, Captain J. P. Jenkins. Jenkins' surgeon general, Alex Foster, inspected each man and, once he found them free of sickness, handed them over to the oldest soldiers Liam had ever seen. He was also surprised to see several women and their children milling about on the deck, curious about the arriving prisoners. The soldiers marched Liam and his fellow inmates down to the prisoner quarters where, below deck, they were escorted to their allotted area. They were the last to be put aboard, and Liam estimated the prisoner population to number at least two hundred. Several older soldiers came down with Captain Jenkins, and one of them shouted over the prisoners' commotion. 'All right. Listen up, you lot. The captain wants to talk to you.' The men quieted down and turned to hear the captain address them for the first time.

'Gentlemen, my name is Captain Jenkins. As the captain of this ship, the Mermaid, I have been given the responsibility to transport all of you safely to the Swan River Colony in Western Australia. I intend to get all of you there healthy and well. With a bit of luck, the journey will take us about three months if the weather remains with us. You will be assigned sleeping quarters, clothes, and work duties. We have four schoolmasters ready and willing to teach you reading, writing, and arithmetic, skills you will need for your future well-being, once your sentences are completed. We will observe religious services every Sunday on deck, weather permitting. You will be fed three times a day, with much better food than where you've just come from. I guarantee you that.' There was considerable guffawing and shuffling about from the prisoners, many in disbelief that they were being treated like human beings for the first time in years. 'We will not put up with any insolence, disobedience, or profanity. Any misbehaviour shall be dealt with severely. The guards will now direct you to your sleeping quarters and issue you clothing, eating, and sleeping supplies. Good day gentlemen.'

When he left, the senior guard shouted for quiet once again. 'Gentlemen, we're going to divide you into groups of eight. We call this grouping a 'mess'. Each mess will appoint a spokesman, should you have any grievances. As you can see, the bunks are grouped in fours on either side of the deck. Each set of eight will consist of each mess.' He walked over and lifted a mattress from a bunk. He turned it over and pointed to a number on the mattress. 'Can you see this number?' Everyone nodded. 'Every mattress, sheet, pillow and blanket have a number giving us a record of each convict's belongings. If there's a theft of anything, we will look at that number and be able to identify the culprit immediately. He will be severely dealt with by flogging or worse.'

The guards then divided the men into groups of eight and assigned them to specific bunks to avoid complaints about bunk choices. They handed each man a white canvas bag and a large linen towel. Liam opened his bag to find a jacket, coarse woollen trousers, a waistcoat, a pair of shoes, a stitched worsted cap, two pairs of drawers, two worsted woollen stockings, four handkerchiefs, and a comb. This unexpected bounty elevated everyone's mood. The men were allowed to move freely about the area, and there were no chains in sight. Most of the prisoners were not used to this kind of treatment nor had they expected it, as they'd languished in prison awaiting transportation to Australia. For the first time in a long while, they felt that they were not being treated like human waste. Indeed, they felt human again.

Liam was shown his bunk, third up from the floor. He climbed up and was grateful to find there a mattress, a pillow, and two flannel sheets. Ten inches above him was the fourth bunk. The five-foot length bunk would oblige him to sleep in an almost foetal position, but having a mattress, pillow, and clean sheets and blankets, for the first time in years, pleased him to no end. Once the eight men had located their bunks, the guards showed them that they were built in such a way that they would become a table during the day, with four seats at each side of the table. 'Now sit down and decide who will be your spokesman,' said the guard. Liam and the seven other men in his mess sat and looked at each other. Liam was the only Irishman in the group. All in their early twenties, most were hardened by their rough lifestyle in Britain, largely because of the industrial revolution which was well underway there.

New machines were replacing the need for large numbers of men to work the farms, so they drifted towards Britain's larger cities in search of jobs. But finding a dearth of jobs there, they stole to survive. Anyone who stole more than a shilling, a large amount of money at the time, or anyone caught stealing livestock was sentenced to transportation to the colonies. This was a convenient way to empty prisons and prison ships, thus saving the government money, and ridding Britain of some of its troublesome lower classes, while fulfilling their agenda of populating Australia.

'Gentlemen, I would be honoured to be your spokesman.' Liam looked across the table at a fresh-faced and bearded, lean young man, barely twenty. 'John Atkins Faught.' He rose to his feet to introduce himself formally, smiled, and shook hands with each of them. He was a smallish man about five feet two, with a pleasant face and piercing grey eyes. He was clearly more refined than the rest of them. His hands were soft, definitely not accustomed to any hard labour. The men shrugged, glanced at each other, and nodded.

Just then, the ship heaved a little, and they heard shouting and orders coming from the top deck. The ship swayed as it pulled away from the dock. After a few minutes, they felt the vessel turn and then pick up speed when the wind caught its sails. Finally, they were on their way. As the Mermaid sailed west down the English Channel, the wind started to pick up; the seas became increasingly rough when the ship entered open waters. Within hours the Mermaid was caught in a huge storm, and half the convicts were throwing up from the heaving of the seas. The captain decided to wait out the storm in Spithead Harbour. It was extremely cold and everybody huddled in their bunks under their warm woollen blankets.

The next morning, everyone was rousted from their bunks and given mops and buckets to clean up the vomit from the night before. The guard inspected the floor and wasn't satisfied. 'Not good enough chaps. Everything's gotta' be spick and span or the surgeon general will punish you with smaller rations. He doesn't want anyone getting sick and putting us all at risk, so clean your mops and do it again.' Reluctantly they complied. When he was satisfied at last, they went to the prisoners' galley for breakfast, each man devouring his allotted pint of gruel, tea, and a biscuit.

Directly across from the prisoners' galley, towards the bow of the ship, Liam saw the ovens used to prepare meals for the soldiers and their families. Then, as marvellous aromas wafted towards him, he learned of one more cooking area. It was the galley where the captain, the surgeon general, and the ranking prison guards and their families took their meals. Clearly, one of the sheep had been killed, and these people were enjoying fresh meat. This contrast in meal quality added one more indignity, not just for the convicts, but also for the wives and children of former convicts who were making this long journey to be reunited with their now-free husbands and fathers. Once they had served out their sentences, the former convicts worked to pay for passage of their families to the new world. Most of them had nothing to go home to, and they could build a better life for themselves and their families as free men in Britain's newest colony.

On the Mermaid, each prisoner was issued cooking and eating utensils which included a pint mug made of tin, spoons, plate and dish. Knives and forks were issued at every meal and collected afterwards for security reasons. Liam accepted the duty of collecting and washing utensils, mugs, and plates, mainly because it kept him on the main deck in the fresh air for a little longer each day. The eating routine was strict: breakfast at seven forty-five, dinner at noon, and supper at four. Compared to what Liam had been eating in Dublin and London, these rations were satisfactory, but there wasn't much variety; they had cured beef or salted pork, broth, and tea or cocoa, every day for dinner.

They sailed again the next day, heading west along the Cornwall coastline, and within hours were forced into Falmouth Harbour for shelter. Liam saw two soldiers escort ashore a woman and her children. 'Two of her children have measles,' said a nearby soldier. 'We can't have anyone spreading sickness on board.' As they watched the frantic woman begging not to be sent ashore, the soldier continued, 'Pity really, she was going to join her husband in Western Australia. Now she'll have to find her way back to Portsmouth and wait for another ship.'

After five long and tedious days, they set sail again, but the wet weather and squally seas impeded progress. Measles broke out again, and many of the passengers became fatigued and weak. Doctor Foster issued an order stating that everyone on board was to take a daily dose of fresh lemon juice. This would prevent scurvy, from a deficiency of vitamin C.

Monday was bath day for the convicts. Awakened before dawn, they were walked down to the washing area to bathe in clean salt water, as approved by the surgeon. Although each prisoner was issued a scrubbing brush, no soap was issued. Razors with a small sliver of soap were provided for shaving twice a week. Once shaved, the convicts returned the razors to their guards.

A soldier's wife gave birth to a baby daughter who died shortly after the birthing. Everybody was called to assemble on deck a few hours later, where the captain, with a clear and solemn tone of voice, conducted a dignified service. During the sad ceremony, Liam's thoughts wandered to his little son Tomás. *Will I ever see him again? Will Máire tell him about me?* They all watched as the tiny infant was committed to the sea.

At their dinner table that night, Liam was getting to know the other seven men in his mess. John Atkins Faught was the most distinguished looking and educated of them all. Most of the others were rough and tumble, bawdy-mouthed, working-class Englishmen.

One of them, a chap called George Wheeler, was gentler than the others and seemed shell shocked. He wasn't adapting at all to his new reality. He never spoke and never went above deck, unless ordered to. And everything he ate, he threw up. Tonight, George hadn't touched a bite. 'What happened to you, George?' asked Liam. 'Why are they sending you away?' 'They said I stole a lamp from a shop, but I didn't. The shop-keeper gave a description to the police. They saw me walking down the street and brought me before him. He said it was me, but it wasn't. I didn't have the lamp. They searched our house and never found it. My mother begged them not to send me away, but they didn't listen. Now I'll never see her again,' and he burst out crying. 'Try and eat somethin' mate. Ya need to keep strong,' said one of the prisoners. George got up from the table, and walked away, utterly beaten.

'And you mate,' said another prisoner, looking at John. 'You don't look like a thief. What happened to you?' Stroking his wispy youthful beard, he said, 'My story is as old as Adam and Eve.' He stretched his elbows out on the table and clasped his hands together, resting his chin on them. He paused for a moment and said, 'I was trying to impress a young lady.' The men were intrigued. 'And they sent you away for that? Was her father a judge or somethin?' quipped one of the soldiers. 'Well, not quite. I was an apprentice printer in Ipswich, and I became enamoured of a girl called Elvina. I thought she'd think more of me if I looked more impressive. So, I stole some stationery and forged an order for jewellery, a watch, and a pair of boots. Unfortunately, I got caught. They sentenced me to ten years' transportation for forgery. But first they gave me nine months in solitary confinement, then time in Parkhurst gaol for juvenile offenders. I was there until I turned twenty.' 'Wow, mate, that's tough. Nine months' solitary, and ya still seem rather sane. How d'ya manage that?' asked another prisoner. 'I read my Bible,' he said. 'I actually have it almost off by heart. That's what kept me from going insane. Mind you, I had my moments.' Liam was impressed with this young man. He had an enthusiasm and a gentle honesty that he'd rarely seen in any of the Englishmen he'd met in Ireland. He'd accepted his lot and simply got on with it. John didn't look down on any of his fellow convicts.

Besides the prisoners aboard, Liam counted thirty-two sailors, thirty older guards with their wives and children, and several women. Some of the women were the wives of convicts who had served their sentences in Australia and were now free men. Convict ships were also known as 'bride ships'. Women were enticed to emigrate to the new colony to address the gender imbalance. Convict women were transported to Australia, just like the convict menfolk. While orphaned girls between the ages of fourteen and eighteen were given assisted passage from the workhouses under the Earl Grey Scheme of 1848 to 1850 while others voluntarily travelled there – all hoping for a brighter future.

The sailors, Liam noticed, looked like nomadic wanderers who had left their homes a long, long time ago, and now had no strong ties to any place. They worked hard, showed affection for no one other than their fellow sailors, and mainly kept to themselves. Their shipboard quarters were even more cramped than those of the convicts. They slept on the rigging and spare sails above deck. Though uncomfortable, it was better than being below in harsh weather, where the sickening smell of vomit, and spilt buckets of sewage from the heaving seas, was almost unbearable.

Harsh weather and unbearable heat were the two scourges hardest to deal with. Ventilators, ingenious devices situated in many quarters, allowed the exchange of foul air for fresh, while keeping rain, sea spray, and seawater out.

Assigned to the convicts' cook in the galley was an old guard by the name of Tommy Steel. He was a jovial man of about forty, but he looked much older. He was about five feet eight with a face weather-beaten from years of exposure to the relentlessly searing sun. Years of demanding work had taken a toll on his back, and he had a slight limp from an old war injury. As he washed dishes and utensils after each meal, Liam got to know Tommy. Curious to know why there wasn't one soldier under the age of forty on board, he'd commented, 'All the guards are older than any soldiers I've ever seen.' Willing to talk about his past and future plans, Tommy laughed. 'We're what they call pensioner guards. I joined the army when I was sixteen. Fought in Afghanistan and China, didn't I? I done my twenty-one years, and they pensioned me off. So now I'm bringing my wife and two children to Australia. We're expecting another child. Our job is to guard you lot, and once we get to Australia, we'll each receive a two-room cottage and some land to grow our crops and livestock. I had nothin' back home except a lousy pension that went nowhere. Who wants a beaten-up old soldier like me? I couldn't find any work. Once we get to Australia, all we have to do is be willing to help if any trouble breaks out in the colony. I want to give my family a better life than what we had back home.'

Liam envied Tommy, on his way to a new life with his wife and children. How he wished Máire and Tomás were on this ship, sailing together to a land with new opportunities – a second chance, just like Tommy and his family. Strengthening his resolve, he vowed that someday he would do the same thing. They would not beat him down. Ships went both ways.

At breakfast the next morning, a young convict snapped and began to scream at the pensioner guard assisting the cook. 'This food is shit. I wouldn't give it to my dog.' Several soldiers ran up, grabbed him roughly, and dragged him to the ground. 'Fuck you,' he screamed. 'Fuck you all.' He was brought before the captain for his insolence and foul language. All of the prisoners were marched to the front of the ship where they saw a tiny, cage-like iron box. The soldiers opened the door and placed the prisoner in it standing up. Then they locked the door, rendering the prisoner completely immobile. Depending on the weather, anyone thrown into 'the box' would either freeze or be roasted. 'Gentlemen,' bellowed Captain Jenkins, 'this is the pound. Anyone found guilty of insubordination, theft, foul language, or abuse to any fellow traveller, man or woman, shall be sentenced to the pound for a period of time reflecting the crime. In this man's case, twenty-four hours. This is a warning to you all that there will be no mercy.'

When many of the prisoners, lazy, diffident, and generally up to no good, reacted as though the captain's warning was a joke, Captain Jenkins shouted, 'Below all hands.' This was his subtle reminder that, if one prisoner stepped out of line, they all would suffer. The men were escorted below; today, they wouldn't be allowed to roam about freely on deck.

Over the first few weeks, travel was slow with storms forcing them into one harbour after another for shelter, and at a speed of about three knots an hour, they weren't making much progress. Nevertheless, rain or shine, the convicts swabbed the decks daily.

When the captain at last determined that no one on board was ill, the convicts' work was rewarded with a gill of cape wine, served after dinner to everyone on the main deck. Before long, some of the sailors and pensioner guards took out their fiddles, bones, and tambourines, and a lively sing song began. Some of the women sang their party pieces and, though some were rather bawdy, for a little while the music brought Liam bittersweet memories of home. The nostalgic songs expressed the same emotions as all the old songs Liam had grown up with. He listened to English, Scottish, and Welsh songs. Their themes of achingly-beautiful longing for home, regrets for love lost, and sadness coursed through the words he heard. Through his tears, Liam began to realise that people everywhere had the same dreams and regrets and, like everywhere else, some people were good, and some were bad. Eyes closed, he imagined Tomás, without a care in the world, playing his button accordion, Colm, frantic as usual on the spoons, and little children happily twirling about. He remembered Máire on the dance floor that first night, dancing happily with her innocent smile. With the wine helping, he smiled for the first time in a long time. It felt good.

Liam's reverie was gently interrupted by one of the most

beautiful melodies he had ever heard, played on the violin by one of the pensioner guards. He was transfixed, as the magnificent notes rose and fell pleasingly. The soothing sound of crashing waves, as the ship carved its way through the ocean, provided a surprisingly delightful accompaniment. Everybody listened attentively to the haunting melody filling the night air. Liam closed his eyes allowing the music to consume him. As the music started to rise and reached a crescendo, he imagined Máire and himself back home in his favourite spot, looking out at the ocean. *Máire, sitting on the grass, smiling her gorgeous smile, leaned over and kissed him gently. She pulled away slowly, looked at Liam and said, 'I miss you Liam.'* 'I'm here Máire,' he said softly, and he could feel her lips on his. He held her close and kissed her softly. Pulling away, he faced her and began to unbutton her blouse. He kissed her on the neck, and she let out a little moan as they slowly fell together. He kissed her with a hunger that she had never felt in him before. 'I want you,' she said. For those few beautiful moments as his fantasy played out, all was right again. Liam was in Galway making love to his wife. At the end of the guard's song, the sergeant shouted, 'Below all hands!' brutally pulling Liam back to reality. Everybody applauded the violinist and, reluctantly, began to go below to sleep.

    Liam approached the guard shyly. 'What was that song called? 'That's Bach,' said the guard. 'That's what?' 'Johann Sebastian Bach. It's his *Air on a G String*.' 'It's magnificent,' said Liam. 'Yes, it is. Bach was a German composer in the seventeenth century. He wrote a lot of great music.' 'I'd like to hear more,' said Liam. 'Well, we have a long time before we get to Australia, and I know a lot of classical music. Have you ever heard of Mozart?' 'No,' said Liam.

'Beethoven?' 'No,' Liam admitted. 'Don't worry, son,' said the guard kindly. 'Before this journey is over, I'll introduce you to all the great masters.' Liam went below deck realising that there was much to learn about the bigger world beyond Galway's Atlantic shores.

Climbing up into his bunk, he heard George Wheeler moaning in his bunk directly below. After four weeks of not eating or drinking, poor old George was in a bad way. The surgeon had done everything he could, but George continued to weaken. John Atkins Faught read his Bible to him every night, giving him comfort and urging him to ask God for forgiveness to save his soul.

Little more than flesh and bone towards the end, at night George cried out weakly, begging the Lord for mercy and to take him home. 'Please try to get this to my mother, and I'll be eternally grateful.' Being the only one of them who could read and write, John Atkins Faught had written George's final message to his mother in a heartfelt letter. George died in his sleep that night. The next morning, his body was covered with the Union Jack and placed on the hatch which rested on the bulwark. Captain Jenkins read passages from his Bible, and solemnly, George's body was committed to the deep. John Atkins Faught wrote this poem the following day:

> Despised by all those from whom love was due
> Bereft of all those whose love he well knew
> Friendless and alone from his country he's sent
> To toil in some distant land, 'til his life he had spent.
>
> The shock too severe – his nature gave way
> He sank under the weight from premature decay
> His spirit has fled from all troubles and pain
> To his maker returned – in sweet peace to resign.

No useless coffin did his body enclose
The funeral knell bespoke, his death's last repose
Closely shrouded in his hammock, he was borne towards his grave
Covered o'er with the colour, he was launched in the wave.
The waters' closed o'er him, he sank in the deep
Without a tear being shed, or no one to weep.

During one of the worst storms Liam had ever experienced, Tommy Steel's wife was in the final stage of giving birth. The ship heaved violently from side to side, as Doctor Foster, valiantly trying to keep his balance, attended her. She gave another huge push, and the head appeared. When Mrs Steel gave a final push, the surgeon gently assisted with delivering the baby. 'It's a girl,' said the surgeon, cutting the umbilical cord. Mrs Steel fell back exhausted and waited to hear her new daughter's first cry, but it never came. The surgeon cleared the baby's mouth, spanked her softly, and wrapped her in warm woollen blankets, to no avail. The baby was lifeless. 'I'm so sorry, Mrs Steel,' said the surgeon, 'I'm afraid your baby is stillborn. Situated at the rear of the ship to avoid the worst rolling and heaving of the sea, the ship's hospital was just ten by fifteen feet in size. Waiting at the hospital door for news of his baby, Tommy heard his wife's labour screams dissolve into those of sorrow. The surgeon stepped out to tell Tommy of his baby's death and invited him in. Mrs Steel lay on the lowest of three iron bunks. Tommy knelt before his bereft wife and, setting aside his own heartbreak, tried to console her. 'It's going to be all right, Lizzie. We have two fine daughters; sure, we can try again.' Tommy and Lizzie Steel's baby daughter was buried at sea that afternoon, with Captain Jenkins once again reading scripture.

The routine of school one day, work the next, began. For work, the convicts were allowed to choose from among several possible jobs: swabbing the decks, working in the kitchen galley, sewing military suits and duck canvas trousers, shoemaking, and knitting socks. Liam chose galley duty and knitting. Already adept with knitting needles working with rough Connemara wool, he knew the various stitches, so it wasn't a huge transition to knit with the even rougher Scottish worsted wool. He daydreamed of his family as he knitted, trying to imagine what his son looked like now. He didn't once doubt that he and Máire had survived. Colm would never allow anything to happen to them, and Seán would be true to his promise to take care of them. The sea was perfectly calm again, and a full moon lit up the endless ocean.

As he and Tommy Steel were washing supper dishes, Liam took in Tommy's demeanour as he shuffled around the tiny galley; his hunched shoulders seemed lower than usual. 'I'm sorry about your baby.' Liam could feel his pain, remembering the heartbreaking times for his parents, when four of his siblings had died, either stillborn or shortly thereafter. 'Thanks Liam,' said Tommy, his lips tightly clenched, trying to keep himself together. 'How's your wife?' asked Liam. 'She's as good as she can be,' he said. 'She's had a bad feeling about it right along. She never felt the baby kick, like when she had our other two daughters. The doctor said she bled a lot and was lucky to be alive, but I know Lizzie. She's a tough one.' 'I'm glad to hear she's all right.' 'We're lucky we have a surgeon on board. If she were on one of those coffin ships, she'd have probably died. On those ships, they don't give a shit about anybody. They get paid full fare before they leave England or Ireland.' 'Is that so?' 'Yes, those bastards don't care if the people make it or not. The more they throw overboard, the faster they get to America.' 'I didn't know that' said Liam, wondering how many of his old friends, who might have boarded those ancient, barely sea-worthy ships, had made the crossing to America alive. 'On these ships, they don't pay the owners the full amount, until every one of you makes it over alive and healthy.' 'Well, that's good to hear.' 'They tell me that one in every four dies on those old ships. It's a disgrace,' said Tommy. Liam appreciated Tommy's decency and respect for his fellow man, regardless of creed or country. Liam felt a curious irony about his own situation, and as a convict being transported to a penal colony, he received rations and was treated better than those fleeing for their lives on the coffin ships to America.

With the ship making timely progress at about seven knots an hour, school began in earnest about two weeks into the journey. It was conducted by four elderly schoolmasters under the supervision of an old pensioner guard called Sergeant McCabe. McCabe sincerely desired to improve the convicts' chances once they arrived in Australia, so he consistently encouraged those students who were motivated to learn. Many of the others didn't give a damn, but they were forced to learn, nonetheless. Books were distributed to the convicts who could already read. Liam, being next to illiterate, was determined to learn to read and write. John Atkins Faught volunteered to be an assistant teacher, and spent hours every night patiently helping Liam get better at reading. John's parents had given him pens and paper for his long journey, knowing that he had kept a diary of his life for as long as they could remember. For Liam this was a godsend, allowing him to practice writing on the many pages John was kind enough to share with him. Over time, they became good friends. Liam told him all about his past life, about his beloved Máire and son Tomás back home, and about how he was captured. One night, to encourage Liam to persist when he was finding these exercises difficult and frustrating, John said, 'When you have perfected writing, I will post a letter from you to Máire.' 'You could get a letter to Máire?' asked Liam stunned and excited at the possibility of getting word to her that he was still alive. Then, well aware of their oppressors' cruel ways, he said, 'They won't allow her to see it.' 'I'll send it first to my sister in England. I'll instruct her to send it to Máire from there. Nobody will suspect it's from you. They'll think it's from one of your family in England.' 'I do have an uncle in Manchester.' 'Fine then. Just give me his name and address, and she can put it on the envelope.' This was all the encouragement Liam needed, and with only the dull light of two oil lamps at either end of their prison quarters, Liam wrote and wrote, determined to succeed. He went to sleep that night composing his letter to his beloved Máire.

The weather became increasingly warmer as they made steady progress each day. One afternoon, just before sunset, there was great excitement on the top deck as dozens of dolphins appeared from nowhere and swam parallel to the ship. The sailors harpooned two of them, and everyone sampled the exceedingly tasty dolphin meat that night. Liam thought its reddish-black-coloured meat tasted like beef liver. As the weather became sultrier and more oppressive, tempers ran short. A soldier was 'boxed' for abusing his wife – solitary confinement for twenty-four hours. Liam saw numerous multi-coloured birds, as they passed unfamiliar but scenic shorelines. One of the sailors hooked an albatross which had flown too close for its own good. It was the biggest bird Liam had ever seen, its wingspan measuring over nine feet from tip to tip. The weather became increasingly warmer each day sailing from the Northern Hemisphere to the Southern Hemisphere. They stopped in the Canary Islands and the Cape Verde islands for supplies of fresh water, food and some timber before heading around the southern tip of Africa, heading into the Indian Ocean. Liam saw the water change from a cold blue to a peculiar green as the weather became milder and more comfortable. That night, he was in absolute awe as he witnessed the most amazing lightning show he had ever seen, accompanied by frighteningly loud and frequent thunder.

After six weeks of school and John's nightly tutoring, Liam was beginning to read well. He was also learning rudimentary mathematics. He had just eight weeks left to learn as much as he could. He was also knitting industriously and handing out the finished socks as needed. There were no complaints.

After a few more weeks of steady sailing, Liam heard talk of being near an island in the middle of the Indian Ocean called St. Paul. He understood that Australia was then about two thousand miles away. Wine was served at dinner on the odd occasion, afterwards, the music started once again. The longer they were at sea, the more relaxed these nights became for the men. As singing and dancing with the single women had by now become commonplace, Liam could see several of them pairing off with the sailors. Such offenses by the convicts and sailors were generally treated leniently. John Atkins Faught, however, was appalled by the loose morals of many on board traveling to a new life in Australia. His strong faith was evident as he voiced his disapproval to Liam after observing the night's debauchery. 'They are destitute of any morals and use such obscene language, they are a disgrace to their class, both men and women. It may be a good thing for society that they be exiled, and it is no wonder that such should have happened to them,' he huffed. In John's eyes it got worse as the weather became unbearably hot and humid. He was appalled watching everybody sitting and lying about almost naked, until the order for bed was given, which was always complied with, albeit reluctantly. As Liam practiced his reading and writing, as well as his daily knitting, as well as cleaning the convicts' galley twice daily, the Mermaid made swift progress, sailing at eleven knots.

By far, Liam's favourite book was Charles Dickens' *Oliver Twist*. It exposed the world to the awful conditions of orphaned children deprived of food, warmth, and decent shelter in London's criminal underbelly during the first half of the nineteenth century. Liam identified with Oliver, the hero of this classic tale of good versus evil, rich versus poor; and he wondered if he would ever be fortunate enough to meet his own Mr Brownlow, the man who rescued Oliver and offered him the hope of a brighter future. His new friend John Atkins Faught came close. On the Warrior, that hellhole of a prison ship where he had barely survived the longest nine months of his life, Liam had met many of the criminal types which Dickens portrayed. He thought of all that had befallen Ireland over the last hundred years, everything that now was the cause of his being torn away from everything and everyone that mattered.

Liam became a voracious reader, opening his mind to the works of William Shakespeare. With John Atkins Faught's constant help and encouragement in discerning the meaning of his texts and poetry, Liam came to appreciate Shakespeare's ability to convey a seemingly complete range of human emotion and conflict. John introduced Liam to the great English poets of the day, and William Wordsworth became his favourite. Wordsworth's, *I Wandered Lonely as a Cloud* captured exactly and wonderfully how Liam felt about the beauty of nature. As he read the verses over and over, learning them by heart, two of the poem's verses became his favourites:

> I wandered lonely as a cloud
> That floats on high o'er vales and hills,
> When all at once I saw a crowd,
> A host, of golden daffodils;
> Beside the lake, beneath the trees,
> Fluttering and dancing in the breeze.
>
> For oft on my couch I lie,
> In vacant or in pensive mood,
> They flash upon that inward eye
> Which is the bliss of solitude;
> And then my heart with pleasure fills,
> And dances with the daffodils.

In a pensive mood, Liam considered all that he had to be grateful for: the patience and generosity of John Atkins Faught; the arithmetic, reading, and writing instruction he'd received from the schoolmasters; his friendship with Tommy Steel; the pensioner guard's exposing Liam to the beauty of classical music, and Captain Jenkins' humane treatment. Towards the end of this journey of a lifetime, Liam had become a more self-confident and worldly-wise young man.

Part Seven

Dingoes, Whales, Potato Orphans, and a Letter

After weeks of sailing the vast emptiness of the Indian Ocean, there was great excitement on the ship when finally, in early May 1851, land was sighted. Except for poor old George Wheeler, every one of the two hundred convicts arrived alive and healthy. Many of them were actually healthier than they had been for years, thanks to three meals a day, good hygiene, and the strict work ethic imposed upon them.

Captain Jenkins congratulated the convicts for making two hundred grey suits, three hundred fifty duck trousers, and knitting dozens of worsted socks. 'It was a productive four months,' he said. 'Soon, I shall formally hand you over to the Governor of the Swan River Colony. Many of you will be assigned to the construction of buildings or farming. The rest of you will be assessed for other sought-after skills and held in the Round House until needed.' He issued each convict his discharge papers, listing for the governor the man's name, crime, and sentence. Liam noted that, on his papers, there was no name listed, just that he was from Ireland, and sentenced to life for theft.

Soon, the ship docked at the mouth of the Swan River in Fremantle. A local doctor came aboard, inspected every convict, and declared them fit to land. Captain Jenkins shook Governor Charles Fitzpatrick's hand, and the convicts, now formally transferred, were escorted off the ship.

Liam wasn't greatly impressed with his first view of Australia. The soil was sandy and poor for as far as he could see upriver and completely different from the green, rocky lands of Connemara back home in Galway.

John Atkins Faught and Liam disembarked together,

thinking that they would never see each other again. Liam had finished his letter to Máire a few days before. 'I promise I will get this to Máire,' said John. 'I don't know how long it will take me, but I give you my word that I will send it.' Liam was grateful to him, for Máire would know for sure that he was alive, had made it to Australia, and was determined to come back to her someday, somehow.

The familiar atmosphere of the ship and its lenient ways were now replaced by armed soldiers shouting orders to walk in a straight line to a building about a half mile down the road. They marched into a large empty building where six men were seated. Ordered into six lines facing the seated men, one by one they were interviewed. Liam was behind John in the line. Each man could hear the convict in front of him being interviewed.

'Jeffrey Smith, you have been sentenced to seven years for theft. Can you read or write?' 'No, sir.' 'Do you know anything about farming?' 'No, sir.' 'What did you do back in England?' 'Nothing, sir.' The man wrote a few lines on Jeffrey's paper, stamped it, and said, 'Go over there to that man, and give him this.' Jeffrey left, and next up was John Faught.

'John Atkins Faught, you have been sentenced to ten years for forgery. Is that correct?' 'Yes, sir.' 'Can you read or write?' 'Yes, sir.' 'What did you do in England?' 'I was a printer, sir.' Impressed, the man nodded his head and wrote it down. 'Anything else?' he asked. 'Yes, sir. If you look further down on my file, you will see that Captain Jenkins appointed me as a part-time teacher on the ship. I helped the other convicts learn to read and write.' The man glanced at John's file and nodded his head as he read the paragraph stating how helpful he had been during the journey. He stamped his papers, and in a friendly manner said; 'Okay Mr Faught, I'm sure the town officials can use you in some capacity. Please wait in that room over there.' 'Please, sir,' said John, 'the gentleman behind me was the best student I had. He is an excellent reader and writer, and I find him to be of the highest moral standards. I believe him to be as honest as the day is long.' The man nodded, dismissed John, and signalled Liam to come forward. Liam handed him his papers, and the man opened the first page. 'What is your name?' he asked, puzzled that it wasn't written there. Liam figured that nobody cared about who he was anymore, now that he was in Australia. 'Liam O'Donaghue sir,' he replied proudly. 'You can read and write?' 'Yes, sir.' 'Have you any special skills?' Liam had often told John about his love of horses, and what he was able to get them to do. 'Be sure to tell them about your skills with horses, otherwise they might sentence you to hard labour for the rest of your life.' 'Horse trainer, sir,' said Liam.

The man duly wrote it down and stamped Liam's papers. 'Wait in the room over there with your friend.' Liam was delighted to join John and a few other fellow convicts seated there. He noticed that most of them were the same men who had been less disruptive and, like himself, had attended classes diligently.

Presently, the sixteen of them were marched over to a circular prison gaol aptly called the Round House which had been built in 1831 using convict labour and other arrivals. As they walked up the steps of the fortress-like limestone building, Liam saw large, menacing cannons facing out to the harbour. They all admired the gaol's uninterrupted views of Cockburn Sound. Then Liam saw its immense, forbidding wooden doors, and felt as though he was about to enter Kilmainham gaol in Dublin again. *I hope to God we'll be treated better here.*

They were marched inside to an open area surrounded by high walls lined with eight prison cells and a gaoler's residence. Liam and John were to share a cell and were pleased to be treated well by the guards; they also found the food to be decent. Several days later, a guard came for John and, once again assuming that they would never see each other again, they quickly said their goodbyes. John's parting words were, 'Good luck old chap, keep the chin up.' Grateful for all that his friend had taught him, Liam thought, *If only every Englishman could be like him.* He lay back on his bunk, alone again, and quietly shed a tear.

Liam spent a long, and thankfully uneventful, two weeks alone in his Round House cell, reading the last book John had given him: Charlotte Bronte's masterpiece, *Jane Eyre*. Liam loved Jane's story, dealing with the English class system and the same abuse that he and his family had also endured. He wondered if he would ever be free of it. He easily related to the social issues of her time, her troubled upbringing and sad love story, ultimately leading to a happy ending. This plot resolution gave him the hope he needed to continue to pursue his dream of returning home to Máire and his son.

As one day followed another, he began to wonder if he'd ever get out of gaol. Early one morning he was awakened by a prison guard. 'Okay, O'Donaghue,' he said gruffly, 'you're outta' here.' He walked Liam to the prison doors and shouted an order to open them. When Liam stepped out, he saw three burly men on horseback waiting for him. One of the men held the reins of a fourth horse. 'Welcome to the Swan,' said the biggest man of the three. 'O'Donaghue isn't it?' he asked in his clipped English accent.

Liam nodded. 'Well, you'll be workin' for Mr Dunsley from now on mate, biggest farm for miles around. We were sent to get ya. Reedy's the name, Jack Reedy. This is Murdock, and that's Bald Paddy.' Liam looked at Paddy who had the thickest head of hair he'd ever seen on an Irishman, and all he could do was shake his head and laugh. 'Jealous bastards that's all ye are,' shouted Bald Paddy. 'So where are ya from?' asked Paddy warmly, in fluent Gaelic. 'Connemara.' 'I'm not too far from ya.' 'Is that so?' said Liam, answering in Irish. 'Yea,' said Paddy, 'Mayo, God help us.' 'Dunsley told me you're a horse trainer,' said Reedy. 'Yea, I've trained a few,' said Liam modestly. 'Well, we love our nags over here mate,' said Reedy, 'and Dunsley has a few beauties that'll keep ya busy, this one included.'

Liam took the reins and patted the horse; he whispered a few words in its ear and jumped up confidently. It had been almost three years since he last rode, and it felt good to be on a horse again. This one was a little bigger than a Connemara pony, but it was every bit as wild looking. The saddle was the finest and most comfortable he had ever been on.

'That's a brumby, mate,' said Reedy. 'They're wild, feral horses from the bush. They brought horses over for farming and transport, and some of 'em escaped and bred like crazy.' 'I've never heard of a brumby,' said Liam. 'It's some sort of an Aboriginal word meaning wild horse,' said Murdock in a distinct Scottish accent. 'What's an Aboriginal?' asked Liam. They all laughed. 'Laddie,' said Murdock, 'you've gotta' lot to learn.' As they set off towards the sandy road to head upriver, small mountains looming in the distance, Reedy saw that Liam handled his horse with the ease of a master. 'Dunsley will have plenty of work for you mate.'

After a few miles' riding on flat, marshy ground, Liam noticed a change in the terrain. The soil along the river looked a little finer and more fertile. Farther inland, even richer cultivated farmland came into view. There, he saw seasoned farmers, equipped with four strong horses, thrashing rich golden wheat. This land was clearly far superior to Connemara's rocky fields that he and his family had toiled for years to cultivate. And there were prime healthy sheep everywhere.

'Tis fine land, isn't it?' said Bald Paddy. 'If we only had the likes of it in Mayo.' 'They're fine-lookin' sheep, too,' said Liam. 'The Dunsleys brought them over with them from England. They're called Leicester and Merino sheep. They do very well here. When they came here, they brought everything over with them, sheep, horses, cattle, farm implements, seeds, everything to get started.' 'How long are ya here?' asked Liam. 'Ten years. They gave me seven for a bit o' trouble in London, but I'm a free man now.' 'Why don't ya go home then?' 'Sure, why would I want to go back? There's no one left; they're all dead or scattered everywhere. They took our farm, and I went over to London to save a bit for me passage to America but, before I could get there, I got caught for a bit o' stealin'. Nothin' much mind ya, but they still sent me away, the bastards. I've got a few acres of my own here now, and I do a bit o' work for Dunsley every now an' then to keep me goin', so this is where I'll stay.'

'I'll tell ya one thing,' said Murdock. 'The climate's better here than in Scotland. Sometimes in the summer it gets way too hot, just for a couple o' months, but the rest o' the time it's perfect.' 'Dunsley has a few thoroughbred horses; they're his pride and joy,' said Reedy. 'If ya know yer stuff, ya could be training 'em. That's why Dunsley asked the magistrate for you.'

Liam appreciated their warm welcome, gruff as it was, realising that just a few short years ago, they were the ones making this same journey into the unknown. They tried their best to make the start of his exile in this new land as normal a beginning as they could. Once again, Liam was grateful for the good word John Atkins Faught had put in for him. He would at least be working with his big love – horses.

Riding along the narrow dirt road, Liam observed trees, the likes of which he'd never seen before. They had massive trunks with thick, white branches. Totally dried-out and grotesque looking, the branches shot out wildly in different shapes and sizes. Even though they looked dead, the trees still had fine green leaves, and their flowers were multi-coloured. 'Eucalyptus trees,' said Paddy, amused as he watched Liam taking in their random shapes. ''Tis fine timber. Good for fencin'. We chop 'em down, and they grow back like mad. I tell ya, ya can't kill 'em. We use 'em for windbreakers instead of the stone walls like back home. And the blowies hate the oil we get from them.' 'The blowies?' 'Yea,' said Paddy, 'biggest feckin' flies I've ever seen. If ya don't have the oil on ya, they'll suck the blood right out o' ya. I tell ya, they leave the blackies alone, but they love us.' 'Blackies?'

'You'll be meetin' 'em soon enough,' said Murdock. 'You'll be livin' with 'em,' said Reedy. 'They're called Aborigines. We just call 'em blackies. They're a merry bunch who come and go as they please. They don't understand us, and we don't understand them. They didn't like us when we came first, taking their hunting lands and all, but now they work for us, if you could call what they do, work.'

Is there any place in the world where a man can be free, and isn't told what he can or cannot do? Liam wondered.

Liam learned that the coastal Aboriginal peoples suffered devastating changes in their lifestyle as soon as the first British settlers arrived. The British hunted and killed them without mercy and forced many of the survivors to work for them. They destroyed their tribal ways and culture to a great extent, driving them off the most desirable areas and forcibly pushing them into desert lands the Europeans didn't want. Liam could relate totally.

After about twelve miles' riding, they turned up a long and narrow dirt road, tree-lined with neat fencing on both sides. Liam saw lush green fields spreading out in all directions before him. There wasn't a rock in sight. Situated in an expansive green clearing at the end of the road, stood a large, two-story, timber house, with a large front porch. Flanking it were several smaller buildings, and farther to the left was a level, fenced-in field, large and circular.

Then Liam saw it – the most beautiful horse he'd ever seen. Standing about five feet tall, it wasn't much bigger than his beloved Bridgey. It had silky black hair, a fine chiselled head, a long arching neck, and a high-carried tail. It weighed about a thousand pounds and, rather than trot, it seemed to float gracefully around the field. 'That's Rhapsody, Dunsley's pride and joy,' said Paddy. "Tis an Arabian stallion. Isn't he glorious?' 'He is indeed,' said Liam admiringly. 'He's a mighty jumper, and he just explodes with speed when he's let loose. Dunsley breeds him with his best mares. He's got some fine foals from him and they're always strong and fast.' Liam spotted several jumps laid out just like back home. 'His daughter jumps, and she's in all the shows every year.' 'I'd like a chance to ride him myself,' said Liam excitedly. 'Well,' said Reedy, 'I think that's what Dunsley's brought ya here for.' Liam's whole demeanour brightened. *This could be worse*, he thought. As they rode over to the impressive stables, Liam got his first look at where he'd be spending time for the foreseeable future.

'This is Dunsley's stud farm,' said Reedy. 'He hopes to

breed some great Australian winners.' Liam was impressed by the stable's sturdy timber structure and high cathedral ceiling. It had a stone floor with sixteen neatly-designed stalls, eight on either side. It was much larger and better organised than Kitchener's stable back home. To the right, a half wall opened out to a paddock where several thoroughbred horses and a few fine-looking foals were grazing.

Liam unsaddled his horse and led her into her stall. In the next stall, shovel in hand, and sloshing around in the muck barefooted, was an older man barely five feet tall. He had black skin, wild grey hair, and was almost naked. Liam was seeing his first Aboriginal person. Busy cleaning, the man seemed content and ignored him. Liam noticed on the man's back what he thought were ugly scars from floggings. On his journey from England, he had seen several convicts punished with the dreaded stockman's whip. He was later to learn that the scars he saw this day were the initiation marks of the man's tribe. 'Okay, Irish,' said Reedy, 'come on, I'll show you your quarters.' As they exited the stables, Liam took in the striking expanse before him, miles of glorious green ranchland as far as he could see. Eucalyptus trees seemed to be everywhere, even ascending the far-off majestic hills.

Liam saw two buildings behind the main house, one large, the other small. Reedy walked Liam to the larger one, which was basically a huge room filled with assorted farm machinery. Sleeping cots were to the rear; in the centre was a cooking area with a large, rough wooden table and chairs. 'This will be yours mate,' said Reedy, pointing to a single cot in the far corner. It was longer than his bunk bed on the ship, and thankfully, no one would be sleeping a mere ten inches above him! In the opposite corner was a trough filled with water. 'This is where you can wash and shave. Dunsley expects us to be nice and tidy at all times. The blackies hate soap and water; they think washing is pure torture. They hate our clothes and never wear boots, so you don't have to hide yer stuff.' Liam had been told by the pensioner guards on the ship, that Australia was inhabited by hostile savages. Yet as he looked at them looking back at him, he sensed nothing aggressive about them at all.

'The stud master, Robert Martin,' said Reedy, 'will meet ya tomorrow and put ya to work, so I'll leave ya alone for a while.' Free to roam about, Liam returned to the paddock to watch the thoroughbred horses. With his trained eye, he could see that the foals would grow up to be fine runners. Spotting Rhapsody again in the nearby fenced-in field, Liam was mesmerised by his sheer perfection.

'He's a champion three-year-old,' said Bald Paddy walking over to Liam. 'He covers all our mares here, and Dunsley hires him out to accommodate other mares as well. See that brown one over there?' Paddy pointed to a stallion in the paddock. 'They send him in to tease the mare, and just when she's ready, in goes yer man Rhapsody, and does his business. He's getting more ass than anyone in Australia, the lucky bastard.' Paddy let out a huge belly laugh, and Liam laughed, too, but realised that he had a lot to learn about thoroughbred horse breeding.

'C'mon, ya must be starvin',' said Paddy. Liam followed him back to the building, sat down, and ate one of the best meals he'd ever had – fish soup, delicious mutton chops, melons, grapes, and a sweet red wine that he learned was from Dunsley's own winery. For the first time in years, Liam went to sleep on a full stomach and hoped he'd dream about Máire.

Liam awoke to yet another new experience. He was neither too hot nor too cold. He realised how steady the weather had been since he arrived two weeks ago – a new sensation so welcome from the sweltering heat of the last few weeks on the ship, and definitely so different from unpredictable Ireland. He smelled fresh coffee, washed up, and had his first breakfast of warm soupy stew.

'Mornin',' said Bald Paddy, greeting him in Gaelic. He, Murdock, and Reedy sat across from Liam. 'Looks like 'tis a grand mornin',' said Liam, enjoying a mug of warm coffee. 'Ah sure now, wouldn't ya love a bit o' that old Galway mist on your face and a taste of that salty Atlantic air on yer lips?' asked Paddy. He was feeling sentimental with a welcome fellow Irishman around for a change. 'You can shove yer Irish mist up yer fat Irish arse,' said Murdock in his pronounced Scottish accent. 'If I went back to Scotland, my arthritis would be back in a week, and I'm not talkin' January; I'm talkin' about the middle o' fuckin' summer!' 'Well, be that as it may, gentlemen,' said Reedy, 'we have to leave you two lovebirds at it.' Then turning to Liam with a smile, he said, 'The stud master wants to see you.' 'Where is he?' 'Over in the paddock. C'mon, I'll bring ya over.' 'What's he like?' asked Liam, as they walked out into the already-hot morning air. 'He's fair I suppose,' said Reedy with a little hesitation. 'Certainly, knows his stuff though. He's been with Dunsley from the start; brought him over with him actually. Just remember, he's not on your side. As long as ya do what he says, you'll be fine.'

They walked the short distance to the circular paddock with its white double fencing, and there Liam got his first glimpse of Robert Martin, the man who would become his mentor for the foreseeable future. It was a heartwarming sight for Liam – a trainer holding a long rope, as his horse trotted around and around in a circular motion, kicking up sandy-brown dust. Liam's eyes fixed on the perfectly-groomed mare gliding poetically around the paddock. *There isn't a poor old shaggy Connemara pony in sight,* smiled Liam nostalgically. His heart raced with anticipation. Martin shouted familiar instructions to the magnificent animal, and Liam could see that Martin knew his stuff.

As they got closer, Liam took stock of his first impression of the man: medium-sized, mid-forties, muscular, and balding with long stringy grey-blond hair. His dark leathery, weather-beaten skin, which sagged, made him appear older than his years. He was 'no great looker,' as Josie would say. Seeing Liam and Reedy approach, Martin shouted orders to the horse which stopped immediately. He tied her to the fence. 'G'day.' He stretched out his hand to Liam. 'Robert Martin.' Liam shook Martin's strong, rough hand, 'Liam O'Donaghue.' 'Welcome to Australia mate. They tell me you have some horse training experience.' 'I've got some,' said Liam, modest as always, 'but I can see I've gotta' lot to learn.' 'Well, say 'hello' to Eclipse. I hear you've already met Rhapsody.' 'Yes, sir. He's a beauty.' 'Well, this is Dunsley's favourite female, apart from his wife. She's a three-year-old, thoroughbred filly. 'Eclipse,' said Liam, admiring the animal. 'That's an unusual name for a horse, isn't it?' 'Dunsley named her after a famous horse who won eighteen races in England about a hundred years ago.' Liam gawked in awe at this magnificent, perfectly-bred chestnut filly. She had a distinctive, white blaze down her perfect head. 'Dunsley bought her from his friend, James Osborne. He was a governor here in Western Australia. He did a lot for this area. Good man. Retired back in England now, but he bred several racers including Eclipse.'

Martin handed the training rope to Liam, and he immediately sensed her agility and spirit. She trotted around the circular paddock, clearly anxious to cut loose and gallop. 'She's no Connemara pony, that's for sure,' said Liam in sincere admiration. 'Yea, you gotta' watch her. Control her speed. That's for later.' The mutual respect between horse and trainer soon became evident to Martin. The horse readily responded once Liam got a handle on the feel and subtle rhythm needed for this exercise. 'Well,' said Martin, 'I can see you got the touch all right. Let's see what sort of rider you are.' Martin shouted orders to a stable boy to saddle up a horse. Soon he emerged from the stable with an older stallion standing over fifteen hands. The stable boy handed the reins to Liam.

Leading him through the paddock gate into a sizable fenced-in, flat area set up for racing, Liam whispered to the animal and gently stroked his proud head. He put his foot into the fanciest stirrup he had ever seen and pulled himself up to sit higher than on any horse he had ever ridden before. And the saddle was perfect. Liam gave the horse a small kick and soon was doing what he was born to do. Ride! As the horse quickened to a gallop, he showed his true pedigree by holding his speed far longer than any pony Liam had ever trained to race. Exhilarating.

As the magnificent animal gave Liam the ride of his life, the only thing missing was the rugged vista of his beloved Galway and, as Bald Paddy said, the taste of Atlantic mist on his lips. Instead, he ingested a huge blowie and learned the hard way to keep his mouth shut and breathe through his nose while riding horses in the dry Australian heat. Loving every second riding this hot-blooded thoroughbred, Liam wanted to know all there was to know about world-class horse breeding. He felt this was his destiny; this was 'it', and he just knew in his bones that he wanted more, a lot more. As he trotted back to the paddock, Liam was aware that Martin was watching his every move. He hoped Martin would think enough of how he handled himself to take him under his wing and teach him everything.

'Well, mate,' said Martin, as Liam dismounted and handed the horse over to a stable boy, 'you're one of the best that's come here in a long time. I'll be glad to have you by my side. And just to let ya know before ya get too excited, this is the good part. It's costing Dunsley a bloody fortune breeding and training future champions, so most of the time you're going to be out herding sheep. He depends on wool and sheep sales to keep his stable going. The most boring part of it all is coming up in a few weeks – gathering them all up and herding them to the fair in Fremantle. So, like the rest of us, your ass is gonna' be sore by the time we get back.' Liam was delighted by Martin's encouraging words, even knowing how his ass would feel after a few days of hard riding.

A few weeks later, Liam, Murdock, Bald Paddy, and Reedy, rode out and herded wandering sheep back to the enclosed paddock. They swigged down pint after pint of life-saving water in the sweltering heat as they gathered Dunsley's flock of fine, fat, market-ready, thoroughbred Merino sheep. Several Aboriginal men began shearing the sheep and baling the valuable wool for the trip to Fremantle Harbour for export to England.

Each night, after a hearty dinner of kangaroo tail soup, and mutton washed down with generous amounts of Dunsley wine, they fell asleep exhausted. They hadn't left yet, and Liam's ass was already killing him!

The sounds of noisy bullock drivers cracking whips and shouting orders woke Liam before dawn the next morning. He was amazed by another new Australian experience: sets of ten huge bullocks being expertly tied up to large drays. They carried a total of twelve massive bales of wool between them, weighing nearly two tons. *Everything is bigger here*, he thought admiringly. He washed up, ate breakfast, and eagerly looked forward to his return trip to Fremantle.

As his new friends and a few young Aboriginal men began shepherding the flock of about fifty sheep, Liam saddled up to help keep the animals on the primitive, dry and sandy path to Guildford, their first target of the day. Guildford was the loading point for agricultural produce that would be shipped down the Swan River to Fremantle. To haul heavy equipment of any kind through the swampy land from Guildford to Fremantle was impossible, thus the river route.

Liam got his first look at three beautiful-looking animals. Not quite dogs, he observed, they looked more like foxes, same colour, but taller. He noticed that the three of them were not herding sheep like dogs back home, they were just tagging along beside Murdock, Reedy, and Bald Paddy. He admired their lean, hardy bodies, raised ears, bushy tails, and broad heads that seemed out of proportion to their bodies.

'Mornin,' said Murdock, 'are ya ready for yer first trek to Fremantle?' 'Yea,' said Liam as he guided his horse to the opposite side of the path to Murdock. 'I like yer dog.' 'That's not a dog mate, that's a dingo, very different to a dog.' 'How so?' 'They're only found in Australia. They say they could have been descendants of dogs and wolves through interbreeding. The Aboriginal peoples use them to hunt, and they're spread all over the country. Farmers shoot them as pests for attacking their livestock, but we keep these as companions. We've trained them since they were pups. They're very protective and loyal. They have a wild nature, very different to most dogs, so you have to know how to handle them. They make great watchdogs and even living blankets.' 'Living blankets?' 'Wait 'til tonight,' said Reedy. 'When you're freezing your balls off, we'll be nice and warm wrapped around our dingoes.'

Liam looked down admiringly at the dingoes who seemed to act exactly like sheepdogs, following their masters obediently. 'Don't be fooled at how calm they are,' said Murdock. 'The Aborigines use them as hunters for rabbits, feral cats, and foxes. They hunt in packs and can tear a sheep apart in minutes. They can burrow down rabbit holes, and when the poor old rabbit comes out the other side, the other dingo is waiting for him and rips him to shreds. They can spot a lizard way off, and they're right on him in seconds before he can escape; they're that fast.'

The searing sun was merciless as they trudged along slowly. Every white man was clothed from head to toe. Scarves covered their mouths to prevent ingesting the ubiquitous blowies or swallowing mouthfuls of foul-tasting, dry dust kicked up into painful eye-watering clouds by the sheep, bullocks and horses. The young Aboriginal men were almost completely naked and barefoot as usual, oblivious to the mid-morning blistering heat, seemingly without a care in the world.

Finally, after crossing over the Helena River and flats on a fifteen-hundred-foot barge built by the newly-arrived convicts, they came to the busy inland town of Guildford at the confluence of the Swan and Helena Rivers. Liam saw a mishmash of early shanty houses and buildings. Disappointed, he hoped Fremantle and Perth would be more exciting.

He noticed dozens of convicts doing the backbreaking work of laying down measured broken stones on top of more stones, tamping it all down, and then, under the searing sun, pouring boiling tar on it to bind it all together.

Once again Liam was grateful for the good word his friend John had put in for him when they arrived in Australia. *I could have been one of those poor bastards.*

It was the noisiest and busiest farming scene that Liam had ever seen. Bulls were everywhere – bellowing, snorting, and grunting angrily at each other. Liam could tell from looking after Kitchener's cattle that they were all in foul mood, shaking their heads and swishing their tails. He counted around ninety teams of cattle and carts being unloaded at Guildford pier that Wednesday. 'It'll be the same thing tomorrow,' said Bald Paddy. ''Tis mad so it is.'

The bullocks and drays pulled up to several small boats, and Reedy shouted orders to everyone to start unloading the heavy bales of wool onto the boats. Once loaded, Murdock and the teams of cattle and their drivers turned around and headed back to the ranch. Liam and Bald Paddy's job was to keep the sheep calm and together, until it was their turn to load them aboard, and then to stay with them all the way.

Liam was well used to controlling sheep, and ever the master horseman, was in complete control. Soon they got the word to load, and the sheep were predictably easier to board than the terrified cattle; once they got a few on board, sheep being sheep, the others followed. As soon as everything was loaded, Reedy gave the signal to go, and the boats headed down the Swan River for the ten-mile trip to Fremantle Harbour.

Slowly heading downriver, Liam began to despair of ever escaping from this isolated place. He watched the fertile soil change to marshy swampland as Guildford faded into the distance. Then, after they turned a bend, there wasn't a single soul or animal visible for miles. He recalled what Bald Paddy had told him one night when he'd asked him why he hadn't tried to escape. Realising what Liam was thinking about, Bald Paddy gave him the tough love advice to forget any notions he might have about escaping. 'The only ships that ever come here are British ships full of convicts, nothin' else. Ever. Without papers or money, you've no chance. If you went inland, you'd be dead in a few days, as there's nothing there but thousands of miles o' desert. Nobody will come after ya; they'll just assume you're dead out there somewhere, so they're not going to put themselves in danger. Either way, it's impossible.' Liam thought about this and figured that his best chance to escape would be by boat somehow. They would assume he'd run right into the hell that's the Australian desert and died, as he'd never be stupid enough to think that he could get onboard a British ship. The only thing going for that plan was knowing that no one would chase after him. Unfortunately, he had plenty of time to figure something out.

After several hours, they pulled up to the docks of Fremantle. There, Liam saw mountains of wool, sandalwood, and wheat, and hundreds of sheep, soon to be loaded onto the convict ships that had brought them all on their one-way journey to the other side of the world. Liam looked in awe at some of the biggest fish he had ever seen. They were stacked on top of each other and filled big sections of the pier. *They have to be two to three hundred pounds each. Colm would be amazed,* he thought. They were way bigger than any dolphins he had ever seen. The convicts were doing all the heavy lifting. Reedy was all business with the port superintendent, weighing the wool, counting the sheep, and getting a bill of sale.

Liam saw young Aboriginal boys fishing from the pier. They were doing well, catching herring and thin, ray-finned fish that looked like pike to Liam. Later he learned that they were called garfish. The freshly-caught fish were immediately cleaned, cooked, and sold to the hungry farmers and boatmen. Liam enjoyed a delicious meal of fish, accompanied by salad and slices from huge watermelons grown by the convicts.

'Okay,' said Reedy, 'saddle up and head for Perth. The quicker we do, the faster we get back.' 'I thought that was it,' said Liam. 'Nah, we have to go to Perth to get Dunsley's money,' said Bald Paddy. 'They do all that sort of business in Perth.' Liam watched the shanty houses and dirt streets of Fremantle fade away as they headed north.

Josie and Órla were preparing dinner when they heard a knock on the door. 'God bless all in this house.' They looked up from scrubbing potatoes and saw Dinny Mac the postman with his usual friendly smile, standing in the doorway. He was drenched from the afternoon's rain. 'I've a letter here for Máire from England; I hope everything's all right.' 'Oh my God, there's somethin' wrong with Séamus or Sheila,' said Josie, thinking of Tomás' brother and his wife in Manchester, their only kin in England. Josie knew that she couldn't trust the postman to read it to them, as he was the biggest gossip for miles around. She always said, 'If ya want everybody to know yer business, tell Dinny Mac to keep a secret.'

Getting herself all worked up, Josie shouted, 'Bríd, go find your Da and Colm and tell them to come home immediately. Go on away now.' Bríd ran as quickly as she could towards the Kitchener mansion and found Tomás pitching hay in a barn. 'There's a letter from England,' she screamed excitedly. Tomás stuck the pitchfork into the hay, and he and Bríd ran home. When they returned, Colm was already there. They took turns looking at and touching the manila envelope with its impressive stamp. It was the first letter they had ever received. The fact that none of them could read it infuriated them all. 'We'll have to wait until Máire gets home so Tomásheen can read it for us,' said Órla.

They were always entranced whenever little Tomás would come home with a book given to him by one of Harry and Tomás' tutors to encourage the boys to read. After the nightly rosary, he would help pass the long winter evenings by regaling them with his reading, one great novel after another. Little Tomás was becoming a real character when he read to the family. He loved hamming it up with his captive audience, unaware that he was also helping them improve their English. Colm's favourite was a just-published book Tomás had brought home: *The Whale* by Herman Melville, a book later to be introduced to Americans as *Moby Dick*. Colm lost himself in the brilliant story of Captain Ahab's obsessive quest to seek revenge for the whale which had taken his foot on a previous hunt.

'With the help of God, Séamus and Sheila are all right,' said Josie. She looked out the half door with her rosary beads clicking away, reciting decade after decade, and praying that Máire and Tomás would soon come into view. 'Maybe somebody had a baby,' said Órla hopefully. 'Well,' said big Tomás, 'we'll know soon enough.' 'There she is, thank God,' said Josie excitedly, grabbing the letter.

After another busy day's work at the mansion, Máire was crossing the little bridge with Tomás and looking forward to dinner. She became alarmed when she saw an excited Josie running towards her in the pouring rain, her white apron billowing wildly in the wind. Josie waved something in the air. Máire's immediate thought was that there must be something wrong, for Josie was always in the cottage preparing dinner when Máire and Tomás came home from work. *She must have been waiting by the half door for ages until she saw me*, she thought. W*hat's got her all excited?* Finally, Josie reached her and breathlessly gave her the big news. 'There's a letter here for ya,' she said, nervously waving the envelope. 'The postman said 'tis from England and 'tis addressed to you. We're worried sick that somethin's happened to Séamus or Sheila, but we can't read it. Tomásheen, will ya read it for us?'

Big Tomás, Órla, Aoife, Bríd, and Colm were sitting at the kitchen table waiting for them to get home, unable to eat a thing until they heard the news about Tomás' brother or his wife. Máire had little Tomás sit down and handed him the letter. 'Tomás, please read this letter to us from your granduncle in England.' Tomás took the letter from his mother, and as he slowly and carefully opened it, the only sound in the hushed cottage was the comforting crackle of the turf fire. They waited with bated breath to hear the news from England. Tomás innocently began reading. Nobody was prepared for the first three words that came from his lips:

My Dearest Máire,

Everybody froze. Máire sat up straight as a rod and gasped loudly, her hand instinctively covering her mouth. Groaning loudly and uncontrollably, she suddenly bent over shaking her head violently, rocking back and forth in an overwhelming state of shock. As her tears began, her quivering hand still firmly holding her mouth, she pulled herself up abruptly and looked pleadingly at everybody for reassurance about what she had just heard. *Could it be? Did I hear right?*

Órla ran to her, hugged her tightly, and full of emotion, could barely get the words out herself, 'He's alive Máire, your Liam's alive!' Josie fell to her knees blessing herself repeatedly, reciting the Hail Mary, as her husband tapped lovingly and comfortingly on her shoulder. He finished the second part of the Hail Mary prayer, rosary-like, as they had done thousands of times before. He tried to hold himself together while he grasped the startling news that everyone's daily prayers had been answered. Liam was alive! As it was with the rest of them, tears poured down Colm's face hearing those three beautiful words. He shook his head in shocked admiration at how cleverly Liam had managed to get this letter back to them without anybody suspecting a thing. *Horse, ya never lost it boy.* And he coughed a tearful smile.

Poor young Tomás, frightened and confused by their reactions to those first few powerful words, thought he had done something wrong. Seeing how puzzled little Tomás was, Máire pulled herself together, rose from the table, and hugged him tightly. She pulled away after a few seconds, bent down and said, 'This letter is from your father. He's alive, Tomás. Your father is alive.' 'But you told me he drowned,' he shouted. 'I know, Tomás, I know.' Tomás angrily pulled away when she tried to hold him. 'We had to say that to keep everyone safe or we would have had to leave here.' 'But you told me. You told me,' he cried. Colm, Tomás' father figure since Liam was sent away, came over, sat him down, and said, 'Tomás, I've told you so many stories about your father, but there's lots more you don't know. You're becoming a man now, so it's time to tell you what really happened to your father when you were very young. And it's time to let you know everything he did for you and your mother, but first your mother needs you to read the letter.'

Over the years Colm had told Tomás about many of the wild things he and Liam had done, always reminding him how great a man his father was, but leaving out what had happened, and why he was sent away. Tomás idolised Colm and, trusting his uncle's reassurances, began to calm down. Máire gently raised his lowered little head and gave him a smile. 'Okay Tomás, start again. We want to hear what your father has to say to us.' Once again, Tomás raised the letter and began to read. Nobody heard the crackling turf fire, nor the pouring rain and gale-force winds outside. The only sound they heard was Tomás as he began to read.

My Dearest Máire,

I am writing to let you know that I arrived safely in Australia in May 1851. I am very grateful to a fine Englishman, John Atkins Faught, himself a fellow convict, who taught me to read and write during the four-month long voyage, thus this letter which he kindly helped me get to you.
I know that I have brought many hardships on you by being away. For that, Máire, I am truly sorry. I could not stand idly by, seeing the injustice and cruelty all around us. I only hope you can understand this love I bear for my fellow Irish men and women, which forced us apart.
I swear to you and Tomás, if I have to spend the rest of my life trying, I will come back to you both. Sometimes I dream beautiful dreams of you and me together. We're in our favourite place, lying together as we did in happier days gone by. I'm holding you, loving you, delighting in just being with you. I hear you saying, 'Come back to me Liam, I miss you.' Sadly, the dreams are always too brief. Tomás, my son, I'm desperately sorry I wasn't there to hear your first words, or watch you grow up. I'm sure your mother is raising you with dignity and honour, and I look forward someday to seeing the fine young man I'm sure you're becoming.
Colm, I think of you often. Together with my love for Máire, remembering our mad days growing up has given me the strength

to carry on. I wonder did you find the love of your life like I found Máire?

Mam and Da, Brid, and Aoife, I miss you all so very much it hurts.

Máire, know that you're my last thought before I go to sleep each night, and my first each morning. You are strong Máire, so very loving, funny, and kind. I consider myself lucky that you are, and always will be, the love of my life.

I hope our love, the most perfect love I have ever known, will somehow carry you through the days until we are together again

Your loving husband,
Liam

There was a long silence as everybody listened to Liam's letter. Máire didn't want his beautiful words to ever end. Her anger and resentment about what he had done, causing her and Tomás such awful loss, dissolved as Tomás read those loving words to her. She knew she would have the whole letter memorised quickly, and it immediately became her most prized possession.

'He's only been in Australia for six months,' said Colm angrily. 'They must have kept him in prison in England for a long time, the bastards.' 'He's gonna' come back to us Máire,' said Josie. ''Tis a miracle.' 'He's smart Máire, very smart. He always was,' said big Tomás. 'And an Englishman helping him get the letter to you, can ya imagine that! An Englishman helping an Irishman! There's hope for us yet, thanks be to God. He's gonna' come back to us Máire.' Tomás was already getting out the poitín and started pouring everybody a generous portion. He looked at his grandson and said, 'He'll come back to you Tomásheen. You heard what he said in the letter, and I know my son. What he promises, he'll do. He'll come back to us all, with the help of God. Come on, lift yer glasses with me and let's drink to Liam.' 'To Liam,' they all said with deep emotion. 'Sláinte,' said Tomás. 'Sláinte mhaith,' they all replied. 'Tomás,' said Máire, 'read it again please.'

Later, as little Tomás slept soundly, the family talked into the wee hours of the morning about the great news the postman had delivered that day. Eventually, Colm and Órla went next door to their little cottage and tucked their baby daughter, already fast asleep, into her cradle without awakening her. Soon, they all drifted off to sleep, exhausted after all the drama and excitement. All except Máire. Quietly rocking in one of the rocking chairs, the only two things she had kept from their cottage, she gazed at the soft glow of the fading turf fire, hearing Liam's words over and over. She couldn't believe the beautiful things he had said to her. She tried to imagine her Liam befriending an Englishman, 'a fine Englishman', as he had put it, who had taught him to write so beautifully. *How did that happen?* she wondered. *They must have helped each other on that long journey over. What did they talk about? Did Liam tell him everything? What is Liam doing in Australia? Is he farming?* Her last thought as she finally drifted off to sleep was of the two of them sitting happily together in their rocking chairs.

Liam's first experience of Perth was the luxuriant perfume of roses filling his nostrils. He smiled remembering what his mother called them – 'the queen of flowers'. She was absolutely right, and he wished she could enjoy the sight and aroma of these beautiful roses herself, flourishing in such fertile soil. It was a nice moment, briefly bringing him back to someone so near and dear.

As they entered the town, Liam saw it as small, remote, and rustic, with a village-like atmosphere. Scattered single and two-story brick and stone residences, surrounded by gardens full of beautiful flowers, led down to the water's edge. The main streets were macadamised, stone upon stone and tarred, while the minor streets remained primitive with loose sand offering its usual quota of dust.

In this remote settlement, he saw the hustle and bustle of convicts constructing impressive-looking buildings which reflected the culture and aspirations of the British Empire. These buildings of gothic-like architecture were cast in a pleasing mellow colour. They would become fine structures, such as those he had seen on his walk from Kilmainham gaol to the docklands back in Dublin. As he looked out at Perth's beautiful harbour with its fine sandy beaches, turquoise waters, and the comfortable afternoon breeze coming in from the ocean, he thought, *Someday it'll be a fine city for any man, a man who's free.*

They rode up what seemed to be Perth's Main Street, and straight ahead saw men lined up to enter a large, two-story brick building. Dozens of horses were tied up outside the building, and police were admitting the men in single lines only. 'Wait here 'til I get paid,' said Reedy, and he took his place in the queue.

Bald Paddy dismounted and walked to the other side of the street where a man was selling Australia's biggest morning newspaper, the *Morning Herald*. 'Dunsley reads this from cover to cover the second we get back. He'd have a stroke if we forgot to buy it.' 'Can ya read?' asked Liam. 'Nah,' said Paddy, 'Her Majesty wasn't kind enough to teach us on our way over.' Liam had heard from the pensioner guards on board the ship about the public outcry by the British public to the awful mistreatment of the earlier convicts, almost on a par with those coffin ships from Ireland. Thankfully, by the time Liam was shipped over, a more benign approach had been adopted. 'Could I have a read of it so?' 'Go ahead, but don't mess it up or you'll be hearing from Dunsley.' Liam opened the paper and the headline read:

COULD BATHURST BE BIGGER THAN THE SAN FRANCISCO '49 DISCOVERY?

As he read on, Liam learned about the gold rush going on just 200 miles from Sydney. He read about men making fortunes overnight as they found huge gold nuggets in the rivers and rocks around the area. There were stories of men with Irish names, obviously former convicts, having as equal a chance as anybody, as they panned for their own eureka moment:

> A wonderful lot of fellows with local nicknames and likable ways, all digging for gold, including a wily old Irishman called 'Paddy the Flat'. Unable to read or write, gold seems to have levelled all distinctions, making them as good as their former masters. They don't depend on their masters' speculation, nor the doubtful payment for work performed in paper and bills. At once the acknowledged medium of exchange throughout the world comes into his possession, and he fears not bankruptcy or bad debts.

As Liam read on, he had his own eureka moment: escape to Bathurst, make his fortune, and return to Ireland. 'Hey Paddy, how far is Sydney from here?' 'Ah, just twenty-five hundred miles,' he joked. 'A couple o' days ridin' an' you'll be making yer fortune like the rest of them, no bother at all to ya.' Bald Paddy was very much aware of what was happening on the other coast, and he knew exactly what Liam was thinking. 'C'mere an' let me tell ya somethin'.' Paddy quickly burst Liam's bubble. 'Get that idea outta' yer head right now boy, you're not talkin' Galway to feckin' Mayo here, no no no,' he laughed, 'twenty-five hundred miles across nothin' but desert. Forget it Horse, nobody's ever done it and lived to tell the tale. Impossible boy, just forget about it.' But those gold mines could be Liam's ticket home. He was determined to find a way to get to them, deserts or not. Liam read the newspaper from cover to cover. Soon, Reedy came out, and they all headed back to Fremantle to spend the night and then catch the river boat to Guildford the next morning.

At nightfall everybody bedded down in the open air. The temperature dropped and, just as Paddy and Reedy said, Liam froze. He saw the dingoes lying right up against Reedy and Bald Paddy, exactly like warm blankets, just as they had said. Within minutes they were both snoring blissfully. As Liam shivered in the darkness, unable to fall asleep from the cold, he decided he'd get a dingo as soon as he could.

He finally drifted off to sleep but was awakened a few hours later when he felt something cold crawling up his leg. He put his hand down to shoo away what he thought was a frog but, to his horror, found he had taken hold of a large snake. Jumping up screaming, he swung it to the ground awakening the others. Then, in the moonlight, he saw it coming at him again, not realising he was probably covering the nervous snake's escape route. Just before it could reach him, one of the dingoes grabbed it by its tail. The snake gave a whiplash-like jerk, and the dingo lost its grip. To everyone's relief, the snake slithered quickly away into the darkness. 'Are ya bit?' screamed Bald Paddy. 'I don't think so,' said Liam, trying to calm down. 'Are ya sure?' Paddy roared. Liam did a quick body check and nodded nervously. 'Good,' said Reedy. 'That could've been an Australian brown snake. One bite from that and you're done mate!' he said reassuringly. Liam was wide awake for the rest of the night, even more determined to get his own dingo immediately, or sooner!

The next night he was delighted to sleep in his own, safe, comfortable bunk, sore ass and all. The following morning, after their eventful trip to Perth, Liam was roughly shaken from his deep sleep by Murdock. 'Dunsley wants to see ya.' As he pulled himself up, Liam could feel every bone in his body ache. 'Why so?' he asked. 'I dunno,' said Murdock. 'Maybe it's got somethin' to do with the race next week.' Liam had heard all the excitement about The Town Plate, the biggest race in Western Australia. He knew that Dunsley was entering his pride and joy. 'If Rhapsody wins it, he can charge even more for stud fees,' said Murdock. 'He wants you and Martin in his office at nine sharp.'

Liam washed up, got ready, had some breakfast, and prepared to meet his new master. The story on Dunsley was that he was strict but fair, generous when he could be, and of course, obsessed with horses. Like most other entitled Englishmen of his time, he had no problem with cheap indentured labour, no matter the colour of their skin. He took it as his right that he, an enlightened modern Englishman, was superior to anyone beneath his class. What was his was his, and everybody he controlled could help him get more.

Liam went to the paddock where Martin was watching a stable boy giving Rhapsody his daily walk. Everything about the magnificent horse mesmerised Liam: his confident presence; magnificent black colour; the perfect motion of his strong straight legs; and the equal length of his neck, back, and hips in perfect balance with each other – a true athlete. 'There's something about the outside of a horse that's good for the inside of a man,' said Martin, looking admiringly at

Rhapsody. 'It's an old saying, but it's true.' Liam knew exactly what he meant. He was at his most calm around horses. 'Well, are ya ready for this mate?' asked Martin. 'What does he want from me?' asked Liam. He had been at the ranch less than six months and knew he still had a lot to learn. 'I told him how impressed Reedy was with everything you did on your first ride, and he's thinking of having you join us for the trip to Perth. He wants to meet you first, of course.'

Liam was delighted at the chance to experience his first ever horse race. Nervously he walked over to Dunsley's house. He had already seen the outside of it many times, and it wasn't at all as grand or imposing as Kitchener's mansion back home, but it was a fine, sturdy-looking, two-story timber house. Its elegant wraparound porch was positioned to face the paddock so that, while he smoked his fine cigars in the evenings, Dunsley could watch his beloved horses.

Martin knocked, and Dunsley opened the door within seconds. 'Gentlemen, come in,' he said warmly. A fine looking, fifty-something man as tall as Liam greeted them. Dressed in rather old-fashioned brown cotton breeches, loose fitting cream cotton shirt with fuller sleeves and fold-down collar, and wearing dusty, well-worn black leather riding boots up to his knees, Dunsley wasn't what Liam had imagined a big landowner to be. 'I hope you're settling in well,' he said, without shaking Liam's hand. 'Please come in.' When Dunsley led them into his dark, stained-oak study, Liam was impressed. The walls were full of paintings of English horses, some in country meadows, magnificent stallions standing proudly in their prime, and others with exciting, though faded, English horse racing scenes. 'Robert tells me you're quite the horseman.' 'Yes sir, ever since I was a young lad I've been ridin' Connemara ponies.' 'Yes, I've heard of them, quite like our brumbies here I believe.' 'Yes sir. They're every bit as wild as the brumbies, a few hands smaller, but once you've broken them in, they're excellent for ridin' and jumpin',' 'Well,' said Dunsley, 'you'll be breaking in quite a few brumbies for me over the coming years.' Liam winced when he heard 'over the coming years,' but he kept his composure. *Once again,* he thought, *somebody thinks he owns me.* 'Robert suggested that coming along with us next week would be a good experience for you, and if we're to keep Rhapsody calm and relaxed, he'll need every bit of trained help he can get.' 'Yes sir, he's a magnificent animal. He's fiery and rarin' to go all the time. They all have their own different temperaments. Mr Martin and his team have done a great job gettin' him to this level. I think he's just about ready. There's an old Irish saying, 'There's no luck where there's discipline,' and I'm very impressed with what I've seen here so far.' Dunsley had seen and heard enough from Liam in this informal interview to agree with Martin's opinion of him. 'Well then, good enough.' He turned to Martin and gave him instructions. 'Robert, get this man familiar with Rhapsody and his jockey, and let's show Perth what a champion we have.'

Liam's eyes were drawn to a verse he saw above Dunsley's desk. It was written in white ink on a three by three-foot piece of brown leather, simply hammered into the wall.

> In the steady gaze of the horse shines a silent eloquence that speaks of love, loyalty, strength and courage. It is the window that reveals to us how willing is his spirit, how generous his heart.

'You can read? asked Dunsley surprised. 'Yes sir, I like poetry. Do you know who wrote it? I'd like to read more of his work,' said Liam. Dunsley was taken aback, trying to take the measure of this seemingly refined new convict, standing tall, handsome, and obviously intelligent. *Quite unlike the rest of them*, he thought. *Not only can he read, but he appreciates poetry*. Dunsley felt slightly inadequate as he failed to quickly come back with a good answer. 'I never thought about it actually. I just like what it says. My wife gave it to me for one of my birthdays.' 'Yes,' said Liam, 'they're a mighty animal for sure, and whoever wrote it certainly knew horses'. 'Yes indeed. Well, that will be all then. Thank you, Robert,' and they both walked out.

'So, tell me, what's he up against?' asked Liam, considering Rhapsody's chances as they walked back to the paddock. 'Well, there's a fellow called Cowell up in Avon Valley. He and Dunsley are good friends, but they're always competing with each other. He's got a fine stud farm, but I think Rhapsody can do it.' 'How long is the race?' 'Two miles, with maybe five or six horses,' said Martin. 'Mother of God,' said Liam absolutely shocked, 'in this heat?' 'Yea, they've gotta be pretty hardy. Dunsley is trying to form a turf club in Western Australia to change the rules so they can shorten the course. It's way too long.' 'And what's the course like?' 'It's pretty good this time of the year, the best in the colony, they say. It's about four miles from Perth on the left bank of the river. A lot of the ground around here is too heavy, but the stewards did a good job selecting it.'

When they reached the paddock Liam got his first look at Rhapsody's jockey as he was walking the horse from the paddock. Liam marvelled at Dunsley's choice – a baby-faced young man who looked like he was twelve years old. Liam learned later that he was a twenty-five-year-old fellow convict from London. He was barely five feet tall, weighed no more than seventy pounds, and was bowlegged, *the perfect jockey*, thought Liam. 'Say hello to Big Norman,' said Martin, enjoying Liam's efforts not to laugh hearing the name. 'Liam O'Donaghue.' He extended his hand and, as he towered over him, Liam shook the softest hands he had touched since Máire's. 'Dunsley saw something in you three years ago, didn't he mate?' said Martin admiringly, putting his hand around Norman's shoulder. 'You started training first as a stable hand, then as a hot walker, then as an exercise boy, putting you on the best runners in the stable. You've won three of the last four races, haven't ya Norman?' 'Yes sir.' 'I'm impressed,' said Liam. 'Dunsley wants Liam to come to Perth with us next week and help us win,' said Martin. 'He trained ponies back in Ireland.' 'Nice to meet ya mate,' said Norman confidently. He spoke with a heavy Cockney accent that Liam was familiar with from all the Londoners he had met on the ship.

Martin bent down beside Rhapsody and clasped his hands. Norman placed one foot on them and pushed himself up for his morning gallop. Soon Liam saw what Dunsley had seen three years previously, as Martin put Norman through his paces. First, a quarter mile, then a half mile, and finally a one-mile gallop, timing him at each distance with another invention Liam had never seen before – a stopwatch. Liam had, of course, seen large clocks before, but he was fascinated by the large second hand spinning around a small circular silver timepiece, which, with one quick press of Martin's thumb, was able to start and stop the time to the second.

Liam, a gifted horse whisperer, could read Rhapsody's mind as he started his gallop. He felt certain that this wonderful racehorse instinctively knew his own power and agility, yet was waiting for his rider to tell him exactly when to unleash his tremendous energy. That rare understanding between horse and jockey was a beautiful thing to watch. 'He's ready all right,' said Liam. 'Yes, he is,' said Martin. 'It's taken three years of hard work gettin' him to this level; now all we've gotta' do is keep him nice an' relaxed 'til Sunday.'

Waiting to witness his first thoroughbred race felt like months for Liam. He marvelled once again at how seriously everybody took racing when he witnessed another first: Rhapsody slowly being rolled out of the stable like royalty in a horse trailer. A modified four-wheeled timber cattle trailer, it was drawn by three heavy-duty horses, two in the lead and one by the front wheels. Heavy blankets lined each side to protect his majesty. 'They call it 'vanning',' Martin explained. 'This setup will spare him the wear and tear of the journey and prevent anything happening to him getting on and off the boat. We had a desperate disaster two years ago when a champion filly slipped getting off a boat. She was injured so bad we had to put her down. 'Twas awful.' Martin looked at Liam with a wry smile. 'Funnily enough, her name was Maid of Erin, so everybody is vanning now; can't take any chances.'

Liam saddled up, better prepared this time for the unrelenting sun, dust, and ever-present blowies. He also packed warm blankets for the overnight stay at the racecourse. He joined Robert Martin, Big Norman, and the horse carrier driver, and set out for Perth with a few Aborigines walking behind. Dunsley and his wife followed in their stately carriage.

Liam was now more familiar with the route as they headed towards Guildford. They got the horse carrier on board without incident and headed down the Swan River. While Dunsley and Robert Martin were engrossed in conversation on one side of the boat, Mrs Dunsley remained in the carriage. Liam had yet to meet her.

Liam leaned absentmindedly on the boat rails, gazing out at the riverbank. 'How long did they give ya mate?' Startled, Liam looked around and saw no one. 'How long did they give ya?' Liam looked straight down to his left and saw Norman staring up at him like a little boy. 'Life,' said Liam. 'Sorry mate,' said Norman shaking his head. 'What did ya do to get life? Kill someone?' 'Nah, I didn't kill anyone. I got caught trying to steal some grain to feed my family. 'They gave ya life for that?' 'Yea, what about you?' 'We were caught doin' a house. Me mates got away, but I couldn't run as fast as them with a heavy bleedin' chair on me back. They gave me seven years.' 'Why didn't ya just drop it and run?' 'The gaffer would've killed me.' 'The who?' 'The boss. He expected us to deliver when he sent us out.' *Mother of God*, thought Liam, *Oliver Twist*. 'Are ya gonna' go back?' Norman, turned and looked proudly at Rhapsody. 'Nah. I've nothin' there now, nothin'. I left home when I was fifteen. I went back a few years later and there was no one there. I couldn't find anybody. They were all gone, probably dead. Dunsley says that, if I keep winnin', he'll put a word in for me to the magistrate and try to shorten my sentence. Then I'll be a free man, an' I'll ride for the highest bidder.' 'I hope so,' said Liam, sorry to hear Norman's story. *At least, he has a plan, and sadly, I don't. Not yet.* 'So, who gave ya the name Big Norman?' asked Liam. 'Who d'ya think? The one and only Bald Paddy!' said Norman laughing. 'The night I won my first race I got a bit carried away, drunk outa' me mind I was. And in front of everybody, I shouted out at the top of me voice, 'Wha d'ya think of that, ya Bald Paddy bastard?' 'He shouted back, 'Oh, you're a big man now Norman. Look everybody – it's Big Norman! Everybody had a great laugh and it stuck ever since.' 'Well, he got ya back pretty good didn't he?' 'Yea,' said Norman laughing, 'he sure did.'

When they reached the racecourse, Liam sensed the atmosphere there to be far more genteel than it had been at the frenetic fair day in Fremantle. And he could smell the money: ornate carriages; fancy tents dotting the racecourse perimeter; elegantly-dressed ladies in comfortable chairs protecting themselves from the boiling sun with colourful umbrellas; tables groaning with food; jockeys everywhere; and beautiful horses, of course.

'There are four races today,' said Martin. 'We're last.'

Liam saw a tent where, for the day's first race, people were frantically placing bets, before the starting gun went off. 'He's doing some business isn't he?' asked Liam. 'Yea he certainly is,' said Martin, 'and as well as that, every owner has to put in from five to ten pounds, depending on the race. We're in the top race of the day, so Dunsley has to shell out ten pounds. The bets start at one shilling, but there's no limit to what anyone can gamble.' 'That's a lotta' money,' said Liam. 'Yes, it is, but apart from the winning bets, all the money goes to one of Dunsley's old friends.' 'Why so?' 'Over the years all the early colonists became good friends. They went through a lot, helping each other survive some pretty bad times. One of them invested everything in land and property and ran into trouble when we had one of the worst droughts ever. It lasted several years and it broke him. This fundraiser will allow him and his wife to live quietly and comfortably for their last few years.' Liam remembered how all the nearby landlords back home shared their farm equipment and even their tenants. *Nothing's changed,* thought Liam. *They stick together like glue wherever they rule, and everyone else be damned.*

He watched as five horses lined up for the first race of

the day, and he could see that they were nowhere near Rhapsody's class. Three of them were already sweating and fretting no matter what their jockeys did to calm them. He could see the mad look in their eyes. 'They're three of the wildest divils that ever looked through bridles,' shouted Liam to Martin above the screaming and roaring of the crowd. 'Horses know they're going racing and some will spend their energy too soon,' said Martin. As Martin anticipated, none of the horses in the anxious trio won. With each race, the calibre of horses improved. Finally, it came to the big race of the day, and five exquisite thoroughbreds began to line up.

'I tell you,' said Dunsley proudly, as he looked at Rhapsody waiting calmly for the starting gun. 'He's a wonder; I don't see a horse here who can beat him.' Once they were all aligned, the steward fired his gun, and the race began. Though the four other jockeys crouched down in their saddles, Big Norman rode upright, as he'd done the first time Liam had seen him ride. And though Liam had never witnessed such an unorthodox style, he certainly wasn't about to give him any tips about horse riding! A superb judge of pace, Norman stayed behind the two early frontrunners.

Liam watched in admiration as Rhapsody took long smooth strides, each one nearly twenty feet long, one hundred fifty strides a minute – *perfection*, marvelled Liam, *poetry in motion*. He could see Rhapsody's big bright eyes, keen and alert, his ears pointing forward and moving in all directions. Clued into what was happening all around him, he looked confident and in control. With the two horses still in front as they passed the halfway mark, Norman kept up his steady pace. The two horses in the rear fell further behind. The crowd was in full roar, rooting for the horse they had put their money on, as the three frontrunners rounded the final corner. With a quarter mile to go, each jockey signalled his horse to unleash its full energy. Rhapsody answered Norman's call mightily, reaching nearly forty miles an hour in six strides. Passing the second horse easily, he quickly caught up with the frontrunner. Norman had the reputation of coaxing his horse to close with a devastating final burst and, sure enough, with the two horses matching each other stride for stride in those final few yards, he crossed the finish line, winning by barely a head.

Liam had never seen anything so exciting. He heard the crowd roar as Norman led Rhapsody into the winner's enclosure. Dunsley and Martin jumped for joy. As Norman grinned from ear to ear, standing straight up in his saddle, hands in the air, triumphant, Liam knew beyond any shadow of a doubt that he had found his destiny. All he wanted to do, now and forevermore, was breed horses and race them.

Celebrations lasted long into the evening, with plenty of food and wine for everyone. Even here, though, boundaries were strictly enforced – owners, trainers, and their families in one section, while all the others, even Norman, the hero of the day, stayed in the area with the Aboriginal peoples.

That night, Liam got his first taste of Aboriginal culture, when a song-man started chanting in a style somewhat similar to old-style, traditional Gaelic singing. Shortly after, another Aboriginal man started to beat two sticks together in rhythm with the singer. Then, listening with fascination, Liam heard the strange, low, monotonal sound of what the Aboriginal peoples called a yidaki, a didgeridoo. The beatings of the sticks and the yidaki sounds were timed in precise rhythm with the song-man's chants.

'The Aboriginal peoples search for bamboo trees hollowed out by termites and use them for their ceremonies,' said

Norman. Liam was mesmerised by the sound and, when they finished, he approached the young man, barely twenty, who had been playing the yidaki, and asked if he could have a look at it. With a huge smile, the man handed the five-foot-long instrument to Liam and showed him how to hold it. Liam saw that it didn't have a mouthpiece like his tin whistle. The man shaped his lips and started blowing as if he were playing the yidaki. Looking at Liam and nodding his head, he encouraged Liam to give it a try. Liam blew into it and suddenly a sound like a low wet fart came out of the instrument. Living in the moment, his cares forgotten, Liam let out a huge belly laugh and handed the instrument back to the young man, shaking his hand and thanking him. Surprised by this gesture from a white man, the young man started his droning sound again. Shaking his head, Liam smiled in admiration of the man's skill, patted his shoulder, and sat next to Norman again. 'Hey mate,' said Norman, 'we don't mix with them, all right?' 'Why not?' 'It's either us or them.' 'Whad'ya mean? They're just playing their music,' said Liam. 'They'd gut ya in a second if they got the chance.' 'I dunno',' said Liam. 'From what I heard, you can't blame 'em. When ye came over first, ye massacred them, and then ye pushed the rest of 'em off what used to be their lands.' 'They're savages. They think we're fools working hard to make a life here on the farms. No matter how we try and teach them, they won't give up their lazy ways. They don't ever wash themselves; they don't wear proper clothes or bother to learn English.' Liam looked at the men, laughing and playing together without a care in the world, and he remembered similar happy nights at all the great céilís back home. Norman, even though he was brought up in the slums of London, still had the superior attitude that his ways were better than the ways of those he considered beneath him, without ever bothering to understand their way of life. *This is just like it is back in Connemara.*

Watching them enjoying themselves in their own way, Liam, exhausted from the day's excitement, was determined to learn more about their culture. Now though, he needed sleep. Wrapping himself tightly in the blankets he'd brought, he hoped no snakes would be visiting his bed.

Edward Kitchener had a problem. Though he'd had an unusual, but brief, run of bad luck, he knew he couldn't return to Dublin without likely getting beaten up, but Dublin was where the big gambling money in Ireland was. Once his luck turned around, he knew he could pay off his debts quickly, but money from the rents and cattle sales wasn't due for weeks.

When Edward was given the gift of a year travelling Europe before starting Trinity, he did the exact opposite of what his parents had hoped he would do. Instead of learning how important a good work ethic was, he went straight to Paris where he frequented its popular gambling halls and, of course, its seedy red-light districts. His favourite game was poker, and he was becoming increasingly better at it. He studied the great gamblers of Europe. They played every night, gambled carefully, and frequently won. He studied the gamblers' body language meticulously. Along with his mathematical ability, he was also blessed with an almost photographic memory. Soon, he was able to calculate who had a good hand, and who was bluffing. He had found his calling – professional gambler. *To hell with Trinity,* he thought arrogantly. *I'll make my fortune my way.* But he still had that pesky problem – getting his creditor's 'heavy' off his back.

Harry's routine ran like clockwork. He rose early, had

the same breakfast every day, and then started practicing piano until lunchtime. He ate the exact same meal again, then practiced for another four hours until dinnertime. He did this, seven days a week. The constant 'noise' from Harry's practising was driving Edward crazy, now that he was back in residence in Galway as the new Kitchener landlord. Suddenly, in a flash of genius, as he would boast about later, it came to him:

HARRY KITCHENER
BOY PRODIGY IN CONCERT

It was time for Harry to go on the road! Edward could see it now – Harry, a sensation at all the big houses, performing his first Irish tour. He remembered the enthusiasm of the crowd which had attended Harry's first concert in the family's drawing room, the smallest in Galway. *I could charge fifteen shillings a ticket. My God, I could make almost a hundred pounds a night!* He considered the huge drawing rooms in Dublin's fine mansions. *Why didn't I think of this before?*

Edward became increasingly motivated. Harry would be the solution to his immediate cash flow problems. The possibility of Harry's bringing in a hundred pounds a night, plus the evening's gambling potential, was getting him more and more excited. As Edward saw it, his biggest problem would be persuading his mother to go along with his plan. He was now in charge of the daily running of the estate, but he knew he couldn't get Harry to do his bidding without his mother's support.

He remembered the shows he'd attended in Paris and the big posters advertising various concert hall acts. He needed two things: a decent review from a respected source, and an agent to book the tour. The posters would follow. He approached Mrs Best to get her advice about a music critic. She loved the idea that Edward was helping Harry pursue a possible music career. Unaware of his real reason for doing this, she suggested bringing Harry to Dublin to perform and inviting the *Dublin Times* music critic, whom she knew, to attend. She kindly volunteered to write a letter of recommendation. 'If he gives Harry a good review, everybody will want to hear him.' *This is getting better and better,* he thought. *Now, how am I going to break it to mother?* His mind was going a mile a minute. He had a brainstorm – get Mrs Best to approach Elizabeth and encourage her to do it. 'Mrs Best, would you mind discussing this with Lady Elizabeth? I think the suggestion coming from you would be a huge help, after all you've done for Harry.' 'Why Edward, I'd be delighted.' Reverend and Mrs Best were invited to dinner the next evening! After the usual pleasantries, Mrs Best brought up the recommendation that Harry go to Dublin and be heard by *The Dublin Times* critic. 'Thanks to Harry's dedication and hard work, he deserves to be heard by bigger audiences. A positive review by this gentleman would open doors for Harry's future.' *I couldn't have said it better,* thought a delighted Edward. *Mrs Best, I love you. Please keep going.*

Elizabeth, still in mourning, enjoyed the thought of getting away for a while. *I could do with a little distraction right now,* she thought, *and so could Emma. And it would be good for Harry to get a positive review. It would certainly improve his prospects of attracting more advanced piano teachers to give him master classes, as Mrs Best advised.* 'Well, I suppose a trip to Dublin would do us all some good,' she said. 'Fine,' said a delighted Edward. 'I'll set it up as soon as Mrs Best hears from the gentleman.' 'We will of course be obliged to bring

Tomás,' said Elizabeth. 'Harry won't play unless Tomás is present.' Edward had forgotten about Harry's strange obsession with Tomás. This meant that Máire would have to come along too; with the extra lodging and food costs involved, his gross takings from the concert would be reduced. *Hopefully, the mansions will have spare staff quarters available, but if that's the only way to get Harry to perform, so be it*, he thought. He didn't consider for a moment how Máire would react to such a situation. She had no say whatsoever.

Expressing an interest in hearing this eight-year-old boy prodigy give his first Dublin concert, the music critic's response to Mrs Best's letter was clearly positive. He was especially excited after reading how Harry was already performing piano works that some professional pianists wouldn't dare tackle because of their almost impossible demands of fingering and speed. Edward promptly contacted one of his college friends, Robert Archibald, 'offering' him the first exclusive premiere performance of his brother's classical career with the proviso that Robert guarantee an audience of at least one hundred people, that tickets be priced at fifteen shillings, and that he cover all lodgings and expenses. This proposal appealed to Robert's parents, who could of course boast that they were the first to 'discover' this young, classical prodigy.

Finally, everything was arranged for the last Saturday of the month, three weeks away. This would give all of Dublin's high society plenty of time to be invited. Edward was disappointed it couldn't happen sooner, but by then he would have enough rent money to pay some of the money owing to his creditor and hold his 'heavy' off until the day after the concert.

Edward sent a letter to the music critic asking him to

recommend an agent and invite him to the concert as well. Thankfully the agent agreed. Robert's parents had guest rooms available for Elizabeth, Emma, Harry, and Edward. A spare bedroom for staff in the Archibald's basement would be arranged for Máire and Tomás. Everything was all set. Now it was time to break the news to Máire.

Since receiving Liam's letter, Máire was almost back to her old self. She had hope and a renewed enthusiasm for living, as opposed to just existing. Liam was alive; he promised to come back to her; and he reminded her of what they had and still have, despite the distance between them.

As she was preparing dinner, the butler appeared in the kitchen doorway. 'Máire, Mr Kitchener wants to see you in his study immediately.' She cringed knowing she would have to be alone with him. Apart from during meals, she was grateful not to see much of him, as he was usually out with Bishop getting acquainted with the daily running of the estate. Besides increasing everybody's rents, he was anxious to see where he could increase productivity throughout the vast estate. His engineering studies, together with embracing cutting-edge farming techniques, gave him the potential to be a successful landlord. Sadly, for everybody, farming bored him totally. It was all about the gambling.

Máire walked down the long hall to the study and tapped quietly on the open door where she saw Edward reading at his desk. He stood, gestured for her to enter, and closed the door behind her. As always, he had that sly smile on his face. This is the first time she had been alone with him since Kitchener died, and she wondered how he would behave as her landlord and not as the landlord's son. 'Máire, at the end of the month, Harry is giving an important concert in Dublin, and we'd like you and Tomás to come along with us.' She tried not to laugh at the 'we'd like you and Tomás to come along with us' part, knowing full well that, if Tomás didn't go, there wouldn't be a concert. 'I think you might like a visit to Dublin. It has to be a long time since you were there last,' said Edward. 'Mother and I are planning to bring Harry and Emma to the Dublin Zoo. I think Tomás would like to see all the animals there too. It's quite a sight.' 'Yes sir, I'm sure it would be.' *Oh, you're good,* thought Máire, *making me out to be the unreasonable one if I object.*

A visit to Dublin after all these years was indeed appealing. She could show Tomás all the sights of the city, and she knew how excited he'd be at seeing lions, tigers, and giraffes for the first time. She knew it was settled anyway, and this was just his way of giving her notice of his intentions. 'I would hope that it wouldn't be too long a trip sir. I have so much to do here every day.' 'Well,' he said, 'you wouldn't have to cook any meals while we're all away, and I'm sure Tessie could keep the fires burning until we return. I expect we would be away no longer than a week. Harry's only doing one concert.'

Knowing that Elizabeth was coming gave Máire some assurance that Edward wouldn't try any of his old tricks. Still, up and down to Dublin in a week was going to be very tiring for everybody. 'How are we going to get there, sir?' asked Máire, remembering her last, long, open-air Bianconi coach trip. 'We'll bring our coach, and the Stuarts are allowing me to borrow theirs for the occasion. They're all excited about this opportunity for Harry, so it will be a comfortable journey. Máire felt better knowing that the journey would be as comfortable for Tomás and herself as for the Kitcheners. With any luck, it might just be the two of them in the coach for the trip. Of course, Tomás could hardly wait when Máire told him that they were going to see elephants, giraffes, and monkeys. That night, he began counting down the days.

Off to Dublin, Máire and Tomás did have the coach to themselves – almost. The Kitcheners' suitcases took up one whole bench and almost the entire floor area, but at least it wasn't the Kitcheners themselves, especially Edward. Edward's 'one week' turned into a good nine days. It was three and a half days to Dublin and the same coming home, plus the two days there. On the way to and from Dublin, Edward cleverly treated Máire and Tomás to the same comfortable lodgings as his own, knowing that this treatment would make Máire more amenable to the idea of traveling to Harry's future concerts. Elizabeth offered Máire several of her dresses and some of Harry's outfits so that she and Tomás would better fit in with her high society friends.

The Dublin Zoo was a huge success. The boys were enthralled by the fierce lions and tigers. They roared with laughter and mimicked the funny way the penguins walked. They looked up at the giraffes in awe. The boys' reactions gave Máire and Elizabeth countless moments of light, mother-to-mother conversation. Although Harry was out of his routine, he showed no signs of anxiety as he enjoyed these amazing sights for the first time. Edward was absent, making final arrangements for tomorrow night's concert.

The next morning, while Harry practiced with Tomás beside him as always, Máire was free to ramble down Dublin's Georgian streets. She walked the perimeter of the magnificent gardens and lake of St. Stephen's Green. Access to this twenty-two-acre park, in the centre of the city's largest Georgian square, was exclusively for the use of the people living around it. Each owner had his own key. Looking through the park's iron fencing, Máire saw lovers basking in the sun, and it was at times like these when she felt at her lowest. She could be in the kitchen working all day, seeing virtually nobody, and she'd be fine. But seeing couples lying on the grass, carefree and laughing together, gave her a profound sense of loneliness. *Where are ya Liam? Will I ever see your face again?*

She watched two majestic swans swimming with their cygnets. They looked so perfect. She knew swans mated for life and were a symbol of love and fidelity because of their long-lasting relationship. When a duck approached the cygnets too closely, the male swan viciously attacked it, protecting his family. This display gave her comfort and renewed her resolve not to entertain overtures from local suitors; several had indeed tried to court her over the years. No, she would wait and hope and pray for Liam's return.

The concert in the grand hall of one of the most prominent families in Dublin was about to begin. It was a sellout. If one received an invitation to the Archibald house, one accepted it, as it was THE place to be seen. Edward had chosen well. Everyone who was anyone was there, curious to hear this young English prodigy. Elizabeth, Máire, Harry, and Tomás waited in the anteroom. The elegant drawing room's beautiful grand piano had been tuned that afternoon and Harry loved playing it. 'Are you nervous Harry?' asked Elizabeth. 'No mother, I'm ready.' Elizabeth looked at Máire with tears in her eyes. She didn't have to say anything. They both knew how improbable this victorious event would have seemed just a few years ago. They were both grateful for how far Harry had come, beating all the expert opinions that he would be a 'vegetable' all his life. Yet here he was, this child prodigy, not yet eight years of age about to give one of the most amazing concerts anyone present was ever likely to witness. *Love is the answer to everything,* thought Máire.

And never give up. 'Okay Harry,' said Edward, poking his head in. 'Good luck. You'll be wonderful.'

With everyone seated, Mrs Archibald welcomed her guests. 'Good evening, ladies and gentlemen. Thank you so much for coming. It gives me great pleasure to introduce to you a wonderful young boy from Galway. He is the son of our friends, Elizabeth and the late William Kitchener. Ladies and gentleman, Harry Kitchener.' Everybody applauded as a shy little boy, his head down, took his seat at the piano. As he effortlessly played several Bach fugues and some of Beethoven's most complicated piano pieces, his mature style and technique quickly impressed the audience. Applause grew louder at the end of each piece, and everyone marvelled that he played it all without music in front of him. As he came to the impressive crescendo of his final piece, he mesmerised all present with his fast-flying octaves, played with a beautifully-even tone. The room erupted with the same appreciation he had received for his first concert back in Galway. Mrs Archibald's youngest daughter presented a bouquet of flowers to Harry, as he received a sustained standing ovation. Harry was a huge hit! Máire looked at Harry, enjoying the attention and appreciating the applause. He had a big open smile on his face. *Miracles do happen*, she thought. The *Dublin Times* review two days later was lavish in its praise.

SEVEN-YEAR-OLD PRODIGY DELIVERS VIRTUOSO DEBUT

His finely controlled touch, clarity, and polished performance belied his young age. His interpretation of Beethoven's dramatic 32 variations in C minor was more than up to the challenge, with a virtuosity seldom seen on stage no matter what the age.

His robust technique, delicate colourings, and respect for the score, made all the pieces spring to life. His keen intelligence, strong technical command, and stamina, bode well for the future of this fine young boy. Harry Kitchener's debut performance does indeed entitle him to join those rarified ranks of 'child prodigy'.
James Claxton, Music Critic

Edward now had his entree to the fine mansions and concert halls of Ireland. The agent couldn't wait to begin Harry's triumphant concert tour, and he had even more ambitious plans than Edward did.

After hearing about the substantial amounts of money that were now possible, Edward's opinion of himself made him even more unbearable, if that were possible. Everyone wanted the child prodigy, and they were prepared to pay well for the privilege.

It took about a month to line up Harry's first nine-concert tour. With all the travelling required, it would involve being on the road for three weeks, beginning in Galway, then Limerick, Tralee, Killarney, Cork, Waterford, Kilkenny, Carlow, and finally, two already sold-out Dublin concerts.

Elizabeth was unaware of Edward's big plans. He broke the exciting news at breakfast one morning. She was agreeable to Harry's doing a concert now and then, but as Edward well knew, nothing like what he had just planned. 'Edward,' said Elizabeth, 'why didn't you discuss this with me? I forbid you to do this.' 'Mother, I thought this is what you wanted – get Harry out as much as possible with people. Isn't that what you said?' cleverly twisting her words. 'I definitely did not mean a concert tour. How long will this take?' 'It's only three weeks.'

'THREE WEEKS?' she exclaimed furiously. 'Harry couldn't possibly do this. You saw how anxious he was coming home from Dublin. Three weeks is simply impossible.' 'But mother, there's a guarantee of at least fifteen hundred pounds, plus expenses. We need the money for several upgrades I wish to do here.' Elizabeth was stunned hearing of such a large amount of money. She knew of Edward's plans to modernise the estate, and this windfall would go a long way towards fulfilling his ambitious goals. She was caught between concern for Harry's wellbeing and not wanting to dampen Edward's newfound enthusiasm to upgrade the estate. He had never shown any interest before, and she didn't want to quash his plans. She knew William would have been delighted with Edward's finally showing an interest in the welfare of the estate. 'How do you intend to do this?' asked Elizabeth. 'I can't leave the house for three weeks. Who will look after Harry and keep him calm for so long? He's never been away like that before. He might refuse to do a concert one night. Then what will you do? Once he decides on something, there's no persuading him to change his mind. You've seen that over and over. Surely you can shorten the number of concerts to two or three. I think Harry could do that without becoming too anxious.' 'You're right mother,' said Edward. 'I should have discussed it with you before I signed the contracts.' 'Contracts? Do you mean he has to do it?' 'Yes, mother, I'm afraid so.' 'Oh Edward, what have you done?' He knew, of course, that had he discussed a three-week tour with her, she would have refused to consider it. *She has a point,* he thought. *What if Harry refuses one night to perform? What will I do then?* 'Yes mother, I'm afraid I signed the contracts for the nine concerts. Tickets are already being sold. He's already sold out for two shows in Dublin.' 'Oh my God, Edward. What have you done?'

Practicality and common sense were never a part of Edward's makeup. He wasn't used to considering other people's feelings and needs. He selfishly lived his entitled life, thinking of no one but himself. Now his mother made all the sense in the world. He would have to devise a plan to keep Harry happy and calm. He had three weeks.

Edward thought he had it all figured out: he had asked Harry who his favourite piano teacher was and had hired him to accompany Harry on the concert tour. Once they arrived at the various concert halls and drawing rooms along the way, he could keep Harry busy learning new pieces and encouraging him to keep practicing his scales and arpeggios. This would give his brother somewhat of a normal routine, as well as more lessons than he would normally have taken. He knew this would please Harry.

Once again, Máire was summoned to Edward's study, and she had the same reaction as Elizabeth when she heard about the three-week tour. However, unlike Elizabeth, she had no say in the matter. Even so, Edward knew that he had to keep Máire as happy as possible, since she was the key to Harry's remaining calm throughout the long journeys and concert days. He knew how adept she was at handling Harry, and now he had the money to offer her hotel accommodations similar to those he'd arranged for himself, Harry, and his tutor. 'I will double your wages while we're on tour and pay for nice lodgings for you and Tomás,' he said. He hoped this enticement would soften her negative reaction when she heard they would be away for three weeks. 'Mother says it's vital to keep Harry calm throughout the tour, so I'll be counting on you and Tomás to carry on as normally as you can – as if we're at home.' *You arrogant son of a bitch,* thought Máire. *The last time was hard enough, and that was only a week. The journey home was a nightmare when Harry became more and more upset. And now you're asking ME and a little boy, not you or Elizabeth, to keep him from exploding. This is a catastrophe-in-waiting.* 'I think three weeks is too long for Harry to be away from home sir,' said Máire, echoing Elizabeth's concerns. 'Well, that's what it is, I'm afraid. I'll expect you to do your best.' Máire was furious.

The short ride to Galway for Harry's first concert was uneventful. Held in a prominent judge's drawing room, it was a sellout. Some of those who had attended his first concert had spread the word. Once again, Harry received a sustained standing ovation.

Unbeknownst to Máire, while Harry performed, Edward and six of the wealthiest men in Galway were in a serious poker game upstairs in the judge's study. Edward had arranged a similar game in the remaining nine venues as well.

Without a doubt, he had become one of the best poker players in Ireland by now, and he did well on his first night's 'poker tour'. Hand after winning hand, Edward accumulated more and more money. So, once he had a really good hand, he could raise the stakes so high as to force most of the players to concede. *So far so good,* thought Edward; tonight's winnings almost equalled Harry's ticket sales. Máire, Tomás, and the piano tutor, were doing their job well, and Harry was content. *Roll on Limerick,* he smiled smugly, silently toasting his victory with a snifter of brandy.

Two nights later, Harry had another triumphant concert, and Edward did equally well again. As a treat, after Harry's master class, Edward arranged a visit to the stunning St. John's Castle in the heart of medieval Limerick City. With a well-placed bribe, the five of them were given permission to explore the seven-hundred-year-old Norman towers and fortifications on the banks of the River Shannon. Atop the towers, they enjoyed stunning views, and Tomás and Harry had fun touching the swords and crossbows of the old Norman soldiers.

Harry's concert that evening was magnificent. Once again, Edward did equally well in his card game. *Two down, seven to go. We're going strong!* crowed Edward. Tralee was another resounding success for Harry. Edward suffered his first loss so far, but not by too much. He was still way ahead. The cards just didn't fall his way.

There was much anticipation about the concert in Killarney in two days' time. Harry was scheduled to play in the newest and much talked-about mansion in Ireland – Muckross House, set on an eleven-thousand-acre estate situated between two of Killarney's beautiful lakes. They arrived late in the evening, after the long day's coach ride from Tralee. The two little boys were fascinated by the profusion of mounted deer heads displayed on the front entryway walls. They were especially taken by an enormous rack of antlers from an Irish Elk, which was extinct. Harry couldn't take his eyes off it.

Unknowingly, the piano tutor served as a buffer between Máire and Edward on the long coach rides; conversation was minimal. With Edward reading the morning paper, and the tutor writing his thesis for Trinity college, Máire was free to drift off to happier days.

After a light supper they all retired to their bedrooms – the finest Máire had ever experienced. The one she and Tomás would share had a large four-poster bed. Its heavy, red velvet draperies framed tall windows which overlooked manicured gardens, these leading down to a lake. It was simply magnificent. The night's quiet was shattered by a scream coming from across the hall in Harry and Edward's bedroom. Harry's piercing, high-pitched cries were pitiful. Máire quickly put on her robe and, with Tomás trailing, knocked on their door. 'He had a nightmare,' said Edward, looking helpless. Harry kept up his terrified screaming. 'What is it, Harry?' asked Máire. 'Did you have a bad dream?' She stroked his forehead. 'Tell me what's wrong Harry.' 'I dreamt that the elk was chasing me, and I couldn't run fast enough.' 'It's all right Harry. It was just a bad dream,' said Máire. Harry sobbed. 'I ran into the water, and he pushed me under. I couldn't breathe.' 'You're okay now Harry. That old Elk isn't around anymore. They found his antlers in a bog. He's been gone a long, long time, and he won't be coming back ever again. You're safe now,' said Máire, patiently stroking his hair and holding him close as she would Tomás. Harry, calmed now, Máire and Tomás turned to go back to their room. As she was leaving, she glanced at Edward. There was no 'thank you for saving me.' Rather, he had a disgusted look on his face, furious that his night's sleep had been interrupted. *God spare me,* she thought, *and we've still two weeks to go.*

Harry was not okay the next morning. He refused to get out of bed and wouldn't eat a thing. Edward tried to persuade him to get up for his piano lesson, but nothing he tried would convince Harry to cooperate. Edward called for Máire to intervene. 'I've seen him like this many times,' she said. 'He'll get out of bed when he's ready, and not a second before.' She relished seeing Edward sweat as it got closer and closer to concert time.

As people began arriving for the concert, Edward went up to Harry and demanded that he get up. Harry wouldn't budge. He wore his familiar stubborn face which meant

'NO.' 'Get out of bed right now,' Edward shouted. 'There are people waiting below for you to play for them. Come on Harry, get up. HARRY, GET UP!' It was useless. Harry just sat up in bed, hands folded, looking down.

Edward went down to the waiting audience and announced that, because his brother had suddenly taken ill, he couldn't perform for them. He apologised profusely. Embarrassing for all concerned, this turn of events was especially infuriating to Edward, as he had to refund everyone's tickets, and even worse, would lose the night's anticipated poker winnings.

The next four concerts went on as planned. Harry was sensational and received rave reviews from everybody attending. With the agent receiving myriad requests for return bookings, Edward knew that his brother was pure gold.

For the final night's concert in Dublin, Edward had arranged his biggest poker game yet. So, while Harry enthralled everybody downstairs, Edward was having a wild run of good fortune with several well-known Dublin socialites. Every hand he was dealt came up flush. He was in complete command. In the last game, all but two of the players folded – Edward and a gentleman who had been losing heavily and consistently. Holding a straight flush, his best hand of the entire evening, the Dublin socialite was convinced that Edward was bluffing. Unfortunately, though, he was out of money to call Edward's bluff, so he took out a pen and paper and wrote a few lines. He tossed the paper into the middle of the game table, looked around, and announced, 'Gentlemen, if I lose this game, I deed my house to Mr Kitchener.' Stunned, his friends earnestly pleaded with him. 'Henry, for God's sake, my good man. You mustn't do this. Please think of Harriet downstairs,' said one. 'I know you've lost a lot tonight. We all have, but your house? Henry, please don't do it. It's not worth it,' said another.

Henry Cox wouldn't listen; he had lost too much to back down now; he had a perfect hand. He looked at Edward to see how he was reacting to possibly losing such an enormous amount of money, almost the entire evening's take. Edward wore his practiced poker face, revealing nothing. 'I call,' said Henry and, with complete confidence, proudly showed a straight flush. The men looked at Edward, waiting for him to reveal his hand. He glanced at each of them in turn and then broke his poker face with a sly smirk. He held back for a few seconds, building the drama as he had seen the professionals do in Paris, and then, slowly revealed the best, once-in-a-lifetime hand a player can hold in poker – a royal flush. Henry was absolutely stunned, and everybody saw the terrified sense of dread on his ashen face. As Henry's tears flowed, slowly building to the cries of an utterly defeated human being, Edward gleefully scooped up all the money and the note. Henry Cox went home that night and shot himself. Edward had his townhouse.

Six months went by, some slowly, and some more quickly as Liam became accustomed to the routine of a horse and sheep farm. He loved breaking in the brumbies. They bucked and kicked with the same wild and fiery spirit his beloved Connemara ponies had. He rode several up-and-coming thoroughbred stallions and fillies, and he steadily learned more and more about effective horse breeding techniques. Now that Dunsley had cemented his reputation by winning the premier horse race in Western Australia, he and Liam had interesting conversations as they watched Rhapsody and other thoroughbred stallions siring fillies provided by other colonists. Their relationship grew further during the endless hours they spent training future winners.

To Liam's surprise, Dunsley had a genuine interest in the history of the indigenous Australians. While he loved to talk horses with John Martin, Big Norman, and fellow horse breeders whose visits were a welcome but rare occurrence in this remote outpost, none of them seemed to possess Liam's curiosity and intellect. 'I can understand why they don't farm like we do,' said Dunsley. 'This weather can break a man real fast. Food production here is a very risky business. When drought comes to one area, they simply move back and forth depending on the weather. We obviously can't do that and, unlike us, they can survive in the desert. They know how to detect water and hunt, and they know what's edible and what's poison, so they can survive the lean years.' 'That makes sense,' said Liam, recalling that Dunsley's friend had gone broke during a sustained drought. 'But they don't raise horses or cattle or have plants as we know them, so they're limited in what they can grow, right?' 'Precisely,' said Dunsley. 'This is the last continent in the world to be occupied by Europeans. The Aboriginal peoples have been cut off from the rest of the world for thousands of years. Their hunter-gatherer lifestyle and their minimal temporary shelter needs make a lot of sense'. 'Originally, though,' said Liam bravely, 'they lived on the most fertile lands here, before they were taken from them by the white man. It would seem that they learned to survive in the desert because they had to, not because they wanted to.' Dunsley took it well. 'I can't dispute that, but I find it fascinating that there is less cultural change here than on any other continent.' Liam thought for a moment, then surprised Dunsley with an interesting observation. 'When

I was repairing ships on the London docks for the better part of three years, there were people coming and going every day from all over the world. They brought supplies, they tried out new inventions, and they all worked together solving big problems. If you're cut off from that sort of give and take, how can you develop?' 'Very true,' said Dunsley, impressed by Liam's theory. 'It also didn't help their having thousands of miles of uninhabitable deserts, impeding interactions between the tribes. For thousands of years, they travelled around in their own little world, small groups with their own walkabouts. They were hostile to other tribes who invaded their territory. Did you know that they don't have a written language?' 'They don't?' 'No. It's all handed down orally. They don't see any need for it. Anything that would not enhance their way of life is ignored. Anything worth remembering is remembered. They simply accept now and don't question it, thus they don't have a word for "why".' 'Why not?' asked Liam. 'Asking "why" is offensive to them. They believe that time will reveal the answer, so they don't worry about it. They accept things and people as they are. What is, is. It's as simple as that, they live in the now.'

Liam could relate to this notion: he could do nothing about the past, and there was no guarantee of a free future, so he tried to accept the now as best he could. 'Did you know that there are about two hundred thousand words in the English language?' asked Dunsley. 'No.' 'Do you know how many the Aboriginal peoples have?' 'No.' 'They only have about three thousand.' 'That's pretty basic, isn't it?' 'Yes. For example, they have no words for left or right. They just point with their lower lip.' 'I haven't noticed them doing that.' 'It's very subtle. They don't have a word for time or for days of the week either. It's all about now. They can't change the future, so they don't worry about it.' Liam thought about that for a while as he watched Norman on a gallop. 'In a way, 'tis a gift, isn't it?' 'Yes, quite a different culture altogether. I quite admire them for that.'

Sharing space in the large stable, Liam was soaking up Aboriginal culture. Fascinated by the sound of the yidaki, he was determined to learn how to play it, and by now he had befriended Kumba, the young man who had introduced it to him at the Perth races. Once again, the power of music brought two completely different cultures together. Naturally, not sharing in Liam's concept of time, Kumba didn't know his age, but Liam estimated that he was about twenty. Standing about five feet five with blue eyes and skin as black as night, Kumba had slightly-curly blond hair, long and matted.

Always wearing a friendly open smile, Kumba, meaning black fruit tree, had worked for Dunsley for several years and had learned some basic English. His father was a 'Wati,' meaning an elder, well respected by his tribe. Each evening after work, with Kumba's patient help, Liam practiced and became increasingly better at playing the yidaki. The other Aboriginal people, including Kumba's father, were suspicious of this white man who showed no hostility or superiority whatsoever towards them, while appreciating their music and trying hard to learn it. Their initial fear began to diminish, as Liam even began to speak some basic Aboriginal sentences.

He learned that, in fact, they used to farm some perennial crops such as yams and tuber potatoes, contradicting Dunsley's theory that they had always been hunter-gatherers. Liam sensed that perhaps this belief was an attempt to assuage Dunsley's guilt about dispossessing them of their fertile lands, pushing them into the inferior arid wastelands of his country.

Liam noticed that Kumba cowered in fear every time he passed a certain tree as they walked the horses. 'What is it Kumba?' In his broken English, Kumba explained that, whenever his people displeased the white man, that was the tree where they would be chained by the wrists and ankles and left to dangle all day in the hot sun. Once again, Liam took the side of the underdog and was determined to show them that not all white men were cruel. He asked Kumba if he could address the tribal elders, as he had something important to tell them at their next ceremony.

After a week, when Liam had begun to think they wouldn't allow a white man to attend, Kumba said that the elders had made their decision. 'Tomorrow.' The following night, when farm work was done and all the tribesmen were present, the ceremony began with their traditional moment of silence; this was a mark of respect to allow the gathering area to become accustomed to their presence. Wati let out a small cough to signal that it was now permissible for Liam to speak, but rather than talking, Liam played the yidaki for several minutes.

By now they were all aware that this strange white man was learning their yidaki, but in the solemn presence of all the elders, without a single white man present other than Liam, the mood took on a serious tone as Liam droned on, trying to convey the right and respectful sounds that Kumba had patiently taught him. They knew he wasn't like the other white men. He didn't look down on them but treated them as equals; he ate with them and tried to talk to them in their own language, something no other white man had ever done.

When he finished the song, Liam handed the yidaki to Kumba. 'Sorry, sorry. Ngayulu, ngayulu,' he said. Everybody looked at each other in surprise at hearing a white man speaking their language. He had their attention! He had practiced a few sentences with Kumba and, with his help translating, Liam apologised about the treatment their people had suffered at the hands of the white man. He told them that where he came from, his people too suffered the same treatment from the white man.

The elders nodded to him, acknowledging their understanding that he was speaking from the heart. They beckoned for him to continue. He told them about his people far away being pushed off their lands and into the badlands of his country. He explained that this was why he and the other men were here. He told them that not all men with white faces were bad, and that this was his reason for calling them all together.

There was a long silence, then the banging of sticks began and they started on their yidakis. The ceremony continued until Wati gestured for them to stop. He stood and told Kumba to ask Liam to come forward. Liam rose and walked solemnly over to Wati and all the other elders. 'Yagan,' said Wati smiling. He signalled for the music to begin again, and the song-man started chanting. Then the Aboriginals started blowing their yidakis. Two others started banging on their sticks, and the ceremony continued. 'Brother,' said Kumba smiling. 'Yagan, brother.' Liam smiled knowingly and said thank you to Kumba, aware that Kumba would not reply. He had learned that, as a part of their culture, they were expected to give and share what they have. Words like please or thank you were, therefore, meaningless to them. Liam, a stranger in a strange place, was now family and considered a brother.

Liam's time in Australia had been a period of unexpected

enrichment: he'd enjoyed foaling season at the horse farm, witnessed the amazing results of mating one thoroughbred horse to another, learned volumes about ranching in extreme climates, and mastered the yidaki and the basics of the Aboriginal language. He was intrigued to discover that some of their native customs mirrored the ancient native laws of Ireland known as the Brehon Laws, which had long been in practice before British rule. 'Whoever comes to your door you must feed him and care for him with no questions asked' was one of the ancient Brehon laws. The Aboriginal peoples had shown Liam nothing but kindness. When an Aboriginal man or woman died, the tribe had a wailing session similar to the Irish tradition of 'caoiners' hired for a wake. Liam saw that the people wailing would lie face down in the sand at a burial. He laughed to himself when he remembered his uncles' lying face down on the floor at a wake, after collapsing from drinking too much poitín! One custom he found to be uniquely different: When an Aboriginal man died, his wife was not allowed to speak to anyone for a year. Sadly, Aboriginal women were considered to be very much inferior to men. Although the ancient Irish lived in similarly primitive dwellings, when it came to women and marriage, Irish women enjoyed considerably more equality than Aboriginal women. Eight hundred years ago under Brehon Law on the first of February, each year, a husband or wife could decide to walk away from their marriage union, no questions asked.

Day by day Liam gained greater acceptance by Kumba and his tribe. He was invited to share 'damper,' where they lit a small fire in the middle of their huts and, using flour and water, made a kind of flat bread, baking it in the hot ashes of the fire. They taught him how to hunt with a boomerang. After months of practice, he was able to throw a boomerang about three hundred feet and drop a kangaroo, hitting it precisely in the leg or knee. He also learned how to throw a boomerang into a flying flock of birds, and almost every time, drop at least one. He watched in awe as Kumba, a master hunter, threw his boomerang over a flock of ducks. It hovered perfectly over them. Mistaking it for a hawk, as Kumba had intended, the ducks dove towards hunters waiting with nets and clubs. Liam was the only white man in his time to ever participate in this remarkable hunting method.

Liam tried to grasp their beliefs. They called it Jukurrpa, dreamtime – in a manner similar to Ireland's Brehon laws, Jukurrpa established moral, practical and spiritual laws governing Aboriginal societies. It included much knowledge and stories held by the elders. Jukurrpa is based on the belief that ancestral beings helped to create features on the land, including waterways, plants, animals, hills and valleys and people. This Liam thought was similar to the Tuatha de Danann, who form part of the folklore of the indigenous supernatural people of Ireland. Kumba explained how the low mountain ranges of Perth, known as the Darling Ranges, were actually the body of Wagyl – a huge ancestral being, serpent-like who meandered all over the earth creating land and rivers.

After supper, one of Liam's last duties was to ensure that all of the horses were settled down for the night. Leaving the barn where he and all the workers slept, he passed Bald Paddy having his last smoke of the day outside the barn. As he walked through the long stables, stroking several of the prized stallions and admiring the mares caring for their new foals, he heard a blood-curdling scream. It seemed to come from Robert Martin's cabin at the far end of the stables. He heard Martin cursing loudly and then a heavy thud. Liam rushed to the front of the stable and shouted to Bald Paddy. 'There's somethin' wrong at Martin's place. Get the lads.' Running to Martin's cabin, he could clearly distinguish that the pained screams were coming from a girl. Following the sounds, he rushed into Martin's bedroom. His massive frame filling the doorway, Liam stopped in his tracks, stunned by what he saw: Martin on the bed raping Kumba's sister, Maali. What humble, tattered clothing she had was torn away from her breasts and hiked up above her hips. Liam saw her tear-stained face and look of terror as she fought her abuser. Disbelief and anger overtook him; he rushed Martin, grabbing him by his shirt and wrestled him off Maali. 'Get the fuck out of here; this is none of your business,' shouted Martin, obviously drunk and sweating profusely. He pushed Liam against the wall and moved to mount Maali again. Disgusted, Liam hit him with a right hook, and Martin went down in a heap. Martin wiped the blood off his mouth, gave Liam an evil smirk, and shouted, 'You fucking bastard, do you know what you've just done?' He charged at Liam again, slamming him against the cabin wall.

Bald Paddy, Murdock, and Reedy rushed in and pulled them off each other. A terrified Maali, holding onto whatever dignity she could muster, tried to cover her body with the few scraps she had left of her clothing. Crying, she ran from the room. 'This is the biggest mistake of your life,' said Martin, as Dunsley came into the room. 'She's only fifteen you bastard,' screamed Liam. Maali's job was cleaning Dunsley's and Martin's homes. But after Martin's few brandies at Dunsley's, Maali was in the wrong place at the wrong time. 'Tie him up,' said Dunsley, and reluctantly, Murdock and Reedy went to hold Liam. 'What's this?' said

Liam, shaking them away. 'HE was raping her. I saved her. Tie THAT bastard up.' With an agonised look on his face, Bald Paddy said, 'I'm sorry Horse,' as they grabbed him roughly and tied his hands behind his back. 'Jesus Christ, Dunsley,' pleaded Liam, 'come on, you can't do this, this is wrong, all wrong.' 'No one is allowed to touch my manager. NO ONE,' shouted Dunsley. 'So, she's worth nothing?' spat Liam. 'Not worth dying for,' said Martin, confident that he had Dunsley's full support. 'Dying for?' asked Liam shocked. The gravity of what he had done began to sink in. 'I see,' said Liam bitterly. 'Ye never change do ye? There's one law for you, and one for everybody else. Whatever ye decide it to be.' 'Take him away,' ordered Dunsley.

They brought him to a small hut and locked him in for the night. Liam couldn't believe what had just happened. *Martin couldn't be right, could he? They're going to kill me over this? He was raping somebody. I saved her. Jesus,* he thought, *Bald Paddy, Murdock, and Reedy tied me up. My friends tied me up!* It slowly dawned on Liam that his friends couldn't help him. Abandoned, on his own, he slumped to the floor.

The next morning Martin and two of his cronies dragged Liam out to the tree so feared by the Aboriginal people there. Martin didn't say a word to Liam. Exactly as Kumba had described, they chained his wrists and ankles, hoisted him up, and left him dangling in the tree to face the punishing sun all day. Nobody was allowed to talk to him or give him water. After a few hours, Liam's tongue felt like a rock. Sometime during this, the longest day of Liam's life, he heard Dunsley shouting up at him. 'Why didn't you just walk away like Robert said, you stupid bastard?' Liam could barely open his eyes. Dunsley raged on. 'I was about to appoint you to be Robert's right-hand man; you would have had your own cabin. I was going to ask the magistrate to commute your life sentence. She's only a blackie. Why did you have to ruin it all for yourself?' 'She's a human being,' whispered Liam, barely able to talk. 'You're so fucking naive. Haven't you seen that they care more about their fucking dingoes than they do about their women?' 'She's only a child,' pleaded Liam. 'She's a fucking BLACKIE,' Dunsley roared with pure hatred, 'and now you're going to hang for her. Was it worth it?' 'You're going to hang me for that?' Liam was shocked to hear that he was indeed going to hang. 'If I show you any mercy, it's only a matter of time before all discipline breaks down, and we could face a mutiny here. I can't allow that; not even for you.' 'What a waste,' were Dunsley's last words to Liam, as he shook his head and walked away. He was the absolute master of his land – judge, jury, and executioner.

As the sun and dehydration took their toll, Liam experienced a constant, splitting headache. Between temporary blackouts and hallucinations, he tried to grasp the reality that they were going to hang him. He thought of his promise to Máire that he would return somehow; now he would never see her or his son again. *So, this is it? Me hanging from a tree because I saved a girl from being raped.* He cried out in desperation.

Come nightfall, Bald Paddy disobeyed Dunsley's order and quietly approached the dreaded tree where his friend was now tied. He looked up at Liam's swollen, sunburned face. 'I'm sorry Horse,' he said, speaking in Irish. 'There's nothin' any of us can do. Why the hell didn't you just walk away?' 'I couldn't. She's Kumba's sister,' said Liam barely able to whisper from dehydration. 'He was like a wild animal. She's only fifteen, I couldn't walk away. I couldn't.'

'They're going to hang you tomorrow,' said Bald Paddy, crying, and hating how helpless and ashamed he felt. 'Jesus Paddy, will we ever be free of them?' said Liam bitterly. 'I know,' said Paddy, a huge lump in his throat. 'This is all I have; the same goes for all of us. If we leave here, we've nothin'. I'm so sorry Horse. I'm so sorry.' Liam could see Paddy's tears. 'Will ya be there tomorrow? I want to die looking at an Irishman.' Paddy choked. 'Yes,' he said, broken-hearted.

At a safe distance from the ranch, there was a long meeting of the Elders that day, convened by Kumba and Maali's father. They argued back and forth for hours, until eventually Kumba was summoned. 'Yagan out,' said Kumba's father. 'Get him to water,' he commanded. 'Give him when he at water,' and he handed Kumba a small but heavy leather pouch. The elders knew there would be repercussions if they saved Liam, but they could see that clearly, he was different from other white men. That was the tremendous sacrifice they, especially Kumba and his father, were willing to make for Yagan, their brother. As Kumba took the pouch, he saw that his father had been crying. He realised then, that by freeing Liam, he himself could never return. He would never be able to see his parents or sister again. He wept as he looked at his father and all the other elders in the room. He truly considered Liam his brother and, knowing that he was now Liam's only chance, he dutifully nodded his head. He visited Maali one last time, and seeing her swollen face as she moaned quietly, curled up foetally, he was certain of what he had to do. He said goodbye to his brokenhearted mother and began preparing for Liam's rescue.

No guard was posted. Nobody would consider helping Liam knowing the backlash they would face from Dunsley.

At around three that morning, with all of their dingoes far away so that they wouldn't bark, Kumba and some of his friends cut Liam down from the tree and carried him off to a hidden place. There, Liam desperately drank water as the men rubbed cream on his blistered face, an immediate soothing relief. The men knew that, if they stole horses, several in their tribe would be hanged, so they had to walk. And to avoid retribution, they had to make the escape appear that Kumba acted alone. They shouldered Liam for a couple of miles, heading out for Guildford. As Liam slowly recovered some strength, they said their goodbyes and headed back. 'Thank you,' said Liam. They looked at Liam and said, 'Yagan,' smiled, and then vanished into the night.

Kumba and Liam walked the now familiar path. They had taken it often to Fremantle and Perth, delivering sheep and wool. Reaching Guildford a few hours later, they knew they couldn't take the boat; not being on their usual run, they would have been caught and returned to Dunsley immediately. Stopping to rest, they ate food Kumba had brought and talked about a route through the swamplands between Guildford and Fremantle. By now it was daylight, so they would be able to see where they were going. And though it was only ten miles downriver, they were forced to go miles out of their way through the spongy, snake-infested swamp, following the firmest ground they could find.

It was nearing dusk when they reached Fremantle Harbour. From a safe distance, Liam saw two massive ships docked at the wharf, vessels similar to the one that had brought him to Australia. To check out the origins of the ships, they waited until dark, and then they joined everyone roaming freely on the wharf. They approached the first ship and saw the British flag flying from its mast. Soldiers guarded the boarding gate, checking the papers of sailors coming and going. Nonchalantly they passed the British ship and approached the second one which was considerably larger. Fluttering in the breeze from its rear mast was a flag Liam had never seen before. It was the same red, white and blue as the British flag. Rectangular in shape, it had horizontal red and white stripes. In its upper left-hand corner were multiple white stars on a square, dark blue field. He didn't see a single soldier aboard and, to his surprise, saw men of all colours leaving and boarding the ship without being asked for papers.

Liam stopped one of the men who had just disembarked. 'When are you setting sail?' 'First light tomorrow,' he replied, in an accent Liam had never heard before. 'Where are you heading?' 'The Pacific. We're a whaling ship; we picked up supplies here.' Liam had heard about such ships. He couldn't believe his good fortune, and he knew this was his escape. His only escape. He had to get on that ship. 'American?' he asked. 'Yep, Massachusetts.' Liam knew of Massachusetts. It was where Úna and Paudie Casey had immigrated to live with her uncle so many years ago. 'Boston?' asked Liam. 'New Bedford.' 'Are they looking for any extra workers?' 'No, we've got a full crew.' 'Could I talk to somebody? I need to get outta' here.' Glancing at the British ship, he asked, 'You're Irish, aren't you?' 'Yes,' said Liam, wondering if he was going to raise the alarm. Much to Liam's relief, he said, 'My father's Irish. He came over in 1805 from Galway. Do ya know it?' 'Yes, friends of mine left from there about ten years ago.' 'Well, he told me what the English did to Ireland.' 'They're still doing it,' said Liam. 'Yea, I can see that.' They heard British soldiers shouting orders as they passed. 'Look, there's an officer down there. He's the one you should be talking to, not me. Either him or the captain. And come to think of it, I think he's Irish.' 'Thank you,' said Liam. 'You're welcome, I hope you make it.'

Liam was pleasantly surprised by the man's friendliness and openness and wondered if this was the way all Americans were. Kumba and Liam approached the officer who was having a smoke at the end of the wharf. 'Sir, my name is Liam O'Donaghue. I was wondering, are you looking for any help on board. I know my way around ships,' said Liam positively, but in a humble tone. 'No, son,' said the older officer, 'we have a full crew right now.' Liam persisted. 'I know how to mend sails. I can cook. And I can read and write. Unimpressed, the officer said, 'I'm sorry,' and started walking back to the ship. Liam saw his last chance evaporating, and now his only option was to head across the desert, definite suicide as Bald Paddy had said. Kumba watched the officer walk away, and when he saw the defeated look on Liam's face, he reached into his pocket and gave Liam the pouch his father had given him. Opening it, Liam couldn't believe what he saw – several gold nuggets in assorted sizes. 'Where did you get these?' he asked Kumba, astonished. Kumba smiled. 'Noongar have gold,' he said, referring to his people. He pointed his lower lip to the officer almost at the ship.

Liam took out two decent-sized nuggets and ran after the officer. 'Excuse me sir,' said Liam as he caught up with him, 'would these get me on board?' The officer looked at the gold nuggets, estimating that even sharing them with his captain, he was looking at the equivalent of at least a year's pay. 'Come with me,' he said. They walked on in silence. 'Wait here,' he said, leaving to board the ship. After a few minutes, the officer came down the gangplank with another man. 'This is Captain Larsen,' said the officer. The captain looked Liam up and down. 'Looks like you need to get outta' here,' he said, seeing Liam's red blistered face and torn clothes. 'Yes sir,' said Liam. 'Show me the gold,' he said. When Liam handed Larsen the gold, his eyes widened. These were the biggest nuggets he had ever seen. The captain beckoned to his officer to follow him. 'Just a second,' he said to Liam, handing him back the nuggets. The men walked up the wharf, just out of earshot. Liam could see both men in deep conversation mulling over the proposal. Then he saw them nodding their heads as they turned and walked back. Frustrated, he couldn't read their faces. These were hardened sailors who had seen and done it all, and Liam's life depended on whatever Larsen said next. 'Look, we're going out to sea tomorrow, and we won't be coming back to land for months. We can get you to America, but it could be three years or more. That's it.' Liam's whole body shuddered with relief; he was getting on. He took a few short breaths and looked at Larsen, nodding his head. His hands trembled in grateful disbelief as he handed the gold to Larsen. 'Okay then,' said Larsen, 'let's get you on board.'

Liam turned to Kumba, knowing his farewell to his great friend would be one of the hardest goodbyes he would ever be forced to say. 'Kumba go with Yagan,' said Kumba seriously, without his usual big open smile. 'What?' asked Liam, shocked. 'Kumba go with Yagan,' he repeated, but now with a worried face. Suddenly it made sense. Because he'd saved Liam's life, Kumba couldn't return to his family. What could he do? Where could he go? Spend the rest of his life going walkabout? Liam looked expectantly at Captain Larsen. 'I'm all the family he has.' The captain shrugged and gestured to them both to go aboard.

'There's a letter for Tomás from Australia,' said the postman. 'Come on inside and tell me,' said Josie, excited that Liam had managed to send another letter. But the postman quickly dashed her hopes. 'It's from Bridget Dowd.' 'Bridget Dowd?' asked Josie, blessing herself. 'Mother of God, I thought she was dead.' 'Well, she must have been picked to go to Australia,' said the postman. 'We'll have to wait until Máire comes home, and Tomásheen can read the letter,' said Josie.

Everybody had assumed that Bridget was dead, along with her parents and eight brothers and sisters. Like so many others, they had been evicted from their home, mercilessly thrown out into the Irish countryside in the dead of winter for not paying their rent.

As a last resort, like most desperate Irish peasants, the Dowds had probably gone to the Galway workhouse in search of food and shelter. It was a miserable choice: die on the road or die in those disease-ridden buildings which had become horribly overcrowded during the worst years of the famine. The inmates were forced to break rocks, build roads to nowhere, and carry out many other pointless physical tasks for pennies a day. In their last desperate search for food, families entered these huge, austere buildings. Men and women were immediately separated from each other, as were brothers and sisters, never to see each other again. Children were pulled from their mothers as young as two years of age. They were packed into long, cold dormitories with forty to fifty people in each dormitory, often four to each bed. Some healthy families were fortunate to be given passage to America and Canada through the generosity of local benefactors, who showed some Christian charity towards their fellow human beings, but these lucky few were very much the exception. Most people who entered Irish workhouses succumbed to dysentery, scurvy, typhoid and measles while cholera swept through those overcrowded prison-like buildings.

During the famine, Earl Grey, Secretary of State for War and the Colonies, fashioned a plan to ease the overcrowding in Irish workhouses, while providing servant staff and future wives for Britain's newest colony. Smallpox-free, healthy, usually orphaned girls, some as young as fourteen, were shipped to Australia to address its acute shortage of women. Between 1848 and 1850, approximately four thousand Irish girls were sent to Australia. They became known as the 'Potato Orphans' or 'Famine Orphan Girls'. Most girls found employment within weeks of their arrival as domestics or indentured servants, while others worked as cooks at the gold fields. The luckier girls married after their period of indenture was over and many of them spent the rest of their lives in remote farms or outstations, often being the only European women for hundreds of miles.

When Máire came home from work at the mansion, Josie stepped over to her and put her arm around her shoulder. 'Máire, there's a letter from Australia.' Tensing, Máire pulled away and looked expectantly at Josie. 'I'm sorry Máire,' said Josie. 'It's not from Liam. 'Tis from Bridget Dowd.' 'Mother of God,' said Máire, clearly disheartened. She took a deep breath, 'I thought she was dead.' 'We all did. She must have been picked to go to Australia.' 'What was she, sixteen years old?' asked Máire. 'I think so. She was the eldest child, a fine strong little girl as I remember.'

Máire looked at the creased, stained letter that had come all the way from Australia, so unlike the pristine letter she had received from Liam via England. It had the same Queen Victoria stamp, but it was heavier than Liam's. As before, everybody eagerly waited for little Tomás to read it to them. As he carefully opened it, money fell to the floor. Colm jumped out of his seat and picked it up. 'There's four pounds here!' he exclaimed. Everybody was shocked at such a huge amount. He placed it on the table, and they all stared in amazement at the most money they had ever seen. 'Okay Tomás,' said Máire, 'please read the letter.' Sitting tall in his chair, Tomás, 'the scholar,' as they called him, began to read Bridget's amazing story:

Dear Ma,

I'm sending this letter to Tomás O'Donaghue so he can give it to you when you come back from the workhouse. After they took me away, I was put on a boat to Australia. It took nearly three months. After I stopped crying, it wasn't so bad. There were about two hundred girls and some convict wives and their children on the huge sailing ship.

I looked after a girl called Anne Deely. She was only fourteen. Her tears flowed down her freckled face every night as she cried herself to sleep. The food was much better on the ship than in the workhouse. There was a teacher who tried to teach us to read. She beat us if we made mistakes, but I am able to read and write a little now.

It seemed like we sailed forever. Sometimes it was very cold, other times it was too hot.

When we arrived in Sydney, we were marched up from the quay and people spat and shouted names at us. We were so frightened. They walked us up to a big building where we slept on hard iron beds. They taught us needlework and how to clean houses.

Every morning, we got up early to get ready for the people who came to give us work. We had to make sure our clothes were clean so they would hire us. They brought six of us at a time into a room and men asked us questions. Somebody took Anne Deely away and I never saw her again. Anybody who came from a farm was taken away quickly. I heard that these girls were taken hundreds of miles into the bush to marry farmers.

I got a job in Ipswich, a small town about five hundred miles from Sydney. I am a domestic, and I get paid eight pounds a year. I put money in the envelope so you could buy food. I will send more next year. I miss you all so much.

Your loving daughter,
Bridget

There was a long silence as everybody thought about Bridget and all the other girls: poor, alone, and shipped to the other side of the world. Máire tried to imagine how they must have felt, taken from everything they had ever known, despairing, lonely girls, many just teenagers. The realisation that Bridget didn't know that she was the only surviving member in the Dowd family of eleven, made her letter all the more poignant. 'May God give her strength to carry on,' said Josie. 'What will we do with the money?' asked Colm. 'We'll send it back. We'll get Tomásheen to write a letter to her letting her know about her family,' said Josie. 'God knows, she'll need the money herself over there, even though the news will break her heart, she needs to know, the poor girleen. May God be merciful to her mother and father and all her brothers and sisters.' Máire went to sleep that night grateful to Bridget for giving her a little more information about what Liam faced on his long, forced journey to Australia.

'McCarthy's the name,' said the officer, leading them up the gangplank. Then heading below deck he said, 'You're going to be in the forecastle.' 'The forecastle?' asked Liam. 'Yes, you'll see,' said McCarthy. He led them into a narrow, triangular-shaped room under the main deck in the front of the ship. 'This is where the ordinary crewmen live and sleep.' 'Get these men some clothes,' barked McCarthy to one of the sailors. Liam saw narrow bunks lining the wall, bunks similar to those on the convict ship, but there the similarities ended. The boat was filthy. The walls were black and slimy. The air was foul, as was the language. He saw large rats and soon learned that cockroaches, bed bugs, and fleas were a way of life here because the oil and whale blood were never completely removed from the filthy decks.

McCarthy led them to the two last bunks at the very front of the ship. They were empty because, once the sea got choppy, anybody trying to sleep in them endured the worst rocking on the entire ship. They didn't have to unpack. They had nothing except Kumba's boomerang and club. When they heard the orders to man all stations, they put on their welcome change of clothes, and went on deck to watch the sailors unfurl the smaller sails as the ship slowly left the wharf and headed downriver to the ocean. Standing on the deck to begin his long journey home with no chains on his feet, and no soldiers shouting orders, Liam was exhilarated. *I'm a free man*! he thought, choking back tears. And as they finally left the mouth of the Swan River he whispered, *Máire, I'm coming back to you.*

After just two weeks at sea, Liam had already learned much about whaling ships. There was big money in whale hunting. Whale oil was used for candle wax, as a lubricant in machinery, and for oil lamps – especially sperm whale oil, which burned cleanly and brightly. They called it liquid gold because it got the highest price on the market. Whale oil sold from one pound to two fifty a barrel, so it was a luxury only the rich could afford.

Though separated from their families for years, whalers could make more than landsmen, but working conditions were brutal. In tiny, flimsy open boats, the men hunted sixty-foot-long, eighty-ton sea monsters with huge, lethal tails and razor-sharp teeth. It was a strange way of life, and only the hardiest and most adventurous of men survived it.

Meals and quarters reflected the ship's class structure. The captain, of course, had his own suite in the rear of the ship where he enjoyed the smoothest sailing conditions. The officer mates, like McCarthy, had smaller cabins, also towards the back of the ship. Harpooners, cooks, cask makers and the blacksmith had midship bunks. The ordinary sailors slept in the worst section of the boat, right up front, as did Liam and Kumba.

The whaling ship had a deep hull to hold hundreds of barrels of whale oil. It was specially designed to get close enough to whales for the kill, with the minimum amount of crew required, to afford the ship's owner a greater profit. Lashed to the highest mast was a barrel in which a spotter stood and looked for whales.

Thirty-five men and five women were aboard. One of the women was the captain's wife who also served as the ship's nurse. Two of the women were married to two of the officers; one was married to a harpooner, and the fifth woman was married to a cask maker. These women chose the discomforts of life at sea over years of lonely separation from their husbands. Four thirty-foot whaleboats swung from davits, while two spare boats were stowed atop each other midship, on the top deck.

Liam found that, sadly, the food for the ordinary sailors had nowhere near the quality of food on the convict ship. It ranged from barely edible to revolting, but the men's hard work gave them hearty appetites, even for the repetitive fare of greasy pork, potatoes, hard biscuits, and cockroach-laden molasses used to sweeten their tea or coffee. The captain, his officers, and the more specialised crewmen enjoyed the best food: poultry, pork, and clean vegetables. Though the men were packed into cramped quarters, the sailors learned that it was wise to tolerate each other's racial and personality differences because any insubordination resulted in a flogging by a multi-tailed whip called a cat-o-nine.

Liam learned that Captain Larsen started as an ordinary sailor and had worked his way up to become captain of his ship. He was impressed with that concept, for he had grown up being told that he had no chance of ever getting ahead because he was born Irish. Even so, Liam was beginning to learn that cultural stereotypes and bias persisted everywhere; black and brown men were limited in potential for advancement.

In the late afternoons, sailors came up on deck and smoked their pipes. They talked, read, and mended their clothes. Liam was delighted when some of them broke into lively singing and dancing. He heard black men singing about slavery in America and was fascinated by how well and expressively they sang, naturally relating to their stories. Liam had been hearing wild tales about whaling and couldn't wait to witness an actual hunt.

When they returned to America, each man would receive a 'lay,' a percentage of the profits. The ship owner would naturally receive the lion's share. The captain earned one eighth of the lay. On a full ship he would earn approximately six thousand dollars. Then the percentages would drop depending on seniority. The ordinary seaman might earn five hundred dollars for several years' work, sometimes ending up in debt to the ship's owner when cash advances for families back home and tobacco, boots, or clothes would be deducted from his lay.

Early one morning Liam awoke to the shouts of the whale spotter. 'THERE SHE BLOWS!' While everybody scrambled to man their stations, Liam looked out and saw nothing. After a few minutes, the ship turned to where the spotter pointed, and then he saw it. He couldn't believe how colossal it was, spouting enormous amounts of water into the air. 'He's a forty barrel,' shouted a sailor. 'He's a what?' asked Liam. 'He'll fill forty barrels of oil. He's a sperm whale. They're the most profitable.' 'Why so?' asked the forever-inquiring Liam. 'They have fatty oil in their heads, barrels of it. It's the most valuable oil and will fetch the highest price on the market.'

Liam was impressed by how remarkably literate and relatively well-educated most of the crew were. Although these men went off to seek adventure, hunted the biggest game, visited islands and faraway places that no one ever saw, and dallied with exotic women, most found misery and disappointment in this occupation and gave up after one or two voyages.

When the captain ordered that all boats be lowered, Liam got an up-close look at whaleboats. They were sturdier than Colm's currach, but not by much. About thirty feet long and six feet wide, each of the boats was painted front and rear with bright colours for easy identification at long distances. Each boat had a mast, sail, rudder, paddles, and oars. The oars were the longest Liam had ever seen – about twenty feet long. Liam and Kumba watched as the boats were lowered into the water. Six men got into each boat

– four rowers in the middle, a harpooner up front, and an officer at the rear.

After about an hour's hard rowing, they reached the whale and succeeded in driving two harpoons into it. When, after a short while, the whale started to feel the harpoons, it took off at full speed. The wounded animal tried to escape by diving deeply, pulling taut the hemp line attached to the harpoon. The sailors frantically wet the hemp rope to prevent it from smoking and possibly breaking as it ran out rapidly.

The other boats launched their harpoons when the whale resurfaced. The besieged animal circled the perimeter of the four boats roaring loudly and spouting blood-reddened water high into the air, drenching some of the sailors. When the four boats went in for the kill, several of the sailors, knowing precisely where to aim, pierced the whale with long lances. Finally, the whale lost its strength and slowly turned over, 'fin out,' as the whale hunters called it. All six men in each of the four boats started rowing back to the mother ship, towing the whale behind them. Liam watched as they made slow progress straining with every bit of strength they had, dragging eighty tons of deadweight through the water.

When at last the whale was brought alongside, it was secured to the ship with a hefty chain. 'All hands,' shouted the captain. With sharks swarming around the bloody whale, a particularly brave sailor mounted the corpse to insert a huge hook into its head. The sailors began to hoist the whale up out of the water, so that the butchering could begin. As they pulled, they sang a lively sea shanty.

HAUL THE BOWLIN' THE FORE AND MAINTOP
HAUL THE BOWLIN', HAUL THE BOWLIN'

HAUL THE BOWLIN' THE BULLY BULLY BOWLIN' HAUL THE BOWLIN', THE BOWLIN' HAUL

The singing seemed to put life and strength into every man, and each strong pull brought the whale closer to the rigging. More strong ropes tied it up against the ship. With a huge cutting apparatus, they started removing large strips of blubber off the whale, lifting them on board with an enormous hook. There, the strips were cut down to suitable sizes for the next stage called 'trying-out,' the process of boiling oil from the blubber. Liam remembered butchering cows back home, but this was butchering on a huge and disgusting scale. There was blubber everywhere, its smell most foul.

Everyone on board spent the next three days cutting and boiling the blubber, working round the clock in six-hour shifts. Everybody and everything were drenched with oil. The workers reluctantly swallowed their meals, for all they tasted was whale oil. There was no escaping the obnoxious smell.

After the whale was gutted and the 'trying-out' finished, the workers tossed what was left of the carcass overboard to waiting sharks and scavenging birds. Their final step was cleaning the ship with a strong alkali and sand. Only after the cleaning were the men allowed to wash and put on clean clothes and, thankfully, to eat again without the ubiquitous taste of blubber.

'How often do ya do this?' Liam asked an exhausted sailor. 'We did this nearly one hundred fifty times the last time out.' Liam now understood why men didn't sign up for numerous whaling trips, but for many it was one of the few roads to prosperity open to them.

Sure enough, the first hunt Liam witnessed was followed by one after another, and the ship's hold filled with more and more barrels of oil. Like the others aboard, Liam and Kumba became accustomed to the pervading smell of whale oil and partially-decomposed blubber in the hull. 'Ship ahoy,' shouted the spotter. Everyone came on deck to see another whaling ship in the distance. 'It's Thanksgiving,' said one of the sailors. 'Thanksgiving?' asked Liam, unfamiliar with the word. 'Yes. A group of pilgrims broke away from the Church of England and landed in Plymouth in 1620, not too far from New Bedford. They shared a meal with the local Indians who helped them survive their first winter there. So, every year, we give thanks.' Liam could relate to the fortune of those early pilgrims who had escaped their country's oppression. He also remembered his own 'Thanksgiving' – breaking bread with the Aboriginal people, and Kumba's having saved his life, while putting his own life in mortal danger.

Within a few hours, the two ships were parallel to each other. They dropped sails and came to a slow crawl. Mrs Larsen, seated in a wicker basket known as a gamming chair, was lowered from the ship to a whaleboat and rowed to the other ship. The other ship's crew lowered their chair and lifted her aboard. The other ladies followed one by one, and soon, most of the crew rowed over to the other ship to celebrate Thanksgiving. Liam got his first taste of mince pie laid on especially for the occasion, and soon, with music filling the deck, everybody enjoyed this brief respite from the monotony of whale hunting.

On a hunt a week later, one of the sailors became entangled in the hemp line attached to the harpoon and drowned when the whale dove to escape. This was the first fatality ever on Captain Larsen's ship, and it cast a pall over the entire crew. Once again Liam attended a burial-at-sea service.

Ever the adventurer, Liam offered to take the dead sailor's place on the next hunt. 'I can row as well as anybody; I did it all the time in Ireland,' he told Officer McCarthy, exaggerating his skills somewhat. 'My brother was a fisherman. We were always out,' he said, 'and you're short a man.' McCarthy saw before him a strong, sturdy man offering his services, a man who didn't have to step up. They'd had a deal that didn't involve Liam and Kumba's working in any way, but he was indeed short a man. And, impressed by how Liam and Kumba worked every bit as much as the other sailors cutting up the blubber, he didn't have to think too long. 'Okay, be ready next time,' he said. Delighted, Liam wondered if Kumba might be interested. 'Kumba, do you want to go?' 'Kumba no. Yagan go,' was Kumba's quick and emphatic reply.

'THERE SHE BLOWS,' shouted the spotter a few days later. Excited, Liam prepared to board one of the whaleboats. 'You're with me,' shouted McCarthy. 'She's a Baleen,' yelled the spotter. Liam sensed that everyone was more excited than they'd been on any of the previous hunts. 'A Baleen?' McCarthy explained, 'Baleen whales have a cartilage in their mouths which filters out little fish. It's called baleen. When we cut it out and clean it, it has numerous uses: for corsets, hoops, bodices, undergarments, bristles for brushes, ribs for umbrellas, carriage springs, and fishing poles. It sells for three dollars a pound. One whale could be worth as much as fifty thousand dollars.' 'Mother of God,' said Liam. 'That's a fortune!' 'So, let's go get it,' McCarthy said confidently, and they lowered themselves into the whaleboat.

McCarthy stood on a narrow piece of wood at the rear and started giving orders as the four men rowed away from the ship. The harpooner in the front of the boat was also in charge of steering it. Liam admired the boat's sleek lines, which gave it speed and manoeuvrability. Though he had no problem rowing towards the whale, sadly, the exercise brought back many memories of fishing alone in the currach, none of them pleasantly nostalgic.

Soon, they reached the whale and Liam gasped at the colossal size of this gigantic king of the seas, especially as compared to their tiny whaleboat. As before, two harpoons pierced the whale. After a few moments the whale angrily reared out of the water, a terrifying monster rising from the deep. Liam saw its bulging black eyes peer at his whaleboat. Within moments, its huge tail rose into the air and crashed down, barely missing them but causing a huge wave which overturned the boat and tossed them into the sea. Liam surfaced quickly to see the whale racing forward dragging the two boats behind. Flailing about to stay afloat brought Liam back to the day Colm almost drowned. Thankfully, this water wasn't as numbingly cold at it was in Ireland. The men struggled to keep their heads above water. The whale dove again, and the hemp ropes uncoiled furiously. Suddenly everything was ominously quiet. As the nearest whaleboat crew scrambled to pull the men out of the water and help them back into their boat, the whale, with a fury and power that Liam had never seen before, resurfaced headfirst directly under Captain Larsen's boat, pitching everybody into the sea. Roaring like a lion, it smashed the boat to pieces with its tremendous tail; Larsen and his men, pulled beneath the raging water, didn't have a hope. Again, the whale raced ahead until all nine hundred feet of hemp rope was pulled out of the two whaleboats. Then it dove once more and disappeared.

The sailors recovered three bodies, but Captain Larsen's wasn't found. In complete shock, the men rowed back to the master ship, slowly and in silence. In this sombre quiet, Liam counted his blessings. Captain Larsen's uniquely-coloured whaleboat was not one of the three returning boats. Liam saw Mrs Larsen on deck holding her hand to her mouth in fear, as she saw that it was her husband's boat that was lost. Not seeing her husband on any of the three boats, nor among the three bodies being lifted on board, confirmed tragically, that her husband was lost at sea. In a moment of controlled but grieving kindness, she asked Officer McCarthy, the second in command, to take over for her husband.

McCarthy was first tasked with presiding over the moving ceremony to mourn the ship's unspeakable loss. Liam and Kumba watched as the three sailors were placed in the middle of the ship's deck. Their bodies had been sewn into makeshift canvas shrouds, weighted with lead to help them sink. A wooden plank was placed over the side of the ship. Captain McCarthy recited a passage from scripture and then the sailors placed one of the bodies onto the plank. They raised their end and the remains dropped over the side into the water. They repeated this twice more in solemn silence. Then, knowing that the ship was about a week out from Adelaide, McCarthy decided to put in there to hire more crew and purchase supplies, and to allow Mrs Larsen to disembark. There, she would await a ship that would take her home to America.

As a small token of gratitude from Captain McCarthy, Liam and Kumba were allowed to move into the steerage section of the ship where the harpooners and cask makers bunked. It was an irregularly-shaped, midship compartment. Once the eerie feeling of sleeping in the drowned harpooners and sailors' bunks faded, Liam and Kumba spent a most enjoyable week. They slept well and ate in the main cabin after the captain and first mates left. Generally, they were served the same food as their superiors. Cockroach-free molasses for their tea and coffee was an especially welcome change.

Liam now had a difficult choice to make; whether he should stay on board and hope to get to America in a few years or whether he should he disembark in Adelaide and head for the goldfields of Bathurst. Bathurst was the topic of many a conversation with gold having been discovered there in the early 1850s. Staying on the ship until it arrived in America would leave him penniless. Trying his hand at gold mining would at least give him a chance at making some money. He was also well aware that, lacking papers, he wouldn't be allowed to board an English ship. What to do?

One late afternoon, when Liam asked Captain McCarthy how near Sydney they would be once in Adelaide, McCarthy showed him a map of Australia. From his monthly reading of the Sydney paper, Liam knew that the Bathurst goldfields were about two hundred miles west of Sydney. 'I'd say Adelaide's about eight hundred miles from Sydney,' said McCarthy studying the map. He saw the defeated look on Liam's face. 'Listen, we've just chopped off seventeen hundred miles for you,' he said encouragingly. 'Have you any gold left?' 'A little,' said Liam. 'How far can a horse travel in a day?' asked McCarthy. Liam had told him about his passion for horses. 'On flat land, on a good horse, I'd say about thirty miles or so,' said Liam. 'So, about a month?' Turning to the map again he said, 'Look here.' He pointed to Adelaide and ran his finger over to Sydney, 'Looks like you've got some mountains east of Adelaide, but it looks pretty flat after that.' 'Yes, it does,' said Liam beginning to get excited. 'So go get yourselves a few horses.'

For the remaining week, Liam focused on planning the long journey from Adelaide to Sydney. The atmosphere on board the ship remained one of shock and sorrow. Nobody aboard had ever experienced the tragedy that had befallen them. A dead whale was the designed and assumed outcome, not a dead captain and crew.

Adelaide couldn't come soon enough for everybody to let off some pent-up steam. Nobody saw Mrs Larsen for the remainder of the journey. She mourned quietly in her cabin. When they reached Adelaide Port on the mouth of the River Torres, Liam saw land far more fertile than any he had ever seen at the Swan Colony, and he noticed how much more developed this port was than Fremantle's. There wasn't a single British warship docked at the impressive wharf. People were coming and going noisily but in a relaxed manner. He liked what he saw. As he was saying his goodbyes to his fellow crew members, Captain McCarthy approached. 'A word please,' he said, beckoning Liam to follow him to the quieter side of the ship. 'We've been told that there are no ships sailing to America from here. They frequently go to England, but to get Mrs Larsen back to America, first she has to get to Sydney.' Thinking that McCarthy was about to ask him to take Mrs Larsen along with them, Liam began to panic. McCarthy continued, 'She's in no state to sail to Sydney on her own; she's in a really bad way.' And then his heartbeat quickened when McCarthy made an amazing offer. 'So, we all agree that the best solution is for you to accompany her and get her on a ship to America.' Liam was speechless. *Sydney! America! Home! What was I thinkin'? Eight hundred miles on horseback when there are ships all around me sailin' to everywhere? How stupid are ya, Horse? Sure, don't I have some gold left, probably enough to get us both to Sydney you amadán!'*

McCarthy saw Liam's excitement grow at the thought of not having to traverse the eight hundred miles to Bathurst. 'You get Mrs Larsen safely on her way to America, and you get to Bathurst quicker. What's wrong with that? We'll pay your passage and board in Sydney until you see her safely on her way.' *This is getting better and better*, thought Liam. *Finally, my luck is changing.* 'Mother of God! Thank you, sir,' said Liam excitedly, fully aware of how huge a favour McCarthy was doing for him. 'You're a good man,' said McCarthy. 'You have the makings of a whaling captain in ya if you'd ever be interested.' 'You can have it,' said Liam laughing. 'Well, there's a ship sailing to Sydney in three days' time. I've given the crew the day off before we get back to work tomorrow. Why don't you join the crew and me in Adelaide today? This is our first time here.' 'I'd like that,' said Liam, admiring McCarthy's decency. They walked down the gangplank, entered waiting carriages, and headed down the Port Road for the nine miles or so to Adelaide.

Here, as in Fremantle, Liam saw sheep and wool being loaded onto ships. The December Summer weather was agreeable as they passed acres of wheat farms and vineyards. Then, arriving in Adelaide, they found it to be a bustling city with wide streets and impressive buildings. 'We're the first city in Australia not settled by convicts, but by free men,' said the innkeeper proudly, as they enjoyed lunch. 'There are no transferred convicts in South Australia. We bought land before we came to Australia. We needed labourers, so we paid for healthy men and women of good character to be shipped over free of charge. Our only condition was that they repay their fare by working for us for three or four years. They paid us back, saved until they could buy their own land, and then employed others.' The entire crew explored the elegant Victoria Square and the four smaller squares of beautiful Adelaide, the city named after King William IV's wife. After a memorable night of wine and song, they headed back to the ship.

The following morning, Liam was introduced to Mrs Larsen in the luxury of the captain's stateroom. 'Mrs Larsen,' said Captain McCarthy, 'this is the gentleman who will escort you to Sydney.' Seated on a sofa, Mrs Larsen offered her hand. 'I'm sorry about your husband ma'am,' said Liam, shaking her hand, happy to see that no bowing was expected. 'Thank you.' 'Don't worry about a thing Mrs Larsen, I'll be happy to look after ya.' 'I appreciate that very much. And your name?' 'Liam O'Donaghue, ma'am.' Captain McCarthy gave her a respectful smile, gestured to Liam to follow him, and they left.

Mrs Larsen stayed mostly to herself on the journey to Sydney, so Liam had the most leisurely sail of his lifetime. As a regular passenger, and not a prisoner, he and Kumba had a comfortable cabin, and were astonished at the luxury of it, especially being able to imbibe in fine Australian wines each evening in the ship's plush dining room. The contrast between this vessel and the convict and whaling ships was so striking that Liam felt guilty enjoying it. *Máire, I know how hard you're working for the Kitcheners at this very moment. I only wish you could be here enjoying this with me instead.*

Kumba was squirming – uncomfortable in the suit

Liam had bought him; Captain McCarthy had said that he wouldn't be allowed in the dining room unless he was properly attired. Once seated at the table, he quickly kicked his shoes off and did his best to figure out the formal assortment of knives, forks, and spoons. 'Kumba no like,' he complained. 'Don't worry Kumba,' Liam laughed. 'We'll be a long way from all this in a few days.' Liam took full advantage of the ship's library and eagerly read recent copies of the *Morning Herald*, familiarising himself with the latest world news. While he was relieved to learn that the famine in Ireland was finally over, he was stunned and shaken to read that millions had died or emigrated. Millions! Huge numbers. Cold facts in black and white. Liam could put familiar faces on some of the souls in those abstract numbers: *Peig Shea – the O'Flaherty family – did Mrs O'Flaherty make it to America? I wonder if Mary Lowry and her five children survived – sure, we kept them in their home – but food? Who else among the dead did I know? Are my family and friends still alive? Mother of God, with those numbers is there anybody left alive in Ireland?* He wished he could get another letter to Máire without raising suspicion. *But Máire, did you even get it?* He would give anything to receive a letter from her – ANY news of his family.

When they finally sailed into Sydney Harbour, Liam heard church bells ring out, announcing the one o'clock hour, followed by two answering blasts from the horns of the many ships tied up at the wharf. 'That's the signal that all work is suspended for an hour when everybody eats lunch. It's a tradition here like the siesta is in Spain,' said one of the passengers. Liam, of course, had to ask what 'siesta' meant. Soon they docked, and Liam was taken aback at the bustling wharfs where warehouse workers busily loaded and unloaded huge amounts of sheep and supplies, dwarfing anything he'd ever seen before.

Liam and Kumba helped Mrs Larsen disembark, stowing her luggage on a carriage waiting to take them to their hotel. Mrs Larsen's America-bound ship would depart in three days' time. As they moved along George Street, Liam couldn't believe the opulence of what he saw – myriad fashion shops, huge mansions, and inviting inns – obvious signs of wealth, all clustered together. That evening, the trio ventured to a nearby inn and enjoyed dinner on Captain McCarthy.

Over the next two days, Liam and Kumba saw several hard-faced men, bronzed from the sun, recently arrived from Bathurst, some of them, sadly, squandering their whole year's earnings in just a few days in Sydney. From these men, Liam learned about the most important provisions for the long trek to Bathurst and the best places to get them. 'The first thing you'll need are two good horses. Don't let those bastards sell you any old nags. Be sure to buy colonial half breeds. They're fine hardy climbers and able to endure great fatigue in this damned heat,' said one of the men. 'And don't pay any more than fifteen pounds a horse.' They also learned where the gold buyers were and that the going rate for gold was around fifty-nine shillings an ounce. 'You can buy what you need for panning when you get there,' said another. They told wild stories of men earning fortunes striking gold on their first day's panning, and they told of the heartbreak of many, many others. 'If you're willing to use a pick and spade, dig, drive a barrow, splash ankle-deep in water all day, bear sleet and rain, sleep in damp blankets at night – thankful that they're not entirely saturated – then give it a go,' said one of the men. 'If not, get a job here in Sydney,' he advised. After all Liam had already endured, he felt certain that he could do this, especially having his friend Kumba with him.

Finally, they escorted Mrs Larsen to her ship. Liam was impressed to see that it was a modern steamship similar to one he had worked on in London, and he was delighted that they were finally in commission. This one had three sailing masts, and Liam marvelled that it would only take a month to cross the ocean to San Francisco, as compared to the three long months it had taken for the Mermaid to travel from England to Australia. This was all thanks to the extra power of steam engines, allowing such ships to continue their journeys when storms raged or when winds died down for days or sometimes for weeks. Smiling, Mrs Larsen thanked Liam and Kumba, shaking their hands, and finally the men were free to travel to Bathurst.

By late 1850, Ireland's great hunger was mercifully coming to an end. Both the O'Donaghue and Donnelly families had miraculously survived, thanks to Máire's constant supply of smuggled nourishing food and the extra fish that Colm was able to deliver without getting caught. Yet so many around them had died or attempted to leave for America and Canada with nothing but the clothes on their backs. All that remained of their existence were stone walls, the little that was left of them, defining their little plots of rented land. This was their humble legacy.

With the lands mostly cleared of tenants, now, Edward Kitchener had taken full advantage of grants the government was offering to change from the old, restrictive farming methods to more modern and profitable grazing and pasture farming. By now, Edward had largely handed the daily running of the estate over to Bishop, but he still kept a close eye on all of the estate's financial transactions. It was a profitable arrangement both for the estate and for his professional gambling career, as it allowed him to spend considerable amounts of time traveling to various gambling events in Dublin. There he enjoyed the luxury of his finest victory so far, Henry Cox's townhouse. Elizabeth was appalled when she heard about the townhouse affair. She didn't learn about it from Edward, of course, but in a letter from a friend of the Cox family in Dublin. Elizabeth liked Harriet Cox and felt immense guilt about Henry's suicide, but there was little she could do. She appealed to Edward to return the townhouse to Harriet, but he adamantly refused. 'I did nothing wrong, Mother,' argued Edward. 'He could have folded but he didn't. It was his fault, not mine,' such was Edward's amoral, narcissistic justification. Edward Kitchener was becoming one of the wealthiest men in Ireland thanks to his gambling talents.

Colm and Tomás and the few other surviving Kitchener tenants had toiled hard and long to adapt their landlord's holdings to this new methodology, but it was heartbreaking. They'd cleared their old friends' tiny hovels, remembering happy times shared there. And almost worse was removing the stone walls which had once signified an Irish presence, to make way for huge fields to maximise the Kitchener family's profits.

Colm and Órla's daughter Chara was the delight of the entire O'Donaghue family. She was now almost four years old and was as gregarious and outgoing as Colm. Órla did her best to hold her back, while Colm left her free to chat with everybody. She charmed anyone who would listen to her. Máire looked forward to coming home every night to listen to how her day went. It was hard to get a word in, once she got onto whatever interested her that day. She had inherited the black Irish look of the O'Donaghues. With her beautiful green eyes, thick black hair, peach-coloured skin, and her outgoing personality, it was impossible not to be completely entranced by her.

Máire was the official family hairdresser. Every month she would cut everybody's hair, but it was impossible to get Chara to sit still for more than a few seconds. Máire would chase her until she stopped, then cut a little. Then she'd be off again, stop, and Máire would cut a little more. Everyone loved her game, and the more everybody laughed, the more Chara ran. She was her father's daughter! Her free spirit raised them up a little every night. Young Tomás took it upon himself to read in English to Chara in the evenings. He was the only one of the family who could read both in English and in Irish. Máire was doing her best to learn, too, and with Tomás' help, was coming along slowly. She was thankful that Tomás had his father's patience.

Colm and Órla asked young Tomás to only speak English to Chara, so that she would grow up being bilingual. The world was changing quickly, and they realised that their daughter would have a better chance to get ahead if she spoke English fluently.

Part eight

Cradles and Snakes

Liam and Kumba walked to the gold buyer's store. Liam had three decent-sized gold nuggets left. The buyer weighed them carefully, all the time watched by Liam and Kumba. Both had heard the stories of the unscrupulous gold traders and merchants. Some of them used faulty, deliberately adjusted scales. Others were known to grow long fingernails in an attempt to conceal the smaller gold flakes and nuggets under them during the weighing process, thereby paying out for a lesser weight. After some time examining and musing on the nuggets, he came back with his offer. 'You have thirty-one ounces here, young man. I'll give you fifty shillings an ounce,' offered the gold dealer. 'Fifty-nine and you have a deal,' said Liam, forewarned being forearmed. 'Fifty-five,' said the dealer. 'Fifty-seven or I'll go elsewhere,' said Liam, enjoying the haggle. 'Fifty-seven then,' said the dealer. 'That comes to one thousand seven hundred and sixty-seven shillings.' As he started to count out the money and place it on the counter, Liam glanced at Kumba who just smiled, shaking his head proudly. Aboriginal peoples admired gold and opals for their beauty, but they knew that the white man lusted after them as possessions. It was the classic culture clash: 'I have enough for today' as against 'I need more for tomorrow.'

In the Aboriginal peoples' thinking, possessions didn't improve their lives, so they weren't important. They would never exchange their own free life for the white man's laborious existence; they considered white men foolish to work for more than they could consume.

The buyer kept counting and counting, until finally he handed Liam eighty-eight pounds, three shillings and five pennies – a small fortune back then. Liam was giddy with excitement having such an enormous amount of money in his pocket for the first time in his life, all thanks to Kumba and his father. He was delighted now that he had chosen to get off the whaling ship to try his hand at searching for gold. Now, he could purchase all of the equipment and horses needed to give him a decent chance. Increasingly, he was feeling like a free man again.

Sure enough, there were plenty of horses for sale and Liam chose two fine, healthy, colonial half-breeds. After purchasing sturdy saddles, blankets, and other goods for the ten-day journey to Bathurst, he still had more than half of his money left. Liam and Kumba rode along a road built and paved by convict labour, which extended well into the rich lands beyond Sydney. They passed settlers selling dairy and farm produce to diggers on their way to and from Bathurst. At nightfall they arrived in the tiny river town of Paramatta, where they spent their first night at a dismal-looking inn. The owner obviously made more money selling liquor than bedrooms, which were a big letdown compared to the luxurious ship's cabin and hotel rooms they had just left. Even so, tomorrow's journey would lead the men into some harsh outback, so they relished what few comforts the inn did offer.

Getting an early start the following day, they passed through the town of Liverpool. Heading for Goulburn, they traversed the richest lands Liam had ever seen. As they passed several drays and carts laden with merchandise of every sort for digging, Liam became more and more excited. He had as fair a chance as anyone to strike it rich, and he was willing to endure any hardships to make his fortune. Then he would return to Ireland and finally be together again with Máire and his son. Under the stars in the outback that night, Kumba, used to the strange noises of the bush, snored peacefully. Liam on the other hand, recalling that unwelcome snake visit, put in a rather sleepless night.

The next morning, on the road to Penrith, they began a gradual climb, passing through several forests. Elegant homes built on open glades cleared by early colonists dotted the area. As they moved along, in what seemed a split second, a band of about a hundred Aboriginal peoples appeared from behind rocks and trees along the riverbank on the edge of a large forest. Completely naked, they wore brightly-coloured feathers, and their entire bodies were painted white. Pointing their spears and boomerangs menacingly at Liam and Kumba, they screamed and roared, stomping down the high, dry grass. 'Tell them we mean no harm,' said Liam. 'No can,' said Kumba. Several older men came forward and danced and howled as they raised their spears aggressively. 'They're going to kill us,' Liam screamed. 'Tell them we have food.' 'No can,' said Kumba, and in his broken English he tried to explain to Liam that he didn't speak their tribe's language. Suddenly it made sense. Liam remembered his conversations with Dunsley about how, for thousands of years, these tribes had been cut off from each other. This tribe was completely different from the Noongars, so of course Kumba didn't speak their language.

Liam dismounted, grabbed his tucker bags, and waved them. The tribe members lowered their spears and an older man came forward. He picked up the food, and then excitedly pointed with his lower lip at Liam's coat. He shouted something, and the men raised their spears again. 'Give coat,' said Kumba. Liam pointed to his coat and looked at the old man. The man pointed again with his lower lip. Liam took his coat off and threw it towards the old man who quickly picked it up and began to cut off its buttons. When he had removed them, he turned and showed them to his men. They obviously liked the shiny silver buttons because they lowered their spears. The man put the coat down, and still looking at the buttons, walked back to his men. Liam smiled at the man and shook his head. With that, the tribe members quickly disappeared back into the forest. Liam speculated that they hadn't been speared because, seeing Kumba, they recognised him as one of their own.

The following day, off in the distance, they saw a towering challenge, the magnificent Blue Mountains, and they hoped that there was some sort of trail over or around them. These mountain ranges were unrelentingly arduous, except for the nomadic tribe members who came there to bury their dead in hidden caves. Liam and Kumba slept that night in a cave reeking of bat and kangaroo droppings, but apparently no bones from dead Aboriginal peoples. They struggled on slowly the next day, following a desolate road which led to a river. There, in a sort of floating bridge fastened to a cable operated by one man, they crossed the river, along with several animals and vehicles heading to Bathurst.

The road ahead became increasingly steep and rugged. Everyone seemed to be heading towards Bathurst. It certainly was a 'gold rush' as the newspaper had described. They passed a heavy dray, which on level ground would require a team of just two bullocks to pull it, but such was the incline on this long, steep hill, that thirty bullocks were straining under the load, their drivers shouting and cracking their whips savagely. When at last they reached the summit, twenty-seven hundred feet above sea level, the air was thin, and all was quiet. For the night's lodging, they'd been told of a place a few miles east of the summit, the Weather-

Board Inn. Thankfully, it was far better than the one in Paramatta, and it had a tremendous view of the Cordillera Mountains in the distance.

The next day they rode through thick forests and mountain valleys. Liam was increasingly grateful to Kumba's father's life-saving gift of gold, since the closer they got to Bathurst, the more expensive everything became. That night they had the unexpected expense of paying one pound for stabling their horses in addition to the cost of their own lodgings at the Rough Inn. And rough it was! Liam's excitement grew daily, and the road became busier and busier the closer they got to Bathurst. They passed the time riding alongside several horse teams, who invited them to sleep under the shelter of their drays, rather than be drenched by the often-rainy nights.

Skirting the base of the Blue Mountains the next day, they rode through the remote Pulpit Hill, surrounded by massive granite and basalt rocks. Soon, three thousand feet above sea level, they reached Mount Victoria Pass. Carved out by convict labour, it was a truly striking monument to all those unfortunate souls who had cleared the path. They were now only seventy miles from Bathurst.

Passing through the Vale of Clwyd they came across the Shamrock Inn Cottage in the town of Hartley. In a burst of nostalgia, Liam booked a room there, enamoured by the name, and they enjoyed their most comfortable night's lodgings and sleep since leaving Sydney. The Shamrock Inn was solidly built on high ground. From its huge wraparound porch, travellers could look down the valley at the thick forests in the foothills of the towering Blue Mountains. Liam knew that beyond those majestic, far-off mountains, lay the goldfields of Australia.

The next day they rode on through high gorges until, finally, the land levelled out on the eastern side of the mountains. The streams glided more quietly through verdant pasture lands, with a nearby forest supplying plentiful timber for fuel and building. Liam noticed that people were settling here, as houses, ploughing, and fencing appeared frequently. As they rode on, the land reminded Liam of Connemara – there wasn't a tree in sight for miles. In an ugly, arid-looking area, they crossed a wide, almost dried-up river. Liam had been told that, once he reached this river, he was only thirty miles from the goldfields.

Riding in the extreme heat of the day was particularly taxing on Liam, leaving him exhausted and nearing dehydration. Kumba, though, seemed unaffected by the journey. Using his efficient boomerang skills and perfect aim, he supplied plenty of rabbits for meals. Liam was grateful for the food and amazed that Kumba always knew exactly where to burrow to find welcome, life-sustaining water. *I was so lucky to get on that whaling ship*, he thought. *I wouldn't have had a chance crossing twenty-five hundred miles of desert, even with Kumba.* That night, sleeping under the moon and stars, Liam dreamed of all that lay ahead of them tomorrow.

Riding all day, it was nightfall when they finally reached Bathurst. Liam couldn't believe what he saw: hundreds and hundreds of tents that made it look like a military encampment, their campfire smoke curling up the sides of the hills, and fierce-looking men from many countries, with wild beards and pirate-like costumes. Yet, as the men smoked their pipes and played their music, Liam heard only quiet conversations and hearty laughter. As Liam and Kumba slowly rode down the almost two-mile-long dirt road, its sides flanked by tents and small clumps of trees, he was impressed by the order that prevailed. At the end of the 'street,' they saw a makeshift police barracks next to the commissioner's quarters, followed by the post office, then stores of every kind imaginable, selling every form of camp provisions: food stores, butchers, bakers, and gold buyers. Out front, each store flew a colourful flag on a long pole. The variety of colours added a festive atmosphere to the entire scene. Gold buyers displayed placards outside their tents announcing their purchase offer; today it was fifty-eight shillings an ounce.

Turning around, they rode back again even more slowly, this time taking in the tent town's wild men who were sitting around campfires, gazing at the sky, and wondering if tomorrow would bring a lucky strike. Just up ahead and to his right, Liam heard the distinctive sound of an Irish tin whistle, its plaintive, sad tune filling the nearby area. He followed the sound and saw four men sitting at their campfire. Three of them were smoking their pipes, while the fourth continued his slow air. Liam recognised the melody, dismounted, and started singing along in Irish. It was the first time he had sung in years, and it felt liberating, despite the nostalgic lump in his throat at hearing a song he loved after all these years. Everyone turned and listened to this new 'blow in' pouring his heart out with a true Irish musician's feel for this traditional song. Liam finished to appreciative applause. 'Come over here and talk to me, boy,' said the tin whistle player in Irish. Liam saluted the other three men as he and Kumba joined them at the campfire. 'Joe Brady,' said the obviously overweight Irishman. 'They call me Fat Brady, though I don't know why, the bastards,' he laughed. 'And this is Drunkin' Duncan from Scotland, Herman the German, and Big Jim from America.' Laughing at all their nicknames, Liam introduced Kumba and shook hands with the men. 'Liam O'Donaghue from Galway,' he said, 'but they call me Horse.' 'So where in Galway are ya from, Horse?' asked Fat Brady, and thus started another great friendship between two Irishmen on the absolute other side of the world. 'Big Jim, boil the billy there will ya,' said Fat Brady. The American got a small pot of water and put it over the open fire. This would be Liam's first cup of tea with some of the greatest friends he would ever have. Liam gave them a rundown of his story, and they couldn't believe all he had gone through. He was equally fascinated when they regaled him with their own stories. Fat Brady was a convict of course, also from Connemara like Liam, but now he was a free man having served his seven years.

Duncan McKenzie was a friendly-looking young man from Scotland, with a fierce head of red hair and a big, thick, foxy beard. He had such a strong accent, that it was almost impossible for anyone to understand a word he said. He didn't drink, thus his nickname Drunkin' Duncan! Once he read about the Australian gold rush, he decided to give it a go, make his fortune, buy a farm, find a woman, and settle down here.

The longing for loved ones back home was the common theme Liam heard among these men. For so many of them, finding gold was their last hope of ever returning. Most of them knew they probably would never make it back, and this gold rush was a way of getting a decent start to their new lives here.

Herman, the German was an engineer from Berlin. Bored with his job, he'd decided he needed some adventure in his life. He was a medium-sized, studious-looking young man, with thick glasses. Jim Sullivan was an Irish American from

California. In his forties and taller than Liam, he was the oldest in the group. He looked like he could manage anything or anyone. He wore a broad-brimmed California felt hat, red shirt, and heavy denim pants, held up by a broad leather belt, its buckle a brass snake. He had done well in the 1849 California gold rush, and now he wanted to try his luck further afield. He was keenly interested in world history, especially that of his ancestral homeland.

'So, you're going to give it a go?' asked Big Jim. 'Yea, I'm going to buy whatever we need tomorrow and find a spot.' 'Well,' he said, 'pan with us on our lot and save yourself the money for a license.' 'Thank you,' said Liam. 'I appreciate that.' 'Yea, be here tomorrow at eight or so,' said Drunkin' Duncan, an' I'll go with ye to make sure ye get everythin' ye need. Then we'll get ye started.' 'Look,' said Fat Brady, pointing to a spot to the right of their tent, 'There's room enough for ye to pitch yer tent here by us, if you'd like.' And so, thanks to the modest Irish tin whistle and the international language of music, Liam was beginning his hunt for gold with four seasoned, friendly men, who would shape his destiny.

Settling into his lodgings on the outskirts of the goldfields that night, Liam relished his first impression of the thousands of men sharing their next adventure in Bathurst. They truly were a disparate crew, hailing from all over the world. That night, Liam saw a man pay his bar bill in gold dust and other men examining a sizable nugget, each giving his expert estimate of its worth. Liam felt more alive here than he had in years. He was ready to go to work. It was up to him now. That, and a little bit of Irish luck.

True to his word, Drunkin' Duncan brought Liam and Kumba to the general provisions store the next morning, and Liam used up almost the last of his money buying everything he needed to get started. Kumba wasn't interested in the least in panning gold, so they bartered – they would work during the day, and Kumba would be their cook. Liam and Kumba set up their tent, their home for the foreseeable future, and then stabled their horses and walked to their new friends' allotted stretch of the river.

The license for their section of the slow-running creek cost thirty shillings a month. Diggers, as they were called, resented this license fee, and there were rumours that the government intended to increase it even more, to three pounds a month. Expensive as it was, with so many prospectors digging in such a relatively small area, the licensing did bring order to what would otherwise be a chaotic situation.

'Mornin',' said Fat Brady, 'are ya ready to make yer fortune?' he teased. 'I certainly am.' Liam saw an amazing sight down by the creek: dozens of men were in the shallow part of the creek panning, as Liam intended to do, while hundreds of others were divided into teams of four and panning with a machine Liam had never seen before.

'Say hello to a gold cradle, or what they call a rocker box over here,' said Big Jim. 'It was invented during the California gold rush and recently made an appearance in the gold fields over here. It can do more than twice the work a single man can do, and with much better results.' It really did resemble a baby's cradle: a high-sided wooden box about four feet in length, open at the top and sides. Attached to the bottom were rockers, and at its top end a wooden handle. To work this 'machine,' rocks and stones were put into a smaller, sieve-like box mounted at the top. As Fat Brady poured water over the stones from a bucket, Big Jim rocked it from side to side using the wooden handle. The larger rocks were trapped in the top box. Smaller stones and, hopefully, gold flakes, forced by the water, fell to the lower section. There, a dense canvas cloth sagged in the middle, trapping gold flakes, tiny pebbles, and sand particles.

From time to time Big Jim would toss aside the strained rocks and pebbles and then carefully shake the contents of the canvas cloth into a bucket. Later, with practiced skill using mining pans and water, they would remove the brown sand to reveal the hoped-for, heavier-than-sand, gold flakes. All this time, Drunkin' Duncan and Herman the German were delivering buckets of rocks and stones they'd dug beyond the steep riverbank. Liam was impressed watching them keeping the operation moving efficiently, carrying the buckets on their heads. All four men, working flat-out from sunrise to sunset, ended the day wet and spattered with sand and mud. Vulnerable to sudden and frequent weather changes, the men took few breaks. Liam looked around at all the other four-man teams doing the same thing – a hive of organised activity.

Fat Brady showed Liam how to pan, and soon he had the knack, standing knee-deep in the creek in search of his fortune. 'Dig up some sand there, Horse, and put it into your pan. Keep the pan submerged all the time and make big circular motions. The movement of the water removes the lightweight sand, slowly but surely. Gold is way heavier than the sand, so if there's any there, it has no choice but to sink to the bottom of the pan.' Then continuing to add water, Fat Brady gently moved the pan forward and backward, emptying even more sand. 'This is what they call "walking the sand".' They watched with hope for glints of yellow flakes, but all that was left were tiny grains of sand.

'No beginner's luck this time, Horse,' he said, 'but ya get the idea.' Panning away for hours, Liam hadn't yet seen even a hint of yellow, when, late in the afternoon, he finally spotted his first gold flake, clearly visible amongst the brown sand particles. He was almost as excited seeing his first tiny piece of gold as he was when his little cottage extension was finished. His new friends laughed watching his first thrill of the hunt. They had all been there and knew exactly how he felt. Liam carefully put his treasure in a small bag and continued panning, eventually ending up with two more slightly bigger flakes and a few tiny gold particles. He was happy with his first day's panning and, after this hard day's work, he realised that, while there was nothing romantic at all about gold digging, the rewards could be great.

Famished, the men ate grilled mutton chops that night and drank from a rum keg. Kumba's meal was a tremendous success; prior to tonight, every man had been his own cook. After dinner, Liam asked Fat Brady if he could borrow his tin whistle. Fingering this cool, slender tube, for a moment, he was home again. It had been too long. He closed his eyes, paused, and let fly with a lively reel. He felt rusty as his fingers weren't as nimble as he would have liked. Several others, hearing Liam's lively music, joined their campfire. This was an unexpected treat after a hard day's work. Everybody applauded. 'Mother of God, Horse,' said Fat Brady admiringly, 'where did ya learn to play like that?' 'Yerra,' said Liam modestly, 'my father taught me and my brother how to play.' 'Well don't stop now,' said Big Jim, thrilled to hear music from his grandfather's homeland. Eyes closed as always, Liam began to play a beautiful slow Irish air. Fat Brady soon joined in, singing in Gaelic in the old-style Irish tradition. Soon, the hardened faces of the gold diggers softened, as they were carried back to their home countries for a few precious moments.

'Any man who works hard for a year can support himself for three years,' said Drunkin' Duncan, chatting by the campfire after the short concert. 'But if he gets lucky, the sky's the limit.' 'Why did ya pick this spot, Jim?' asked Liam. 'It has the same look as where I found gold in California; granite and quartz rocks on either side of the creek, and porphyry.' 'Porphyry?' asked Liam. He was never afraid to ask a question and was always eager to learn. 'Well, they're extremely hard rocks containing crystals. I'll show you tomorrow. Gold doesn't occur in the rocks; it's dispersed through the quartz veins in those rocks. They could be anything from the particles you got today to pieces weighing many pounds. For thousands of years this creek has flooded and, when it does, it becomes a raging river pouring over the rocks above us there, pulling rocks and stones along with it. It roars over large boulders and passes over deep pools where the flow slows a little, allowing heavier gold particles to suddenly drop and become embedded into the rocks. We look for those dried-up pools and dig into them every day, hoping to find the big nuggets.' 'And have ye?' asked Liam. 'Yea, we're doing okay,' said Fat Brady. 'We've agreed to pan together for another six months; then we'll figure out what we all want to do. We're averaging about two hundred ounces every ten days.' Liam was impressed; his take was way less than that. 'We're making about eighty pounds a week, so, yea, we're doing fine. We haven't found a huge nugget yet, though.' 'Herman, the German is our money man,' said Drunkin' Duncan. 'He brings it to the local government official here. The officials take their ten percent, of course, and they bring it to Sydney under armed guard every week.'

Liam was impressed with the whole setup, and even though his gold-digging luck hadn't been great so far, he was encouraged to keep going after hearing these numbers. He had to chip in his share of gold to pay for their weekly cost of butcher's meat, sugar, tea, and flour, further diminishing the small amount of gold he had accumulated over the past few weeks.

The next day, Liam decided to take Big Jim's advice, and he poked amongst the rocks, rather than panning in the water. He looked for fresh holes that might not already have been worked over, digging into small crevices with a small pick. Every few minutes, he transferred the sand and gravel from his bucket into his mining pan. Inspecting it closely, he separated the particles with his jackknife so that he wouldn't have to keep going back to the creek for water. He blew off the dust and, every now and then, he discovered the odd gold particles.

Every night the men discussed their day's panning, and it was becoming more obvious to Liam that his daily yield wasn't anywhere close to what they were accumulating working as a team. Liam's favourite part of the day was enjoying the company of his new friends, as they talked and sang around the campfire every night. He heard several gold digger songs, one of them becoming his favourite:

COME LET US ROUND THE BUSH FIRE THRONG
AND CLOSE THE LABORING DAY.
LET'S PASS THE JEST AND JOCUND SONG,
TO WHILE THE NIGHT AWAY.
THOUGH BUSHMEN WE, WITH PIPE AND TEA
ALONE TO CHEER US UP,
YET STILL WE'LL SING, AND PLEASURE BRING,
WITHOUT THE SPEAKING CUP.

Every night, sheltered by his tent, Liam wrapped himself in his blanket and, feet towards the fire, lay down on the bare ground, surrounded by men of all characters. Hostilities between the white man and the Aboriginal peoples continued intermittently in the goldfield areas, but many of the gold diggers employed a practical solution; rather than being speared for their tucker bags as they dug further and further from the camp, they bartered their tobacco and flour for a steady supply of freshly-caught fish.

Over the weeks, Liam got to know more about his new friends. He discovered that Big Jim was extremely proud of his Irish roots. He gave Liam a history lesson about the American struggle with the English. 'The farmers and shop-keepers revolted against the high taxes in 1775. The Irish didn't have a hope, being so close to England, but thankfully, the English couldn't send reinforcements as quickly as that over there. The revolutionaries picked them off one by one. They couldn't miss, as the English insisted on wearing their red coats all the time. It took a long time, but in 1783, they finally won their independence from England.' 'Ye were lucky ye're so far away all right,' said Liam. 'Yep, and California just became a part of the United States in 1850.' 'What's it like?' asked Liam. 'Well, there's nobody telling me what I can or can't do. It's up to me how hard I want to work. My wife Maria and I have a nice farm in Sacramento. We bought it with the money I made in the California gold rush. My brother and his wife live next door and are helping Maria look after our farm while I'm away.' With that, for weeks Liam peppered Big Jim with questions about everything having to do with America, and Big Jim was happy to oblige.

Liam's luck changed a few days later when he was once again searching for a dry hole in the rocks that hadn't yet been picked over. He'd found a spot to relieve himself, and as he was scouring his surroundings, looked down, and saw his first decent piece of gold. It was embedded in the exposed root of a tree. Excited, he picked it up. Rough and uneven on the edges, it was about three inches long and of varying thickness with a small piece of quartz embedded in its thickest part. *Mother of God,* he thought excitedly, carefully weighing it in his hand, *it must be at least four ounces. I've just made my first twenty pounds.* He searched the entire base of the tree, finding several more grains. It was the best piss of his life!

Every Sunday, a clergyman visited 'the diggings,' as it was called, and conducted a worship service which was always well attended. Liam and his fellow diggers earnestly prayed for luck.

Liam savoured the long walks he shared with Fat Brady each evening, always chatting comfortably in Gaelic. Both from Connemara, they had a lot in common. Like Liam, Brady had also been torn away from his family, trying to save them during the famine. 'I'll tell ya, Liam, as soon as these six months are up, I'll be on a boat home,' he said. 'I'll buy my land back and grow old watching my grandchildren grow up free, beholden to nobody.' 'You're a lucky bastard able to go home,' said Liam. 'If I go back they'll hang me. The more I hear about America, the more I think that's where I'm headed. I'm thinking of sending the money back for Máire and Tomás to join me there; I can't get on a ship home.' 'Sounds good,' said Fat Brady. 'So, how'd ye meet?' Brady enjoyed listening to Liam's story – he had plenty of time to tell it all.

At dusk the next day, the men washed their mud-spattered bodies in the creek and took a little breather before heading back to camp. Everything was quiet in the early night's stillness, until Fat Brady, his pant legs rolled up, took a few steps backwards out of the creek and inadvertently stepped onto the tail of a snake. He watched in horror as the startled snake reacted in a purely instinctive display of self-defence. It raised the front of its body off the ground in an s-shaped coil and, without hesitation, lunged – sinking its fangs deep into Fat Brady's thigh. It happened in seconds. Brady let out a terrified cry as he'd recognised one of the deadliest snakes in Australia. 'I'm bit, Jesus, I'm bit,' he screamed. ''Tis a brown snake, oh God Almighty!' As the snake scurried away, the men rushed to his aid, knowing he was a dead man if, indeed, it was an eastern brown snake. Alarmed by Brady's screams, there was an instant cacophony of screeching birds, and loud cries of small animals scurrying through the long grass. 'Are ya sure t'was a brown snake?' knowing what was going to happen to his friend if it was. Big Jim looked at Fat Brady's thigh, and saw that the bite mark was small, consistent with the fangs of an eastern brown snake. As they eased their friend down onto a patch of soft sand, Big Jim shouted, 'Can anyone help us here?' Several diggers came to Brady's aid, but there was nothing anyone could do. His leg was already paralysed, as the venom coursed through his body. 'Jesus,' screamed Liam helplessly, 'isn't there anything we can do?' Fat Brady felt the venom attacking his muscles; it was exactly how he had heard a bite from an eastern brown snake would feel. Knowing what would quickly follow, he told his digger friends crowding around him to leave. He wanted to talk to his team. The men said their goodbyes and walked away. Holding back tears, his team listened to Fat Brady's final words. 'Lads, you're the finest people I've ever known. I'm gonna' miss ye.' 'Will ya stop with that talk,' said Liam. 'You're gonna' be fine.' He couldn't accept what he knew was going to happen, especially not to his friend. 'No, damn it, I'm not,' Brady said beginning to cry. 'I'm done lads. I can't feel my legs anymore, an' I'm cold.' 'We're gonna' miss you, too, you fat bastard,' said a crying Drunkin' Duncan, realising that his friend was indeed slipping away. 'Horse, I want ya to have my papers. They're in my satchel back at the camp. It's the only way you can get back to Máire and your son.' He looked at Liam and gave a quick laugh between his tears, 'If ya don't mind being called Pat Brady.' *That's our Fat Brady,* they all thought, *still keeping his sense of humour 'til the very end.* 'I'd be proud to carry your name, Pat,' said Liam, holding back tears. He was stunned by Pat's amazing gift. He would now be a free man with papers to prove it. He could sail on any ship to England without fear of being caught. 'Horse, will ya do me a big favour?' 'Anything, Pat, what is it?' 'If ya get back to Ireland, will ya try to find Nora and give her my share of the gold? Tell her I did my best. Will ya do that for me?' 'I promise I'll get it to her. You can be sure o' that.' 'Good man, Horse.' He weakly shook Liam's hand. 'Good luck, Herman, good luck, Jim, and you, ya bastard,' looking at Drunkin' Duncan. 'I hope ye all hit it big,' and slowly, he faded away.

Stunned, wordless, the men stood looking at Pat's body for several minutes. In shocked silence they carried him back to camp, laid him out in his tent, and then, into the late hours of the night, sat around the campfire drinking and telling stories about their friend. 'Well,' said Big Jim, looking at Liam, 'we'll be needing another man now, so how about it? There's no one he would have wanted more to join us than you.' Ironically, the tragic death of their good friend, now gave Liam the opportunity to earn a lot more money working with them, instead of panning on his own. 'Thank you,' said Liam raising his drink. 'Here's to Pat Brady, a fine Irishman.' They raised their mugs in honour of their friend. 'To Pat Brady.'

The following morning, they carried Pat to a little makeshift diggers' graveyard and buried him. Several fellow diggers who knew Pat attended. Big Jim read scripture from his Bible. 'Spout it out in Latin. The old bastard would appreciate that,' shouted one of the diggers. Liam nodded his head in agreement, remembering all the Latin masses with Father Murphy. Pat Brady would have known all the Latin responses, too. As they lowered his body into the grave, Liam played the slow air he'd heard his friend playing when he met them all that first fateful night. They took the day off in his honour.

The next day, Liam began panning with his friends. Assuming Herman's former position, he joined Drunkin' Duncan in bringing rocks and stones to Big Jim who constantly shook the rocker box. Herman the German took Fat Brady's place pouring water into the top box. As the weeks passed, Liam's cache of gold increased steadily, working with the team.

'You know you can't stay in Ireland,' said Big Jim chatting by the campfire one night. 'Once you go back to your wife, they'll arrest you; Brady's papers won't protect you there.' 'I know,' said Liam. 'You said you'd like to have your own horse farm someday.' 'Yea, someday, somewhere.' 'Horse breeding in Sacramento is beginning to get pretty big. I was thinking of going into it myself when I get back. I'll have a bit of money to buy a few decent horses to get started. Maybe we could do something together.' 'Wow,' said Liam.

'In Sacramento? I heard Kentucky was the place for horses.' 'Yes, but they're not your type there,' said Big Jim. 'They're not?' 'No, they're mostly Protestants from Northern Ireland. You wouldn't be welcome there.' 'I see,' said Liam. 'Look, in Sacramento, the weather's great; it's good, flat land, and we could help each other. You, me, and my brother.' Liam thought about this prospect and about all it would entail – go to California, buy some land, get to England, get back to Connemara, and then try to persuade Máire to leave everybody to go to California. 'You'll be a free man in America, Horse, and it's up to you how far you want to go. Only one person will have the authority to tell you what to do – you, and no one else.'

Over the last few months in the goldfields of Bathurst, Liam had gotten used to working for himself. Here, they were all in it together to better themselves, not to enrich their landlords. Nor was he an indentured servant to Dunsley. Now he was Liam O'Donaghue, a free man among fellow free men. And now, here was Big Jim, a fine human being, an Irish American, offering to help him start a new life in America. He wondered how many poor souls that emigrated during the famine had an opportunity like that offered to them. *Not very many,* he thought. He liked the idea.

A few weeks later, Liam woke up nauseous and weak with a massive headache. He apologised to the men and took the day off to rest. Feeling somewhat better that afternoon, he felt strong enough to grab his pick, pan, and satchel, and go for a walk. Still weak, he slowly climbed the creek's bank and walked farther from the stream than he had ever gone before.

Sitting on a rock to rest, he took out Fat Brady's tin whistle and started to run up and down the scale. It wasn't as fine an instrument as his own, but it felt good to be able to play again. As he took a deep breath, he got a fit of coughing. He stood up, staggered around the rocks coughing violently and, finally, began to breathe easily again. He sat down again, closed his eyes, and took a few deep breaths. When he opened his eyes, he thought he was hallucinating; he saw a long vein of yellow embedded in the rock facing him. Wide-eyed he focused on the big quartz boulder. Sure enough, there it was – glittering in the sun – a beautiful vein of yellow gold. Without even standing up, Liam broke off a chunk with his pick, revealing a sight he would never forget – right there in front of him were three smaller blocks of quartz containing more gold than he could ever imagine in his wildest dreams. There, jammed in by the elements for thousands of years, was the answer to his prayers. For a few moments he stared at the rocks in complete shock, crying, laughing, jumping for joy, and thanking God. He began chipping away at the first of the blocks, pulling away heavy chunks of gold weighing several pounds apiece. 'Mother of God, Mother of God,' was all he kept saying as he kept picking. More and more gold kept falling away from the rock. And there were still two more big boulders with the same yellow veins revealing themselves in all their beautiful glory. He thought of his mining team, *There's plenty for all of us here.* Gathering up what he had collected so far, Liam made sure of his bearings and headed back to the creek.

With hundreds of sometimes frustrated gold diggers all around them, Liam had to think through his next move. He wanted to run back to his friends, screaming, roaring, and waving the huge gold nuggets in the air. That's how he felt. But this huge news would spread like wildfire, and soon every gold digger from miles around would be searching those boulders, searching for his strike. So, Liam returned to the creek, waved at his friends, and continued on back to camp.

Bursting to break the fantastic news, Liam managed to wait until after dinner to say, 'I've somethin' to show ye lads.' But he knew that there were all sorts of unsavoury characters in the surrounding tents. It didn't take a genius to know that some of them wouldn't think twice about slitting another man's throat, if there was big money involved. Liam had selected the smallest nugget, which was about a half pound in weight. 'Lads, before I show ye what's in my hand, I want to warn ye. Don't get excited. Stay calm. All right?' 'Vat is it?' asked Herman the German, in his strong accent. 'You've gotta' stay calm and quiet,' said Liam, looking at each of them. 'All right?' 'Will ya show us for God's sake?' demanded Duncan anxiously. Liam extended his clenched hand. 'Lean in,' he said. They did, and he slowly opened his fist, revealing the huge gold nugget. Stunned as expected, they bent farther forward for a closer look. As the men became louder and louder staring at the nugget, Liam indicated with his other hand to hush them. 'My God, Horse, where did you find this?' whispered Big Jim excitedly. 'I went for a long walk today. I got a fit of coughing, so I sat down on a rock, and it was right in front of me,' said Liam as he handed around the chunk of gold. 'This is over half pound weight,' said Herman. Liam smiled. 'Yes, and there's more.' 'There's more?' asked Big Jim. 'Go into our tent. Kumba wants to show you something,' said Liam, enjoying the drama. They all began to stand. 'Easy lads. Calm, remember? One at a time,' ordered Liam. Big Jim went first. When Kumba opened the satchel and revealed the huge nuggets, Big Jim nearly had a heart attack. Used to dealing in ounces, Herman and Duncan had a similar reaction. For these men all working together, finding one hundred fifty ounces in a week was considered a decent return for their efforts. They were staring at many years of arduous work. 'Congratulations, Horse,' said Big Jim. 'I guess you'll be leaving us then, huh?' Liam waited for Herman and Duncan to sit down again. 'No,' said Liam, 'tomorrow we're going to pick up the rest of it.' 'Jesus,' said Big Jim, 'there's more?' 'WE'RE going to pick up the rest?' said Drunkin' Duncan excitedly. 'You said 'we'?' 'Yes,' said Liam, 'there's enough gold there for all of us – more than we could ever spend in our lifetime.' 'How in God's name did ya find it?' asked Big Jim. Liam told them the whole incredible story. They could hardly believe it. 'If only Fat Brady was here.' said Liam.

They spent most of the night devising a plan of action. To avoid suspicion, they agreed that Liam should go back alone and bring back as much gold as he could carry until he had picked the boulders dry. They would continue as usual. Once that was done, they decided that they would all leave together and bring the gold directly to a dealer in Sydney.

It took Liam four days of picking away at the boulders, until he was sure he'd gotten everything. He poked around in nearby rocks but saw no more yellow flecks. Of course, they all had to see where this amazing, life-changing place was. So, once Liam had finished all his picking, they all went for a 'walk' on their last day at the diggings. Spreading word that they were leaving because of Fat Brady's death, the men began saying goodbye to their digger friends. Early the next morning, they collected their horses from the nearby stable and purchased a donkey to carry the gold. Continuing to deflect suspicion, they sold as much equipment as they could to their fellow diggers, happily discarding whatever was left a few miles down the road.

The journey back to Sydney was virtually downhill and trouble-free all the way. Once in Sydney, they stayed in the city's best hotel. Again, to avoid drawing attention to their good fortune, they decided not to bring the gold in all at once. Over the next few days, they spread out to all of the banks and dealers in town. When finally, they had sold almost all of the gold, they divided the proceeds five ways. Liam insisted Kumba get his share. Each man was wealthy beyond his wildest dreams.

Over dinner that night, the men discussed their plans. Herman the German was going back to Berlin and, if the girl he left behind was still interested, he would propose to her. Liam and Herman had spent many hours discussing the advent of steam engines for ships, and Herman was convinced that he could transfer that idea to coaches. His father owned a coach-building company. Now he had the money to hire the best minds in Germany to make his idea a reality.

Drunkin' Duncan liked what he saw in Sydney and decided to remain there and maybe open a few hotels. 'I like the weather here a lot more than in Scotland,' he laughed. Liam thought of his Scottish friend Murdock back at the horse farm. *And poor old Bald Paddy and Reedy. If only I could get some money to get them outta' there. Maybe later,* he thought.

'So, Liam,' said Big Jim, 'are you going to join me in Sacramento? We could do some really big things now.' 'I've been giving it a lotta' thought,' said Liam, 'and the more I think about it, the more I like it.' 'Great,' he said, delighted. 'Well then, I'll treat you and Kumba to some nice cabins to San Francisco. How does that sound?' 'That sounds good to me,' said Liam. 'Kumba, whad'ya think?' Kumba smiled and nodded his head.

Herman, the German was the first of the men lucky enough to set sail. It was bittersweet saying goodbye to their great friend and watching as his ship sailed out of Sydney Harbor. It would travel first to England and then on to Germany. Liam, Kumba, and Big Jim had a ten-day wait for their ship to San Francisco, and Drunkin' Duncan remained with them until their departure.

They had a busy time preparing for their trip: everyone needed a long-overdue visit to a barber shop and attire befitting their new station as *nouveau riche* gentlemen. When Drunkin' Duncan shaved off his wild, foxy beard, his haircut revealed quite a handsome young man. Liam decided to keep his beard, though he had it tidied up. Big Jim had the most complete makeover. He shaved off his long, greasy beard and requested a tight, businessman haircut. Kumba chose several outfits in colourful combinations. He kept his beard and matted, semi-curly hair. He didn't buy shoes, though. He hated wearing shoes.

Everybody had a good laugh when they met for dinner that night, decked out in their new clothes. The mood was jolly; everything had come together in more ways than the men could ever have imagined in their wildest dreams.

'My God, Big Jim,' said Drunkin' Duncan, 'you look like a banker.' Big Jim laughed. 'Well not quite, but I am an accountant. And who are you? Have we met before?' he teased, looking at the cleaned up and dandy Duncan and Liam. 'And look at you, Kumba. The girls are going to fancy you in America, but where are your shoes?' 'Kumba no like,' he replied. They were an impressive-looking group of men, tanned and fit, and all of them in the prime of their lives.

Hearing that Big Jim was an accountant, Liam asked, 'Do you think you could help me get some money to my friends back at the horse farm?' He'd told Big Jim the whole story about Murdock, Bald Paddy, and Reedy. 'Well, the bank manager knows me by now, for God's sake,' said Big Jim. 'I'm sure he'd like some of his money back,' he laughed. Between the four of them, they had cleaned out almost every bank and gold dealer in Sydney. The next day they visited a bank, and Liam deposited enough money for his three friends to begin new lives, unbeholden to Dunsley ever again. Liam smiled, imagining their reaction when they each received a letter from the Perth bank manager. 'Good luck, from your friend Horse,' was all he wrote. 'You're a good man, Horse,' said Big Jim, as they strolled back to their hotel. 'They're good men,' said Liam, delighted to be able to help them. 'They deserve it.'

The next few days were taken up with helping Drunkin' Duncan check out prospective hotel sites and meeting with potential investors. While Duncan certainly appreciated Big Jim's expertise, Liam valued this preview of his talent for figures. 'My brother is a lawyer. He lives in Sacramento but has his office in San Francisco. I think he'll be a big help with investing our money. I trust him completely. He oversees investments for wealthy clients, so he already has connections. He's going to shit when he hears our story.'

Hearing all the options now available, Liam's head was spinning. He thought of Colm. *He has to come back with me. My God, the things we can do together.* 'The area's going to explode, Horse,' Big Jim continued. 'There's talk of a new railroad line going from New York to Sacramento. Though it won't be built for a few years, we could get in now and buy land where they say it's going to come through. Hell, maybe we could even invest in the railroad itself.' 'Mother of God,' answered Liam, 'all because I had a fit of coughing.' 'Well,' said Big Jim laughing, 'every time you cough from now on, check all around you, under the table, under the chair, check everywhere.'

Liam got a taste of what was to come the moment he boarded the ship; everything was bigger and better than anything he had previously experienced. The positive and friendly attitude of the American crew was remarkable, and the cabin and dining room were sumptuous. He definitely liked the taste of first class and began to relax more as he grew accustomed to his new plush surroundings. He could not wait to spoil Máire. In Sydney he'd had a little heart-shaped locket made from the first few flecks of gold he'd found. He also bought a simple gold chain necklace for it. *I'll give it to her on the ship before we go to dinner on our first night at sea.* Liam hoped he would have time to buy Máire a fitting wardrobe in England before they set out for America.

During the month-long sail to San Francisco, Liam came to know Big Jim very well. He enjoyed discussing anything and everything, especially horses. He was a thinker like Dunsley. Over dinner one evening, Big Jim said, 'You know, things might have been different for the Aboriginal peoples if they'd had horses. Much of the Indian culture in the U.S. was based on horses. These animals gave them the ability to move swiftly across the Great Plains of America. Horses revolutionised farming and transport, of course. Perhaps, if there hadn't been horses, America and the world might have looked like Australia did before the Europeans came. It's hard to imagine what history would have been like without them. Horses truly changed the world.' 'For good and for bad,' said Liam. 'My father told me about Cromwell and his cavalries. They moved across the country so fast; the Irish didn't have a chance to escape.' 'I know about Cromwell,' said Big Jim. 'Good for England; bad for Ireland.' 'Mind you,' said Liam, 'even though he died of natural causes, two years later his body was removed from its burial place in Westminster Abbey. He was tried for treason, hung in chains, and beheaded.' 'Pretty nasty business,' said Big Jim, 'but, giving them their due, Kings James I and Charles I are credited with starting the importation of higher-grade horses into England, in the early seventeenth century. They bred prime imported stock with their best native horses, and their offspring evolved into the thoroughbreds we have today.' 'I didn't know that,' said Liam. 'Well, that's what they say. So, Horse, have you ever heard of harness racing?' 'No.' 'I think you'll find this interesting, then, and another possibility to consider. In harness racing, horses move at a specific gait pulling a lightweight, two-wheeled cart called a sulky. The sulky driver sits on a narrow bench on the cart. Harness racehorses have shorter legs and longer bodies than thoroughbreds. Trained to trot rather than gallop, they're cheaper to buy. In America,' said Big Jim, 'harness racing is bigger than thoroughbred racing. I was considering going into it before we met. Now it's up to you – whatever you want to do.' 'I dunno',' said Liam. 'We have the money now to develop thoroughbreds. I learned a lot in Australia, and I'd prefer to do that.' 'So,' said Big Jim, 'it's the sport of kings you want then? That's what they call it you know.' 'You know I hate the word 'king,"' said Liam. 'All right then,' said Big Jim, 'let's go and become kings.' Liam shook his head smiling.

'The climate in California is much milder than it is on the

east coast. This gives us a huge advantage when it comes to developing and building up our horses; they can spend more time outside. Before I left, I heard that the going rate to cover a mare by a top horse was seventy-five dollars. The charge for boarding a mare, until they were certain that the breeding had been successful, was seven dollars a month' 'Mother of God,' said Liam, 'that's a fortune.' 'So, Horse, let's build the best stud farm in America and set our covering fee at one hundred dollars and our monthly boarding fee at ten. Our expenses will exceed profits at first, for sure. In fact, they'll be absolutely enormous, so maybe we could also do some harness racing to cover those initial costs. By the way, what colours will we have?' 'I didn't think of that. Dunsley's were blue and white.' 'What about green for Ireland?' said Big Jim. 'And gold for what got us started?' 'I like it,' said Big Jim. 'Green and gold it is. Now we need a name. There's already a racecourse in San Francisco called Pioneer Course, and they're planning another, so our timing is perfect.' Liam's head was spinning when his head hit the pillow that night. He couldn't believe all this was happening. Soon, Máire and Tomás would share in his good fortune, and hopefully, Colm.

Weeks of running up and down the banks of the creek carrying buckets of rocks and stones on his head had put Liam in the best shape of his life. After a few days of dining on sumptuous food though, Liam felt sluggish, so he decided to run the length of the ship several times, twice a day. For the first time in his life, Liam was in First Class. Second Class and Steerage passengers were not allowed to enter the First-Class area. Every day, for almost an hour, Liam ran down the stairs to the Second-Class section, ran around that area and then ran back up to circle First Class again. Finishing this routine, he'd wash up, eat breakfast, and head to the ship's small library. He enjoyed its extensive book collection and the wealth of current magazines and newspapers available there.

One morning, as he ran down to the Second-Class area, he heard cheering and yelling. Running aft to where the noise was coming from, he saw a thirty-foot-wide circle of people, mostly men, watching two men fighting. The onlookers were cheering wildly. Having been in his share of fistfights over the years, Liam saw that this wasn't a common brawl. *There must be rules to this,* he thought. *There's no hitting or kicking, no gouging out eyes, no biting, and no grabbing the other man's private parts.* Fascinated, Liam saw that the first objective of each fighter seemed, simply, to get his opponent to the ground. Next, it appeared that the prevailing fighter, having a good enough hold on his opponent to keep him pinned to the ground for several seconds, won the round. Then the fighting started up again for a few more rounds, each of them timed and controlled by one man. Liam saw people placing bets as two more fighters stepped into the circle to face each other.

Liam, impressed by all of this and typically curious, wanted to try it. He approached the winner. 'Well done,' he said. 'Good fight.' 'Thanks,' said the fighter. Liam heard his American accent. 'Liam O'Donaghue,' and shook his hand. 'Jack Parks, my pleasure.' 'What part of America are ya from?' 'Massachusetts.' 'Boston?' 'New Bedford.'

Hearing New Bedford, Liam figured the man to be a whaler. He'd heard about the problems whaling captains had trying to keep their crews from jumping ship once they heard about the gold rush near Sydney. 'So, you're a whaler then?' asked Liam, smiling. 'Was a whaler,' said Jack. 'Never again. My friend and I spent the last year in Bathurst and made more than we ever made in years of whale hunting. When we land in San Francisco, we're going to stay there and set ourselves up in business. We don't know what yet, but we'll figure it out. We're sick of the wretched winters in Massachusetts.' 'I spent a few months on a whaling ship myself, and I just came from Bathurst. I agree with ya. Give me Bathurst any day,' said Liam. 'Did you do all right?' 'Yerra, all right I suppose,' said Liam, modest as always. 'Listen, I never saw fighting like that before, and I'd like to try it.' 'It's called "Folk-style Wrestling" – it's very popular in America,' said Jack. 'You look like you could handle it, but you wouldn't have a chance to make any money if you didn't know how to use and break out of all the different holds involved. You have to know the moves.' 'I don't want to make any money out of it. I'd just like to learn a little bit, that's all,' said Liam. 'Well, when you get to America, you could join a wrestling club and learn it. There are clubs everywhere.' 'I'd be willing to pay you to teach me,' said Liam. Always thinking of ways to make some extra money, Jack figured, *Why not?* 'How about a dollar a lesson?' said Jack, expecting Liam to balk and haggle. 'How about two dollars?' said Liam, shocking Jack. 'Deal!' 'So, how about tomorrow after breakfast?' 'Fine, I'll see you then,' and so, another unlikely friendship grew out of Liam's unceasing curiosity.

The next morning, using techniques worthy of any excellent teacher, Jack outlined the essence of wrestling for Liam. 'Securing the fall and learning to escape from your opponent's control are the main goals of wrestling. That's what wrestling's all about. No holding below the waist is allowed, and no grabbing your opponent's leg.' The men were well matched in height and weight, so in skirmishes with Jack, Liam quickly learned the rules of wrestling and became adept at applying them. They could spar without Liam being overpowered by Jack's body strength. Liam learned the full range of moves and holds. His favourite hold was the Half Nelson. Jack demonstrated by passing one hand under Liam's arm and locking it around Liam's neck. Meanwhile, he held Liam's other wrist so that he couldn't move or peel his hand away. Then he turned Liam over on his back and pinned him to the ground. Liam learned how to counter the Half and Full Nelsons and the best ways to fall to avoid breaking his neck.

For three weeks, Jack, delighted by the unexpected extra income, gave Liam a wrestling lesson every day. Though neither man had anticipated it, a strong friendship evolved over that time – so much so, that Liam invited Jack and his friend to come and work for him and Big Jim. *Anyone who has worked on a whaling ship and panned for gold knows the meaning of hard work*, thought Liam. *We'll need men like that to get everything up and running.* By the end of the three weeks, Liam had become a decent Folk-style Wrestler.

The weeks flew by as Liam kept up his routine of running, wrestling, and then reading in the library every day. He enjoyed the variety of exotic new food dishes offered at dinnertime and was amazed that there were so many ways to cook and serve meat. There were so many choices that even Kumba found foods he liked. And dinnertime conversation was always lively and enlightening. Everyone around him, passengers and crew alike, was cheerful and friendly. He wasn't used to the positivity of it all, and he began to believe what Big Jim had said, 'There's nobody to tell you what to do and when to do it. It's all up to you. That's America.' It was a liberating breath of fresh air for Liam.

When the ship sailed into beautiful San Francisco Bay, Liam could clearly see the impact the California gold rush had had there. It was all hustle and bustle, but not in the grimy way he had experienced in London. As they neared the dock, he saw large population settlements and expansive building projects in progress. Liam agreed with Big Jim's opinion that the time to invest their fortune in California was now.

The news of gold had brought approximately three hundred thousand people to California from the rest of America and abroad. This population explosion was a contributing factor in California's abolition of slavery in the following years, and of quickly achieving statehood. Big Jim had explained all of this to Liam during their passage over, and these pivotal events were largely responsible for Liam's decision to settle in California. 'I want to hire people, not own them. I've had enough of that to last a lifetime.' An Irish American, Big Jim knew exactly where Liam stood, and he agreed with him completely.

Shortly after disembarking, the men headed for Portsmouth Plaza in the heart of San Francisco's commercial district and arrived at the plush office of Big Jim's older brother Ben. As Liam entered, he was amused by the look of shock on Ben's face, delighting in his younger brother's safe return from Australia. After emotional hugs and a little catching up, Big Jim introduced Liam and Kumba. 'This is my older brother Ben. Ben, these are my friends Liam O'Donaghue and Kumba.' As Liam shook Ben's hand, he compared the brothers. Ben could easily have been Big Jim's twin – same height, weight, and looks, although Ben seemed to be more intense and reserved. He hadn't gone through what Big Jim had in the goldfields of California and Australia. These experiences had put a few years on Big Jim's handsome face. Neither did Ben have Big Jim's sense of humour; he was all business. 'Ben, I think you'd better cancel the rest of today's appointments,' said Big Jim. 'We have a bit of a story to tell you.' Over the next few hours, as they shared their amazing story, Ben's right leg twitched with nervous excitement, and as the incredible story unfolded even further, it twitched even faster. 'I'd like to divide my share with you,' said Big Jim. When Ben heard these words and realised the immensity of what his brother was offering him, he nearly fell out of his chair. Rising to hug Big Jim with heartfelt gratitude, his legs gave out and he fell into his arms. 'Liam is going to Ireland for his wife and son and is hoping to persuade his brother to come over too, so that we can all go into business together.' 'Why don't you just send the money and stay here? That will take you months,' said Ben, thinking as practically as any lawyer would. The romantic that he was, Liam replied, 'I promised Máire I'd come back to her.' The men went for a celebratory lunch and discussed their plans for buying land in Sacramento. 'Gentlemen,' said Ben, 'you're not going to believe what landed on my desk last week.' 'What?' asked Liam. 'I'm managing a delinquent loan sale for thirty thousand acres in the valley. It's not too far from our land in Sacramento.' 'Can we afford it?' asked Liam. 'With your money, you could afford three hundred thousand acres.' 'Mother of God,' said Liam. 'Could we go see it?' 'What're you doing tomorrow?' asked Ben jokingly. After lunch, Big Jim gave Liam a quick tour of San Francisco. He loved its eclectic mix of architecture, its steep rolling hills, and its bay views – especially from California (Nob) Hill.

Over the next two days, they travelled by coach to Big

Jim's welcoming home. Although, around the campfire, he had often talked about his Mexican American wife Maria, he hadn't mentioned how beautiful and gracious she was. They had no children. Liam suspected Big Jim wasn't home enough.

The following day, they went to see the land that was for sale. It dwarfed Kitchener's Galway holdings. The last owner had raised cattle and harvested farming grasses to feed them. Located on the northern fringes of Sacramento, some of the land was undesirable hardpan where a dense layer of soil underneath the topsoil made it impervious to water. Even so, Liam felt he could make it work since the land was near the Sacramento River.

As Liam scanned the vast expanse of land, he already imagined a self-contained horse farm. In his mind's eye he pictured where the fenced exercise areas would be. There was plenty of land to grow all the hay and oats he would need to feed the horses, as well as all the crops and vegetables needed to sustain his family. He would build a state-of-the-art stable for his thoroughbreds, a shop for his blacksmith, additional barns for the farm's workhorses and for feed storage and living quarters for jockeys and labourers.

Looking up ahead, he noticed a particularly impressive piece of land, a good two acres or so, which sloped gently towards an expansive valley. The far side of the land was lightly forested. He walked up the little incline to admire the view, turned around, and saw a deep green valley stretching out before him. *This could be Ireland,* he thought. From deep within, a wave of emotion surged. Discovering the immense amounts of gold was an abstract experience for Liam, joyous though it was. But this was land, and land defined an Irishman. It was in every Irishman's blood. *This is my land,* thought Liam. *Nobody can take it away from me. If God allows it, I will grow old here with Máire by my side and we will share in the joy of watching our son and grandchildren flourish here.* As Liam wept tears of gratitude, Big Jim walked up to him and stood quietly, a witness to Liam's emotional epiphany. With a quick swipe of his hand, Liam dried his tears.

'Well,' said Big Jim, 'what d'ya think? Will it work?' Liam's smile was his answer. In a burst of nostalgia, and even though it didn't look at all like where he came from, he said, 'I'm going to call it Connemara,' said Liam. 'Well then, let's build the finest Connemara horse ranch in the world.' 'This is where I'll build our house,' said Liam excitedly. 'I agree,' said Big Jim. 'It's a perfect spot, and I have the architect that will make it happen.' 'That's grand,' said Liam. 'I'll have Jack Parks and his friend get started while I'm away. He told me he built houses before he tried whale hunting and gold digging.' 'Fine,' said Big Jim. 'I have a good crew as well. They built my home and my brother's. Hopefully, we'll have it ready for you when you return. And when you come back, we can travel to Kentucky and New York, even Europe, to buy the best horses available.' 'When I get back, I'll never set sail again. Never,' said Liam. 'Yes, I understand. By the way, a bit of good news, Ben told me they just opened up a racetrack here in Sacramento.' 'That's great,' said Liam. 'In a few years, all going well, we can start from there and build up.' 'You handle the farm's layout and the selection of horses. Those are your strengths. You obviously have the eye to spot superior physical qualities in horses. Ben and I will look after the business side of things.' 'I appreciate your faith in me,' said Liam, 'but be forewarned. We might breed a foal from two prized thoroughbreds that couldn't outrun a fat man running downhill!'

Big Jim laughed. 'After all you learned in Australia, I'm certain that won't happen.'

On their way back to his ranch, Big Jim regaled Liam with a tremendous horse racing story. 'I'm from New York originally. I came to California for the gold rush in 1849. My getting involved with horses began on Long Island in 1842. There was a well-publicised horse race planned between two champions: Boston from Virginia and Fashion from New York. The papers built it up as the great clash – north versus south. It was the biggest horse race in history up to that time. Seventy-thousand people came to the Union Course on Long Island. Seventy-thousand! Can you imagine that? Carriages of all sizes of the rich and famous lined the streets. Thousands more came by train. There were so many people trying to get there that thousands of people missed the race completely. The excitement was astounding. Boston was a perfect-looking chestnut stallion which had won thirty four-mile races. Word was that Boston's original owner had lost him as a two-year-old in a card game to repay his debts of over eight hundred dollars. They said Boston was difficult to train and had a terrible temper. His trainer said, 'The horse should be castrated or shot – preferably the latter.' Fashion was a beautiful filly which had won many of her races, but Boston was the favourite. The crowd surged onto the track upsetting both horses. The scene was chaotic. In all the confusion before the race started, Boston cut a long, jagged gash on his hip against a rail. Even so, he led for three miles, but Fashion won by sixty yards, setting a world record for that distance. It was the most exciting thing I ever saw. I've been drawn to horses ever since.'

Liam and Kumba spent the next two weeks as guests of Big Jim and Maria. Ben drew up the legal papers, which they all signed, including Kumba. Liam guided Kumba's hand, signing his name on the legal documents. Kumba couldn't understand that he was now a 'partner' and had trouble grasping the white man's legal need for signed land ownership.

Liam met Big Jim's architect and together they designed his future home for Máire and Tomás. Liam liked the design and floor plan of Big Jim and Maria's inviting two-story, timber home, but he wanted a few changes for his own – most importantly, no more tiny windows! He commissioned the architect to include three of the largest windows he could find, so that Máire could admire the beautiful view of the very Irish-looking valley from her kitchen sink. The architect thought it would be too big, but Liam insisted. In fact, he ordered bigger windows all around. He'd loved Dunsley's wraparound wooden porch and helped design an even bigger, wider one, encircling the entire house, so that from every vantage point, he and Máire could sit and enjoy watching their family as they grew up. Remembering that Dunsley's porch had no protection from the sun, Liam co-designed an imposing high-roofed porch similar to the one Kumba and he had seen when they stayed at the Shamrock Inn on their way to Bathurst. Liam loved Big Jim and Maria's bedroom and bathroom suite. He had never before seen the likes of it, so he ordered a similar one, adding a few ideas of his own. He meticulously designed a large library with floor-to-ceiling bookcases. Liam added a sprawling family room to the plans, its exterior wall completely windowed with double doors opening onto the porch. This room would be ideal for family parties and dancing. By the time Liam finished explaining his design requests, his planned home no longer compared to Big Jim's rather modest house. It was a mansion.

While the architect worked on preliminary sketches, Liam took Kumba out to show him where the home would be built. He looked at Kumba, who had never asked for a single thing since the night he'd saved Liam's life. Because of Kumba's brotherly sacrifice, everything Liam now had – his life, his wealth, his chance to reunite with Máire – was finally possible. This fine young man had given up all he had ever known: his family, his friends, his entire way of life. He'd selflessly joined Liam in an odyssey of sacrifice, survival, and amazing experiences beyond either of their wildest imaginations. And now they stood together on a hillside in America. In humble gratitude, Liam was thrilled to be able to give a gift to his Aboriginal brother. He turned to Kumba and said, 'After all you've done for me Kumba, I would like to build you your own house.' Kumba chuckled, thinking Liam had spoken in jest. Saying nothing, Liam returned his brother's smile. Kumba searched Liam's face and realised that he was serious. This wasn't a joke. Stunned, Kumba looked out at the vast land before him, and thought of his life in Australia. He had never lived in a 'proper' home. He grew up under the harsh rule of Dunsley who, with the Redcoats' help, had forcibly and ruthlessly cleared his tribe off the best lands, their tribal lands, the lands where his ancestors had lived for thousands of years. Repeatedly he had witnessed the white man's terrible cruelty. When he was working, he was forced to live in a large, extremely basic building. His family's home was a tiny dirt-floored shed. There, he had been brought up in the old Aboriginal ways: the language, customs, and beliefs, as taught by his father and the elders of his Noongar tribe.

Kumba realised that, beginning with the night when he helped Liam escape, he had been privileged to come to know well another sort of white man, one who was selfless, generous, and decent. Because of their friendship, he'd come to appreciate a sense of freedom and self-worth he had never experienced before. He'd enjoyed unimaginable comforts he never knew existed. He'd observed many people whose culture and customs were remarkably unlike his own. And along the way, like Liam, he had learned much about himself, especially about how much he could endure. Kumba could see that he was a changed man, and he liked the man he saw. He turned back to Liam with a look of disbelief, his eyes welling up at the thought of a promising future. Liam placed his arm around Kumba's shoulder and said, 'I saw the way you looked at Maria's maid Isabella, and I saw the way she looked at you.' Kumba grinned, then shyly lowered his head, and pointed his lower lip to the right of where they were standing. 'So,' asked Liam, 'you'd like to live next door to Yagan?' Kumba answered with a wide-open smile. 'Not big like Yagan,' he said modestly. With Liam's arm still around Kumba's shoulder, they turned to face the valley lying before them. 'Kumba,' said Liam, 'You can marry, and our children can grow up together here. Let's go in and talk to the gentleman with the pencil.' With Liam's help and the architect's expertise, Kumba designed his own house, his way. In a huge leap of faith, Liam also commissioned the architect to design and set in motion the building of a home for Colm, next door to Kumba's.

Part Nine

The Air That Binds

Returning to San Francisco, banking finances tended to, Liam booked his and Kumba's passage to England. He held onto a decent number of pounds and gold, more than sufficient to get him to Ireland and return with his family. He also had Fat Brady's money. He looked forward to fulfilling his promise to Kumba that he would show him his country, and he decided that he would do for Kumba what John Atkins Faught had done for him on their journey to Australia as convicts; he would teach Kumba how to read and write.

Soon, Liam and Kumba were back on the city's docks and boarding the ship to Southampton, a recently-built combination steam and sailing ship called the Chusan. It was owned by the Peninsular and Oriental Steam Navigation Company. (P&O) The English-built iron ship was capable of reaching as much as fourteen knots. Liam was excited to be on one of the most modern ships in the world. It had three masts and a midship steam funnel.

Within a day of departure, Liam was down in the boiler room checking out the steam engines, marvelling at the many improvements that had been made since the days he'd worked on ships' engines in London. He was delighted that the 800-horse-powered engines would cut more than a month off of what would normally be a four-month journey.

Besides being extraordinarily fast, the Chusan was the first ship to operate regular mail service between England and Australia in 1852. It was also the first oceangoing liner to make passage via the Cape of Good Hope on a regular basis, and it did it in eighty days.

When Liam and Kumba boarded, they'd noticed that, because the ship frequently carried vast amounts of gold to London, it was heavily armed with a thirty-two-pounder cannon, four broadside guns, and six swivel guns. Liam learned that, on their way to England, they would pass through pirate-infested seas. He was thankful that the added speed of the steam engine reduced the chances of their being ambushed. A sailor told Liam about an unfortunate ship called the Madagascar which had set sail with five tons of gold. It too, had been heavily armed, and its crew were all experienced sailors, but the Madagascar simply disappeared, never to be seen nor heard from again. There were rumours that a gang of desperados, already aboard, had seized control of her at an opportune moment. It was widely believed that they had massacred the passengers and crew, sailed into a remote harbour, secured the gold, and then destroyed the ship. *That's all I need now*, thought Liam, *to be ambushed by bloody pirates!* Because of the Madagascar saga, security had been beefed up. Before boarding, people were required to show their papers. Once again, Liam was grateful to Fat Brady for his last dying gift – his freedom papers. Kumba had no problem. He was assumed to be Liam's slave.

The Chusan was considerably smaller than the ship that had brought them to San Francisco. Just one hundred fifty feet in length, it appeared more yacht than ship-like and was considerably quieter than the bigger steamship. Liam enjoyed the most comfortable slumber of his life in his roomy cabin, since its modern, wire-spring mattress reduced the effects of vibration. In the morning, he and Kumba folded the bed away, allowing free access to the cabin's desk, so that they could sit side by side to read, write, and study. Liam had perused the ship's remarkable library and, at the recommendation of a fellow passenger, an American, had chosen Washington Irving's *Rip Van Winkle* to read with Kumba.

Liam's biggest challenge was Kumba's deep-rooted cultural belief that learning to read and write wouldn't enhance his life. So why learn? Drawing from his time living amongst the Aboriginals, Liam understood Kumba's reasoning, but he recognised how much he himself had evolved since leaving Ireland, so he patiently tried to change Kumba's mind and get him interested in at least making an attempt to read. 'Ya know Kumba, the wife in Rip Van Winkle's story was a real nag, and I don't blame him for hiding from her.' Kumba laughed. 'On the other hand, I can't wait to be with my wife, and reading this story has helped me appreciate all that I have. I've learned things from books that have helped me survive all the hardships I've experienced. We're partners now in America, Kumba. We can build something way better than Dunsley's place; and it will be ours. We need to watch everything that's going on carefully. Your being able to read and write would be a significant help. I really think that, if your father saw where you are now and how far you've come, he'd want you to do this. Your parents and Maali would be proud of you. Wouldn't it be nice to write a letter to Isabella? I'm sure she'd love it.' Kumba didn't seem too excited about this prospect, but Liam persisted. He remembered his own frustration when first learning to read on the ship to Australia, and now he appreciated John Atkins Faught's extraordinary patience even more. Liam was determined to prevail and started at the very beginning. He began by showing Kumba how his name looked in print, getting him to name each letter, and sounding out the word. He did the same with HORSE, and several other words well known to his reluctant student: SHIP, SAILOR, FOOD, and SHOE.

With Liam's enduring patience, encouragement, and loving perseverance, Kumba became excited when, finally, it started to come together for him, and he began to read several words and string them together meaningfully. Liam had Kumba read a new paragraph each day, over and over, trying to get Kumba to sound out the words. He did this faithfully every morning after breakfast, promising Kumba that, once he was able to get through just one paragraph on his own, he would stop torturing him for the day.

Over the weeks, and then months, Kumba was doing well enough that he could read and enjoy many of the children's books in the ship's library. Liam was delighted to see that, as Kumba became more proficient in his reading, he seemed to hold his head up a little higher. They finally finished *Rip Van Winkle*.

Rip's story was an inspiration for Liam. He tried to imagine falling asleep under the tyranny of a king, and waking up twenty years later, free, and no longer a royal subject. *I haven't been out of touch with my family for twenty years, but these almost-seven long years have certainly felt like it. I hope that, like Rip, my family will soon be able to wake up free from their oppressors.*

There was no steerage section on the Chusan. This was the ship favoured by wealthy passengers emigrating to America and by successful gold diggers heading home. There were no inner-tier cabins. Outside cabins lined both sides of the ship, affording the cabins great light and air. Liam and Kumba dined in the elegant dining room each evening. Beautifully furnished, with white and pink-toned marble columns, it extended the full breadth of the front of the vessel and measured about fifty-feet-square. Magnificently ornate sofas had been arranged around the sides of the room, and its main tables were beautifully set and decorated.

Liam delighted in quiet satisfaction at the reaction Kumba's presence caused each evening at dinner. Slaves, as they assumed Kumba to be, simply didn't dine in the main dining room. It just wasn't done. Nor did slaves walk amongst passengers on the forward, first class promenade. Nor should they be seen in the ship's music salon with its white, marbled panels and carvings traced in gold. Yet, Liam and Kumba enjoyed every facility aboard as a twosome! Many of the other passengers couldn't get used to it. *Money is power,* thought Liam, *and nobody can do a thing about it.* He loved it! Ever the rebel, he proudly conversed in his heavy Galway accent, and, capable of discussing any matter under the sun with learned confidence, Liam held his own at dinner each evening. Eventually, Kumba's friendly smile and gentle manner won over most of the passengers.

Liam felt uncomfortable spending the last few hours of each evening enjoying brandy and cigars in the luxuriously-fitted smoke room. Though most of the male passengers did this, it was just too rich for him. There was also a limit to how much he could take of their exaggerated gold-discovery stories. He preferred being out on deck alone, watching the moonlight as it reflected on the endless ocean. He wished Máire was by his side. The soft evening breezes and soothing ocean waves always brought her closer. Alone, he played his tin whistle. *Soon,* he thought, as his musical prayer reached towards the Heavens.

Liam looked forward to the resident classical pianist's performances every night in the elegant, generously proportioned music salon. It brought him back to balmy nights on the Mermaid's deck, listening to the works of some of the world's greatest composers, played on the violin by that kindly old pensioner guard. Once again, hearing Bach's *Air on a G String* on the salon's grand piano, Liam wept. He recalled the melody's profound impact on him when he heard it for the first time with his friend John. He wondered how he was getting on. Now he heard the perfect accompanying arrangement to the inspired melody, and his respect for Bach grew even greater.

Even though Fat Brady had been impressed by his tin whistle playing, Liam realised how rusty he had become from not having played for so long and from all the abuse his fingers had suffered during those seven hard years of manual labour. He decided to try to get his own playing back to where it used to be. The music room was closed to the public during the day, and Liam was allowed to practice there to his heart's content. As the weather worsened the farther away from America they sailed, Liam spent more and more time practicing. He hoped that, by the time he reached Ireland, he would have his technique and flexibility back. *Da would expect no less*, he thought.

Liam inevitably got to know Captain Down who couldn't get enough of Liam's whaling adventures. 'Now that's what sailing is all about,' enthused the captain. Liam confided in him his plan to return to Ireland to meet up with his wife and son and bring them to America. Liam asked what he thought would be the best and fastest way to sail from Southampton to Galway. 'I would suggest you charter a ship yourself. Do you have the means to do that?' 'Yes sir.' 'You'll have to return to Liverpool. it's the only port with shipping to San Francisco due to the California gold rush.

I'd imagine a week is all you'll need. There are always a few ships in between voyages. If you have the money, you'll have a ship.' *Money really is power*, Liam smiled to himself. He couldn't wait.

Finally, late one afternoon, they sailed into Southampton's Port, a major naval shipbuilding port on the south coast of England. From the deck, he saw immense bales of wool ready for export and the off-loading of huge casks of wine. As promised, Captain Down kindly brought Liam to the local booking office near the docks. 'The only ship available right now is a small cattle ship,' said the agent. 'It brings cattle and sheep over from the islands. It's a solid ship, sir.' Liam and Captain Down went to have a look at it anchored farther up the dock. It was a small, sad-looking, two-masted vessel. 'It's not the prettiest,' said Down, 'but I think it can do the job.' They returned to the booking agent. 'Can it get me to Galway and back to Liverpool in a week?' The agent cocked his head in puzzled thought. 'If you leave first light tomorrow morning, you'll make it over and back in seven or eight days. The weather's holding steady, so you should be fine. I'll contact the captain right away, sir.' Liam said a grateful goodbye to Captain Down and then discussed the price with the agent, paid a deposit, and got a recommendation for a nearby hotel on French Street where he'd await confirmation from the ship's captain. Within two hours, Liam received a message from the booking office saying that everything would be ready to set sail at first light.

Liam and Kumba decided to celebrate at a fashionable restaurant near their hotel. On the back of the restaurant's menu, an interesting story about Southampton's maritime history caught Liam's attention. The story gave a nod to the fact that the Vikings had attacked England and

Ireland. He read that, according to legend, while he was in Southampton, the Viking King Canute sat on the shore and commanded the tide to stop and not get his regal robes wet. The tide, of course, ignored him. Canute used this example to show his people that, though he was their king, he was not all powerful. 'One historian,' the menu read, 'quotes King Canute as saying, 'Let all the world know that the power of kings is empty and worthless, and there is no king worthy of the name, save Him by whose will, heaven, earth and sea, obey eternal laws.'

Liam found it difficult to sleep that night, knowing he was just days away from reuniting with his beloved Máire and their son after all these years. No matter what he endured, year after lonely year, what always kept him going was his deepest yearning, no matter how impossible it seemed, to return to Máire and Tomás. But now as he lay awake in the darkness of his hotel room, so tantalisingly close to home, serious doubts crept in. He had all these grand plans for his family's future, but everything depended on Máire and Tomás' agreeing to leave Ireland for good. *Surely Máire knows I can't stay in Ireland. She and Tomás will have to leave everything behind. What if she won't come? I can't force her. And Tomás? I'm going to drag him away from everybody and everything he knows.* He tried to picture Tomás. *He's about ten years old now,* he thought. *What am I going to say to him? 'Hello Tomás, I'm your father. We're going to America now; say goodbye to everybody; hurry up now.' And will Colm come? What if he's married? Will his wife want to leave her family?* Liam tossed and turned, finally drifting off for a fitful few hours.

Liam and Kumba left their hotel after a miserable night's sleep, and the dreary morning's drizzle did nothing to improve Liam's mood as they walked the short distance to the inner dock. The captain and three crew members greeted them. 'Mornin' Skipper, Captain Baynard at your service.' With raggedy clothes and filthy beard, this was the most unlikely looking 'captain' Liam had ever set eyes on. He looked more like a gold prospector than a ship's captain, and his crew members looked even worse. Sceptical, Liam was reassured somewhat by Captain Baynard's sailing skills as he and his crew successfully steered a course through the busy sea traffic of Southampton's booming port. And to Liam's great relief, Captain Down's opinion of the ship was correct; it responded swiftly to all of the captain's commands. The bracing sea air lifted Liam's spirits somewhat, and he began to relax as they headed out into the major shipping lanes of the Solent, the strait separating the Isle of Wight from the mainland of England.

Over the obligatory cup of tea, Liam learned about Captain Baynard's noble family and its British nautical history. 'I'm named after one of my ancestors, Robert Baynard, who defeated the infamous pirate Blackbeard. He was a captain in the Royal Navy, so he was. He lured Blackbeard into a battle off the coast of Carolina in 1718 and killed him.' Liam was amused by the marked contrast between this Captain Baynard and his famous ancestor. Rough and smelly with a heavy black beard and a clearly anti-traditional swagger, this Captain Baynard could be a present-day pirate himself. *I hope we won't need any pirate tactics when we get to Galway!*

When the water became increasingly rough as they sailed out of the English Channel and into the North Atlantic Ocean, Kumba became violently seasick. Liam felt sorry for him, so far away from his natural environment. He remembered how deathly dehydrated he'd been during their days riding horseback in the boiling Australian sun. Kumba, though, never seemed to suffer ill effects. He always knew which roots to burrow into and, mercifully, find lifesaving droplets of water. Now the opposite was happening. Liam was fine and Kumba just wanted to die. Captain Baynard prepared a concoction of raw ginger and chamomile tea to help ease his nausea. Liam helped Kumba drink the tea and said, 'Just another few days and we'll be there.' As his friend lay on the deck groaning, Liam had second thoughts about having brought him along, but he had talked so much about Ireland, he felt Kumba should see where he'd come from. He wanted Kumba to meet his family, and he wanted them to meet Kumba, his Aboriginal brother – the man who had saved his life and who, in so doing, willingly gave up so much of his own.

Apart from Captain Baynard who had a tiny cabin, they all slept on deck. It had been a long time since Liam had experienced the Atlantic's cold damp nights, and he just about froze. *This,* thought Liam, *is worse than steerage! I wish I had my dingo to keep me warm.* He remembered Murdock's droll comment about the cold, 'If I return to Scotland, my arthritis'll come back in a week.' He wondered if any of the three of them would be returning home, now that they'd have the money for it, and he smiled, remembering some of the good times they'd shared.

Apart from the now-ruined clothes on his back, he had one suitcase full of the new clothes he'd purchased in Sydney. When he rejoined Máire after all these years, he wanted to look his best. He took out Fat Brady's tin whistle to play a tune, but his fingers were numb with the cold, so he tucked it back into his inside pocket. Shivering, he finally slept.

When screeching seagull cries woke Liam, he beheld a sight he thought he'd never see again – the green hills of Ireland sparkling in the dawn's sunlight. He rose and walked to the railing to take it all in. As they entered Galway Bay's welcome harbour, he closed his eyes, inhaled deeply, and filled his very being with fresh Irish mist. Liam gazed at the breathtaking views, so deceptively wild and free. Then, pointing towards the hills of Connemara in the distance, Liam turned to Kumba. 'There's where I lived.'

'Mornin' Skipper,' said Captain Baynard, handing Liam a welcome cup of strong tea. 'How long has it been since you've been back?' 'Nearly seven long years.' 'I take it your departure was compliments of Her Majesty?' 'It was,' said Liam. 'They sent my lad away too,' said Captain Baynard, sadly. 'I'm sorry,' said Liam. 'For how long?' 'Seven years, but they won't ship him home, the bastards.' 'I know,' said Liam. 'Where did they send him?' 'Sydney. I hear they have 'em digging roads there. That's a killer so it is.' 'Does he know how to sail like you?' 'He's a better sailor than me, so he is. They caught him pocketing a gentleman's wallet. He wanted money to fix the sails after they were ruined in a bad storm. He never did anything like that before. Broke his mother's heart, so it did.' Liam told him about his experience when he'd first arrived, of having been asked if he had any special skills. He felt sure that Captain Baynard's son would have been taken aside, as Liam had been, to await sailing work. Liam explained that it was unlikely he would be doing hard labour like digging roads. Captain Baynard was impressed. 'Thank you, sir. I'll tell the wife what you said. It'll make her feel better. She hasn't been the same since.'

As they began to dock, Liam noticed that the pier wasn't as busy as he'd expected. 'Pull in here at the start of the pier,' ordered Liam, 'and don't leave the ship. Be ready to leave at a moment's notice. Have the gangplank ready. I won't be here long.' 'Aye aye Skipper,' said Captain Baynard, enjoying the drama of it all; this was so unlike his usually-boring cattle runs.

Dressed in his finest clothes, Liam presented his papers to the customs superintendent. 'Welcome home Mr Brady,' said the smiling Galway man. He seldom saw a fellow Irishman dressed in such fine clothes. 'And who is this?' asked the superintendent, looking at Kumba carrying Liam's suitcase. 'This is my assistant.' The superintendent had never seen an Aboriginal man before. He looked Kumba up and down, shrugged, and waved him through. Liam hired a driver and the largest coach available on the docks. He and Kumba boarded and they were on their way. *So far so good.*

As Liam left Galway city and entered the countryside, bitter memories came flooding back – he remembered being chained like an animal on those same roads. Even though it was years ago, it was all still vividly embedded in his psyche. Looking back now, he wondered how he'd made it to Kilmainham gaol alive. As the coach wended through the post-famine lands, passing the sad ruins of what once had been cottages, Liam sensed the cries of poor unfortunate souls, evicted and starving, pleading for help. He became increasingly apprehensive at the lack of people on the road and in the fields, and he worried about what he would encounter when he came to his family's cottage.

Sadly, England still ruled Ireland, and Liam was no longer welcome. Nothing had changed in that regard. But, given everything he had seen and experienced, learned and endured, he began to realise how much he himself had changed. Now, sadly, he felt very much a stranger in his own country. His singular mission now was to find Máire and Tomás and get them out of this never-ending Irish nightmare. Coming within sight of the first few cottages on Kitchener's land, Liam's heart sank when he saw that all their roofs had been burned and that most of the stone walls had been levelled. He saw no signs of life at all.

By now the famine was well and truly over. But the curse of emigration still hung over the land, as the heartbreaking memories were too much to bear for so many people. Even now, harbours were full of ships carrying destitute Irish families to America and Canada. Liam's carriage passed wheat fields and grazing cattle on the land that used to be his family's. *It has to be Da and Colm still farming*, he thought, becoming a little more hopeful. The coach neared their little bridge. Liam knew that, once they crossed it, all of his hopes, doubts, dreams, and prayers, would be resolved. He braced himself for what he was about to see, his heart pounding. Slowly the coach turned the corner and moved up the gentle incline of the bridge. *I love you, Máire, my own sweet Máire. I've imagined this moment so many times. I was so afraid it would never happen.*

Liam trembled with anticipation when they reached the top and he looked about. The torment of years of loneliness, longing, and despair vanished when he saw the O'Donaghue cottage still intact. He fell back in his seat with grateful relief. When the coach rolled to a stop, Liam drank in the sight of their tiny addition – his wedding gift to Máire. 'I thought I'd never see this again, Kumba,' he cried, stepping down. The half-door was closed though, strange for such a clear, sunny day. His stomach tightening, Liam placed his hand on the door and pushed it open slowly. No one was home. Scanning the room, he saw children's clothes scattered about, and then, when his eyes fell upon a cot near the bed, his heart sank. It was the cot he'd built for Tomás. *That cot's too small for Tomás.* Then he saw that the rocking chairs Colm had given them as a wedding gift were gone. Standing there again, after all this time, and looking at what used to be their home, Liam was overcome by a sickening, stomach-wrenching, helplessness – *Máire has married again. She didn't get my letter.* He slumped into a chair, utterly defeated.

Painfully, as the tears started to flow, he tried to accept the fact that nearly seven years had been too long a time for Máire to be alone. Maybe she had never forgiven him for his being a member of the Irish resistance and so had gotten on with her life. He couldn't count the times he'd told himself how lucky he was that she'd married him in the first place – *me, of all people. She's a beautiful looking woman, and she had every right to marry again. There must have been men coming from miles around after I was taken away. She knew she would never see me again, and like everybody else, assumed I was probably dead. Nobody comes back from Australia. Shit, I might as well be dead; I'd be better off.*

He got up and went next door. Once again, nobody was there. The turf fire smouldered. Looking around, he saw the rocking chairs. *Colm kept them,* he thought, *or maybe Máire didn't want to be reminded of our times together.* Then he saw something uniquely special and his heart lifted – Tomás' button accordion. It was exactly where he always kept it, on top of the dresser, ready to play. *Da's alive and still living here!* Heartened, he stepped over to the turf fire and lifted the cover of the simmering pot. The wonderful aroma of his mother's cooking wafted up. There was no mistaking it. *Mam's alive too! But Mother of God, where are they?*

When Liam came outside and looked around, Kumba pointed with his lower lip to the last cottage at the corner of the road. Someone was sitting outside by its door. Liam bounded over and recognised old Mrs Joyce, enjoying a little fresh air. She'd already seemed old to him when he was growing up, but now she looked terribly ancient and feeble. Downcast and trancelike, she sat in her rocking chair, barely moving back and forth. 'God and Mary be with you Mrs Joyce,' said Liam in Irish. She didn't respond. Liam said it again louder and got a fright when she looked up. She was skeletal – utterly gaunt, with deeply hollowed-out eyes. 'Who are you?' she asked weakly. 'I'm Liam O'Donaghue.' 'Who?' she said, thinking she hadn't heard correctly. 'Liam O'Donaghue,' he said louder. 'You're not Liam O'Donaghue. Sure, he drowned.' After a few more efforts, Liam realised he was getting nowhere. 'Where are the O'Donaghues?' 'They're down in the church at Father Murphy's wake.' 'Thank you,' he said, relieved.

Liam and Kumba ran to the coach and headed back across the bridge. Liam was sorry to hear that poor old Father Murphy had died. He'd been everyone's rock throughout the famine years and for many years well before those hungry years.

While Liam was truly grateful that his parents were still alive, he was bracing himself for the sight of Máire with another man. On the carriage ride to the tiny church, his thinking went wild. *She's alive. Thank God. So, too, is Tomás, hopefully. Horse, no matter how much you want her, you have to let her go. You've been away too long. Get ready to see her married and with someone else's child.* 'Oh God Almighty,' he cried out. 'No, no.' Kumba had seen that same despairing look on his friend's tortured face before, when he'd rescued him at Dunsley's stud farm. But this time, he felt powerless.

When they came to the little church, Liam recognised his family's donkey and cart, set amongst the neighbours' carts. It was a comforting sight; everyone was safe inside. He heard the mourners singing a traditional air, a sound which brought back comforting memories of the many years he'd gone to Sunday morning mass with his family. Though the small church was packed to the door, Liam pushed his way through the little front entrance. When he saw the looks of disgust on the men's faces as he passed them, Liam knew exactly what they were thinking, his being dressed in such fine clothes. *The English bastards won't even leave us in peace at Father Murphy's wake.* He made it far enough inside the church to stand at the back. From there, he tried desperately to spot his family, but everyone was standing for the hymn making it difficult for him to see. Father Murphy's humble pine coffin was in the centre aisle, at the foot of the altar.

Liam's heart raced. When the hymn ended, everyone sat, and then a young boy shyly stepped up to the altar and faced the parishioners. Liam saw him turn to a woman in the second row where she gave the boy a discrete nod of approval. Then Liam looked back to the young boy as he began to play. He was a slender, broad-shouldered lad with a full head of wavy black hair. His stance became more confident as he started to play a slow, beautiful air. Liam's mouth opened in shock. *Mother of God. It's Tomás!* His heart welled up as he heard his son playing the same piece he'd played at Paudie and Úna Casey's wake so long ago. He stood there transfixed, marvelling at how Tomás had changed into a such a fine-looking young boy. His last memory of his son was of a three-year-old toddler. His heart burst with pride hearing his Tomás playing so well. *Máire knew that air,* he thought. *She hummed it to our son as a lullaby. She must have taught it to him.* Liam pulled out his tin whistle, clenching it tightly. He raised it to his lips and hesitantly began to play, but after a few bars, he choked up, barely able to breathe, caught up with the love of seeing his son after nearly seven long years. His hands shook; his fingers went limp. Then he took a few deep breaths to calm himself down and began again.

The parishioners listened contentedly to the sound of two tin whistle players playing in unison. This wasn't anything unusual amongst the locals; they appreciated someone giving little Tomás support as he played shyly on the altar. But the sound of a stranger playing the same melody Tomás was playing – note for note – electrified the family seated in the second row. It was the O'Donaghues' family song. They had come to call it *Liam's Air*. Melancholy as its melody was, it was somehow comforting for them to hear little Tomás play it over the years. Máire froze, unable to move. Her eyes were fixed on the handkerchief in her hands. *It can't be.* Colm turned in his seat and scoured the back of the church to find the source of the music. He searched the faces in the back and saw a tall, distinguished-looking man he didn't recognise playing a tin whistle. The gentleman was dressed in fine clothes and had a heavy beard, but there was something in his eyes.

One by one the O'Donaghue family shifted in their pew and turned their faces towards Liam. Colm reached down to ease Máire's hand from the handkerchief and supported her as she stumbled to her feet. She turned towards the back of the church, eyes downcast, afraid she'd look up and not see her Liam. The parishioners sensed that something was amiss and began to turn, one by one, to see what was so captivating at the back of the church.

Wary, Máire looked up, afraid of what and whom she might see. She saw the man playing, but she didn't know the beard, the carefully combed hair, nor the fine clothes. The stance though, the way he held the tin whistle. The eyes looking at her. They bore into her soul. And then she knew. She pushed past Colm and Órla, stepped out into the aisle, and slowly walked towards the 'stranger.' Liam saw her approaching hesitantly and lowered the tin whistle. He took a few steps towards his beautiful Máire and stopped. He let her continue towards him and opened his arms. 'Liam,' she cried, and ran into his strong embrace. His heart was pounding as he held the love of his life again, after all these long years. He desperately wanted to kiss her, but he knew that at any moment now he would meet her new husband. Little Tomás stopped playing and walked past the silent crowd towards Máire and Liam.

Over Máire's shoulder, Liam saw the familiar faces of his whole family approaching to surround him, each one vying for his attention and sharing in the joy of his return. Liam turned and saw Colm, then Josie. 'Horse,' said Colm, crying, 'you're back. 'Tis a miracle!' Liam hugged him, and then embraced his mother, lifting her off the floor. 'Jesus, Mary and Joseph, thank you, thank you,' she cried. 'My Liam, you're home.' 'Welcome home, Horse;' said Tomás, 'say hello to your son.' Liam gave his father a strong handshake and looked down at Tomás holding his grandfather's hand. He knelt down and saw pure innocence in the sweet face of his son. His heart burst with fatherly pride. 'Hello Tomás, you're a fine tin whistle player. I like that song. Did your mother teach it to you?' 'Yes sir,' answered Tomás politely. 'And you remember Órla my wife, and this is our daughter Chara,' said Colm. Liam's head was racing. He looked around and still didn't see any other man near them with a child. *Maybe.* 'Are you,' he choked, 'are you living in the cottage?' 'We are,' said Colm apologetically. 'When we got married, Máire said we could have it. She was living in the big house and…' Liam didn't hear another word of what Colm was saying. *There was no other man! No other child! Máire waited for me!* He turned to Máire, standing there with loving tears in her eyes. 'Hello, Máire O'Donaghue,' he said. 'What took ya so long, Liam O'Donaghue?' Liam took her hand and almost ran out of the church. He stopped to draw her close, smiled lovingly, and kissed her. The congregation followed them out to witness this wonderful reunion.

Nobody noticed Tessie O'Brien slip out the side entrance, her mission: to rush back to the Kitcheners' to let them know that Liam was back. Even though Máire had always treated her with kindness, Tessie had never gotten over being demoted from head housekeeper. With news that Máire had been lying all along about Liam's drowning, she was sure she would get her job back. *Why should she be happy with a man? Her and her son going to Dublin and all around the country, in Lady Elizabeth's fine clothes, when I had to stay here, day in, day out. Well, she's going to get a surprise when they take her husband away. That'll wipe that big smile off her face, so it will,* thought Tessie bitterly. When she saw Edward talking to Bishop in front of the stables, she blurted out the news.

'Saddle up our finest horses,' he roared at Bishop. 'Tell the stable hand to alert the soldiers and get them to come to the Catholic church as soon as possible. Tell them there's a Fenian on the loose.' Edward ran back to the house and grabbed his father's sword. *That bastard! How dare he come* back. *I'll show him,* fumed Edward. *And Máire, that little bitch, lying all this time about her husband being dead.* 'Tessie, go up and tell mother to come as quickly as she can.'

The Irish stable hand quickly saddled a horse. Edward watched as he galloped away. What Edward didn't see was that as soon as the stable hand was out of sight, he pulled up and stopped. He despised Edward, and he knew that, whatever he was up to, wouldn't be good for him or for his people. *Sure, there's no hurry at all at all, especially if he's a rebel,* he thought, and so very slowly, he rode to the military garrison.

In the amazing excitement of the moment, Colm blurted out: 'Say hello to one of our resisters lads.' Everybody was shocked and began to grasp why the O'Donaghues had to tell everybody the story about Liam drowning. At this, Liam's jaw dropped; he shook his head and gave Colm an angry look. Colm immediately realised his mistake. Outside the church, the crowd of parishioners became animated. Despite the sadness of Father Murphy's dying, Liam's reappearance was nothing short of miraculous, and he was one of the resisters! This news galvanised their spirit into one as they regarded their Irish hero, looking so strong and heroic in such fine clothes. It raised them up out of their never-ending despair. People started raising their hands with clenched fists, cheering in emotional defiance. 'Good man, Horse!' shouted someone. 'Welcome back!' said another.

Liam was introducing Kumba to his family when they heard the sound of horses approaching in the distance. They looked back and saw Edward and Bishop galloping towards them. Catching sight of the sword in Edward's outstretched hand, the crowd backed away in fear. Liam pushed Máire and Tomás back, as he, Colm, and Kumba, bravely faced Edward and Bishop.

As Edward charged towards Liam, ready to behead him precisely as his military father had taught him, Kumba stepped forward and let fly his boomerang. The mourners had never seen anything like it. It flew straight ahead as fast as an arrow, hitting Edward's wrist with a heavy thud. Edward groaned in pain and dropped his sword. Bishop pointed his musket at Colm. At the sound of the sword clattering to the ground, Edward's horse flinched and bumped into Bishop's just as he fired his musket, causing him to miss Colm. As Bishop and Edward charged past, Liam deftly grabbed Edward and yanked him off his horse. When they both fell to the ground, Colm ran back and picked up Edward's sword. Bishop turned and charged straight for Colm, intending to hit him with his horse, but Colm ducked, slashing Bishop's leg with the sword as he passed. Bishop screamed in pain, lost his balance, and fell off his horse. Colm ran up to him as he lay there groaning and rammed the sword into his heart. As Liam and Edward struggled to their feet, Edward saw Bishop lying on the ground dead. 'You'll all hang for this,' he shouted, confident that the soldiers were right behind him. 'You're all dead.' Then he charged at Liam, hitting him hard. Liam lost his balance and fell. Dazed, he tried to get up, but Edward quickly moved behind him, got him in a headlock, and started to choke him. Edward pulled Liam around to face Máire. 'Say goodbye to Máire, you bastard,' he taunted, and he tightened his grip. Colm and Kumba ran to Liam's rescue, but no one was more stunned than Edward when suddenly, Liam twisted him around in a classic wrestling move, and slammed Edward to the ground. Then, he deftly caught Edward in a vice grip that even he, 'the champion wrestler in Trinity,' couldn't break free from. Liam's hatred for Edward was unbounded. He symbolised all those years of famine, hardship, and loss. Yet, as Edward gasped for his last breaths, Liam realised he had seen enough of death and destruction these last seven years, and something deep within him – those very same seven years of enlightenment and enrichment, kept him from breaking his neck.

'Stop!' came a woman's scream from the onlookers. 'Stop please. Don't do it Liam.' Liam looked up and saw Elizabeth. 'Why should I stop? He's going to hang us all,' answered Liam defiantly, stirring up his hatred once again, at the sight of Elizabeth after all these years. Elizabeth looked to Máire. 'Máire, please, I'm begging you, he's my son, please,' she pleaded. Every fibre in Máire's being shouted, *let the bastard die*, but she saw the pain in Elizabeth's face. She'd been widowed, and Máire felt that she had suffered enough. 'Liam, she's lost her husband. Don't let her lose her son as well.' Liam looked at an utterly broken Elizabeth, and then at Máire. Máire shook her head and gave him a pleading smile. 'You bastard.' Liam loosened his grip and Edward fell to the ground gasping for breath. Colm kept his sword pointed at him. 'Thank you, Liam,' said a grateful Elizabeth. 'Edward sent for the soldiers. You don't have much time.' *At least she did the decent thing warning me,* thought Liam.

He realised now that everything had changed utterly. With Bishop dead and Edward obviously thirsting for revenge, none of his family was safe. He knew Elizabeth was right. He didn't have much time. Not only did he have to persuade Máire to come with him, but he also now had to get everyone in the family to come with him as well. Immediately. 'I want all of my family and the Donnellys to come here,' said Liam firmly. Colm handed the sword to Kumba. 'If he moves, kill him,' ordered Colm. Between his family and the Donnellys, Liam counted thirteen people gathered before him. He smiled, trying to calm everyone down. 'You are not safe here now – not even one of you. I didn't mean this to happen, but it did. I'm sorry. They'll have no mercy on any of you. You all know that, even though you have done nothing. I have a ship waiting in Galway that can take us all away from here, but we must go now – immediately. I have the money for your passage, for all of you. I just came from America where I bought a farm where we all can live.'

They were stunned. They looked at each other puzzled, trying to process everything Liam was saying to them. *Liam has a ship waiting for us. We must leave everything, and not even go back to our cottages to get precious items.* They shook their heads, as if the proposition was an impossibility. 'Can I go home and get my clothes?' asked Aoife. 'No, Aoife, I'm sorry; the soldiers are coming. I'll buy you clothes when we get to England.' 'But Liam, I can't be going to America at my age,' said Josie. 'Mother of God what are we going to do?' 'Mam,' said Liam, 'I have a fine house in America, with lots of land. We'll all be free, Mam. We'll never have to bow our heads to anybody ever again.' 'But it's too much Liam, give me time to think. Oh, Mother of God, help me.' 'We're going to America, Josie,' said Tomás firmly. 'We've been praying for Liam to come home every day since he left. He can't stay here. Now Colm can't either. After this, there's not a one of us who's safe. We have no choice, Josie. We must leave. So come on now. We'll all be together. That's all that matters.' 'But, but,' said Josie, confused. Come on now, Josie,' said Tomás lovingly. 'Come on now, everybody.'

'What can we do?' asked a neighbour. 'Can we have some shawls to keep us warm at night?' asked Liam. All of the women kindly took off their black knitted shawls and handed them to the O'Donaghue and Donnelly ladies. 'Follow us and leave your carts on the pier, blocking it so the soldiers can't get to the boat. One of you, get all the cattle and sheep you can find. Put 'em on the road and block the Redcoats.' Liam handed money to his neighbour. 'This is for all of you. Thank you for helping us.' Everyone was amazed to see such a huge amount of money. Liam walked over to the exquisite horses Bishop and Edward had galloped up on. He stroked his beard as he inspected them thoroughly. 'We'll take these too,' he said casually. 'You can't take them. They're my finest horses,' shouted Edward desperately. 'I can. And I'm going to take you, too,' said Liam calmly, in complete control. He pulled Edward up by the hair. 'Tie him to the cart.' Colm grabbed Edward and pulled him towards the cart. 'Mother!' screamed Edward pitifully. Bewildered, Elizabeth was stunned by everything happening around her. Although she held an elevated position as Lady Kitchener, she had no control whatsoever over any part of this situation. 'What are you doing, Liam?' 'Once we get safely away, I'll release him. If we're caught, I swear to God the last thing I'll do is kill him. I suggest you hold off the soldiers for as long as you can.' Elizabeth nodded timidly. She knew Liam meant every word.

'Okay everyone,' shouted Liam, 'as many as ye can, into the coach with ye. The rest of ye get on those carts there. Let's go, quickly now, come on.' Josie, Tomás, and Órla's parents got into Elizabeth's carriage. Órla's younger brother John-Joe ordered Elizabeth's driver off and headed out. Máire, little Tomás, Órla and her daughter Chara, Bríd, and Aoife, piled into Liam's coach, and the driver took off with great haste. Colm and Órla's baby brother Packie threw Edward onto the cart unceremoniously and headed out. Liam and Kumba jumped onto Edward's horses.

As he passed Elizabeth, Liam stopped to speak to her one last time. 'You started all of this a long time ago. It's your fault, not ours.' He kicked his horse and galloped off. The rest of the villagers scrambled onto their donkey carts and promptly followed. Knowing the soldiers were coming, they drove their donkeys faster than they had ever done before.

Leaving in such a mad rush, nobody offered Elizabeth a ride. She was helpless, with no one to order around for the first time in her life. Miserable, she began walking the long seven miles to the pier, passing several of her tenants walking the other way. While they were shocked to see her in such a strange and humiliating situation, Elizabeth was mortified to the core.

She was about halfway to the pier when fifteen Redcoats came galloping towards her. They didn't recognise her, but, given the elegant clothes she was wearing, they knew she wasn't Irish. The captain signalled his soldiers to stop. 'Are you okay, Madam?' asked the captain politely. Elizabeth knew that Liam meant what he'd said about killing Edward if they were caught, so she did her best to delay them. She didn't recognise the captain. 'I am Lady Elizabeth Kitchener. Who are you?' 'Captain James Shaw, at your service Madam.' 'I wonder, could you help me please?' 'Yes of course Madam. We were ordered to come to the Catholic church to arrest a rebel on the run, but there was no one there. I assume he's trying to escape by boat?' 'Yes, that's what they are trying to do. Why haven't I met you before?' Elizabeth asked, playing for time. 'We're just over from England, Madam. This is our first week in Ireland.' 'I see,' said Elizabeth. 'Well, if you could help me get to the pier,

I'd appreciate it.' 'Certainly, Madam. Private, give Lady Elizabeth your horse.' 'Yes sir,' said the soldier dismounting. Elizabeth put her leg in the stirrup and pulled herself up into the saddle. 'Bring the Lady to the pier.' 'Yes, sir,' said the soldier. 'Madam, I shall have to make haste to Galway,' said the captain. 'Wait!' said Elizabeth. 'Madam?' 'I shall tell your superior officer how kindly you treated me, Captain Shaw.' 'Thank you, Madam,' said the captain. He bowed his head respectfully and then gave the command to continue on to Galway. The soldiers galloped off, turned a bend, and were forced to come to an immediate halt. Dozens of cattle and sheep blocked the road. 'Get them off the road immediately,' the Captain barked at the farmer herding them. 'Okay, sir. Right away, sir.' The farmer put a half-hearted effort into opening a path for the soldiers to pass. Frustrated, Captain Shaw fired his musket in the air spooking the frightened animals, scattering them everywhere. Slowly the horses inched past, and once again the soldiers galloped towards the pier. Distraught with worry and knowing the danger Edward was in if the soldiers caught up to Liam, Elizabeth looked down at the soldier walking alongside her. She kicked the horse. 'I'm so sorry,' she said, and galloped off after Captain Shaw.

By now, everyone was nearly at the pier. Liam had raced ahead to warn Captain Baynard that they were coming and to prepare to cast off. 'There'll be fifteen people and two horses. Once we're aboard, set sail immediately,' he ordered. 'The Redcoats are coming.' 'Aye aye, Skipper,' said Captain Baynard, and he jumped into action, shouting orders to drop sail, and untie the ropes. The two carriages were almost halfway down the pier, with Colm's donkey and cart not far behind. Once their neighbours reached the pier, the men started untying their donkeys, and quickly pulled their carts into one line, blocking the mounted soldiers' access to the pier.

Liam helped Josie and Tomás across the gangplank, then the Donnelly parents, followed by some of their children. When someone shouted, 'The soldiers are coming,' everyone looked and saw the Redcoats galloping down the road, just seconds from reaching the pier. 'Hurry,' shouted Liam, as everybody scurried across the gangplank. Colm pulled Edward onto the deck and tied him to the rear mast. When everyone was aboard, Liam walked his horse across the gangplank and safely down into the boat. Kumba quickly followed, helped by the crew who were skilful in bringing animals aboard safely. 'Push away,' shouted Captain Baynard, and the ship began to inch away from the pier.

Kitcheners' tenants, and all of the other people who'd gathered for Father Murphy's funeral, stood bravely in front of their carts. Captain Shaw could see the ship leaving the pier, but he couldn't ride up to stop it. He ordered his men to dismount and line up, and to aim at the peasants. 'Stand clear or I'll fire, he shouted!' The peasants knew they would be shot if they didn't disperse, so they slowly walked away, hoping that they had given their friends enough time to get away. With that, the soldiers clambered over the carts and ran up the pier as the ship pulled away.

Aware that they were still well within rifle range, Liam grabbed Edward and at knifepoint ordered him to climb up on the back of the ship facing the pier. 'They won't shoot once they see you,' said Liam, stalling to get out of rifle range. Liam was unaware, of course, that Captain Shaw had never met Edward whose fine clothes were now filthy and ripped to shreds. Captain Shaw just saw an Irishman staring at them, daring them to fire. 'The arrogant bastard is taunting us,' said Captain Shaw, seeing Edward standing there. Just then Elizabeth arrived at the pier and saw Edward positioned at the back of the boat. 'Turn around or we fire,' shouted Shaw. 'Soldiers, aim.'

Liam looked at Captain Baynard. It was all up to him now. Liam's life, and the lives of everybody on board, were now in his hands. Would he turn around? Captain Baynard had his own personal grudge against the Redcoats. He held his course, and the ship kept pulling farther away. Elizabeth looked in horror as she saw the soldiers prepare to shoot. 'Everybody get down,' Liam shouted. 'Don't shoot,' screamed Elizabeth. But it was too late. 'Fire,' ordered Shaw, and a murderous volley of bullets whizzed over their heads. Edward fell into the water, mortally wounded. Before they could reload, the ship had sailed out of reach. 'Is everyone all right?' asked Liam, getting to his feet. He looked around at all the dazed faces and saw that no one had been injured.

As the ship sailed further out the harbour, they heard cheering and shouting coming from the pier. Looking back, they saw their neighbours celebrating the escape of their good friends. The O'Donaghue and Donnelly clans, knowing that they would never see these kind people again, nor ever forget this glorious send off, waved back at their friends, and saw them become smaller and smaller.

Many tears of joy and many tears of pain were shed during the four-day trip to Southampton. Liam held Máire and Tomás close for hours as they sailed south down the Irish coast. All of his dreams had come true, exceeding by far what he'd imagined. Thanks to Edward's forcing his hand, Liam now had his and all of Máire's family together, heading into a bright future, free at last of English tyranny.

'Thanks, Captain,' said Liam, shaking his hand. 'I appreciate what you did back there.' 'Aye aye, Skipper. I wasn't going to turn around for those bastards. They showed no mercy to my son. They ruined our lives.' 'Here,' said Liam, handing him a fine-sized gold nugget, 'you saved all our lives.' Captain Baynard looked at the gold nugget awestruck. 'That will pay off your loan for the broken sails,' said Liam. 'You're a good man, Skipper. What d'ya think they'll do to all your friends back there?' 'I was thinking about that. I'd hate to be that English Captain explaining to his superiors that he shot one of the men he was supposed to be protecting. I'd say they'll do nothing and try to keep it as quiet as possible.' 'I never saw such bravery as those men and women blocking the Redcoats from riding onto the pier. If they hadn't, you'd have been caught. How could I turn around after seeing that?' 'Yes, what they did was very brave, especially after all they've been through,' said Liam. 'We'll never forget it.' 'I wonder,' asked Liam. 'Would you mind allowing Máire's and my parents to sleep in your cabin tonight?' 'It would be my pleasure, Skipper. Just let me tidy it up a little for them first.'

Just then, it occurred to Liam that he had completely forgotten about getting Fat Brady's money to his wife. Everything happened so quickly, that there simply hadn't been time. *I'll hire a private detective in Dublin when I get to San Francisco. Hopefully, he can find Nora Brady in Connemara, if she's still alive.*

At nightfall, it turned cold as usual. Everybody gathered around Liam as he recounted his amazing adventures. He didn't tell them he had found one of the largest gold strikes in history. Huddled together and wrapped warmly in their neighbours' woollen shawls, the passengers found the nights to be just about bearable. Captain Baynard and his crew approached. 'Here ya go, Skipper, compliments of the house.' They handed out mugs and bottles of whiskey and wine to all the adults. 'You've earned it.' 'Sláinte,' said Liam. 'Sláinte is saol.' they answered. 'We just have to get through this for a few days and nights, and then, I promise you a nice surprise when we get to England,' said Liam kindly. 'What surprise? ' asked Aoife. 'Well Aoife,' answered Liam, enjoying talking to his sister again, 'the first thing we're all going to do is go shopping for new clothes for everyone.' The girls beamed with anticipation. 'Then what?' asked Bríd excitedly. 'Well now, it wouldn't be a surprise if I told ye,' teased Liam. 'But I promise you one thing,' he said seriously. 'None of you will ever be hungry again. You will never have to bow to anyone like you've had to do since the day you were born. You may not be better than anyone, but you're as good as any of them. I've learned that in the last seven years. You're going to a country where it doesn't matter where you come from. You have a chance of getting somewhere if you work hard and never give up. So Sláinte and just put up with a few rough days and nights until we get to England.' Liam raised his glass, and everybody drank to the future. 'Tomás,' asked Liam, 'would you play another tune for us all please?' 'What will I play?' he answered, looking to his mother for some guidance. 'Play a lively reel, Tomás,' said Máire, and he did just that. Everybody clapped along happily. 'He's a fine young boy, Máire,' said Liam, welling up. 'You did a fine job.' 'We all did,' said Máire, looking at everybody gathered around the rough wooden table.

After a few long days and nights, they sailed into Liverpool's bustling harbour. Everybody stared in awe at the docks filled with a forest of tall masts. Liam thanked Captain Baynard one last time as everyone disembarked. Kumba held the horses while Liam went to the booking agents office to pay for five luxury cabins on what would be the maiden voyage of a three masted clipper sailing ship called Sovereign Of The Seas. As he was paying for the tickets, he heard the excitement all around him about this brand new vessel. 'It's the fastest ship ever,' gushed the ticketing clerk. 'It can sail at twenty knots, and should reach San Francisco in a hundred days or so.' Liam was impressed. Even better, it was sailing in eight hours. He arranged for the horses to be shipped to New York, then on to San Francisco. Beaming, he returned and walked everybody to the ship. 'This is the Sovereign Of The Seas, our ship to San Francisco. We have eight hours before it departs, so let's go shopping!' Everyone cheered, as they looked in awe at the beautiful ship. Liam hired three carriages and brought them all shopping as promised. The girls eagerly cast off their tattered peasant clothes. More excited than they'd ever been, they chose beautiful clothes, the likes of which they'd only ever dreamed. Josie had the time of her life, excitedly helping them all select lovely dresses, casual and formal. Meanwhile, next door, the men bought modern suits, shirts, ties, and leather shoes. They had a quick bite to eat and then headed back to the ship with their new wardrobes.

Josie was flummoxed when she saw her cabin. 'Mother of God, is this for us?' 'Yes, Mam, 'tis all for you.' 'Oh Liam.' She looked out the porthole, ''Tis beautiful.' 'You must have found a lot of gold, Horse,' said Tomás proudly. 'Enough, Da, enough,' said Liam modestly. He wondered how Tomás would react when he saw the size of the ranch. 'I'll leave ye alone so. See ye for dinner shortly.'

Liam walked down the corridor to his cabin, tapped on the door, and was stopped dead in his tracks when he opened it. There was the sight he'd dreamed of for over six long years – Máire, in a beautiful evening dress. She smiled as innocently as she had the day he first saw her at the céilí, shyly hoping he would approve. 'Mother of God Máire, you look beautiful. Doesn't she Tomás?' 'Yes, eh, father,' he answered respectfully and in perfect English. By now, Liam had heard the fascinating story of everybody's survival and of Tomás' privileged education. He knelt down to his son. 'Tomás, please call me Da.' Tomás smiled and nodded his head. Liam went over to his bedside drawer and took out a small black box. 'This is for you Máire; I hope you like it.' Máire opened the little box and saw a fetching gold locket on a delicate gold chain. Her mouth opened in surprise. ''Tis beautiful, Liam,' she said lovingly. 'It's the first bit o' gold I found. Please, let me help you.' He stepped behind her, gently put the necklace around her neck, and closed the clasp. Máire went to the mirror to look at her gift and began to cry. Liam held her, 'Now, now, no crying tonight.' And then turning to his son, 'Well, Tomás, are we all ready to go to dinner?' 'Yes Da,' he smiled, clearly idolising his father after everything he'd seen him do outside the church. 'Okay so,' and they headed down to dinner.

As they entered the elegant dining room, Liam, Máire, and Tomás saw everybody near and dear to them, safe and secure, each dressed in elegant finery, smiling, and eager to begin a new life. Later that wonderful evening, Colm turned and whispered to Liam, 'We'll look after Tomás tonight, Horse,' and gave him a wink.

Sources for Further Reading

Barrett, Claire. 'How the Irish Are Returning an Old Favor to the Choctaw Nation.' *HISTORYNET*, 15 May 2020. www.historynet.com/how-the-irish-are-returning-an-old-favor-to-the-choctaw-nation.htm.

Crowley, J., Smyth William J. and Murphy, Mike (editors), *Atlas of the Great Irish Famine*, Cork University Press, Cork 2012.

Curtis, Liz. *Nothing But the Same Old Story: The Roots of Anti-Irish Racism*. Information on Ireland, 6th Edition, 1991.

Dawson, James. *Australian Aborigines: The Languages and Customs of Several Tribes of Aborigines in the Western District of Victoria, Australia*. George Robertson, Melbourne, Sydney, Adelaide, 1881.

Fitzsimons, Jack. 'The Thatched Houses of Co. Meath.' *Ask about Ireland*, 9 July 2020. www.askaboutireland.ie/reading-room/history-heritage/architecture/the-thatched-house-of-co/.

Goodbody, Rob. 'Quakers and the Famine.' *History Ireland*, Spring 1998.

Henry of Huntingdon, *Historia Anglorum* ed. and tr. Diana E. Greenway, *Henry Archdeacon of Huntingdon. Historia Anglorum. The History of the English People*. Oxford Medieval Texts. Oxford, 1996.

Igor, Brian. 'Charles Bianconi and The Transport Revolution, 1800 - 1875.' *The Irish Story*, 14 December 2012. www.theirishstory.com/2012/12/14/charles-bianconi-and-the-transport-revolution-1800-1875/#.Xwc5vS1q2hA.

Irish Famine Curriculum Committee. 'The Great Irish Famine'. Moorestown, New Jersey. January 11, 1996. www.nj.gov/education/holocaust/curriculum/IrishFamine.pdf.

John Acton Wroth Papers. Battye Library, State Library of Western Australia.

Kinnealy, Christine. *This Great Calamity: The Irish Famine 1845-52*. Roberts Rinehart Publishers, Boulder Colorado, 1995.

Lynch-Brennan, Margaret. *The Irish Bridget: Irish Immigrant Women in Domestic Service in America, 1840-1930*. Syracuse University Press, Syracuse New York, 2014.

McClaughlin, Trevor. *Barefoot and Pregnant? Irish Famine Orphans in Australia*. Volume 2. The Genealogical Society of Victoria, Melbourne, 2001.

Mangan, James (Ed.). *Robert Whyte's 1847 Famine Ship Diary*. Mercier Press, Dublin Ireland, 1994.

Monaghan, Jay. *Australia and the Gold Rush: California and Down Under, 1849-1854*. University of California Press, Berkeley and Los Angeles, 1966.

O'Mahony, Michelle, *Famine In Cork City*, Mercier Press, Cork 2023 (2nd edition).

'Oliver Cromwell and Family.' *Westminster Abbey*. London, England. www.westminster-abbey.org/abbey-commemorations/commemorations/oliver-cromwell-and-family.

Póirtéir, Cathal (editor), *The Great Irish Famine*, The Thomas Davis Lecture Series, Mercier Press, Cork, 1995.

Sadlier, Richard. *The Aborigines of Australia*. Thomas Richards, Sydney, 1883.

Scally, Robert James. *The End of Hidden Ireland: Rebellion, Famine, and Emigration*. Oxford University Press, New York, 1995.

Steinmetz, Hilary N. (2009). *Rancho El Paso: The World's Largest Thoroughbred Farm* (unpublished master's thesis). California State University, Sacramento, California. www.pdfs.semantic scholar.org /e478/ab5b3adf8b22dbd63d00ea5545c1aff4b094.

'Trinity College Dublin.' *Dublin City Council.* www.dublincity.ie/ image/libraries/dg25b-trinity-college-Dublin.

'Whales and Hunting.' *New Bedford Whaling Museum*, New Bedford, MA. www.whalingmuseum.org/learn/research-topics/ overview-of-north-american-whaling/whales-hunting.

Woodham-Smith, Cecil. *The Great Hunger: Ireland 1845-1849.* Hamilton, London, 1962.